TWO NOVELS BY ANTHONY POWELL

BY ANTHONY POWELL

Two Novels by Anthony Powell

PERISCOPE–HOLLIDAY
49 East 49 St.   New York 17

Venusberg

Agents
&
Patients

All Rights Reserved
Library of Congress Catalog Card Number: 52-12524
Produced by Rinehart & Co.
for Periscope Book Shop and Holliday Bookshop, N.Y.
Manufactured in the United States of America

Venusberg

'Here, according to popular tradition, is situated the grotto of Venus, into which she enticed the knight Tannhäuser; fine view from the top.'

BAEDEKER.

Lushington collected the pieces of typewritten foolscap and shook them together so that the edges were level. Outside, it was raining. The literary editor said:

'Seeing the world broadens the outlook. You can learn a lot abroad. They're a funny lot foreigners. I always go abroad for my holiday. I like it over there. The food makes a change. I shouldn't wonder if it wasn't pretty cold where you're going. Still I expect you'll be sorry to leave old London all the same. We have some fun here when we do. I don't know any town like it. I don't really.'

The literary editor took out his penknife and, breathing hard, trimmed where his thumbnail had a jagged edge. Lushington opened a box of paper clips and took one out. He pressed the paper clip through the corner of the sheets of foolscap upon which he had begun an article, and put them into a small dispatch case. The literary editor finished off the nail by biting it, shut the penknife and put it back into his pocket. Miss Arnold said:

'I expect you'll give up newspaper work when you get out there, Mr. Lushington, and go into business and become a millionaire. All the best men become foreign correspondents for a bit. They say there is nothing like abroad for training.'

The literary editor said: 'They've taken the place of the old diplomat. Better educated. Better informed. Better paid. And, of course, more reliable. But they carry on the same fine tradition.'

Lushington said: 'Well, you will remember about trying to use both those two stories of mine for the feature page, won't you? It would be a great help if you could. I'd be very grateful.'

'I'll have a look at them just as soon as I have a moment to spare, which ought to be some time the day after to-morrow.'

Lushington shut the dispatch case and picked up his hat. Water dripped down the outer panes of the windows, one of which rattled three times at regular intervals. Outside it was winter. Miss Arnold said:

'Well, good night, Mr. Lushington and good luck.'

The literary editor said: 'So long, Lushington, and all the best, and don't forget to put that dope in the post to-night so that Booth gets it in time for the woman's page.'

Taking the dispatch case and pondering in his mind whether he would go home and finish the article and go to bed, or call on Lucy and sit up all night and finish the article, Lushington went down the stairs which were of stone like those of a prison or lunatic asylum and were, in effect, used to some considerable extent by persons of a criminal tendency or mentally deranged. In the atmosphere there was a smell of icy damp paint permeating the rawness of the night. The wind circulated through the corridors and up and down the lift-shaft. He walked down several flights of stairs wondering whether he had remembered to pack his evening shoes. At the entrance the man with the birthmark on his face who sat at a desk in a cubicle and asked people their names and controlled the house telephone without much success said:

'So you're saying ta-ta to us all for a bit?'

'That's it.'

Shaken by a fit of coughing, a bronchial upheaval like a tornado in its suddenness, the man said:

'Grand weather for travelling, I don't think.'

He struck himself several times on the chest and then spat through the door of the wooden cubicle in which he was confined, neatly, and far out into the corner of the passage.

'That's a nasty cough of yours,' Lushington said.

'Rise and fall of the leaf finds out them with weak chests.'

'It sure does.'

'Suffered from asthma since I was a little kid not so high.'

'You have?'

The man passed his hand lightly over his birthmark and said:

'It's the truth. Well I hope it keeps fine for you.'

'And I,' said Lushington, 'hope it keeps fine for *you*.'

He went into the street where it was raining and cold. The lights disappeared suddenly in the windows of the pub on the other side of the road and deciding in favour of Lucy he got into a bus. Inside he tried to think of a joke to round off the article with. The bus bumped along through the rain. No joke quickened within him. It was too cold a night for that sort of joke, one of the good universal kind.

Coming of that professional stock who, like the Jews, live secretly, holding at intervals well-attended family conclaves, remaining securely out of touch with life, Lushington had begun his career in the City.

An almost absolute business inability and perhaps some hereditary flaw in his character had led him to journalism and being ambitious he hoped one of these days to become dramatic critic on a paper with a decent circulation. Meanwhile he was going as special correspondent to a country on the Baltic, the name of which he could never remember. He was a serious young man with a pink and white face who believed implicitly in eventual progress on a scientific basis although he had had Anglo-Catholic leanings in his City days.

There was nothing at all extraordinary in Lushington's appointment to this post. It was the sort of thing that happened everyday. More than this it had been what he had wanted not so long before and was to some extent the delayed action of past intriguing. He was, in short, as the literary editor had said, lucky to get it. But there was a circumstance that gave to the appointment some of the tang of a stale joke, a flavour used-up but at the same time forceful and disturbing like a tune running tiresomely in his head. This significance consisted in Da Costa being honorary attaché at the legation of that same Baltic state. Da Costa was not only an old friend of Lushington. He was also the man with whom Lucy was in love. Lushington could not therefore avoid reflecting on hearing of his good fortune that he was both leaving Lucy and going to a place where he would be reminded perpetually of her feelings for Da Costa.

Lushington and Da Costa had been at school together. Da Costa's setting was similar to Lushington's without being precisely the same. He came of a large and moderately influential family whose possibly Iberian ancestors had made money in India, nabobs under the Regency, and who, marrying with discernment, had formed a vaguely empire-building tradition. Da Costa himself did not belong to this tradition. It embarrassed him a little. But now in the last resort he had found himself unable to circumvent it. After coming down from Oxford he had hung about working at a thesis on comparative religion. And then Lushington had introduced him to Lucy and the trouble had begun.

Da Costa like Lushington was shy. But whereas Lushington's shyness took the form of creeping about rooms pretending that he was really not there at all, Da Costa's manifested itself in shouting loud and laughing and upsetting things to counteract this feeling of personal inadequacy. As it happened Da Costa was good at games and examinations so that his difficulties were pretty fundamental ones and not merely adolescent non-adaptability setbacks. For example unlike Lushington he was bored by the society of women. He could stand them only for an hour or so on end. This was due to an unusual mental orientation or perhaps to laziness because he was not prepared to concede the exactions of time and energy that prolonged intimacy with one would require. In some ways, they attracted him to a considerable extent and once he had been induced by friends to spend a weekend with an intellectually cultured chorus girl. It was not however a success and, in any case, as Da Costa himself used to point out, he had not enough money to prolong the relationship. Then for a short time he was always seen about with a major's widow. But it did not do. There was something, as his friends used to say, lacking. In spite of this and perhaps because of it women liked him. Among them Lucy.

Lushington had met Lucy at the house of the man who wrote the music column for his paper. Nothing had marked their meeting as in any way out of the ordinary. Lushington liked her but it was not until several weeks after this first meeting that he fell in love with her and it was some months later before he had the courage to tell her so. He had never been in love before, except slightly with one of his first cousins, who was already engaged to a man in the Treasury, and he was surprised when he found that Lucy returned his feelings. He was not at all certain what he ought to do.

In due course she became his mistress. She was not a vicious girl but she had had two husbands and had become accustomed to doing as she wished. But all the time she knew that he was not what she was looking for. That was one of the reasons why she would not marry him. Lushington on his side, surprised when he found that Lucy was attracted by him, was amazed when he found himself living with her and before he had begun to consider their relationship as anything less than a phenomenon he had lost her by introducing her to Da Costa just at the moment when he was beginning to feel that she really belonged to himself. He lost her in the sense that she gave him up as a lover. His place was not taken by Da Costa because Da Costa was for a long time unaware how matters stood and even when he became aware took no steps in the matter. Something about his unbalanced manner and respectable background had appealed at once to Lucy but he felt towards her, as towards most of the women whom he met, only an amiable lack of interest. However it flattered him at first that he should have made such an impression on her and then annoyed him when he found that he had caused a great deal of unnecessary trouble and had gained one of those emotional responsibilities which he devoted so much of his time to avoiding.

For a short time the situation had adjusted itself by all three of them going about a great deal together because they liked each other's company and this system enabled Lushington to be with Lucy and Lucy to be with Da Costa. It was a working compromise but it got on everybody's nerves. In the end it was Da Costa who decided that he could stand it no more. He decided to leave England, and his family, who had repeatedly requested in the past that he should do something useful, had suggested that he should join the legation of a relative who was minister at this obscurely northern capital. The idea was fostered by his elder brother who was married and had several children and who had once been called the most popular man in Throgmorton Street. The post of honorary attaché was considered by the Da Costa family to be the very thing. Da Costa himself liked the idea because, being a young man with wide interests, he wanted to see abroad and, although he was unsatisfactory as an attaché, he himself found congenial the purely formal social contacts of his profession which was in this respect a great improvement upon what he had been accustomed to in London. His relative, as it happened, retired soon after his arrival but this was due to a personal whim and was unconnected with Da Costa's shortcomings. In the meanwhile a new minister had not yet been appointed and as the routine work at the legation had to be completed somehow the *chargé d'affaires* made no effort to eject Da Costa during the interregnum.

And now Lushington's newspaper had decided to send him to the same place. He was to stay there for some months and write about the political situations. Undeniably it was a good job. But at the same time there were drawbacks.

2

The bus stopped and Lushington got out and went through the passage with posts across it which led to the square where Lucy lived. The rain was falling in a measured way on the leaves of the trees inside the square's railings. He rang the bell. Then he waited, listening to the rain and the noise of the water running down the wall of the next house where one of the outside gutters had burst. Lucy opened the door herself. She was wearing a dressing-gown over her pyjamas and said:

'Oh it's you, is it? Come in, sweet, but I'm afraid there isn't such a thing as a cigarette in the house.'

'Why are you dressed like this? Are you ill?'

'I'm just going to bed. I'm going to have a bath and then go to bed. Why have you come to see me now?'

She was fair and had short curly hair and she held the dressing-gown tight across her body so that it showed her figure and her round, knowing, little breasts. He went through the door and followed her into the sitting-room. She slipped her arm through his and into the pocket of his overcoat, taking his hand. Lushington put his hat on the table. Then he kissed Lucy.

'Why have you come now?' she said.

She finished kissing him and went away and lay down on the sofa, under a tartan rug, turning sideways and resting her head on the end of the sofa. Lushington took off his overcoat and sat down in one of the armchairs. He said:

'It's settled that I go to-morrow.'

'By train?'

'By boat. I thought I might make a story of it for the paper.'

'Are you glad to be going?'

'I don't mind much either way.'

'Why aren't you glad?'

'Well I shan't be seeing you for some time.'

'You must find someone else,' she said. 'You must really. You can't go on like this. It's absurd. Besides it's awful for me. Can't you find someone else?'

'Perhaps I will out there.'

'It's funny you're going to the same place.'

'It's in the news you see. They've been having political troubles. Revolutions and so on. Front page stuff, almost.'

'Don't go and get shot.'

'I expect I shall.'

'It's a pity I can't come with you.'

'Yes why don't you?'

She pulled the rug almost over her head and turned away from him towards the inside of the sofa, doubling herself up. There was a pause. She lay there looking a little like a sick child, very slight and taking up hardly any room on the sofa. Outside the rain came thudding against the window. Lushington said:

'You haven't told me why you are dressed like that yet?'

'I'm not well. I'm going to have a bath and go to bed.'

'What's wrong with you?'

'I don't know,' she said, 'I'm just not well. I haven't been well for weeks. I hate everything. That's why I'm not well. There is nothing to be done about it. But tell me about yourself. What has been happening? Anything?'

'Nothing much. Except that I'm going away. And I've told you that.'

'Who was that with you when I saw you the other night? In green?'

'I don't think you know her. I met her somewhere. She looks rather nice don't you think?'

'I hate those slit eyes. You're not in love with her or anything like that, are you? I don't trust your taste.'

'No, I'm not.'

Lucy laughed and threw the rug on the floor and stretched out her arms. Then she stood up, still laughing. She said:

'Anyway I suppose I ought to have my bath now.'

'Do you mind if I finish off an article on your typewriter?' Lushington said.

'There's paper in the drawer.'

'Here?'

'Yes.'

He watched her go into the bathroom, a narrow den leading out

of the sitting-room and heard her turn on the geyser. He sat for a few
moments in front of the typewriter thinking of the first time he had
seen her.

At seventeen Lucy had run away with her first husband who was
rumoured once to have held a war-time commission in a guards battalion. Her father, a captain retired from the Marines, who had lost his
wife's money by judicious investments, lived in a bungalow on the
south coast with his eight children and this used sometimes to make
him appear a discontented man. But his wife was a woman who looked
always on the bright side so that in later life Lucy used to say that she
could never remember which of her parents had contributed most
towards her elopement. Lucy had been married at Torquay and her
husband had worn an old Etonian tie which he had seen on his way
there in a glass case on Paddington station. But although he had initiative he was an ignorant and rather greedy man and the marriage had
lasted less than eighteen months.

Not long after the decree was made absolute it became apparent
that she was more than remarkably good-looking. She showed signs of
becoming a film star. But she was a girl who felt that life should be full
of meaning and she broke with her second husband, a film producer,
because he adapted one of the minor classics too freely. After that she
lived on alimony and occasionally had lovers. But somehow it was not a
success although as a sex she liked men and in the evening she used to
sit in her room and play the gramophone or read a book because, although this was not very amusing, it seemed better than going about
with the people who were her friends. She often said so. She often told
Lushington when he became her lover that she felt like this. Also it
filled up the time while she waited for the ideal man, who became as
the months went on an increasingly improbable figure, because her
adventures, particularly those on the films, had caused her to develop a
mild but insidious megalomania. But even after she had decided that
Da Costa was what she wanted Lushington used often to visit her because she could not have Da Costa who was not interested in anyone
at all.

Lushington opened the dispatch case and put one of the sheets of
paper into the machine. Lucy came out of the bathroom and watched
him typing. Clouds of steam began to puff into the sitting-room. She
took up the rug again and wrapping it round her knees sat on the edge

of the sofa. Lushington typed. The article had to be finished somehow. The steam began to fill all one side of the room with fog. Lucy went into the bathroom again and, without shutting the door, turned off the water. He heard her get into the bath and begin to splash about. He wrote:

'. . . and, too, why do people keep on repeating the old, old lie that the only maidens with sex-appeal are the ones who want to always be having a good time? When will all those would-be clever people commence to understand that that girl, who holds our heart in thrall, is the old fashioned miss, who our grandfather loved as she tripped demurely between rose-blossoms, along the garden path, in that quaint old-fashioned frock to meet her sweetheart. After all it is among the kindly, everyday folk that you find garnered-in the best hearts, among those worth-while, simple souls . . .'

He wrote for some time. Lucy splashed about next door. Outside a clock struck. It was still pouring with rain.

Lushington took the last sheet out of the typewriter and read it through, altering 'empirical' to 'real-life.' Then he lit a cigarette. From the bathroom Lucy said:

'It's a new country isn't it?'

'Yes.'

'Who used to own it?'

'Russia. I think Germany had some of it too I'm not sure.'

'Come and talk to me if you have finished.'

He clipped the sheets of paper together and put them once more into the dispatch case. Then he went into the bathroom. Lucy was lying on her back, only her head appearing, the light deflected through the water making it join her shoulders obliquely as if it grew at a sharp angle to the rest of her body. Lushington said:

'I'm going now. Goodbye.'

'Don't go yet. Why go now? I've hardly seen you at all.'

'I've still got some packing to do.'

'You poor darling.'

She sat up in the bath and reached out for the towel to dry her hands and arms. Painfully he became aware of how lovely she was and how much he wanted her. For the moment he was glad even that he was going away where he would not see her so that perhaps by being distant from her he might not want her so much. She threw away the towel and put her arms round his neck and he held the cigarette away at arms length to keep the smoke from her face.

'Goodbye,' she said, 'I hope you have a lovely time.'

'What are you going to do?'

'I may be staying with people in the country for a bit.'

'At the home of that curious new young admirer of yours?'

'I expect so.'

'Is he nice?'

'Yes,' she said, 'I'm very fond of him. He has very nice manners.'

'He has no roof to his mouth has he?'

'The poor boy is very sweet really. He's so young.'

'Well, goodbye,' said Lushington, 'I'll write and tell you all about life out there. How we all are.'

'Thank you, darling.'

He stood there not wanting to go. She said suddenly:

'Do you think he's like that? Always has been? I mean is it really no good? Will it never be any good?'

'Who?'

'Him.'

'No of course not. How absurd. He has had girls. Very dull ones I admit. But women don't amuse him much.'

'He is undersexed?'

'He is not in the least undersexed. You think there is something pathological about every man who does not fall for you.'

'But he doesn't like women.'

'He gets on without them. Some men can. It has been done.'

'Then he is undersexed.'

'All right. He's undersexed.'

She said: 'Don't get angry. All I mean is do you think that one of these days he might begin to like me?'

'I daresay.'

'Do you think so?'

'In the meantime please remember that there is always me.'

'Darling.'

He shut the door behind him and went down the stairs and out into the square. The rain had stopped but water still trickled down the wall of the house next door. A gramophone was playing in one of the basements as he passed and he stood for a few moments listening to it. The curtains did not meet across the windows of the room so that he could see people inside who were dancing. He watched them for a time, oppressed by the recognition that there was still some packing to be done. Then he walked home, posting the article in the letter box at the end of the square.

3

The boat was small. It smelt of cocoanut oil and was to call at Copenhagen on the voyage. Recreation on board was limited to reading in a bunk or sitting in what was called the *smoke saloon* and talking to Count Scherbatcheff. It was also possible to talk to Count Scherbatcheff while walking up and down the deck and this was in fact preferable when the two Danish young men from Manchester University who were interested in radio sat in the smoke saloon with their friend the German commercial traveller. Count Scherbatcheff who was about thirty had a fair moustache and, having studied engineering in Belgium, he sometimes wore a béret with three different coloured buttons in it, each of which stood for something definite in his life. He and Lushington used to lean over the side of the boat and discuss expenses and similar matters.

The North Sea, an engrailed tract of sheet iron, heaved a little. All the sky was grey. Count Scherbatcheff who had stomach trouble of some sort patted the front of his overcoat. He said:

'For example my great uncle was a very extravagant man. He used to have supper parties after the opera. Very often at these parties he would give chorus girls baths of champagne. He would astonish gipsies and such people by his behaviour.'

'Often the only baths that they ever got?'

'I should not be surprised. Moreover in Russia before the Revolution we used to give huge tips. It was absurd. It was unnecessary. I can give you no idea how large they were. Really it was ridiculous. I can remember when I was a schoolboy going out to dinner by myself at Yalta and leaving the waiter an outrageously large tip. A great deal too much.'

Lushington turned up the collar of his overcoat. He hoped that it was not going to be rough. There was a red, weak sun but a cloud was reflected darkly in the metal surfaces of water. The boat heaved again. Count Scherbatcheff, steadying himself with a piece of rigging, said:

'It will be bad in the Baltic. There it will almost certainly be rough.

In the Baltic the sea is often very stormy. I shall not be surprised if the
weather is inclement on this trip.'

They walked up and down the deck. Sometimes other ships passed
on the horizon. It appeared that Count Scherbatcheff was going on a
visit to his grandmother who disliked travelling and, when the Revolution came, had refused to emigrate as far as England or France.

'She is a woman of great obstinacy,' Count Scherbatcheff said.
'Like all my family she is very obstinate. I myself am very obstinate. It
was for this reason that she refused to move.'

'Did she stay there during the Revolution and the War of Independence?'

'Through both. And through the civil war too that followed them.'

'She was lucky to escape. How did she do it?'

'When the trouble began she had been staying with cousins who
had a small estate in the neighbourhood. A house which afterwards
was burned. We Russians are not popular with these people and especially this was so during the Revolution and before the Independence
was declared. My grandmother was out walking one day when she was
thrown from the Nikolai Bridge by some members of the Social-
Democratic party.'

'Into the river?'

'It was the custom. It was from the Nikolai Bridge that Jews were
sometimes thrown.'

'Why?'

'Jews. I cannot say the word. *Les Juifs*. It is hard to pronounce.
Jews. That is how you say it? At times of public excitement.'

'Quite.'

'Fortunately it was summer time and my grandmother swam to
the further bank. The very next week the Bolsheviks came into power
and threw into the river many members of the Social-Democratic
party.'

'And when the Independence was declared I suppose they threw
the Bolsheviks in?'

'By that time,' Count Scherbatcheff said, 'it was winter. Holes had
to be cut in the ice.'

That was how the time passed as far as Copenhagen. They arrived
there at night and the two Danish young men disembarked. The German commercial traveller remained on board but he never spoke again.
He sat alone in the smoke saloon and read the back numbers of *Die*

Freundschaft which he had taken the precaution of bringing with him. Lushington and Count Scherbatcheff walked up from the docks into the town and dined there and went to a cinema. When they arrived back on board they found that there were some more passengers. There was a pile of luggage but its owners had retired to bed.

4

They sailed from Copenhagen early the next morning. Among the new
arrivals was another count. Lushington found this additional count in
the bar. He was a fat man who smelt of brilliantine and sandalwood
boxes and his profession was to sell face cream. He made no secret of
this and at once showed Lushington a sample of the face cream that he
sold. As a slight return Lushington stood him a drink. It was at this
juncture that the new count introduced himself by handing across a
card on which were printed the words *Le Comte Michel Bobel* under
a coronet. Count Bobel also wore a coronet embroidered on the outside
of his shirt immediately over his heart and above it the letter B. It was
embroidered in mauve silk and as he did not wear a waistcoat it was
possible to see it when he opened his coat and rested his hands on his
upper ribs which he did when emphasising conversational points. He
talked French some of the time and said that he was Russian. What
race he actually belonged to it was impossible to say. In face he was
German with thick lips and a roll of fat at the back of his neck but although he talked German he seemed to prefer using French or English
and he had evidently an oriental strain, Levantine perhaps or Armenian,
that through the working of some Mendelian law had given him more
of its colour than his more immediate presumed racial infusions. Lushington said that he himself would not buy any face cream at the moment. Count Bobel said:

'You have seen the ladies, yes?'

'On this boat?'

'Indeed.'

'I have not seen them yet.'

Count Bobel puffed out his cheeks. He was smoking an amber
cigarette which he never removed from between his lips, so that the
smoke from it curled into the eyes of anyone who was standing beside
him, making them smart and water. Lushington edged away.

'You like girls?' Count Bobel said. 'The younger one is magnificent.
Exquise. They came on board at Copenhagen at the same time as myself. They have a great amount of luggage. But even before I had seen

that I could tell that they were ladies of rank. It will be a good voyage.'

Lushington said that he hoped so. He himself was by no means confident after what Count Scherbatcheff had said and besides the wind seemed to be getting up. He tried to decide whether or not he would eat any lunch. He had been trying to decide this all the morning. While he was speculating on this point someone outside began to ring a bell. Making up his mind on the spur of the moment at least to see what the meal was going to be, he said:

'That is for luncheon. Shall we go below?'

'*En avant, mon cher.*'

In the dining saloon the ladies of whom Count Bobel had spoken were sitting at the Captain's table. Lushington habitually sat at the Captain's table and also Count Scherbatcheff but the German commercial traveller and the two Danish young men had not sat there and the German now sat by himself. Count Scherbatcheff was late for lunch and accordingly had his seat appropriated by Count Bobel who parried the efforts of the stewardess to eject him. The Captain, a gloomy Swede, watched the tussle but offered help to neither party and when Count Scherbatcheff arrived he had to sit at the same table as the German. But he sat at the far end of it, away from the German himself, so that he could join in the conversation at the Captain's table.

Lushington looked at the two ladies. One of them was elderly and fidgeted and moped, full of aristocratic worries. The other was much younger, a tall blonde with blue eyes and high cheek bones, dressed in light coloured clothes and looking like the leading lady in a German musical comedy. They were talking German to each other but it was evident that the younger woman had Slav blood. She was not what technically is called beautiful. Her features were not proportioned with enough restraint for that and she was too tall and thin. But she carried with her a certain gorgeousness which was like something that Lucy too possessed and for a moment he was reminded of Lucy although this woman was not like her in appearance nor in manner. Count Bobel, who was still talking English, French, and German indiscriminately, said:

'And so you have been to Copenhagen, ladies? What a pleasant town in which to spend a holiday. I myself envy you.'

They nodded, the elder one examining Count Bobel with apprehension. The younger one turned and looked at him too and in profile her cheek bones and long, blacked eyelashes made an angular pattern against the varnished walls of the dining saloon. Count Bobel when he saw that she was looking at him made his beautiful smile and, eyeing her wedding ring, said:

'And did you in Copenhagen buy many presents for your dear parents, mademoiselle?'

She laughed and shook her head, glancing across the table for a moment to where Lushington was sitting. Her eyebrows were plucked and arched so as to give her an expression of exaggerated indifference to things, but her eyes showed that at some time in the past she had been hurt and made to suffer. Count Bobel said:

'Copenhagen is a very gay city, mademoiselle. I hope that you got into no mischief?'

The Swedish Captain, awakened by the thought of mischief at Copenhagen from the kind of trance into which he was accustomed to fall at meals, said:

'Every year at the same season Frau Mavrin makes this journey. For three years I have taken her back on my vessel. Is not that so, Frau Mavrin? And Baroness Puckler too?'

They said that it was true. They said that they went to Copenhagen to buy their Christmas presents. Neither of them seemed to care much for Count Bobel. Count Bobel himself however was quite satisfied with the impression he had made and asked for a second helping of stew and sauerkraut, saying:

'A thousand apologies, Madame, that I should have addressed you as Mademoiselle but it seemed impossible to me that one so young should be already married.'

Count Scherbatcheff when he arrived used different methods. He was handicapped from the start by being very angry at having his seat taken away from him, but after this initial set-back he settled down into his stride which was to be very attractive and feline and to talk English. He tried Russian at first but this was not well received by the ladies. The old lady, Baroness Puckler, was less chilly with Count Scherbatcheff than she had been with Count Bobel and after a short conversation it turned out that she knew several of his relations although she did not remember the grandmother whom he was on his way to see. But Baroness Puckler made it clear from her manner that in her native town no Russians were to be on her visiting list however friendly she might choose to be to them on board ship. Frau Mavrin treated Count Scherbatcheff as she had treated Count Bobel, eyeing him and laughing at his jokes but not troubling to hide that she took no interest in him at all. Baroness Puckler said to Lushington:

'Does it happen that you know Mr. Da Costa at your legation?'

'I know him very well.'

'He often comes to my house. Ortrud, you have met him too, I think?'

'Indeed he is charming and has such a yellow face.'

'Yes,' said Lushington. 'He has.'

He wondered if Frau Mavrin too was in love with Da Costa. At least it appeared that she had only met him once. He tried to estimate the relationship between these two women. Baroness Puckler behaved like someone who had in her possession a valuable pet, a rare animal that must be looked after constantly in case it should get into mischief or fall into a decline from inattention. But Frau Mavrin as it were produced and did showman for Baroness Puckler and yet it was evident that it was really Frau Mavrin herself who was being exhibited and by her very attentions evading any sentimental restraint.

By the end of the meal everyone was great friends with everyone else. The Captain and the German commerical traveller went away and Frau Mavrin, Baroness Puckler, Lushington and the two counts remained drinking coffee while the two hard-faced stewardesses cleared the table. The boat had begun to roll gently. Frau Mavrin said:

'Sophia, you must tell our fortunes. That will entertain all of us and pass the time.'

'But, my dear Ortrud, do these gentlemen wish that their fortunes should be told? And besides the motion of the boat is beginning to make my head ache. Do not you notice it yourself?'

'You must beg her all of you,' Frau Mavrin said. 'You must press her to tell your fortunes. If you do not do this she will think that you do not wish for your fortunes to be told.'

She looked at Lushington under her heavy lashes and he became aware of contact with her. She dropped her eyes suddenly, like pulling down a blind with a snap. For a moment he felt almost as if he had touched her. Then it was over and he and the counts were telling the Baroness how much they would enjoy a prognosis. They took some time to persuade her but at last she said:

'I will fetch my cards and tell the fate of each of you. It will rest on your heads if I foretell evil things.'

She got up and went to her cabin. Count Bobel moved round to the seat next to Frau Mavrin.

'Like this it will be more convenient,' he said.

The sea had become noticeably rougher and some of the beams in the dining saloon began to creak. Once the coffee cups slid almost off the table and the smell of cocoanut oil seemed to have become more noticeable. There was also an increasingly evil scent of fish. Baroness Puckler returned with a pack of cards. She said:

'They are greasy but always I use them. Those with the second sight often have a special pack that they prefer to use and such are these.'

Count Scherbatcheff said: 'I fear, Baroness, that you will find my fortune a sad one. The fortune of a man who has lost in the gamble for life. A man who in that game had often thrown the zero.'

Baroness Puckler handed the cards to Lushington to shuffle and cut. Count Bobel lit another cigarette and said:

'I am the King of Hearts. That is my representative card. It bespeaks my character. You agree, all of you?'

Lushington made the cards and cut. Baroness Puckler began to lay them out on the table. Frau Mavrin said:

'And are you going to believe what Sophia tells you?'

'I don't know yet.'

'She has the true gift. She never makes a mistake in her predictions. She will indeed tell you the future.'

'How dangerous.'

'Do you think so?'

Baroness Puckler began counting the cards, checking up their relation to each other. She said to Lushington:

'First I will say what stands round you. Like all your countrymen you are a prey to melancholy. The spleen of Hamlet. I see you in a big building. It is a church or a palace. You hurry through it writing in a book. Many people are round you, men and women, and they too write in books. A great noble who has many enemies rules over you all. And now I see you next to a fair woman. But she belongs to someone else. Quite soon there is a journey across water. The fair woman comes in again. I see her standing next to you. You go among a number of people. All of them are talking scandal. The fair woman goes out of your life. No, no. I see her with you again. Perhaps there are two fair women. You will meet a dark man who is displeased about something. Will you cut again? There are troubles and disturbances. Perhaps even death. You will receive a letter from across water. You will have a disappointment. There is a love affair. Perhaps it is one of the fair women. You will make some money. Not much money. A little money. It arrives in a letter. A small sum but you will be glad of it. Perhaps it is the great noble who sends it to you. Cut again and wish. You have wished?'

'Yes.'

Baroness Puckler looked at the card.

'You will have your wish. It will be granted to you.'

Frau Mavrin said: 'I see from your fortune that you are a dangerous man. I am curious to know what you wished.'

'Are you? But if I tell you I shall not get my wish.'

'It is something wicked I feel sure.'

'Perhaps.'

Count Scherbatcheff was next. He cut the ace of spades and before Baroness Puckler could speak he said:

'Ah, yes. I see. You need not explain it. The card of death. My poor grandmother. I knew that it must come sooner or later. But I feel an affection for her. In spite of her obstinacy I am attached to her.'

The rolling of the ship was becoming more and more apparent and with it strange odours floating up from the galley. Some of the cards fell on to the floor and in picking them up Count Scherbatcheff knocked his head on the edge of the table. The rest of them were full of sympathy for him but the rolling continued and occupied their attention. Baroness Puckler lifted her hands to her forehead. Lushington held on to the table to steady himself. Count Bobel took out a pocket comb and began to smoothe his hair. Count Scherbatcheff was too dignified to rub his head but he patted his chest and said:

'I have learned sufficient, my dear Baroness. My poor grandmother. However much I may expect her death it will always be a blow to me when it comes. And now I shall go and lie down for a short time in my cabin.'

He went away suddenly, unexpectedly. He was gone like a flash. They heard a door slam as he arrived below. Count Bobel said:

'It will interest all of you to hear what my fortune will be. I am a person who has had innumerable adventures of all kinds. I am a man of the world. I am interested in everything and naturally a man of that kind is the best subject for the seer. Be sure that you all attend.'

But Baroness Puckler was standing up. She still held her hands to her head. The boat beneath them continued to ride uneasily the swell of the sea. The beams creaked all the time. Baroness Puckler said:

'Another time, Count, another time. Just now like Count Scherbatcheff I go to lie down for a little. Ortrud, I shall see you later.'

Lushington and Count Bobel stood up. Count Bobel said:

'I trust, dear lady, that you are not unwell?'

'It is nothing. Nothing. But I go to lie down.'

Baroness Puckler refused Count Bobel's arm and went away down the stairs that led to the cabins. Lushington, Count Bobel, and Frau Mavrin were left sitting round the table. Lushington himself was becoming aware of a feeling of vertigo but he was unwilling to leave the field to Count Bobel although the Count's presence prevented him from making any headway with Frau Mavrin. She sat in her place, assured of herself, almost lovely, making conversation to them both, sometimes staring from under her long eyelashes. The boat heaved about recklessly. The sensation of vertigo was becoming increasingly apparent. Count Bobel who had left a pile of cigarette ends in the ash tray where they burned on incessantly like a small scented bonfire said:

'You do not mind, Madame, if I smoke a cigar?'

'Not at all.'

'And you, sir?'

'Naturally not.'

'You will smoke one with me. They are good these. They are a special brand. They come from Batavia and are hard to obtain.'

'Thank you, no,' said Lushington. 'As it happens I think I too shall go to my cabin for a little while. I have reached an important point in a book I am reading. It is a detective story and very exciting.'

5

The sea continued to be choppy. The German commercial traveller lay on his face on the leather seat which ran round the smoke saloon, with his cheek pressed against several copies of *Die Freundschaft*. His expression showed that philosophically he had reached the sphere of complete submission to fate. Lushington in his cabin thought about Frau Mavrin. He also thought about Lucy and remembered that she had said that he must find someone else. Later he felt better and ate a little dinner. Count Scherbatcheff appeared again too and said, rather insincerely, that his stomach was in any case so unsettled that it was unaffected by the motion of the waves. He did not accept however the amber cigarette that Count Bobel offered him. Count Bobel therefore smoked it himself and many more after it. He was also heard to ask for cointreau in the bar. The smell of cocoanut oil persisted, especially below deck, but that of fish was kept under better control and towards evening abated considerably.

6

The wind had dropped a little and Count Scherbatcheff said that the worst was past and it would not be rough for the rest of the voyage. The passengers on board now formed a world of their own and it was difficult to imagine any time when acquaintance had not been limited to this half-a-dozen and all life proportioned to the boundaries set by the sea.

Lushington sat with the two counts in the smoke saloon. They were comparing experiences and after a lull in the conversation he said:

'I suppose we are due to arrive to-morrow?'

Count Scherbatcheff who was unwilling to break the thread of the discussion, said:

'After that you never feel the same towards a woman. It happened to me once with a girl of mine in Munich. I never felt the same to her after that. Never. Our relationship was altered. All was spoilt.'

Count Bobel said: 'You should have taken more care, Count Scherbatcheff. With women you can never be certain. Now in London, Mr. Lushington, how is it with girls? Always I collect addresses. Is it true there are no *maisons*? No *quartier reservé*?'

'Absolutely.'

'That I cannot understand. *Comment s'amuse la jeunesse?*'

'This girl I was speaking of in Munich,' said Count Scherbatcheff, who disliked interruption, 'she was a Bavarian girl. An art student. I was passionately fond of her.'

Count Bobel said: 'That is like we Russians. It is always the same. We cast our hearts at the feet of women. It is in our nature to give. We do not know restraint. You western peoples little comprehend our ways.'

'She was beautiful,' Count Scherbatcheff said. 'A girl of good family. A girl whom it would be impossible to forget.'

Count Bobel said: 'I too have lived and loved in Munich, Count Scherbatcheff. Who can forget those summer evenings in the gardens of Nymphenburg? Or sunset through the trees at Schleissheim? Not I

for one. Though it was long ago. I was connected with a pedicure establishment in that city for several months. A certain girl especially I remember who was employed by the same firm.'

Count Scherbatcheff said: 'It is indeed remarkable that you should
mention Nymphenburg. It was in those very gardens that I was accustomed to meet the girl I was telling you of.'

'She was fair,' Count Bobel said, 'and——'

'This girl was dark——'

'Allow me one moment, Count Scherbatcheff——'

'Please, please——'

'And now,' Lushington said, 'I shall walk a little outside before I
go to bed. It is an English custom and besides my digestion requires
that I take some exercise. Good night. Good night.'

It was cold on deck. Lushington went to his cabin and put on an
overcoat. Then he walked to the forepart of the boat and, leaning over
the side, looked at the sea, wintry like that on which the schooner *Hes-
perus* had sailed. He was feeling a great deal better now. The sea was
calm and the hard clearness of the night limited the illusion of space and
accentuated the claustrophobia of sea-travel. The ship seemed shut in
closely by the waves and the bright wastes of stars. The breeze came
faintly across the water as he walked along. He did not at once notice
Frau Mavrin who was standing away from the sea, leaning a little against
one of the nondescript subsidiary structures that overspread the deck.
When he became aware of her he saw that she was watching him. As he
looked she came across the deck towards him and said:

'Do talk to me. I came here for a little before bedtime. It is such a
lovely night.'

'The sea is very calm to-night certainly.'

'Where have you been? I have not seen you since dinner. Have you
been avoiding me?'

'Avoiding you, Frau Mavrin?'

'No, no. It was silly of me to say that. I did not mean that exactly.
And please do not call me Frau Mavrin.'

'I do not know your other name.'

'Ortrud.'

'It suits you. It is a lovely name.'

'Do you think so? Where have you been? Talking to the two
counts?'

'I was sitting smoking with them. That is why I did not see you after dinner.'

'Those two terrible men.'

'Don't you like them?'

Standing beside him she touched his arm.

'You are the only person on board to whom I can talk. That fearful Count Bobel whom I feel sure is not a count at all. And even Count Scherbatcheff many of whose cousins I have met. Both of them made extraordinary suggestions to me as soon as I was left alone with them. But I suppose I should not tell you all this.'

'Suggestions?'

'I am a woman of the world. I know men a little. But is that any reason why they should behave in that way to me?'

'But of course not.'

'With you,' she said, 'I feel safe.'

Not knowing exactly why he did it, Lushington put his arm around her.

'With me,' he said, hoping it would not mean fighting a duel with either of the other two, 'you are safe.'

Later they leaned together arm-in-arm over the side of the boat, watching the sea. Lushington said:

'You are not Russian, are you?'

'Why do you ask?'

'You look a little like a Russian.'

'I am Austrian. You wonder why I am going on this voyage. I will tell you. My family had a small property in Galicia but we lost all our land at the end of the War. My father would not change his nationality. He had been an officer in the K. *und* K. cavalry. You understand? He did not recognise the partition of the Empire.'

'Exactly.'

'So we went to Vienna and my parents kept a pension. I taught dancing. But my father was a man of naturally gay disposition. He rose above his misfortunes and used to lose all the money we earned by the pension and the dancing lessons when he played cards. Then my mother, who was a Pole, became despondent and ran away with a Rumanian financier. It is because I look like my mother that you thought I was a Slav.'

'And then what happened?'

'For a time my father and I lived on the bets he won at the local café. No one came to my dancing class. And then one day a foreign professor arranged to have six lessons. Before he had completed the course I was married to him.'

'Did you teach him to dance after you were married?'

'Never.'

'Why not?'

'After we were married he said that there was no more need for him to know how to dance. He only wished to learn in order to find a wife.'

Again she reminded him of Lucy but because she was different and not because their careers had been a little the same. There was the rather sparkling hardness that gave meaning to what both said but the force behind it here was all instinctive and unsupported by any of Lucy's semi-philosophic buttresses.

'He is a difficult man,' she said, meaning her husband.

'Older than you?'

'Oh, yes. He is difficult, you know.'

'Does he treat you badly then?'

'He does not always understand.'

They leaned there together, looking out towards the sea.

'I was so surprised when you kissed me,' she said.

'Were you?'

'I did not know that Englishmen did that sort of thing.'

'Now you know.'

'Now I know.'

They moved from the sea, more conveniently, to a seat beside the wireless cabin. She seemed to him absurdly slim and yielding beneath her heavy coat. At the same time the deck was not in the circumstances an ideal place. She sat there for a time in his arms. Then she said:

'Which of the two counts shares your cabin?'

'Neither of them. I have a cabin to myself. On the port side.'

'Which side is that? I don't know what that means.'

'There. That side.'

'They say that the sea rolls less on that side. That is the best side to have a cabin.'

'Which side is yours?'

'It is on the other side. At the far end of the passage. But do you find that it rolls much on your side?'

'Not so much as you might think. I am lucky to have a cabin to myself. Don't you agree?'

'Does it roll there more than it is rolling now? What do you think?'

'I don't know. I think it does.'

'It rolls very badly on the side I am on too.'

'You share a cabin with your friend of course?'

'Yes.'

They did not speak for some minutes. The wind was increasing and had begun to blow shrilly through the rigging which creaked and strained insistently. The lights were still on in the smoke saloon. The two counts would talk for some time yet. He said:

'Would you like to come down to my cabin and see if the boat rolls as much on that side as the side that you are on?'

'Yes,' she said. 'It would interest me to see.'

In the cabin, when she gave herself to him, she lost some of her remoteness. This remoteness was a weapon, a protection that she might at any moment reassume. But she put it aside for the time when she gave herself to him. He was surprised and rather shaken, feeling that he had been carried unexpectedly off his feet. Afterwards he watched her. Like Lucy she was thin but she had not Lucy's effortless, quite amateur loveliness. She was like a very spruce animal. Her skin was not so white as Lucy's. It was tawny, almost olive and her hair was not so fair. Resting her arm on his shoulder, she said:

'We must meet again. It is a small place and we shall meet again. I am sure that it will be soon.'

'Yes, soon.'

He kissed her.

'You are in love with someone else already, yes?'

'Why should I be?'

'It came in the cards.'

'So it did.'

'Is it true?'

'No.'

'Yes it is. I know. I always know such things.'

'Why do you ask then?'

'You are in love with someone else and you do this? Are you not ashamed?'

'Anyway I'm not married as it appears you are.'

'She is an English girl and she does not love you. I know it is that.'

'How do you know?'

'I am sure of it.'

'Why should you be interested in it at all?'

'You will see. We will meet again and you will tell me all the story. What do you say to that?'

'We shall see.'

'Now I must go.'

'Don't forget this.'

She laughed.

'How absurd. I nearly left it here. Give it to me.'

She turned and slapped his face lightly. Then she opened the door, listened, and went out into the passage. Her perfume, heavy and disturbing, still hung about the cabin. When she had gone Lushington opened the port-hole for a few seconds but it was so cold that he shut it almost at once. It was rough that night and he could not sleep. He continually thought of Lucy. But he did not think anything definite about her. He merely thought of her.

In the afternoon the air was still clear and they could see a town between the gaps in the islands. The lower part of the town was obscure, hidden in light mists, but there were shapes behind that took on an architectural form. This was their destination. The end of the voyage. Soon they would be set at liberty from the sea. Count Scherbatcheff, who for his health's sake had eaten no lunch, said:

'In the first place let me assure you, Lushington, that the man is not a Russian. It is no doubt equally absurd to suppose that he is a count. His behaviour! Have you noticed it? The way he sits at table. His attitude towards the ladies and especially Frau Mavrin. What could be more repellent? And then the heraldic chinoiserie embroidered all over the front of his shirt. I feel certain that he is a man to be avoided. I take this opportunity of warning you to beware of him. There are a great deal too many men of his type about Europe at the present day passing themselves off as Russians.'

He looked at Lushington through very pale blue eyes. To disembark he was wearing the béret with the enamel buttons on it and a raglan overcoat that hung in folds like a cloak. He shook his head and began to walk up and down the deck, sometimes stopping to stamp his feet or beat his arms across his chest.

The ship sailed on, seeming to approach no nearer the town. The hardfaced stewardesses only shrugged their shoulders when asked what time the voyage was coming to an end. Two hours? Three hours? They could not say. It was later that afternoon in the bar, when the view of the town had been hidden unexpectedly by a muddy haze, that Count Bobel said:

'Count Scherbatcheff is a good fellow, Mr. Lushington. He comes of an excellent family. But he is from Little Russia and like all who come from Little Russia he has very marked peculiarities. Besides you must know that his mother was a Georgian princess. He has moreover learned nothing from our country's misfortunes. We of the Russian nobility must face a new order. Times have changed. We are no longer the boyars of John the Terrible. We must curb our pride. Count Scherbatcheff has not yet learned that. He may have a bitter lesson one of these days. Nevertheless he is a sportsman. *Un bon garçon.*'

'What part of Russia do you come from?'

Count Bobel's eyes narrowed a little. His cigarette hung almost vertically from his upper lip and the smoke from it curled gently into Lushington's right eye. The scent of amber hung all round him in a protective cloud. He said:

'My family had several large estates. But they were in a distant part of the country. At a great way off. As you must know Russia is a very immense country. For a foreigner it is difficult even to imagine the extent of it. And now as we shall be landing in a short time I must inspect again my baggage as it contains commodities about which there may be question at the *douane*. You understand me?'

Lushington went on deck again. Ortrud and Baroness Puckler were there wearing all their coats and scarves and standing beside a cairn of suitcases. The baroness said:

'Always this affair of getting past the customs and the passport officers. But last time we were lucky and it was all over in less than an hour and a half. Let us hope we shall repeat our good fortune on this occasion.'

Ortrud said: 'It is good that we have reached here before the ice. Often at this time it is frozen up. We have had a lucky voyage.'

Only her eyes, blue and lozenge-shaped, appeared above the collar of her persian-lamb coat. Lushington slipped his arm behind one of the suitcases and touched her hand. She caught one of the fingers between two of hers and said:

'We must all meet again when we have recovered from the stress of the voyage, Mr. Lushington. You will come and have dinner with me and with my husband?'

As they went on towards the shore the islands receded from the town and remained to the right and left in the mist among which they had first appeared. The place came into sight suddenly, huddled up, with blue-green spires and a red and gold cathedral. A castle or palace in grey stone was built on a rampart in a part of the town that was on a higher level than the rest of the houses. The boat passed a fort jutting out into the sea and then entered twisting waterways between wharfs. Here there was accommodation for a navy but the docks were deserted. Sometimes decrepit tramps rode at anchor, flying a German or Scandinavian ensign, with frozen washing hanging out to dry attached to the lower rigging. There were streets and houses among the docks and looking between these it seemed that ships were moored in the thoroughfares of the town itself so that quite suddenly Lushington thought again of Lucy, vividly, as if she were standing beside him as they moved forward. These ships among the buildings recalled her to him, bringing back a day they had spent together in the country when, coming through some trees towards the sea, funnels and masts appeared before them a few fields away, rising out of hedges and ploughland, jagged and coloured gaudily against the green damp English morning. These unlikely hulls by some configuration of an estuary had seemed cut off and permanently landlocked, part of the strangeness of the countryside. Liners built up among the hedges. The day had been doubly notable for Lucy's release from the higher pessimism and the ships here now reminded him of her as she had come through the trees with him and stopped all at once, her hair blowing across her face as they stood and looked at the painted funnels.

But that had been months before, he thought. This was another country. Something altogether different.

The ship had ceased to make headway and a motor-boat put out from one of the quays and puffed towards them. An officer wearing a sword came on board and a weary civilian with a shaved head and an eye-glass. This last person carried a heavy instrument as for jacking up a lorry. With this contrivance, which proved to be a survival from the early days of printing, he stamped all the passports which he considered to be in order and at the same time was persuaded by Count Bobel to accept a cigar. At last they landed and Lushington drove to the hotel where he found a note from Da Costa who apologised for having been unable to meet the boat. Lushington had dinner and went to bed early. He was tired after the journey.

The hotel was unexpectedly large with palm trees in pots placed at intervals round the lounge. There were two doors at the entrance, one of them so heavy that only very strong people could get into the hotel at all without help and even those who managed to push it open, unassisted by the hall porter, were often swept back into the street at the very moment when they had seemed on the point of gaining admittance. From the middle of the morning onwards business men sat in the wicker chairs of the lounge and drank coffee or *schnapps* and worked out sums for each other in pencil on the backs of envelopes. Flosshilde, the reception clerk, sat at her desk all day long watching the business men. She had red hair and was fat for her age and she wore an engagement ring made of large imitation diamonds. She spoke a dozen words of all languages and usually she had the lounge well under control. Sometimes, but not often, when the business men were very tiresome, she lost her head and the manager had to be sent for. Now she stood over Lushington while he filled up forms for the police dossier of foreigners.

'See!' she said. 'You have not written. The profession of mother's father?'

'I don't know it.'

'So?'

'No.'

'Write *private* then. And the date of marriage of father and mother?'

'I can't remember.'

'They are truly married?'

'They always say so.'

This was a critical situation. Flosshilde thought. She said:

'Write any time before your birthday. But write it a year before.'

'All right. But give me another pen.'

Opposite the hotel was the National Theatre in stucco, Palladian and undistinguished. In the Russian time it had been the Opera House. Near by was the Bourse. All this was in the Low Town where most of the buildings were modern and the streets were broad. In the High

Town on the other side of the river there were mediaeval houses made of wood and the streets were narrow and broken by steps and archways. The place was quite unreal, Lushington noticed. Flosshilde said that there would be snow soon. When that came this unreality would be absolute, although as a set-piece the scene would remain unstylised. Because the unreality was something in itself. Not the product of historical association nor even the superimposed up-to-dateness. It was related perceptibly to the foreground of sea. The weather was not unpleasantly cold and the air was astonishingly clear. But there would be snow soon, Flosshilde said, because it was already late in the month.

Da Costa's flat was in the High Town. There was a shiny white-painted stove in the sitting-room, built out into the middle of the floor, and a bookcase with all Da Costa's books in it, piled up anyhow, some of them facing the wrong way. It was a large, uncomfortable room, greatly overheated, the sort of room that Da Costa was accustomed to inhabit. Lushington sat there looking through the double windows at the Baltic. Da Costa, a dark young man with a greenish, horse-shaped face, stood beside him, also watching the sea, his mouth a little open as if at any moment he were going to laugh. The two surfaces of glass were faulty in the middle so that the spires of the Lutheran churches seemed to have broken away from their swollen bases as they narrowed up. The spires of the Lutheran churches were green and the Russian cathedral was built of red brick with five gold cupolas. The flat was high up and the sea was a long way off beyond the docks but to the right and left of the town it was possible to distinguish where buildings ended suddenly in stretches of sand and pines. On the other side of the house the bedroom looked down on to a square in which a few market stalls were set up once a week and opposite these was the new railway station, designed on a substratum of *modernismus*, with pylons and tumid, angular caryatids. This was in red stone, the same red as the Russian cathedral, and it stood out uncompromisingly against the sky, which was steel coloured and opaque. Da Costa said:

'Sometimes, as an Englishman, I feel a little inferior about my name in a country where so many people are descended from seventeenth century adventurers and are called everyday names like Baron Morgan or Count Mackintosh. Or even, like the Chilean consul, merely Smith.'

Lushington laughed. He was experiencing the feeling of irritation brought on by seeing again an old friend from whom he had been separated for many months. Da Costa, he noticed, felt the same and Lushington knew that Da Costa was wondering when he himself would begin to talk about Lucy. It was a point upon which he had not yet made up his mind. He was thinking at that moment of his own satisfac-

tion that Da Costa should care so little about her and at the same time
of his annoyance that Da Costa should care so little while he himself
cared a good deal. But he knew by experience that if his own affection
for Lucy ever seemed to show signs of diminishing Da Costa was accustomed to show uneasiness because this seemed to lessen the value of
Lucy's feelings for himself. On that account at least Lushington decided
to say nothing of Ortrud. Besides the thought of her disturbed him and
made him feel curiously more amiable towards Da Costa.

Pope was in the room too, moving secretively as if he were tidying
up, sometimes pausing to examine letters or papers that Da Costa had
left lying about or making scraps of introvert conversation. Pope had
an unhealthy complexion, strangely discoloured, mineral rather than
flesh, and hair so fair that it was nearly white. He hurried about the
room, touching everything. He spoke always gently as if he were talking
to a sick person. Gently but with insistence. Da Costa leaned so close
to the window that his nose touched it and made a steamy mark on the
near pane. At this he retreated his face a little and turned towards the
east where on the high ground beyond the industrial quarter were low,
green-painted buildings like dolls' houses, government offices in the
Russian time, now made into tenements. Lushington watched the
people passing below the window. The streets were crowded at this
time of day, mostly with men in black overcoats and astrakhan caps and
goloshes. There were also staff officers who carried under their arm black
portfolios, and a few boy and girl students in coloured peaked caps on
their way home from the university.

The evening light came into the room with curious slowness,
brightening and emphasising the colour schemes of mauve and Venetian red which the late owner, one of the Rumanian secretaries, had
instituted and which Pope would not allow Da Costa to alter. Pope
began arranging in order of precedence all the invitation cards on the
mantelpiece. When he was satisfied with their sequence he addressed
himself to Da Costa. He said:

'It always interests me to do this, sir. Social life has always had a
great attraction for me and I for it. It comes out in my ways. I notice it
myself when I am dealing with others. It is something in myself. I have
no control over it. By that I mean that I do not try to prevent myself
from exercising this quality because I see that it is a desirable thing that
when such feelings exist they should be encouraged. My family have

often commented on the difference between me and them. For example they always call me the Duke.'

Da Costa laughed. He did not answer or turn round. The mark of steam on the inner window became wider than before. Lushington shuffled with his feet. Pope began to smile quietly to himself and set about brushing crumbs from the table with a rolled up copy of *The Gazette*. Then he patted a cushion and moved it from the place where it had been thrown.

'You see my family think a great deal of me,' he said. 'I often tell them that they flatter me too much.'

Outside the fading evening, giving no warning, had become night. The dark steeples could still be seen among the dim lights. Pope went towards the window and began to draw the blinds. He said:

'I took the liberty of borrowing Freud's *Psychopathology of Life* from your bookcase, sir. It is my free night to-morrow and should like to spend it reading. I often read lying on my bed. I hope you have no objection, sir.'

Da Costa came to with a jerk. He said:

'No, no. Read it anywhere you like. And in any position.'

'Is there anything more this evening, sir?'

'No, that's all.'

'Good night, sir. Good night, sir.'

'Good night, Pope.'

'Good night.'

Pope went away. Da Costa said:

'That was Pope. I've arranged for him to valet you. He doesn't have much to do and he said he'd like to take the job on. I inherited him from the last man who was here. He's a curious fellow as you see. Rather a character.'

'But I don't like characters.'

'I know you don't. Neither do I. But we can't always have what we like. You had better take Pope on. I should perhaps warn you that he is sometimes rather inquisitive. Still he is a good valet.'

'I can't possibly afford a valet.'

'You need not pay him much. You must have someone to look after your clothes. The hotel servants won't touch them. Anyway, I've arranged it with Pope and he is going to call you to-morrow. He's a man with a lot of personality.'

'Why didn't you tell me all this when he was here?'

Da Costa laughed again but without reference to any particular matter. He changed his weight from his right foot to his left and began to whistle through his teeth. Lushington said:

'And how are the Communists?'

'Splendid. They blew up the new gasworks the other day. At least that is supposed. Either they or the works manager who was, it appears, a very erratic man. As everything is blown up it is hard to say. It is a pity because architecturally they were of considerable beauty.'

'Do you ever come in contact with the Soviet legation?'

'Not as a rule. But you ought to. I met one of their secretaries the other day at a tea party. We were both lodged in a corner and he thought I was an American engineer on his way out to some mines in Russia and I thought he was a French author on his way back. They have invented an entirely new form of boredom, like the worst moments of being in the boy scouts at one's preparatory school. He was a fine example of it.'

'Do you think I shall be able to get any stuff about communism for the paper?'

'Oh, yes. Plenty of stuff. There might easily be a revolution. There have been several outbreaks in countries next door. But a political assassination is about the best thing you can really rely on. There hasn't been one for some time and everyone is getting heartily sick of everyone else.'

'What's it like being here?'

'An amusing town. I enjoy it. There is Maxim's and the Café Weber and the Station Restaurant and if you've been to all those you can listen to the wireless. You can pick up all sorts of peculiar places from here.'

He laughed again, deafeningly, as if he were going to go off his head at any moment. Lushington lit a cigarette. Da Costa said:

'Fortunately you have come out here in time for the annual ball given by the nobility. You will be able to write something about that for your beastly paper.'

'Is it a good show?'

'Yes. Excellent. If you like that sort of thing.'

'Where are we going to-night?'

'To the Café Weber and then Maxim's. Maxim's is the night club. To tell the truth I have only been there once myself, and that was the night after I arrived for the first time. Two others are coming to dinner. Curtis Cortney, who is third secretary at the American legation, and a fellow called Waldemar.'

'Tell me about them.'

'Waldemar is a soldier. A captain in one of the two cavalry regiments. The 2nd Uhlans I think. Or perhaps it is the 1st. He isn't really a captain, but he had an appointment at the Ministry of Defence, cleaning out the inkpots or something of the sort, and everybody calls him captain.'

'And Cortney?'

'He is a fine chap too. I believe he's a Southerner, but I can't really remember. Perhaps he isn't. I wish their minister was, though. I like Southerners.'

'What's he?'

'He's whatever you are when you are not a Southerner. He is not a professional diplomat of course, so that one should not expect too much. That's their system.'

'What is?'

'They give their best diplomatic posts to business men who need a rest or lawyers who have flown a bit near the wind in their own country. They send publishers to the more important capitals but the people here have to put up with smaller fry. But you'd be surprised to see how soon most of them pick it up. Still poor Cortney who is of course in their permanent service used to go through agonies with the last minister who could not tie his white tie. It once came undone during a presidential reception.'

'By the way Lucy sent her love,' said Lushington, who was not greatly interested in the administration of the United States' diplomatic service.

'Lucy? Oh did she? How is she? Why doesn't she come out here for a bit?' said Da Costa.

He laughed again vacantly and to prevent Lushington going on about Lucy he began to hum. But his presence, slowly getting to work like the warming up of an engine, had begun to condition in Lushington renewed thoughts of Lucy and, although Da Costa was not the person with whom from preference he would have discussed her, he was the only one available, being almost certainly the sole human being in the country who had ever heard her name. Lushington said, above the humming:

'I thought she was looking better when I came away.'

He was considering other remarks to make with which to follow up this one when the door bell rang. Da Costa said:

'This must be Waldemar. I will let him in.'

He went out into the hall and returned almost at once with a young man in uniform who still had his fur cap on his head. The young man looked nervous. He was clean-shaved and wore pince-nez. His double-breasted military overcoat had a high waist and broad sheepskin collar. He clicked his heels, saluted, and said:

'Waldemar!'

Da Costa said: 'He is introducing himself. This is Captain Waldemar. Captain Waldemar—Mr. Lushington.'

Waldemar said in quite good English:

'Pleased to meet you, Mr. Lushington.'

Da Costa said: 'Take your coat and sword off, Waldemar, and we'll have a drink.'

Waldemar unhooked his sword and propped it up in the corner of the room among Da Costa's shooting sticks and golf clubs. Underneath his overcoat he wore a khaki tunic, well cut but very tight, and a pair of blood-red riding breeches with a yellow stripe down each leg. He seemed rather bothered and passed his hand once or twice round the inside of his cruelly high collar. Then he sat down and said to Lushington:

'You have been playing rugby in England, yes?'

Da Costa, pulling the cork out of a bottle, said:

'No, no. Of course he hasn't. I've told you about that before, Waldemar. You read too many of the wrong sort of English books.'

Waldemar laughed a little and adjusted his pince-nez, but he seemed relieved. Lushington said to him:

'I hear we are going to Maxim's to-night.'

'You like dancing?' Waldemar said. 'There is dancing there. And there are girls.'

'I expect you go there often?'

'No. Not often. Two years ago I was there. It was Christmas time. It was very jocose.'

Da Costa said: 'It's an amusing place. I remember it well. The girls are very good looking. They are mostly Russian I believe. You don't have to dance with them if you don't want to. I expect that bell is Cortney arriving.'

He went out into the hall again and came back this time with an American dressed in the English manner and wearing a small fair moustache, trimmed so that it appeared to be false. Da Costa who was evidently embarrassed by this new arrival as much as he himself embarrassed Waldemar, took the American by the arm and shouted to the others: 'This is Mr. Curtis Cortney. This is a compatriot of mine, Curtis. You know Captain Waldemar already I think.'

Lushington shook hands with Cortney who said with a conversational burr as sweet and low as the *vox humana* of some mighty cinema organ:

'Mr. Lushington, I hope that we shall be great friends.'

Da Costa began laughing again and, standing on one leg, yelled:

'Well, Curtis, what's it to be? A high-ball?'

Lushington said to Waldemar:

'How well you talk English.'

Da Costa said: 'Don't sit there paying each other compliments. Come and help mix these drinks.'

Cortney said: 'So we're going to Maxim's to-night. It's strange that I never seem to go there. Only been there once in all the months I've been here.'

'Lovely girls,' said Waldemar, rather unconvincingly, and there was a pause. Waldemar patted his soft black leather riding boots that wrinkled round his ankles. Lushington said to Cortney:

'Have you been posted here long?'

'Since last fall.'

'How do you like it?'

Cortney said: 'Mr. Lushington, for two years I was at Buenos Aires. Do you know that I just couldn't stop there. I used to wake up in the morning and tell myself that I couldn't stand for those modern boulevards any longer. I used to say why can't I get away to somewhere where there is some history, some romance. And then I got my transfer. Hell, what a day that was, the day I got my transfer. Why there wasn't a happier man in all B.A. And now when I run my tub each morning I can look through the window and see those ancient grey walls of stone and I think of the old-time knights—*ritters*, they call them here—who caused them to be raised and my heart beats maybe a trifle faster and sometimes I can almost hear the clash of swords on breastplates, and I tell myself no, no, all that was in the days gone by. Ah, Captain Waldemar, it's a great heritage this little old land of yours. No wonder you're proud of your independence.'

Waldemar said: 'Yes, yes, Mr. Cortney. You love romance. Like you I too love romance. When I was young also I would think how romantic to go to the Wild West. To fight Indians. Or to be English. To have colonies. Always it was childish dream of mine that I should go out to the English colonies. You understand me? It was not a practical thought. It was schoolboy imagining of mine. The dream of a schoolboy not yet grown up.'

Cortney said: 'Captain Waldemar, that's a great idea of yours but it's not just what I intended to convey. It's a fine viewpoint for a young man though it may not be my own if you understand me.'

Waldemar said: 'Nevertheless the English are an elegant race. A nation of dandies. It was a great surprise to me when I saw English officers carrying walking sticks. Here we may not carry sticks when we are in uniform. It is forbidden. We may not carry sticks unless we are lame.'

Da Costa said: 'Here, drink this, Waldemar, and don't talk so much.'

Cortney turned to Lushington and said: 'I expect I'm just naturally romantic. But that's how the place gets me. And I'll swear it will get you that way too.'

They dined that evening at the Café Weber in a wide room done-up in a modern German style. Da Costa, whose nerves were bad, talked most of the time and laughed at all his own jokes. Waldemar and Cortney were evidently used to him. Both seemed to like him, although Waldemar, regarding him as a typical Englishman and as such prepared for the worst, was a little afraid of him. Waldemar himself was a quiet, studious young man whom circumstances rather than taste seemed to have brought to the high calling of arms. He was shy and his tunic was a great deal too tight and whenever Da Costa asked him whether or not he would eat a certain dish he always said 'Perhaps' as a polite method of throwing the onus of choosing on Da Costa. This had the combined effect of annoying Da Costa and holding up the progress of the meal. At moments even Cortney would say:

'Now then, Captain, show some military decision.'

Cortney at times seemed unnerved by Da Costa's general appearance and manner but most of all by his clothes which, as always, looked as if they had been made by a good tailor for someone of quite different shape. Lushington saw him give sidelong glances at Da Costa's waist-coat which continually worked up above the top of his trousers. The food and wine in the restaurant were like the decorations, heavy and pretentious. As the meal advanced Waldemar became more confident and told them about himself and his life:

'For a year I was in France. At the military school of St. Cyr. One would have to get up at four o'clock in the morning. There was no breakfast. Only very strong black coffee. Sometimes it was too strong for me to drink. There was an English officer there with me. Always he would say that he could not become accustomed to there being no breakfast. He was called Macgregor. It was always that. Macgregor could not become accustomed to that.'

'Ah,' said Cortney, 'you English. You're a great race but you have your limitations.'

11

Maxim's was a small and undistinguished night club with a gallery running round it and, instead of being done-up in modern German, it had been treated freely in the later manner of French second-empire style. The band, who were called *Bristol Mondial Boys*, sat at the end of the room. Their name was written on the drum and they were playing *O Katerina* while a few couples danced. Waldemar said:

'You see they have a telephone on every table. Very modern, you see?'

Cortney said: 'If anyone calls us up you'll have to answer them, Captain. I've done all my telephoning for to-day at the office.'

At the next table two conscripts in baggy uniforms with pinched, intellectual faces stood up to attention and one of them upset his drink. Waldemar inclined his head and they sat down again. Two girls were at the table on the other side. One of them was dark and wore the approximation of a riding habit, an indeterminate affair in bottle green, and the other, a sulky looking blonde with hair *à la pompadour*, was in black evening dress. They were drinking coffee and lost no time in indicating that they would be prepared to accept an invitation to supper.

'Shall we get them over?' said Da Costa, rather threateningly, in case any of the others might say yes, but everyone was opposed to the suggestion. Da Costa who had now become something of the school bully, a nervous state engendered by finding himself in a night club, said:

'Come on, Waldemar, pull yourself together and tell all these waiters that we're not going to drink champagne but they're to get some brandy at once and mind it has a recognisable label on the bottle.'

They sat down and watched the dancers, a mixed party, Waldemar explained, mostly business men with their wives, except a major in the artillery dancing with his fiancée, who played Ibsen heroine parts at the national theatre, and a long way off the American minister who was giving supper to the leading lady from the touring German production of *Gräfin Maritza*. It was some time before Lushington noticed Count

Bobel dancing with an elderly woman, who showed by her demeanour that she was paying for the evening's entertainment. The Count bowed to Lushington as he danced past their table. Da Costa said:

'What curious friends you always seem to have.'

'Not at all. Why should you think so?'

'Who is he?'

'A beauty specialist. A count. I met him on the boat coming over here.'

'A typical acquaintance of yours.'

'Do you think so? In any case I see nothing out of the ordinary in my knowing him. He seemed a very normal sort of person.'

The manager of the place stood near the table moving round it at intervals to examine Lushington, Da Costa and Cortney at different angles. He was not interested in Waldemar. The girls at the next table were not interested in Waldemar either as they and the manager were equally familiar with the rates of army pay. The manager had a moustache, side whiskers and a frock coat. When he had inspected the table from all sides he came very close and said:

'English?'

Da Costa said: 'Yes. Of course I am English. Why do you ask?'

The manager said: 'Very well. Yes, please.'

Da Costa bowed to show that the conversation was at an end but the manager lingered by the table. He seemed to have something on his mind. He said:

'I was officer in Russian army. I was major. I was on general staff.'

Cortney said: 'Well, Major, you've got a nice little place here.'

'Revolution came. All was gone. Now am here.'

Lushington said: 'Rather a change.'

The manager said: 'You want to meet girls. I can arrange it. Good girls. One speak English.'

'Not at the moment.'

This reply appeared so far-fetched that the manager was for the moment at a loss for words. He therefore retreated and consolidated his position. He said:

'I was on general staff. I pass examination staff-school and was breveted general staff.'

Da Costa, whose nerves were showing no sign of abating, said:

'Was it fun being on the general staff?'

The manager said: 'Often when in a new place you feel lonely.

Want company. One girl speak English. I present you. Good girl. *Everyone* say good girl.'

'Not yet.'

The manager seemed perplexed. Someone had made a false move. He showed his teeth again.

'Good girls,' he said, but with a lessening conviction.

This conversation might have continued indefinitely but at that point in its development somebody in the band struck a gong and all the lights went out. A mauve spot-light was switched on to the dancing floor and a fat girl in trousers and a Spanish hat came to the centre of the room and with castanets began to sing:

> '. . . for I'm one of de nuts from Barcelona,
> I *pliquety-plonque*,
> My *casa-bionque* . . .'

As she sang she danced round the room snapping her castanets in front of each table. The audience received these representations stoically with the exception of one of the business men who had had too much to drink and who made faces at her while she was executing these movements for his benefit. After a time the lights went on again and the manager was found to be far away. He was ushering in a new party of clients, two women, a man in a white tie and an officer of some rank with a decoration hanging at his throat. At the next table the two conscripts stood rigid. And then Lushington saw that one of the two women was Ortrud.

She came across the room, moving rather superbly. When she saw them she stopped at the table and held out her hand. As they got up she said:

'I told you that we should meet quickly again in so little a city. You remember that I said that?'

'I am glad it has been so soon.'

'I present to you,' she said, 'Major-General of Infantry Kuno and Frau Major-General of Infantry Kuno. And this is Herr Legation-Secretary Diaz.'

The General beamed. He was rather more than five feet high and he wore white kid gloves. His wife was dressed in a tippet. Mr. Diaz had a hooked nose and a blue chin and was the unathletic sort of Latin-American. The general jingled his spurs, clanked his sword a little so that the sword-knot swung backwards and forwards, and bowed. Ortrud said:

'The Herr Major-General of Infantry speaks only our language.'

General Kuno nodded and showed his teeth in friendship at Lushington who nodded and grinned fiercely in return. Lushington said:

'How is Baroness Puckler?'

'Come and speak to me at my table before you go away from here to-night. I will tell you about her. And besides I should myself like to see you again.'

She put her head a little on one side and smiled. Her party moved on towards their table. The arrival of General Kuno had thrown Waldemar into a great state of nerves. Da Costa said:

'You seem to have more friends here than I have. How did you meet Frau Mavrin?'

'On the boat.'

'Do you make all your friends on boats?'

'Some on trains. But who exactly is she?'

'Who is she? Don't you know who she is? What an extraordinary fellow you are. Her husband is Professor of Psychology at the university here. Didn't she tell you? He's a very clever man. An international reputation, almost.'

'What is she like?'

'What's she like? Well I imagine you know more about her than I do. You were almost alone with her in an open boat for several days. For all the privacy there is on those boats coming out here one might as well be on a raft.'

Cortney, who had been occupied during the past few minutes in glancing furtively at the American minister, who with the help of the German leading-lady was energetically lowering his country's prestige at the far end of the room, began to listen to the conversation again and said:

'If it's Frau Mavrin that you're talking of I'll tell you Frau Mavrin is a great little lady. She's got poise, she's got dignity, she's got sense of position. She's a sophisticate who knows the worth of simplicity. She's a girl any country should be proud of. She's Frau Mavrin and we all of us love her for it.'

Da Costa said: 'Your chief was talking about her the other day and said she was a tough baby, whatever that may mean. He said she was the sort of dame who if she'd been taken in adultery would have caught the first stone and thrown it back.'

'I'll say he sometimes seems to lack a proper reverence for women although he is my chief. But he doesn't mean it. It's just his hard-boiled way of expressing himself.'

Da Costa said: 'Well we all of us have our disillusioned moments. I expect your chief does just like the rest of us. In spite of the fun he seems to be having to-night. Come on, Waldemar. Have some more of this. Don't mope.'

Lushington said: 'She's an Austrian, isn't she?'

'Viennese. I fancy she got rather mixed up in some of the gay life there at one point. *Tales from the Vienna Woods* and so on.'

The band after playing *O Katerina* faster and faster had now switched over to *Komm mit nach Varasdin*. The girl in the riding habit and the one with hair *à la pompadour* got up and began to dance together. They gravitated to the centre of the room where, hovering, they attempted a charleston. Once when they passed the table the cross-looking one said 'Hullo, mister,' to Cortney. Da Costa said:

'Of course they don't really like one coming here much at the legation. In fact when the Old Man was here he once warned me against the place. However Bellamy won't bother even if he hears of it and the new minister is bound to get rid of me any way.'

'What will you do if he does?' Lushington said.

'I don't know. I may go and dig in Crete or somewhere like that. I've always wanted to do that.'

Cortney said: 'Fortunately our service does not enforce such a rigid code of personal behaviour. The American People wouldn't think any the worse of us for coming to a dump like this. In fact they'd think we were crazy if we didn't throw a wild party once in a while. Look at the life we lead. What sort of a week have you got ahead of you? I take it you're going to the d'Almeidas' on Tuesday?'

'And dining with the new Japanese that night.'

'I'm not in on that but there's the Danish *thé dansant* the day after and dinner at the Castellinis' for the Gomez reception and they're burying Parapapadoukos on Thursday and I'm going to play bridge with the Zadeks that night.'

'I'm going to all those so that we shall meet several times. Then I shall see you on Friday night at the Bellamys', I hope, and are you going to the Ninitch lunch at the Café Weber?'

'Naturally and the Jakobsens' that afternoon.'

'That's fine,' Da Costa said, 'because I must have a word with you in the near future about something Bellamy wants to know with regard to imported textiles. I expect some opportunity will turn up for discussing the matter.'

Lushington who had not been listening because he was watching Ortrud and her party said:

'Who is General Kuno?'

Waldemar said: 'For the time he commands the police. He is a very strong man. Some do not like him. During the Civil War he executed many people. But he is not so important now as then. Not so important as some of the colonels. Some of the colonels are very important men.'

Count Bobel who was seated some way off at a table in the gallery appeared to be having an uninteresting evening with his partner, who wore a chignon. He continually turned round and smiled at Lushington and pointed below the gallery to indicate where Ortrud was sitting. Lushington smiled back wanly, hoping that others would not see him.

They watched the dancing. Ortrud went round the room once, doing a tango with the South American Diaz, but as she passed her own table she said something to him and they stopped and sat down. The fat girl appeared again several times, variously dressed in man's evening clothes, peasant costume, and as Columbine. There was also a man who did step dancing and held knives in his mouth. The atmosphere was warm and some ladies were fanning themselves with the paper fans that had been handed round. The manager threw a few coloured streamers, but after a time he became tired of doing this and sat at a table near the band and had some tea.

It was getting late. Waldemar yawned once or twice behind his hand. Da Costa said:

'Is it bedtime do you think?'

Lushington said: 'Before we go I must speak to Frau Mavrin. I should like to see her again.'

As he said this he saw that Ortrud and her party had paid their bill and were coming across the room. General Kuno clattered across the dance floor and once more the two conscripts stood up. Ortrud came to the table and said:

'Will not you and your friends come to my apartment for a few minutes before you go home? Mr. Da Costa and Mr. Cortney and you, Herr Hauptmann, whom I have not met yet? You will come?'

She smiled at the others. She watched them from under her absurdly arched eyebrows. Waldemar excused himself on the ground of an early parade he had unexpectedly to attend the following morning, but Da Costa and Cortney said that they would like to come. Ortrud said:

'Then it will be only you three and Mr. Legation-Secretary Diaz. The General and Madame have decided to go home.'

Everyone bowed to everyone else and after a slight disturbance about the bill in which Waldemar had to act as interpreter they left the table. As they went the girl with hair à la pompadour said: 'Hey, hey, mister, you come with us, isn't it?'

Da Costa said: 'No, Madam, it is nothing of the sort,' and they passed on through the bar towards the door.

In the outer room of the premises the tired, hunched-up man sitting on one of the high stools at the bar turned out to be Count Scherbatcheff, who said:

'Good night, Lushington. I suppose the manager of this place told you that he was a Russian?'

'Yes.'

'I supposed that he would.'

Count Scherbatcheff shook his head gloomily. Lushington said: 'How did you find your grandmother?'

'She was obstinate. She is an old woman and she likes her own way. You are English. In England you do not make scenes. But my grandmother does not try to control herself. She screams. She throws herself on the floor.'

Seeing Ortrud, Count Scherbatcheff jumped off his stool and kissed her hand. Lushington introduced Da Costa and Cortney. Waiters hung round expectantly, hoping that the festivities were going to begin all over again. Cortney said:

'Enchanté, Count. A good friend of mine called Vanoppen married a Princess Alexandrovna Scherbatcheff in Boston the other day. The princess is a relative of yours, no doubt?'

Count Scherbatcheff said: 'No, no. No relation. I know of whom you speak. Nor is she a princess. My grandmother was complaining about her only this evening.'

He leaned against the bar and patted his chest.

'I still suffer a great deal from the stomach,' he said. They commiserated and left him leaning against the bar.

'Poor man,' said Ortrud. 'But my husband would never allow me to bring a Russian into the house.'

Cortney said: 'Count Scherbatcheff seems a splendid fellow. One of the best. But I guess he made an error about Princess Alexandrovna Scherbatcheff. Why, she came from one of the best families in Russia. Vanoppen wouldn't have made a mistake about a thing like that. I know him too well to think he'd done that. But they're strange these old-world aristocrats sometimes in the things they say about each other.'

They managed to get into one drosky. Diaz who was good-looking but of weak character was elbowed away from Ortrud by Lushington and Cortney. Lushington held one of her hands under the rug and wondered whether Cortney was holding the other one. Da Costa from choice sat opposite them. Lushington was relieved to find that Ortrud seemed to know neither Da Costa nor Cortney too well. His own relief surprised him and he speculated upon her friendship with Diaz.

12

The drosky stopped in front of a block of flats in the university quarter. They entered a cramped lift which they worked themselves by pressing a button. At one point it showed signs of stopping between two floors, but it recovered and ascended the rest of the way in short jerks. They reached one of the higher floors at last where the lift came to rest.

The Mavrin's flat was unnecessarily full of furniture and pictures of all sorts, including an oleograph of the Emperor Franz-Josef and a cuckoo clock. Ortrud turned on the light and said: 'A moment and I will make tea. I know that Englishmen always like tea. Am I not right?'

They sat down. Ortrud fetched some cups and saucers. Diaz tried to help her but she told him not to interfere and he retired to sit down with the others. They waited. Then the inner door of the room opened and a tall elderly man with a shaggy moustache and wearing a dressing-gown stood on the threshold. Slowly he came into the room. He was clearly surprised to see so many guests at this hour. He said:

'Ach, Ortrud——'

'Speak English, Panteleimon, these gentlemen are English and do not understand our language.'

'Ach, *so*?'

'Mr. Lushington, this is my husband.'

Professor Mavrin stood there for a few moments collecting himself, rubbing his eyes with one hand and smoothing down his hair with the other. He seemed sleepy. Then he bowed and shook everyone by the hand, and said:

'Gentlemen, I am delighted to see you all.'

Ortrud said: 'Panteleimon, do not you think that your clothes are a little incorrect now that we have friends to see us? A little informal?'

'My dear, I have but now come from bed.'

'But, my dear husband, would it not be right to wear something more in keeping? That is my thought.'

'My dear, you suggest that I put on my clothes again?'

'Mr. Legation-Secretary Diaz has full evening dress. These gentlemen wear the smoking. Should we, their hosts, appear in less?'

'You wish that I put on evening dress again, my dear wife?'

'Would it not be becoming, Panteleimon?'

'Very well, my dear wife. What you think is no doubt best.'

The professor turned to the others. He said:

'You will excuse me for a few moments, gentlemen. I fear that I have appeared in unsuitable attire. It is my hope that you will perhaps forgive me.'

He drew his dressing-gown around him and went through the door by which he had come in. He looked rather noble in his simple dressing-gown, like a mediaeval abbot or one of the Burghers of Calais. Ortrud continued to prepare the tea. Cortney said:

'Frau Mavrin, what I marvel at in this little country of yours is your home life. Now in America, I hope not too late, we are realising what a sacred institution the home is and how it is threatened by the stress of modern life. It is in the home that the children are being raised that the nation of the future will be proud of and it's in the home that the finest flower of our womanhood should find its true place. Now that's a lesson it seems to me that this country will never have to learn.'

'Oh, Mr. Cortney, you are so kind.'

'It's just the truth, Frau Mavrin.'

'But then I am really Austrian.'

Cortney made a few passes in the air as if he were conducting an imaginary orchestra of great size and through his teeth he hummed a few bars of the second strain from *The Blue Danube*.

'That's just it, Frau Mavrin,' he said. 'That's just it.'

Diaz who saw the party developing along lines that no South American could tolerate made some excuse about never drinking tea and after spending what seemed to Lushington an age kissing Ortrud's hand went away. Ortrud said:

'I am not sorry that he has gone. When he first came out here I thought that he was such a nice young man. You understand? He dances well. He is always so attentive. But then I find that I do not like him so much.'

Cortney said: 'Frau Mavrin, you can't be too careful. You must always bear in mind that the attitude of a Latin to a woman is not the one that we Nordic peoples have been brought up to. They do not think along the same lines as we do. They sometimes fail to appreciate that conception of chivalry that is instilled into the Anglo-Saxon from his birth up. Is not that so, Mr. Lushington?'

'Absolutely.'

Da Costa said: 'Come, come, don't forget the hot Portuguese blood that flows in my own veins.'

Ortrud said: 'Ah, I think you are right. I am certainly glad that he has gone. I feel more safe.'

She poured out tea for them and gave them sweet biscuits from a tin box. In this room she looked not at all different from what she had been at Maxim's or on the sea. She was nearly beautiful. Lushington was surprised because he had expected her to change when he had become accustomed to her appearance and when he had seen her in her own surroundings. He watched her while Da Costa, all legs and arms, sitting in an armchair, as if his limbs had been thrown there without arrangement, and Cortney, very upright on an embroidered stool, talked of the bridge tournament that someone was organising and about which they wanted Ortrud to give advice. At last she handed both of them a pencil and some paper and said:

'Come. Write down the names each of you and then compare.'

Lushington was standing apart, examining some of the bric-à-brac that hung about the room. She turned from the others, leaving them writing, and came across the room to him. She spoke to him quickly so that they could not hear. Lushington said:

'Yes. Come to tea to-morrow. To the hotel. I have a sitting-room.'

'You want me to?'

'Of course I want you to.'

'You have thought of me, yes?'

'Yes.'

From the other end of the room Cortney said:

'Frau Mavrin, you'll have to help us with this little problem. The two best players in town have both been divorced from the third best. How is this going to affect the tourney?'

They discussed the problem. The wooden clock on the mantelpiece struck and the cuckoo appeared noisily. Da Costa and Cortney both looked at their watches and began to get up. Ortrud said:

'But you must not go yet.'

'You forget, Frau Mavrin, the affairs of state. The councils of Europe.'

'Then I must see all of you again soon.'

Cortney kissed her hand. Da Costa did not; so Lushington did not do so either. She opened the door of the flat.

'You can work the lift?' she said.

'We will walk,' said Da Costa. 'It is only a few flights.'

'It is easy to work.'

'No, no,' said Cortney. 'We will walk.'

Just as they were leaving the flat the other door of the room they had been in opened and the professor reappeared. He was wearing full evening dress, and when he saw that the guests were going home he threw up his hands.

'Ach, gentlemen——'

'Panteleimon, you are too late. What could have kept you so long?'

'My dear wife——'

'My poor Panteleimon, you have had this trouble and now our guests are departing. I have been the cause of all your trouble.'

'It is no trouble, my dear Ortrud. Only I am sorry that we lose our guests. But wait I will take them down in the lift.'

'No, no, Professor Mavrin,' said Da Costa. 'We couldn't allow that. Not for one moment. We will certainly walk.'

Cortney said: 'Professor, we have abused your hospitality enough for one night. You go right back to bed. Don't you go near that elevator.'

'I insist, gentlemen, I insist,' said the professor and, herding them into the lift, pressed the button.

They reached the hall in safety, although the lift stopped about a foot from the floor and they had to open the gates and jump the rest of the way to the ground. As this position seemed final the professor shook them by the hand and returned to his home by the stairs. Cortney said:

'Well, here I leave you, as my own apartment is just two blocks from this spot.'

They said good night to him. It was snowing a little. As they walked towards a drosky Da Costa said to Lushington:

'I thought you were rather offhand with Frau Mavrin. Did you have a quarrel with her on the boat? Or is that just your way with women?'

13

Lying in bed in his room at the hotel in a dry blackness of heavy curtains and radiators and with a bulk of untucked-in bed clothes continually slipping off him, Lushington considered, through his trance of early morning dozing, whether or not he had behaved wisely the night before. He had come to no conclusions when someone opened the door and turned on the electric light. The glare of the lamp was an agony so that he shut his eyes again but not before he had seen that it was a fair wizened man who had come into the room.

'Who are you?' said Lushington, still with his eyes shut.

'I'm Pope, sir. Pope. Mr. Da Costa's man. I expect Mr. Da Costa mentioned I was going to call you.'

He coughed behind his hand. Lushington tried to adjust his memory. The man's face was certainly familiar, so he said:

'Oh, yes, he did. But you have called me rather early, haven't you? What is the time?'

'Mr. Da Costa told me to call you first, sir. Mr. Da Costa goes to the chancellery rather late sometimes. He said that he thought it would be better if I called you first. Those were his orders.'

'By all means call me first. Very likely Mr. Da Costa does not get up until lunch. But is it necessary to be as early as this? This is an unearthly hour.'

'I'm afraid it would be *very inconvenient* to call you at any other time, sir. I am sorry.'

Pope's eyes narrowed. He looked for a moment, rather wistfully, at Lushington lying in bed as if he were sorry for anyone who had fallen so low. Then he turned away and drew up the blinds. It was still dark outside. Central heating pervaded the room and Lushington's skin felt parched. He lay in bed wondering how expensive the employment of Pope was going to be. He said:

'I suppose it would be dangerous to sleep with one of the windows open?'

'Very dangerous. I did it once myself when I first came out here and they thought I was going to die. The doctors despaired of me. There were three doctors and they all despaired of me. One of them was a very famous specialist out here. A man with a big reputation. Which suit will you wear, sir?'

'The blue one.'

'The one you wore yesterday?'

'Yes.'

Pope hesitated. He said:

'If you did not wear the suit you wore yesterday, sir, I could brush it.'

'All right I'll wear the other one.'

'The brown one?'

'Yes.'

'The brown one needs pressing terribly, sir.'

'I know.'

'Shall I press it for you, sir?'

'Will you?'

Uneasily Pope watched Lushington in bed. He said:

'Would it be better if you wore the blue suit today and then I can press the brown one. Would that be convenient?'

'Yes, yes, I'll do that.'

Lushington turned over with his face towards the wall and thought about Ortrud. He felt certain that he was getting into a mess. He tried to will Pope to go out of the room and leave him in peace. From behind him he heard Pope clear gently his throat and say:

'I believe I saw you at Maxim's last night, sir?'

'I was there. I did not see you.'

'I was in the gallery, sir. I do not go there often. To speak the truth I do not find it a very good entertainment. But I am afraid I am very pleasure-loving by nature. Any gaiety has always appealed to me.'

'Has it?'

'They have a curious custom here,' Pope said. 'In a public place you may ask a lady to dance with you before you have been introduced to her. It took me a long time to get used to that. What tie will you wear, sir?'

'Any tie.'

'The grey one?'

'Yes. The grey one.'

'Or this one, sir?'

'The grey one.'

'Would this one go better with the brown suit?'

'All right, that one.'

'Of course it's a custom that widens your acquaintance a great deal,' Pope said. 'There's no doubt about that, whatever one may feel about the etiquette. But then I like society. I only feel at ease when I am with people. My own family have often remarked on it.'

'Have they?'

'They call me the Duke. Jokingly, of course.'

Lushington said nothing because he was still feeling sleepy and could at that moment think of nothing apposite to say. Pope made a clicking noise with his tongue. He said:

'I'm sorry, sir. You said that you would wear the blue suit and not the brown one. In that case I expect you will like to wear the grey tie after all. They would go together better.'

'Yes, if you think so.'

'And what shirt, sir?'

'The same shirt.'

'It is rather soiled, sir.'

Lushington said: 'I know it is. I like it like that.'

He turned over again and began to doze, abandoning all effort to wake up. He had begun to dream when he felt Pope touch his shoulder and shake him slightly. Not hard but enough to make him feel a little sick.

'What is it?'

'You won't go to sleep again, sir, will you?'

14

Although the snow had come the cold was not excessive. The snow lay on the spires and the red railway station and on the timber warehouses down by the harbour. Lushington used to sit in his room in the hotel and write articles in the morning, going out before lunch to send telegrams to the paper. He found the atmosphere congenial to writing articles about London as if he were still living there. The telegrams were for the most part about communist organisations or anti-communist organisations, according to his mood. These people were having trouble with the Communists and also with the Agrarians and the National Party and the Social-Democrats and the Fascists and more recently with the Jews and Jesuits, so that there was always plenty to telegraph home about and Lushington used to send long expensive cables to the paper which subsequently appeared in two lines, low on the page opposite the sporting news. In the afternoon he collected information. Everyone he met was anxious to give him as much information as possible in order that matters should be reported from their point of view, except Da Costa, who, suddenly seized with a fear that he appeared unimportant, assumed an attitude of secrecy about affairs of state as soon as he and Lushington were alone together, which happened usually for not less than two hours everyday. In public however when thinking of other things he would divulge any information that might be required of him. When Da Costa became secretive Lushington as a reprisal talked about Lucy and also to work off his own feelings about her which, as he now saw Ortrud several times a week, had become quite complex. One or two letters arrived from Lucy telling him what to tell Da Costa about herself.

So the days passed.

In the evening there were usually dinner parties given by members of the Diplomatic Corps or persons connected in some way with the Government. When there were no dinner parties Lushington went to the cinema with Ortrud or played picquet with Da Costa. But there were invitations to dinner most nights and dances or parties quite often as well. The dinner parties began early and ended late but it was possible to feel ready for them when the evening came by spending some of the afternoon walking among the pine forests along the shore.

15

Baroness Puckler's parties were in no way different from those given by members of the Diplomatic Corps. Her husband as a young man had in fact been in the service (of which country no one seemed to remember) although he was retired when, a few years before the war, he had been killed motor-racing in France. Baroness Puckler continued to keep up her foreign connections when she returned home and the circumstance that the province in which she lived had now become a sovereign state was some consolation for the confiscation by its government of most of her money and all her land, because it provided her at the same time with diplomats to entertain. She lived a quiet life, existing on the memories of dinner conversations she had had twenty years before with Bülow or de Soveral, and she kept even her affection for Ortrud within disciplined bounds. The society to which she had been brought up had been taken away from her and destroyed but in its place she had constructed a neat miniature world from which she had found it possible to exclude some of the more glaring defects of the great capitals.

That night Lushington found that he was sitting between Madame Theviot, the wife of the French minister, and a woman whose name he had been unable to catch who was one of the female members of the House of Deputies. Professor Mavrin had been placed opposite and immediately facing him. Out of the corner of his eye he could see Ortrud at the other end of the table. The female deputy was talking:

'We are only a little country. A little new country. You must not be surprised if sometimes we do not seem to do things so well as you big countries who have been big countries for so long. You big countries do not know what it is like to be a little country. We are not used to being even a little country yet. You big countries do all the things so well that we little countries do not so well do yet.'

'Oh, but I am sure that you do. You seem to me to do everything so much better than in the big countries. That is why I enjoy being here so much.'

'Ah, you are too kind. You flatter.'

'Not a bit. Not a bit.'

'Yet it is indeed true that here people are interested in culture and education. We are, I am afraid, what in England you would call highbrows. We must always be modern. Up-to-the-date. We read Shaw and Wilde. Barrie we find too sentimental.'

'Quite.'

'You see I tell you that you may understand our point of view. We must always, as you say, go ahead. We cannot remain inactive. We must move.'

'Exactly.'

On the other side of him Madame Theviot was examining with her fork the food that had been put in front of her. She was a woman of great height, who was accustomed to wear a turban which hinted of Madame Tallien and hot moments under the *Directoire*, while at the same time it diminished in no way the dignity inherent in French official life. She came from Rennes and almost all the fun she got out of life was being rude to the German minister whose surname happened to be of some international significance. She also enjoyed bullying her husband. The female deputy continued:

'You have seen that they play the *Loyalties* of Galsworthy at the National Theatre?'

She leaned across Lushington and said to Madame Theviot:

'*Vous en avez vu, Madame? Le* Loyalties *de Galsworthy au Theâtre National?*'

Madame Theviot paused, the fork at her lips. She looked suspiciously at the female deputy and said:

'*Eh bien, qu'est-ce que c'est que ça, Madame?*'

The female deputy said: '*Dites à Madame de quoi il s'agit.*'

Lushington said: '*C'est un officier anglais qui est très brave et qui volait cinq cents livres d'un Juif qui reste à la même maison dans la campagne. L'officier a sauté dans la chambre-à-coucher du Juif par la fenêtre quand celui-là est au salle-de-bain. Il est découvert parce que la veille il a sauté également sur la bibliothèque du fumoir.*'

'*Hein?*'

'*Et puis le Juif est chassé de son cercle par les anciens camarades de l'école du capitaine qui se tue lui-même.*'

'*Aaah,*' said Madame Theviot, nodding her head with recollections of the Dreyfus case.

'*En effet,*' said the female deputy. '*C'est une spectacle magnifique. Voilà six fois que je l'ai vue.*' She turned again to Lushington and said:

'And what in England are they thinking about the Expressionism?'

'They find it much too subjective,' Lushington said firmly.

Professor Mavrin from his chair opposite said:

'I look forward to talking to you of English literature at some time more than hitherto we have had the opportunity, Mr. Lushington. I tell my wife to invite you. Always it seems that she forgets or you cannot come. It is my wish to discuss with you the novels of Thomas Hardy and his belief in the inevitability of circumstances. We will have a long talk one day on that subject. We will choose a time when we have many hours before us.'

The professor stroked his moustache and repeated the words 'many hours' to himself. He had a sallow face with several lines across the forehead. During the Revolution he had been frequently shot at, and in the end had almost starved to death. He was deflected from Thomas Hardy by the girl on his left, the daughter of one of the judges of the Supreme Court, who began a conversation with him on the subject of proportional representation. Baroness Puckler said:

'You must stay, Mr. Lushington, for the ball at the House of the Knights. It is next month and is a great occasion.'

'I shall certainly stay for it. I have heard so much about it that I shall stay even if I am ordered to go back before it takes place.'

Baroness Puckler said: 'And this year, Colonel, will you join in the mazurka?'

The British military attaché, an obese sapper, who had left his wife and large family in rooms at Camberley, said coquettishly:

'I hope that at least I shall have the pleasure of a waltz with you, Baroness.'

'We shall see. Perhaps I shall dance with General Kuno all the evening.'

Da Costa, who was sitting on the other side of Madame Theviot and who had been engaged in telling her a long story about his experiences at a spiritualist séance at Dresden, where he had once lived with a German family, now turned his attention to the rest of the conversation and said at the top of his voice:

'Haven't you heard that Madame Mavrin and I are going to give an exhibition dance at the ball this year—a new form of the tango—in Argentine national dress? I'm having my spurs specially sharpened for it.'

Professor Mavrin said: 'Mr. Da Costa, my wife has told me nothing of this. My dear Ortrud, have you made arrangements to hire the suitable costume? You must not leave it too late because you know how difficult it is sometimes to procure in this small city such things as fancy dress.'

Ortrud, who was sitting at the other end of the table next to the female deputy's husband who was a dentist and said to be very talented, said:

'But, Panteleimon, Mr. Da Costa is not serious——'

'But, my dear Ortrud, I should be delighted for you to take part in such a display. I should not mind at all. It would please me very much and I am sure that you would sustain such a rôle with great distinction.'

'After that,' said Da Costa, who was laughing convulsively to himself at his own humour, 'after that, General Kuno and I are going to give an exhibition of step-dancing, only each of us will wear the other's clothes.'

'Impossible!' said Professor Mavrin. 'Impossible! No, no! Mr. Da Costa, we cannot believe that——'

'Speaking of General Kuno,' said the military attaché, who disliked Da Costa and considered that he had already gone too far, 'I hear that two men were arrested last night in his house. They had broken in and it is thought that they were assassins.'

Professor Mavrin said: 'And only a few months ago such a thing happened before. In the end someone will murder him.'

Baroness Puckler said: 'No. Now, I do not think so. So often they have tried in the past and always they have failed. They have derailed trains that he was travelling in. They have thrown bombs at him. They have shot at him from behind walls. But always he escapes. I think he will die quietly in his bed at a great age.'

'Why do they try to kill General Kuno?' Lushington said.

Baroness Puckler said: 'During the troubles he shot many Bolsheviks. Many, many Bolsheviks. Once he made a mistake and shot a great lot of men who were not Bolsheviks. There were many hundreds of them. In those days it was hard to tell. Therefore he has enemies. He is head of the police too. That may cause him to be disliked by some persons.'

16

Pope always found difficulty in leaving a room expeditiously. Undisciplined, he gave out vitality in such wrong directions as Da Costa with enormous force. But this electric activity was instantly dissipated on reaching its goal because, strangely, Da Costa possessed against it some effortless resisting power. It was a process comparable to the pouring of liquid on to an inverted vessel. The whole room would be messed up with Pope's personality and Da Costa alone would remain untouched. A certain awareness of this made Da Costa prefer Pope to any other subordinate that he had ever known because through him he became conscious of a sense of power that was rare to him. By Pope his own life was made fuller.

At the moment Pope was making preparations for leaving the flat, delaying the final exit, hovering, toying with the past. He said:

'For example, an amusing thing happened to my grandparents. When they were driving to their wedding the bottom of the cab—one of those old-fashioned growlers, I suppose it was—fell out and they had to run all the way to the church. The cabman was deaf, you see. They couldn't make him hear. They had to run all the way. It was a ridiculous thing to happen. The story is often told in my family. We often laugh over it. It's funny, don't you think?'

Lushington and Da Costa agreed that it was funny. Pope shook his head and laughed. There was a silence. The noise of the trams, clanging along ringing their bells, came up from the street below.

'Funny things like that are always happening in my family,' Pope said.

He watched them for a few moments and then backed with reluctance through the door. They heard him fiddling about with the coats in the hall. Da Costa lit a cigarette. He said:

'He's an amusing fellow—Pope—don't you think?'

'Oh, yes, he is.'

'I don't think he talks too much, do you?'

'Not a bit.'

They looked down at the town's jutting out pieces of grey masonry

67

and the steeples which Pope when speaking to Da Costa or anyone else with whom the simile would be likely to bear weight was accustomed to compare to the dreaming spires of Oxford. There was in fact a distinct resemblance. Lushington said:

'Well, I must be going. I have an appointment.'

'Something nice?'

'Yes.'

'You're lucky. I suppose you've got hold of some woman. Don't get involved in a scandal or everybody will blame me.'

'All right. I'll be careful.'

'And don't forget that we are both dining with Cortney to-morrow night. Black tie. If you forget he'll think I never gave you the message.'

'I won't forget.'

'Oh, and I meant to ask you. Have you heard from Lucy lately? How is she?'

'I had a postcard a couple of days ago. She seemed well. Sent her love.'

'I must write to her,' Da Costa said.

17

They used to lunch together at a little Hungarian restaurant down by the quays where the plat-de-jour was either *goulash esterhazy* or *boeuf stroganoff*, though it was always possible, as a change, to eat *wiener schnitzel*. They sat in one of the cramped wooden partitions into which the room was divided. It was customary to begin the meal with *bouillon*. Ortrud sat next to the wall. Lushington said:

'Where does your husband lunch?'

'At the Café Weber.'

'Every day?'

'Yes.'

'Does he never come here?'

'Of course not.'

'Why not?'

'Because he always lunches at the Café Weber.'

Then one day the professor arrived. They had just finished their *bouillon*. The professor, who was shortsighted, sat down at the next table without noticing them and began to order his food. Ortrud leaned across:

'Why, Panteleimon, what ever are you doing here?'

'Ach, Ortrud——'

'Remember to talk English. Mr. Lushington does not understand our language.'

The professor said: 'It is a great pleasure to see you both here. But, my dear wife, to-day you said that you were taking the midday meal with Frau Koski. You have not by chance forgotten your engagement with Frau Koski?'

'Frau Koski telephoned to put off that engagement. I met Mr. Lushington in the street.'

'Your wife was kind enough to accept an invitation to lunch.'

'Too kind, too kind,' said the professor, 'But now you must both lunch with me. Yes, yes, I insist. Not one word. Mr. Lushington, I invite you to lunch with me and I insist that you accept.'

'Panteleimon, why do you take lunch here to-day?'

'The Café Weber was so crowded when I entered it.'

'Indeed?'

'And then I have a slight *migraine*. I could not tolerate the noise.'

Lushington ate his *goulash* and said:

'Well, it's very nice that you have decided to come here instead.'

The professor had a light lunch of ham and gherkins. He seemed tired but he was in splendid form otherwise and questioned Lushington about the history of the sonnet sequence in English literature. It was one of the professor's outstanding merits that he rarely spoke of his own subject, psychology. He had some coffee after the ham and then said that he must go back to the University to work. Ortrud said:

'This afternoon, my dear husband, I shall spend shopping.'

The professor went away and Lushington and Ortrud continued their lunch. When they had finished they went to a cinema and watched a neatly-put-together film dealing with American lower middle class life. The story, which was credible without being convincing, described the difficulties of a man, a superexcellent dancer, who knew that he could not win the local dancing competition if he danced with his wife because she was so pure that as a girl she had never been taught to dance at all and had evidently been unable to pick up the knack in later life. Since it was imperative that he should win the prize in order to pay for the baby she was about to give birth to he entered for the competition with a blonde girl of indifferent morals. The plot hinged on the arrival of his wife at the critical point of the competition and her swooning away at the degrading sight. A certain air of mystery was added to this drama of domestic relationships by the fact that it had been written as a talkie and was now being played as a silent film with a few captions. When this entertainment was at an end Lushington walked back with Ortrud towards her home. On the way there, turning the corner of some government buildings, they met the professor again. Ortrud said: 'Panteleimon, are you going home so soon?'

'My headache. I go home to lie down for a little. Remember that we have an invitation to dinner to-night.'

'Mr. Lushington was kind and took me to the films.'

'He is too good to you. Mr. Lushington, you are too kind to my wife.'

Lushington walked with them as far as their flat. Then he went back to the hotel to change for dinner. He found Pope sitting at his table writing letters. He dislodged him and began to change. He was dining that night with the Danish first secretary.

He arrived a few minutes too early for dinner, although Cortney was already standing in front of the fire, fingering a new sort of white tie which had arrived for him from London the day before. Their hostess, a little Danish countess, who looked like a squirrel, said:

'The Mavrins are coming to-night, Mr. Lushington. You have met them?'

'Yes, I have met them. As it happens, I saw them this afternoon.'

'She is so charming, do not you think?'

'Yes, indeed.'

Cortney said: 'Mr. Lushington was fortunate enough to travel here on the same boat as Madame Mavrin.'

'So? And he fell in love with her, of course? I am sure you did. Is not that true?'

'But of course.'

'Now, Countess,' said Cortney, 'remember you mustn't make jokes like that in the presence of someone who comes from the New World, where we still try to retain our homely code of morals. In the first place we don't understand them.'

'And then Mr. Da Costa is coming from your legation. I expect you see him sometimes?'

'Yes,' said Lushington, 'I do see him quite often as a matter of fact.'

'To speak of morals,' said their host, 'have you heard the latest story about Madame Gomez?'

It was a good one. Later the Mavrins arrived and the Swedish naval attaché and the daughters of the German minister, and Da Costa, rather late. After dinner they danced to the wireless, except Professor Mavrin who talked with their host about the economics of farming, the collectivist system in Russia, and the methods that obtained in Denmark. Da Costa was in one of his noisy moods and he danced most of the time with Ortrud. Lushington watched her, thin and exotic in one of her exaggerated dresses. He wondered if she was a serious person.

18

Lushington had been lunching at Da Costa's flat and they were sitting there drinking coffee. As usual the room was too hot. Lunch, cooked by Pope, had been good and while eating it they had talked about their friends in London and both had now been left with an inevitable sense of being cut-off, outposts of a mighty empire, pleasant in a way but melancholy, and now they sat in silence smoking. Da Costa said:

'I don't think Bellamy ought to call me a bloody fool. It is not so much that I care whether or not that he should think that I am one, as the appalling want of dignity it argues in a man of his age and rank in the service. I mean if he can't learn to control his temper how on earth can he hope to control the fate of nations?'

'Of course his repressions are something awful,' Lushington said.

'That may be. But if he represses his evil desires he ought to repress his temper as well. After all from the point of view of working with him in the chancellery it would be much better if it were the other way about. And by the same token I thought it very impertinent of old Mavrin to tell Bellamy that Madame Mavrin was free for dinner on Tuesday without consulting you first.'

'What on earth do you mean?'

'Nothing.'

'Anyway,' said Lushington, 'she's not going to dine with the Bellamys on Tuesday. She is going to dine with me.'

'In that case you have supplied the answer to your own question. And now I must go away and do some work.'

'May I stay here and write?'

'Of course.'

Da Costa went away and Lushington settled down to writing articles. He opened one of the windows so that an icy shaft of air blew across one side of the room. He had worked for some time before he noticed that Pope was in the room too. Pope made his presence known by shutting the window and bolting it. After becoming aware of Pope's arrival Lushington continued to write for a little time although he knew that it would be no good. With Pope in the room he could not hope to compose a sentence. Pope crept round by the walls, touching everything. Lushington listened to his movements and at last gave up all effort to work. He pushed back his chair and said to Pope:

'It seems a pity to stay in on a lovely day like this, although it is a bit cold, and so I think I shall go out for a walk.'

He said this although he knew that he was going back to his hotel as quickly as possible so that he might be able to go on writing there. Pope put himself in an attitude of conversation. He said:

'When it is warmer, sir, I always get into shorts after finishing my work and run in the outlying districts of the town. I find it is absolutely necessary for my health. I am not by any means a strong man. I have to take care of my health, and exercise is an absolute necessity. It used to give rise to a great deal of comment when I first came out here. Now, however, people seem to have become more accustomed to it. I once suggested to Mr. Da Costa that he should do the same when he complained to me of a heavy feeling.'

'Did he take your advice?'

'No, sir. He did not.'

'I'm not surprised to hear that he did not.'

'Mr. Da Costa is a strange gentleman if you don't mind my saying so, sir.'

'Why?' said Lushington.

He disliked the idea of prolonging the conversation with Pope but at the same time felt himself unable to resist possible intimate revelations about so old a friend.

'He spends all his time reading,' Pope said.

He shuddered. Expectantly, Lushington said:

'He has always read a good deal. Ever since I have known him.'

'Curious books, sir.'

'Are they?'

'I'm a great reader myself,' Pope said. 'I always have been. But it doesn't *do* to read too much. Otherwise you don't have a healthy mind in a healthy body.'

'I suppose not.'

'I like reading serious books, sir. Books that really teach you something. Books on economics especially. Science. Statistics. Nature study.'

'Yes, yes,' said Lushington.

A straight talk on Pope's literary tastes had been just what he had wanted to avoid but self-respect prevented him from returning of his own accord to the subject of Da Costa's vagaries. Pope stood, resting his hands on the table, staring in front of him with his eyes-that-look-beyond-the-grave expression. He had got started. He rapidly sketched in the plots of a few of the books he had enjoyed during the previous eighteen months.

'Yes . . .' said Lushington, '. . . yes . . . yes . . . yes . . . yes . . . yes. . . .'

Art and letters exhausted, Pope began to roam among the litter of his personal reminiscence, exploring the cramped furtive lanes of memory, winding this way and that through the tinsel by-ways of his past, petting and cosseting his ego, warming it at the glow of innumerable self-congratulatory episodes that had, it seemed, lighted the road. Lushington, realising now that he would hear nothing of Da Costa's secret life, contented himself with the thought that anyway it was probably *The Golden Bough*, merely, that Da Costa spent most of his time reading, and he no longer paid attention to the humming cadences of Pope's saga. Instead he listened to the roll of drums that was sounding from the President's palace, where they were changing the guard. Pope pursued his course:

'. . . during the War when I was in the Army, attached as it happened to the Dental Department, one of the officers had remarked that I was good with my hands, he used to say that no one was any use to him after he had employed me, somehow it had spoiled him, he used to say, for other orderlies with their coarse ways, clumsy blighters jokingly he used to call them. . . . I can remember that at one time I went into the canteen wearing a mackintosh over my uniform and as soon as I spoke two privates who were sitting there sprang to attention. They literally *sprang* to attention. Curious, wasn't it? Don't you think that it was curious, sir?'

'Yes . . . yes,' said Lushington, lost in speculations of his own.

'There it was,' said Pope, 'there it was. You know, sir, at that time my cheeks used to be as red as cherries. Someone once said that I looked the healthiest man in the battalion. He said it wouldn't be going too far to say so. That was during the War, sir. Later when I came out here. . . .'

Led by his train of thought to more immediate problems, Lushington waited for an appropriate break in the cascade of anamnesis and then, like the boy thrusting his hand into the hole in the dyke, stemmed the flood by saying:

'And by the way I must not forget to mention to you about those evening shirts of mine. They are ruined. All frayed. Isn't there anywhere here where they can wash stiff shirts?'

'Nowhere, sir, nowhere. Curiously enough I was just about to tell you that. When I first came out here I thought that I should be forced to wear a false front. You won't believe but I did indeed. A *dickey* I think it is called. But then of course I find that the majority of my friends here, being foreigners, do not change for dinner every night so that in the end I found that by constant complaint the laundry managed a little better. That is the only way I fear, sir. Positively the only way.'

Lushington gathered up his belongings and began to put on his overcoat. Pope helped him on with this with such energy that he was almost pushed off his balance.

'The usual time to-morrow morning, sir?'

'The usual time.'

'Good afternoon, sir.'

'Good afternoon.'

As Lushington left the room he saw that Pope was beginning to rearrange the invitation cards on the mantelpiece. He went downstairs and out into the square. A squadron of Waldemar's uhlans were passing, picking the way between the market stalls, most of which were stocked with holly and stunted Christmas trees. The soldiers were on cobby horses and wore short, heavy overcoats bordered with sheepskin. Lushington, standing on the pavement, watched them walk their horses through the slush and then disappear in the traffic at the end of the square. The pennons of their lances flickered above the tops of the trams. Then they were gone as the riders turned the corner into another street. He heard someone behind him say:

'I too might have ridden at the head of a troop of cavalry. But I have few regrets.'

Turning, he found that Count Scherbatcheff was standing beside him. The Count was wearing an astrakhan cap instead of his béret and he looked even more haggard than he had done on the voyage. His overcoat hung on him quite loosely as if it were suspended from a hook somewhere beneath his neck. His pale blue eyes were sunk far back into his head.

'Come with me a little way. I am going back to my apartment? I know that Englishmen like a walk.'

'Certainly.'

'You will do so?'

'I should like to very much.'

19

They went across the square and down steps towards the river, which they crossed by the Nikolai bridge, walking sharply because the air was cold. On the other side of the river was the poorer part of the town. They passed through this quarter and beyond it, while Count Scherbatcheff told Lushington about his cough and stomach trouble, both of which were worse. He had tried various remedies but none seemed to do him any good. He had hoped that in this climate he would feel better but on the contrary he was worse here than he had been in Belgium. A nondescript outlying district was now reached. This end of the city, not yet completed, was full of tin huts and the shells of unfinished modern buildings. Sometimes they passed piles of empty petrol tins and stacks of bricks. All this was part of an ambitious town-planning scheme. Then they came to an immense block of flats only half of which had been built, the right-hand wing being nothing but girders, although work seemed to have been abandoned on it for these were rusty and some of the masonry was already falling away. They seemed to be making their way among the ruins of another civilisation, now passed away, and of which there would soon be no trace. Count Scherbatcheff stopped in front of the completed wing of the flats and said:

'You will come up for a short time? I should be delighted if you would do so and then we could talk for a little longer.'

They went into the hall which was full of ladders and pails of whitewash and, as there was a notice on the lift saying that it was out of order, they walked up the stairs to the Scherbatcheff flat, which was on the top floor. Count Scherbatcheff took a key from under the doormat opened the door and pushed Lushington in front of him into a room which opened directly on to the landing without any hall or passage. The room was in semi-darkness and several people were sitting in it.

Lushington saw that there was an upright piano along one wall at which a girl of about twelve years old with two long plaits down her back was practising scales. She took no notice of their arrival and continued methodically. Two women were sewing in one corner of the room and a man with a yellow shaved head wearing a grey military

overcoat, turned back showing its red lining, was sitting on a kitchen
chair and looking out of the window. He did not turn round at their
entry so that Lushington could not tell at all how old he was. In another
corner a very old woman was propped up in a chair with a shawl over
her knees. She was wearing spectacles and held a book in her hand although there was not enough light in the room to read by. The outstanding scent among the several odours of the room was that of musk.

Count Scherbatcheff helped Lushington to take off his overcoat
and hung it from a nail that was already supporting the picture of a
saint. He pulled forward a settee and said:

'Sit down. Can you give me a cigarette? I cannot offer you one.
There are never any cigarettes in this house. If I get any my uncle puts
them in his pocket and becomes angry if any of us ask for one. Later we
will have some tea.'

He did not introduce Lushington to any of the people in the room.
No one took any notice of them. The girl with the plaits changed from
scales to five-finger exercises and then stopped and altered the height
of the music stool, after which she went on again. Count Scherbatcheff
said:

'You will agree that there come moments when a man feels that
he can stand no more? I know that you are fortunate. You are English.
You have at least a profession which is not too uncongenial. But you
will understand how it is sometimes with me?'

Lushington looked into the middle distance of the room where
through the shadows he could still see a high-light on the glazed surface
of the unknown man's head. He wondered whether or not this man was
the uncle who always filled his pockets with cigarettes. And then remembering that Count Scherbatcheff required an answer he said something about Russians having lost so much. Count Scherbatcheff said:

'No. It is not that. I used to feel the same when I was in the Corps
of Pages. If anything worse. It is just depression as you call it. And this
damned cough.'

'I can sympathise.'

'And then relations—relations—relations.'

'Yes?'

'You see what I mean?'

One of the reasons why the room was so hot was because brown
paper had been pasted over the cracks of the windows. In addition to
the main stove of the room a small oil stove had been placed in the

corner near the very old woman. This smaller stove smoked menacingly. The very old woman now shut her book with a snap and throwing down her rug almost on top of the oil stove began to move across the room. Lushington got up to let her pass. Count Scherbatcheff said:

'That is my grandmother about whom I have spoken to you. You remember? Her obstinacy. But do not be alarmed. She speaks little English and besides she is deaf. There is no need for discretion. As I was saying to you, at times matters are indeed impossible.'

'Can I help?'

'As you know I am an engineer. But what have I to look forward to as an engineer? Shall I live for ever with these people in this room? Yet when I was young and was to enter the Cuirassier Guards I was the same. I thought always of the interminable round of tiresome social engagements and the tedious duties of regimental life that were before me. I could see no way out. I tell you this that you may understand that it is not merely my adversity that causes these sentiments.'

'Anything special at the moment?'

'Yes,' said Count Scherbatcheff. 'Perhaps it is something special. I have been feeling it more than usual. For a longer time. I will tell you. It is Madame Mavrin.'

'What about her?'

'I have thought of her ever since we were together on board the ship. It is impossible for me to see her. What can I do if I did see her? It is clear that she does not like me. That is one of the reasons why I feel as I do.'

'Certainly that makes things difficult.'

Now that his eyes had become accustomed to the half-light Lushington saw that a young man was lying at full length on the ground immediately under the window and in front of the man with the shaved head. This young man was writing in an exercise book by the light thrown by the oil stove. He was writing lethargically with a stumpy pencil. The girl at the piano still played her five-finger exercises. Count Scherbatcheff said:

'I am aware that in England there exists a somewhat rigid code of morals. But we Russians cannot be bound by convention. It may seem shocking to you that I speak thus of a lady who is already married to another. But at least you will sympathise with me in my despair.'

'Of course.'

'May I ask, do you often meet Madame Mavrin in society? That society from which you know we Russians are for political reasons excluded?'

'Quite often.'

'You will perhaps remind her of my existence? That is all I ask.'

'I will certainly tell her that I have seen you.'

'A thousand thanks,' Count Scherbatcheff said, 'a thousand thanks, my dear Lushington. And now I will weary you no more with my troubles. After all how much more fortunate we are than many. At least we have comfortable quarters. *Enfin*, it is not the Scherbatcheff Palace in Petersburg but that house was more draughty than any other that I have known and its rooms were for ever full of relations whom I disliked. Here at least are only those whom I can tolerate and even feel affection for.'

The very old woman now returned leading with her by the hand two small children. These she put between the oil stove and the wall and opening a cupboard brought out some toys, a tin trumpet and a drum which she gave them. Suddenly the young man who was lying on the floor raised himself to his knees. He banged on his exercise book and shouted at the very old woman. She turned towards him and an altercation began. One of the other women stopped her sewing and in a drawling, metallic voice joined the discussion. The children took no notice and began to play in an appropriate manner with their toys. Count Scherbatcheff shrugged his shoulders and looked at Lushington. He said:

'I can only apologise to you as my guest for this disturbance. It is my cousin. He always complains that he cannot work when the children play. Like all the rest of my family he will not listen to the voice of reason. He provokes all of us. Work indeed! He is only learning shorthand. He seems to think that a sufficient reason for imposing his will on all of us.'

The controversy ended at last, the protagonist being worn down in the last resort by the girl with the plaits, who had now returned to scales. The young man lay down once more on the floor, breathing heavily, sometimes staring and pointing in the direction of the children. Count Scherbatcheff took a bottle of something that he said was good for his cough and poured a few drops on his handkerchief. It smelt potent and Lushington refused it when it was offered to him. Count Scherbatcheff said:

'You will accept a little refreshment? We have no cigarettes but at least you will join us in a little refreshment. No, you must not refuse. I insist. My grandmother will prepare something. I will ask her to do so at once.'

He went across the room to where his grandmother was sitting and shouted in her ear. She shook her head and he shouted again. Once more she shook her head. The noise of the Count's shouting was broken at intervals by the piano and more fitfully by the trumpet. The child with the drum had at last succeeded in forcing one of the drum sticks through the parchment and was laboriously enlarging by hand the hole. Count Scherbatcheff came back to the settee. He said:

'She is hopeless. Hopeless. I ask her to prepare a simple meal for my guest and she at once makes difficulties. We have not got this, we have not got that, we have not got the other. *Toujours les histoires de cuisine.*'

'But——'

'Please. Please, my dear Lushington, that is enough. We may be exiles and in difficult circumstances but at least we have not forgotten the name of hospitality. Ah, why do we live in this accursed country? How could such a situation as this arise in a civilised capital like Paris, London or New York? You will agree that matters have gone a little far when this happens?'

'Really——'

Count Scherbatcheff pushed aside the table so that it came into contact with the end of the piano and knocked some of the books of music from the top of it. This rearrangement of the furniture gave him access to a small door with panels of frosted glass. He opened this door and shouted:

'Katya! Katya!'

Through the door there was a room, a little larger than a telephone box, with a sink at one end of it. In front of the sink an old woman, less old than Count Scherbatcheff's grandmother, but at the same time quite old, was asleep in an upright chair. She wore large carpet slippers and had a handkerchief tied round her head. Count Scherbatcheff took her arm, waking her. She listened to what he said to her, standing in front of him with her eyes upon the ground and her arms hanging limply on either side of her body. Then she spoke at some length and pointed to a pile of unwashed dishes on the edge of the sink. Count Scherbatcheff said nothing. He held out his hands in an attitude of resignation. Then the old woman began to open the cupboards that were all round her and to take things out of them. Count Scherbatcheff returned. He said:

'Now all will be well. If I cannot rely on my relatives, at least one who has been so long in our service as Katya respects my wishes.'

'But I assure you——'

'Not another word. Besides I myself am hungry.'

Katya moved the table away from the piano again and pushed it against the settee. Then she cleared a space at one end of it. There were objects of every description on the table and these she put on the top of the piano that was already piled high with books and music. On the space she cleared she put a plate of chocolate biscuits, some ham, a few pieces of beetroot, a decanter half-full of cherry brandy and a wooden box with a design lacquered on it and with assorted jujubes inside. The grandmother, who had been watching these preparations from her chair, now got up and, again throwing the rug on the floor by the oil stove, she moved across the room. Lushington wondered if she were about to throw him out neck and crop and if so whether or not the rest of the family would help her. But she spoke quite quietly to Count Scherbatcheff. Again her grandson shouted in her ear. And then she began to smile. Count Scherbatcheff himself laughed. He leaned towards his grandmother and kissed her on the chin. After doing this he turned to Lushington and said:

'It is I who must apologise. My grandmother was not at fault. It is all a ridiculous mistake. My grandmother misunderstood me. She is deaf as I told you. She supposed that I wished that you should stay with us for several days, sleeping on the *chaise-longue*. She says that no one may sleep on the *chaise-longue* until it has been mended. Otherwise it will be broken so that it can never be repaired.'

'But how could she think that I could trespass—— '

'Also she supposed that you were a Pole. The Polish consul. She has this prejudice against Poles. But now I have explained clearly who you are. All difficulties are at an end. Indeed if you would like to stay with us for a day or two I have no doubt that the difficulty about the *chaise-longue* could easily be surmounted.'

Lushington was presented to the grandmother who joined them in a glass of cherry brandy. Count Scherbatcheff said:

'It sometimes makes me sad to think that her death was foretold in the cards. But that is mortal fate. We must learn to face bereavement. Much is given that much may be taken away.'

Later on in the evening they played ragtimes on the portable

gramophone and Lushington and Count Scherbatcheff danced in turn
with the girl with the plaits, who was persuaded by the rest of the family
to conclude her practising for that day. Even the young man lying on
the floor gave up his shorthand notes and listened to the music for a
while.

20

Dinner that night at the Mavrins' had not been entirely successful. The professor was undoubtedly prolix in telling an anecdote which Lushington had heard more than once before and Ortrud was in a bad mood. By a mischance Lushington upset a glass of wine over her dress. It was a night when things were not going well. Professor Mavrin did his best but clearly he was too used to Ortrud's ways to be more than a little disturbed. They had left the dining-room. The Professor said:

'It seemed to me that of all the ladies last night the Countess Arnhfeldt was the most beautiful.'

Ortrud said: 'My dear Panteleimon, but how absurd! *Chic*, perhaps, but not beautiful. Her face is like that of a rat. She is well dressed like all Danes. That is a national characteristic. But she has no features.'

She stood there, waiting to be contradicted. Lushington said:

'Not at all. I disagree. I think Professor Mavrin is quite right. She seemed to me to be looking lovely.'

'I suppose you find her very attractive?'

'Yes, I do.'

'What a ridiculous thing to say!'

'My dear Ortrud, Mr. Lushington is our guest.'

'But if he says such ridiculous things——'

'It is not ridiculous at all. I entirely agree with the Professor. Surely you are not jealous of her?'

'Jealous of Countess Arnhfeldt——'

'No, of course I know you aren't really. I was only joking. But to the Professor and myself she seemed clearly to be so beautiful.'

'Certainly, my dear Ortrud, Mr. Lushington is right. You must be jealous. But how silly you are, because you yourself are far more beautiful even than Countess Arnhfeldt.'

'You may think so. Mr. Lushington does not.'

'But, indeed I do. Why should you think that I do not?'

'At least, my dear, Mr. Lushington has a right to his own opinions on such matters. You will grant me that?'

'A perfect right to such bad taste.'

'Bad taste! To think that you are a more beautiful woman than Countess Arnhfeldt?'

'He does not think it. He only says it. I see by his face that he considers her the more beautiful. What a pity that we did not invite her here to-night.'

'But my dear Ortrud, you said especially when I suggested that we should invite Frau Koski, whom I knew to be disengaged to-night, that you would prefer to have no other guests. I cannot understand why you should now wish that we had invited Countess Arnhfeldt.'

'I say so only because Mr. Lushington seems to find her so attractive.'

'My wife, you are exaggerating in the most absurd manner. There is no reason to suppose that Mr. Lushington has any particular wish to see Countess Arnhfeldt at this moment, although I have no doubt that he admires her as much as we all do.'

'As a matter of fact I should have enjoyed her presence very much indeed,' Lushington said.

'What did I tell you, Panteleimon?'

'My dear Ortrud, moderate your tone.'

'*Sei doch endlich still!* Be silent!'

The Professor rose. He said:

'I shall go to my study and complete my work until you are in a better mood. Alone with our guest you will perhaps be able to control yourself with more decorum than in my presence. Mr. Lushington, you will excuse me?'

He left the room with dignity. When he had gone Lushington said:

'Let one thing be clearly understood. I will not have you speaking to your husband in that way.'

'And why not?'

'Because you should show him some respect. He is a very clever man indeed and you speak to him as if he were a schoolboy.'

'He was in the wrong.'

'He was not in the wrong. And even if he had been that would have been no excuse.'

'After all he is my husband and not yours.'

'It is because he is your husband that you should treat him with some consideration.'

Ortrud began to dab her eyes with a handkerchief. She said:

'I know that you do not love me. But do not be so unkind. It was all on your account that I was so silly.'

'Well, really?'

'Yes, yes, you know it. Why do you never consider how I feel?'

'Well, don't cry anyway.'

'I am unhappy.'

'Why?'

'Because you don't love me.'

'But I do. I do.'

'Yes? A little?'

'Yes. A lot.'

When the Professor returned everyone was in a better temper.

21

It was snowing. The flakes were small and those that fell close to the window seemed, as they drifted past, almost black. Flags were flying all over the town because it was Independence Day and that morning there had been a review and the President, standing under the statue of the national poet, had taken the salute of several infantry battalions, a cavalry regiment, some gunner batteries, a few signallers on motor bicycles, and a tank. Great precautions had been taken to prevent a demonstration on the part of dissatisfied minorities or disgruntled individuals who might be expected to shout rude words or to throw bombs. In the end the President himself was entirely hidden by his suite and plain-clothes men, a fact that was unfavourably commented upon by Baroness Puckler, who said that in the days before the war when anarchists were an adjunct to any public function of any importance, no royalty would have dreamed of taking so much trouble to remain alive. But she added that she knew that the men of to-day were of a different mould. Lushington watched the review with her and then came home to write up an account of it. Now he was working while Pope, wearing a tartan tie, stood by the door with one hand on his hip which protruded as if dislocation had taken place. Pope said:

'I had the privilege of meeting a friend of yours last night, sir. A very nice gentleman. A count.'

'Indeed?'

'Count Bobel his name was.'

'Bobel? Bobel?'

'Bobel, sir.'

As it would be useless at this stage to deny that he had ever heard of such a person, Lushington put down his pen and said:

'Yes. I remember that there was someone of that name on the boat.'

'A very nice gentleman, sir.'

'I did not have the opportunity of seeing much of him.'

'Oh, but he said that he knew you very well indeed, sir.'

'He did? Perhaps he was confusing me with someone else.'

'Oh no, I don't think so, sir. As it happened I was able to do him a small service. In the place I met him, it was a species of tavern, and I was there with my fiancée, the Count had forgotten to bring his pocket-book. Both he and the four ladies with him would have been in a very awkward predicament if I had not been enabled to lend the Count a small sum.'

'Much?'

'No, sir. A very trivial amount. But the Count said that, should it happen that he was called away on business unexpectedly, he knew you well enough to be able to say that you would repay me at any time and get the money back from him later, as you would be bound to be seeing him again soon in the not very distant future.'

'He said that, did he?'

'Being a count, sir,' Pope said, 'I took his word. After all, I thought, you can't beat *noblesse oblige*. Not that I myself believe in a system of hereditary titles. I think it a vicious one from start to finish. As a matter of fact I'm a socialist. After all, socialism is bound to come. Bound to. Look at Russia, look at Germany, look at France, look at Italy even——'

Lushington said: 'Before looking at any of these I must make it clear that in the future and as long as I am in this country I refuse to be held responsible for any debts incurred by anyone whosoever. Anyone. Not even Mr. Da Costa.'

'Exactly, sir. Exactly. I quite understand. But as I was with my fiancée who also knows you I felt that I ought to take the Count's word.'

'But I don't know your fiancée. I didn't know that you possessed one.'

'Miss Flosshilde, sir. The young lady at the reception desk of this hotel. With the auburn hair, sir.'

'Oh.'

'You may know to whom I refer, sir.'

'Yes.'

'We hope to get married next year, sir.'

'Next year? Indeed?'

Pope said: 'When my great-aunt died she expressed a wish that I should take the name of my mother in addition to my own. My mother was a Malpas. It was a wish that I hope will be fulfilled when I get married.'

'Then you will be Malpas-Pope?'

'No, sir. Pope-Malpas. Is there anything else, sir?'

Lushington got up from the table. He said:

'Yes. There is. What have the laundry done to the stiff shirt of mine that came back yesterday. What have they done to it? Or rather I can see what they have done to it, but how have they done it? Why was it ever sent there? Can I get any compensation? Have any more clothes been sent there this week? Is that the only laundry? Or have I got to give up changing for dinner?'

Pope made a gesture with his hands indicative of despair. He shook his head despondently at the same time and by this movement dismissed the subject from the sphere of serious discussion. He said:

'You must often have thought it odd that I am not married already, sir. I don't mind telling you it has not been for the want of being asked. You wouldn't believe it, sir, if I were to tell you some of the things that women have said to me. Terrible things. Things that I couldn't speak out loud. Not even to you, sir. But Miss Flosshilde is different. She isn't like that.'

'I'm glad to hear it.'

'When I was last in England,' Pope said, 'I used to take my little nephew, my sister's child, about with me a great deal. You never saw such a fine child. Everyone noticed him. Everyone. They used to stop me in the street or in the park or on buses and trams and say what a lucky man I was to be the father of such a child. Do you know, sir, I used to blush so hotly that they didn't know what they had said to make me go like that? I used to blush all up here.'

'I don't wonder.'

'It was terrible,' Pope said. 'And by the way, sir, I forgot to tell you that Madame Mavrin rang up this afternoon before you had come in.'

'Did she leave a message?'

'No, sir, but I rather think that she was at first under the impression that it was you answering the telephone because she did not ask to speak to you by name. She just began speaking, thinking I suppose, sir, that I was you.'

'Did she leave a message?'

'No, sir.'

Pope coughed very discreetly behind his hand. Then he left the room. Lushington sat down again at his writing table and watched the snow driving past the windows while he tried to compose a letter to Lucy. From the bedroom he could hear Pope humming an individual rendering of *Stenka Razin*.

22

They had walked out of the town by the road which led along the shore. Where this road ended there were pines and beyond them birch trees and among these stood a small palace, built in temperate baroque. This place, used at present for nothing in particular, was spoken of as a potential state institution for mental defectives. Meanwhile it was deserted, though waste paper had been left about on one of the terraces and someone had taken the trouble to overturn and to dismember a colossal imperial statue in bronze which had formerly stood at the end of a vista of trees. Anatomical remains of this were sinking into the turf of the lawn or lying about among the flower beds. The steps of the terrace in front had been broken in places and not yet repaired. From the top of the steps there was a good view of the town where wisps of smoke hung round the shapeless citadel. Out to sea a few boats paused or turned, manœuvring to enter the docks. Beyond were the islands where fishermen and professional smugglers lived. The afternoon was sharp and sunny. Ortrud, who was standing at the top of the steps, said:

'The Deputy-Chief of the Air Service is under arrest.'

Lushington was examining the head of the statue, which lay with its heavy Roman nose buried in the grey brittle grass. Contact with the earth had given the potentate's face an agreeable patina. Beside it was an arm and a hand holding an orb. Further off, an immense top boot.

'Why?'

'He found a man in his wife's bedroom when he came back last night.'

'Did they put him under arrest for that?'

'He shot the man with his revolver.'

'With his revolver? Did he? That was hasty of him.'

'Honour demanded it.'

'Is the man dead?'

'They say he may recover.'

'I always said that it was dangerous to allow people to walk about in fancy dress armed to the teeth. Now you see what happens.'

'Did you?'

She ran lightly down the steps of the terrace and took his arm. Then, leaning against him, she put one foot on the statue's ear under its wig and tried to rock the head backwards and forwards. It moved slightly, nuzzling into the frozen grass. The broad three-cornered hat had kept the snow from the ground immediately beneath the face.

'Are you in love with me?' she said.

'Of course I am. I'm always telling you I am.'

'More than with the girl you left in England.'

'In a different way.'

'Horrible man.'

She turned away, still holding his arm, leading him up the steps towards the upper terrace. They began to walk round the palace which was the size of a small English manor house and had been built as a place of retirement from the bustle of court life. There were nymphs holding flower-pots at intervals round the colonnade but the pots were empty and the glass in most of the windows had been broken. She said:

'I have had other lovers.'

'Have you?'

'Some of them were quite unimportant.'

'I am glad to hear it. Do you count your husband?'

'He is one of the important ones. And you are the most important one of all. Did you know that? That you are the most important one of all?'

The breeze from the sea blew across the gardens and carried some few remnants of leaves, scraps and odds and ends of twigs, across the lawn so that they dashed against the tritons and cornucopia of the fountain. Although snow was lying on the roofs of the town, here it was half melted from the grass. Among the beds without flowers and the chipped cupids, the gnawing of actuality seemed for the moment silenced. In this place which had been left without meaning it seemed easier to feel meaning where there was perhaps none. All was very quiet except for an occasional crackling made now and then as birds flew through the trees, or by the bark or branches of the trees themselves.

'What shall I do when I have to go away and leave you?'

'You must not go. I shall come with you. I cannot allow you to go. But why should we talk about that now? Here England is so far away. And you are not going to leave me yet. You are not going to leave me yet, are you?'

'No. Not yet.'

They went up into the woods beyond the garden and along the paths that led inland and upwards, because the palace was in a hollow. The chilly avenues were deserted. Once a peasant passed dragging some wood on a sledge and, with some obscure remembrance of another epoch, touched his cap. The trees swayed about, uncertainly. She said:

'You do love me, don't you?'

'Yes. I love you.'

'And I love you?'

'Yes. You love me.'

They walked on between the birch trees.

'And now I must go back,' she said.

'Why?'

'Domestic duties. You forget that I am a wife. I must go back to my home.'

'So soon? Can't we stay here for a bit?'

'No. I must go back.'

They turned down one of the paths which led back towards the sea and brought them to the embankment promenade, a walk that had been fashionable before the Independence. But now that the town had been rebuilt no one came here. Instead the people walked up and down the main boulevard. Only a few soldiers were wandering two-and-two along the embankment, their sheepskin caps and long overcoats making them like the accepted representations of Noah and his children. Ortrud said:

'When you are gone I shall come to the Little Palace and then I shall be able to remember you.'

'Will you have to go there before you can do that?'

'Of course.'

'And how shall I remember you?'

'I do not know,' she said. 'Perhaps you will remember me when you see your English girl again.'

'But you are coming back with me to England.'

'Oh yes. I forgot.'

He went with her past the barracks as far as the house in the University quarter. When they reached the door he was going to leave her, but she said:

'Come upstairs with me. I cannot say good-bye to you properly in the street.'

The lift was in almost perfect order on that day and they reached their landing in safety. Ortrud opened the door of the flat and Lushington followed her into the hall. From the sitting-room there came a noise of droning, a sort of sing-song, interspersed with high squeaks. The sound was a disagreeable one.

'What is that?'

'Little Panteleimon.'

'Oh?'

'You have not seen him before?'

'No.'

A child of about five years old stood in the middle of the floor of the room, twisting pieces of his clothes in his hands. Little Panteleimon's face was large and round and he stood there, leaning with all his weight on one leg, gazing in front of him with an expression of convinced and dogged cynicism. He watched them as if he were looking through them at something else in the passage beyond.

'Hullo,' said Lushington.

Ortrud spoke to the child in German. Little Panteleimon fixed her with his fishy wide eyes and moved away slightly, crossing one leg behind the other and pointing his toe in the First Position. He was an elderly, world-weary child dressed in the travesty of a sailor suit. He stood there gazing out at them as if through field glasses. Ortrud said:

'He is shy. Like his father.'

'He looks like his father curiously enough.'

Ortrud laughed. She went across the room and taking the child by the hand kissed him on the forehead.

'Come,' she said. 'Play with this.'

She took Lushington's hat from him and threw it across towards the child. Little Panteleimon did not catch the hat. He stood uncertainly, watching it lying on the floor. Then he moved towards the hat and, pausing for a moment before he picked it up, he began to examine it. Suddenly, very deliberately, he tore off the ribbon that was round it.

'Panteleimon!'

'No, no,' said Lushington. 'It doesn't matter. It's all right. No one will notice that the ribbon is not sewn on if I put it round the hat to go home in. I can easily wear it like that as far as the hotel.'

Little Panteleimon's face began to quiver. It screwed up. He yelled. Ortrud rang and he was removed by the nurse, a square middle-aged woman wearing peasant costume. Soon through the wall between the rooms they heard him stop yelling. The sounds sank slowly down the scale until they had reached the theme that he had been improvising when they had arrived in the flat and here he remained, keening resolutely. Ortrud said:

'You see I have a family.'

'Yes.'

'So I shall not be able to come with you after all. To come back with you to England. You will have to leave me and go back alone.'

'Yes.'

'Good-bye,' she said, in his arms.

'Good-bye.'

'*Mein liebling!*'

23

He walked back through the streets that skirted the University, down past the Institute of Scientific Research, into the central boulevard, crowded at this hour with students in their parti-coloured caps, pacing up and down, seeing life. Some of these were strolling arm-in-arm making progress difficult. A drosky passed containing Pope and Flosshilde and, seeing Lushington, Pope raised his hat a little way from his head like a royalty and kept it in this position as they drove by. Flosshilde smirked and the sun flashed blindingly on her diamond ring. She was certainly too fat for her age. Lushington, gaping after them, got caught up in a chain of students and was carried some little way in the wrong direction. He reached the hotel at last and went through the swing doors. The lounge was full of people having tea or *aperitifs*. Da Costa and Waldemar were sitting at one of the tables, smoking. When he saw Lushington, Da Costa said:

'Come and join us. No, don't get up, Waldemar. But, my dear chap, what on earth has happened to your hat? The ribbon is all coming off. I wish you'd remember that you have to keep up appearances if you are seen about with me. On account of the legation, you know. British prestige and so on. Do make an effort. And have you heard the latest? The funniest thing you ever heard in your life. The Deputy-Chief of the Air Service found the Third Secretary from the French legation in his wife's room and loosed off a revolver at him and the shot broke a window in the house opposite and smashed a picture of Mussolini as it happened to be the Italian consulate. There's going to be the hell of a row.'

'Quite right.'

'You don't seem a bit excited by the news. I shan't tell you my secrets in future.'

'I heard something about it all earlier in the afternoon.'

'You can't have people going about breaking windows even if they are important public figures. Especially if the windows are extra-territorial ones. I must say all my sympathy is with the outraged husband. Not to mention Mussolini.'

Waldemar said: 'Nevertheless it was an unseemly occurrence. He should have challenged the delinquent to a duel in spite of the heavy penalties that attach to duelling for those convicted of that breach of the civil code.'

'What are the penalties?' Lushington said.

'For killing a man in a duel there is sentence of three years forced labour. The law is very strictly maintained. Sometimes in very exceptional cases of provocation, as in this instance of which we speak when one party's honour has indeed been tarnished it might be reduced to half that period. But not often.'

Lushington said: 'In that case, should the situation arise, I shall refuse to run the risk of prison. Everyone at home would be sure to hear of it and no one would ever believe that I had been put there for duelling.'

Da Costa said: 'I hope to goodness Pope does not get himself into trouble of that sort one of these days. I hear that he is a very susceptible man and he is such a snob that it would be bound to be no one less than a minister's wife.'

'I found Pope reading my letters this morning.'

'The man lives on his nerves. Obviously you have got to put up with something from a man as nervy as that. He's an excellent valet. You expect too much.'

'I don't mind his living on his own nerves. I object to him living on mine.'

Waldemar said: 'This Mr. Pope? I often hear you speak of him. He is by chance a secretary at your legation?'

Da Costa said: 'Well, he's not actually that but you can take it from me that without Pope our legation would not keep open for five minutes. It would just cease to exist.'

'Impossible!'

'My dear Waldemar,' Da Costa said, 'it's nothing more than the truth. And now I must leave you because I have a heavy evening before me with the Hedevarys. I believe by the way your pretty friend Madame Mavrin is going to be there. Shall I give her your love? And before I go you must congratulate Waldemar. He has been appointed aide-de-camp to General Kuno.'

'You have? Congratulations.'

Waldemar said: 'I thank you both for your congratulations, gentlemen. It is indeed for me a high honour. May I prove myself worthy of it. And only yesterday I was thinking that General Kuno was displeased with me because not long ago he saw me at a late hour with you in a house of amusement. But now I go no more to such places. They are not for those who would make a career.'

Da Costa: 'You're right, Waldemar. They are not. That is one of the reasons why you see me in that sort of place so seldom. I am ambitious.'

He laughed piercingly and getting up took his hat and coat and scarf from the chair beside him. He spent some time in dressing up in all his clothes and then, waving his hand, he made his way between the tables and the palms. Lushington and Waldemar sat on in silence. Several business men were arguing gutturally in other corners of the lounge and one had put his feet up on a chair and had gone to sleep. Waldemar blinked and moved his feet about. Then he moistened his lips and said:

'You will take dinner with me, Mr. Lushington? It would be a great pleasure. I invite you.'

Lushington said that he would like very much to take dinner and Waldemar suggested that they should go first to where he lived so that he could change from top boots. After that they would dine in the mess of his regiment. He said:

'But first we will go back and you may meet my brothers.'

'How many?'

'They are two.'

As they went along the central boulevard and through the public gardens Waldemar began to speak of his fiancée. She worked in a travel agency and they had not yet enough money to get married, but in two years he would have become a real captain and she would be at the head of her department at the office so that by then, with their combined incomes, they would have enough to live on. In answer to Lushington's question, Waldemar said that he did not mind waiting.

'With such good prospects,' he said, 'we cannot complain at a small delay. You agree that we are very lucky?'

'Very.'

'For few is life so easy.'

The Waldemar brothers lived on the outskirts of the town so that when they reached the end of the public gardens Waldemar decided to take a tram. He sat very upright when they were inside it with his sword held between his legs so that it did not trip up the conductor. He said:

'But it is unsuitable in a young officer to think of marriage. Women should not be allowed to interfere with the affairs. You agree?'

'With what affairs?'

'The duty.'

'Of course.'

'And then the life of a soldier is difficult. There is so much gaiety. Last week our colonel's wife gave an evening festival. All the officers had to be present. Only a fortnight before that the artillery corps organised a dance. Soon there will be preparations for the ball at the House of the Knights. In such an atmosphere of pleasure it is hard to think always of the work that is to be done. And besides one does not readily give up one's bachelor freedom.'

Waldemar pursed his lips. He became lost in thought. Later he said:

'But I am fortunate. Many young officers in my regiment have debts. One I know owes as much as a whole half-year's pay. At least I have not that to reproach myself with.'

They arrived at the Waldemar flat and went into a narrow hall. In this hall there were three pegs and a uniform cap and overcoat and sword hung on two of them. On the shelf above the pegs were three steel helmets and three revolver holsters. Waldemar put his cap and coat and sword on the third peg. Then he led the way along the passage and opened the door at the end of it. They came into a small room with a table in the middle of it at which two young men in uniform were sitting reading. They wore blue breeches instead of crimson ones like Waldemar. When they saw Lushington they stood up, brought their heels together, and bowed. Waldemar said:

'These are my brothers. This one speaks English but not well. Always he studies it but he is not yet proficient. He can read but he cannot speak well. The other one is not clever. He can speak only his own language and German. He is backward. A slow boy.'

Lushington shook hands. He shook hands with the slow boy first, for humanitarian reasons. Everyone stood more or less at attention facing everybody else. It was like an amateur two-minutes silence. At the end of it Lushington said:

'I see that they are not in the same regiment as yourself.'

'This one is in the Corps of Engineers. He that is backward in the 8th Regiment of the Line.'

'Very nice.'

After a while everyone sat down. The brothers were young men on the same lines as Waldemar but both of them were larger in build and had redder faces. They said that they had just come back from barracks and, as for some reason neither of them were dining in mess that night, they had been putting in some serious reading before going out to the evening meal. Waldemar said:

'See, this brother reads an English book.'

He took the English book from the brother who was reading it and gave it to Lushington for his inspection. Lushington looked at the title. It was *The Ordeal of Richard Feverel*. Waldemar said: 'And now you will excuse? I go to take off my breeches.'

Lushington handed back the book to the English-speaking brother. He said:

'A bit of an ordeal for you too, I expect?'

'Please?'

'I say it must have been a bit of an ordeal for you too—to plough through all that?'

'To plough?'

'To get through it.'

'Please?'

'I mean it's not at all an easy book to read, that's all. It's the kind of book that an Englishman might find it difficult to finish. It's a bit diffuse. Not easy to follow. Some of the ideas rather out of date and all that.'

'So?'

'I never got to the end of it myself. Somehow I seemed to lose interest. I don't quite know why, because it's a good book in its way. Mental laziness, I suppose.'

'So?'

Waldemar who had appeared again in the room with some crimson overall trousers which he was engaged in fitting over and buttoning under the soles of his wellingtons, preparatory to putting on both at once, made a shot at possible puritanical motives that might cause Englishmen to fight shy of Meredith and said:

'It is a shocking story, yes?'

'No, no. Not at all. All I say is that some people, myself for example, find it rather an ordeal to get through. Ordeal is too strong a word. I only used it because it was one of the words in the title of the book. I was not speaking seriously.'

'You joke?'

'Yes. I joke.'

Waldemar said: 'It is that which I like so much in you Englishmen. The jokes you have. Always it is the jokes. It is very nice.'

He explained matters to the English-speaking brother and then to the dull one who spoke only two languages. He said to the English-speaking brother:

'It is plain that you do not yet understand the English tongue. Be not so slow. Apply your mind to the study of that most useful language.'

When Waldemar had managed at last to get into his wellingtons he and Lushington left the two brothers, after shaking hands again all round, and walked to the barracks which were only a few streets away. They had dinner in the mess, a long low room with two tables running down it at which rows of stolid uhlans were seated. Waldemar said:

'I will present to you but the colonel and the adjutant. The rest who speak only German would anger you. Later I wish to consult your opinion on the subject of marriage and the relative position of the husband and the wife. I wish to hear your view on so serious a topic. I am glad that we have the night before us so that each can put forward the convictions he may hold on the much discussed perplexities of the married state.'

24

Ultimately it was Da Costa who decided that it would be a good thing to go inland for a week-end's ski-ing. He had said that Lushington must certainly ski at some time before he went back to England and that he himself wished to do something of the sort in the near future because he considered that this might send up his shares with Bellamy who approved of outdoor sports. Lushington, whose mind was seldom free from ruminations as to subjects for newspaper articles, was easily persuaded. Cortney agreed to go with them. In the end all the arrangements for the journey were left in Cortney's hands and were carried out by him with moderate success. They arrived at the place with all their luggage and, although at one stage of the journey Lushington mislaid one of the skis he had hired, this was found later in the dining-car.

This part of the country was more hilly than the land along the coast. There were unending downs covered in snow and clumps of pine trees that stood beside frozen water. In the middle of the day the sun was bright and threw up a dazzling glare from the white slopes and the stretches of ice. Later the wind would get up as the sun began to lose its strength and the surface snow would be blown like dust across the tracks of the skis. There were no houses. As far as the horizon there seemed to be not even a peasant's hut. Below was the hotel and the station with the few outbuildings that belonged to them. The railway line ran as far as a signal box and then that too seemed to disappear in the snow. At certain seasons the hotel was quite full of people but this was the wrong time of year.

All that day they had been out on skis and now they were returning to the hotel. They came down the last incline at full speed and both Da Costa and Lushington fell where the ground rose slightly and then slanted away again suddenly. Cortney at the end of the descent did a christiania and turning watched them get up. Da Costa with his long eccentric face and darkened spectacles was the English milord of almost any French dramatic production. This effect was heightened by his hat, bought in the Tirol, and the short square mackintosh coat with big buttons on it that covered the upper half of his body. Da Costa picked up his Tirolese hat and began to brush the snow off it. Lushington rose from the ground and said, not for the first time that day:

'Why on earth aren't one's feet fixed into these skis as they are in the Swiss ones?'

'It is the custom in this part of Europe. It is easier when you are used to it. You can see whole battalions of troops going through evolutions on these skis. It's a wonderful sight.'

'I can believe you.'

'All dressed in white for camouflage.'

'Touching it must be.'

Cortney was some way ahead of them now. He moved easily on his skis and sometimes burst into snatches of song that lasted for several minutes. His medium was a hollow baritone. If the words were at all familiar Da Costa would join in with a stentorian and toneless lament, like some dreadful manifestation of African grief. These cacophonies echoed across the foot hills and the wastes of snow and pine-trees. At the end of them Da Costa would roar with laughter and try to yodel. The snow was beginning to descend again now in small flakes that blew sharply across their faces and into their eyes. The dusk, the tragic northern shadows of late afternoon, had begun to fall. The sun was already making bright stains on the snow between the stems of the pine-trees and across the ice of the lake. Da Costa said:

'We must press on. We want to get back to the hotel before dark. If one is too late there is often no food left.'

'Do you make a habit of spending your week-ends here?'

'Why are you so bad-tempered? What has happened? Has it come off again?'

'The strap has broken.'

'Can't you fix it so that it lasts as far as the hotel?'

'No.'

'Curtis! Curtis! Cur-tis! Have you got some string? Some stri-ing?'

But Cortney was far away and he could not hear them because he was singing. The throaty words were carried back on the wind and past them:

'. . . *Oh my name is Samuel Hall.* . . .
Samuel Hall. . . .
And I hate you one and all. . . .
You're a bunch of . . .'

'It's no good I'm afraid.'

'No, I'll carry them.'

'It isn't far.'

'Oh, no.'

By the time they had come to the hotel the snow was falling heavily. The hotel was a wooden chalet-like structure standing on a slight eminence and dominating the only other building, the railway station which gave the place its name and which was made for the most part of corrugated iron and barbed wire. As they passed the platform they saw waiting there for the train, due in a few hours time for the capital, a peasant family. Steaming, the peasants stood about or sat on their wooden boxes, so encased in clothes that it was difficult to tell which were women and which men. One of the smaller children raised its arm in surprise as Da Costa passed, but the others were impassive, too far from reality or too near to it to know or care whether this was a human being like themselves who looked so strange. Cortney who had waited for the other two had taken off his skis and was carrying them over his shoulder. He nodded in the direction of the peasants and said:

'See them. The children of the soil. The patient toilers now the day is done. Don't they make you think——'

Lushington and Da Costa walked towards the yard and stacked their skis in the shed. Then they went into the hotel which was almost empty at this time of year. It was very warm inside but none of the doors fitted, so that any sounds that were made reverberated along the wooden corridors. They ordered supper at once and went up to change from their ski-ing clothes. It was sometimes possible to obtain water to wash in before the evening meal.

When he came downstairs again Lushington was surprised to find Cortney in front of the fire talking to Count Scherbatcheff. The Count was wearing his overcoat, although the room was stifling and he explained that he had come up to this part of the country for a few days for the sake of his health. Here the ground was higher and the air was better and the doctor had suggested that a week's ski-ing might do him good.

'My health has been bad,' he said, 'and my relations do not understand me. But I am glad that all of you are here. In the evenings we can talk as we are doing now and it will be less dull than when I was here alone.'

The others had their meal but Count Scherbatcheff refused to eat because he said that he did not feel well. He sat there in his overcoat and drank a little beer and joined in the conversation. The food in the hotel was plain, but not bad although there was a chronic danger that owing to the difficulties of transport there might be nothing to eat at all. This eventuality was harped on by Da Costa who used it as a sort of weapon with which to bully the others and the proprietor of the hotel himself. That evening, however, there was plenty to eat and after dinner they pushed back the table and sat in the dining-room in front of the fire. In answer to a remark made by Da Costa, Cortney said:

'Cute? I'll say they are cute. Why there isn't a town from Maine to California that can't produce a year's debs to rival those of any other town in any other country that you may like to name.'

Count Scherbatcheff said: 'There are times when women seem to me no more than the illusions that the camera throws on the shaking screen. The shadow of life. In the mythology of the Scandinavians they tell of creatures who present to the eye the appearance of flesh and blood and beauty. And yet, going behind them, they are discovered to be flat. They have no substance. They are like pictures hung on an easel that have no thickness.'

'Why, Count, you wouldn't say that if I took you around. And one of these days I will. We three and the Count will throw a wild party. And we'll throw it somewhere the right side of Mason and Dixon. You won't think the girls are illusions there. I'll see to that.'

Da Costa said: 'Personally I absolutely agree with Scherbatcheff. I would rather not. But I do. I should like to have a temperament like that new Spanish secretary. I never saw anything like the success he was having at the Arnhfeldts' the other night.'

Cortney said: 'You've said it. All the pretty women in the place at his heels. Madame Mavrin, Countess Arnhfeldt, Mrs. Mitsu, the whole lot of them.'

Lushington said: 'Countess Arnhfeldt certainly. But I don't know why you mention Madame Mavrin. I didn't notice that she seemed particularly keen on him.'

'You know, Lushington, those dagos have a way with them. We just can't compete. It's one of the things I have had to learn and which you will have to learn too.'

'But just because Madame Mavrin may have danced with him a couple of times I see no reason why you should spread scandals about her.'

'Scandal? Why, I should say I wouldn't spread scandals about her, Lushington. Why, there isn't a lady in the whole town whom I hold in greater respect than Frau Mavrin. I should say not. All I said was that she and a good many more of them seemed to like the looks of that young Spaniard more than I did myself.'

'Well that's just what I said.'

'What are you disagreeing with me for then?'

'I mean that I said that that was what you said before and now you are denying it. I didn't say anything of the sort myself. I don't think it.'

'Don't think what?'

'That Madame Mavrin was getting off with that Spaniard.'

'Neither do I. All I said was that she seemed to like him.'

'You didn't. You inferred that she liked him in a way that she should not do. It's a perfect disgrace. It's fellows like you who start these stories and then trouble follows.'

'But see here, Lushington——'

Count Scherbatcheff said: 'Mr. Lushington is quite right, Mr. Cortney. You spoke no doubt unintentionally but at the same time most improperly of Madame Mavrin. Men have had to fight duels for less. I do not blame you because I feel sure that you were not thinking about what you were saying but at the same time I should counsel that you speak with greater prudence in future.'

Da Costa said: 'I can't imagine what has come over you and Scherbatcheff, unless you have eaten too much and he has eaten too little. Cortney never said a word against Madame Mavrin. Anyway I expect the Spaniard preferred Countess Arnhfeldt. In my opinion there is no doubt at all that she is the better looking of the two.'

Lushington said: 'To say that is merely silly. In the first place she does not look nearly so interesting. Anyway the Spaniard obviously did not think that Countess Arnhfeldt was the more attractive. That was clear from his behaviour.'

'But I thought you said that he only danced with Madame Mavrin twice all the evening?'

'What I said was that neither of them had behaved in a way to provoke the scandal which I thought Cortney was spreading. However as I see that you are bent on circulating a tissue of inventions yourself I will say no more and you can broadcast what you like.'

'But see here, Lushington—and you, Count—you must understand that I never meant a word against Madame Mavrin. I can't see how you can have thought that I did. And Da Costa is quite right. It was Countess Arnhfeldt that he had his eye on and I don't blame him. Much as I admire Madame Mavrin I hold the Countess the greater beauty of the two.'

'Well, if you think that, nothing surprises me.'

Count Scherbatcheff who was having a bad fit of coughing at that moment moved his head from side to side to show that he too found these words incredible, but he was unable to speak the protests that he evidently wanted to make. Da Costa said:

'Come on, let's play bridge. I have some cards here. I can't imagine how all this started. Or why.'

25

Everyone felt better after the week-end spent ski-ing, except Count Scherbatcheff who felt worse. The Count decided that to be left alone in the hotel after the others were gone would depress him too much and so he travelled back with them, sleeping on the floor of the wagon-lit shared by Lushington and Cortney. The journey was not long but the best train went after midnight and Da Costa insisted that they must have sleepers. In the morning Cortney forgot that Count Scherbatcheff was on the floor and put his bare foot on the Count's face when he got out of his bunk but Count Scherbatcheff took this in very good part and said that much worse things had happened to him during the Revolution. Da Costa shared a compartment with a priest who wore a square Assyrian beard. They kept the rest of the train awake all night by arguing about religion in bad French. Both of them looked very pale and bad-tempered the next morning and the priest got up early and stood for the rest of the journey in the corridor and ate something which he had brought with him in a paper bag. When they arrived at the capital Count Scherbatcheff refused all offers of a lift and he was last seen hurrying away, carrying his wicker suitcase which was the size and shape of a coffin and had several straps round it. The others went to their respective homes and all of them met again that evening at a party given by Madame Bitulescu.

26

Lushington, who had been spending the previous two or three days writing up accounts of the ski-ing expedition for various periodicals, was standing in front of the looking-glass in his sitting-room, tying his white tie, and because when someone knocked on the door he thought that the Bellamys might have arrived unexpectedly early, he slipped on his dressing gown before opening it. It was not the Bellamys however. It was Ortrud. She said:

'I came straight up. You do not mind?'

'Of course not. But I shall have to go out in a minute. The Bellamys are picking up Cortney and me in the legation car as we are all going to the same place for dinner.'

'You are going out to-night?'

'I have to.'

'But I am free to-night and we can go out together. You must put them off. You can leave a message at the hotel desk to say that you are ill.'

'No I can't possibly. Besides they may be here at any moment. I told them to come here for a cocktail before we went on.'

'But surely you can put them off? We have not met for so long. You go away to the country and leave me. Would you not prefer to have dinner with me? But perhaps you would not?'

'You know I should. How silly you are. But surely you understand that I cannot do so at this moment. It must be obvious.'

'Not at all. If you were really fond of me you would have suggested it yourself. But I understand. You would rather go out with the Bellamys. Naturally I see that they are more important people than I am.'

'Really, please. Do not be so ridiculous. What has happened to you? This is most unlike you.'

'It is unlike me to want to see you? Do you think that is true? I can remember the time when you wanted to see me.'

'But you know that I want to see you now. I would much rather go out with you than with the Bellamys. But I can't put them off when they may arrive in my room at any moment.'

'No, no. I understand.'

108

'But how can I?'

'No, of course not. Naturally not.'

'Ortrud?'

'Good-bye, then.'

'Please?'

'Perhaps we may meet again some time before you leave.'

'When you are in a less ridiculous mood I hope.'

'And you less rude.'

She slammed the door a little. Lushington went on with his dressing. Pope, who for some reason had put out his dinner jacket to wear that night, had also hidden his white waistcoat but Lushington found it at last in a box on the top of the wardrobe. This was reached by putting a suitcase on a chair and then stepping on to it from the table. As he was climbing down, precariously, from this edifice there was another knock on the sitting-room door.

'Come in.'

It was Da Costa this time, who said:

'I was passing and saw a light in your sitting-room so I thought I'd look in. You don't mind my coming straight up, I hope.'

'Have a cigarette. Take your goloshes off. The Bellamys are coming at any moment. They are giving me a lift in the Rolls and are having a cocktail here first.'

'In that case I don't think I'll stop.'

'Why not?'

'It's not that I dislike Bellamy. On the contrary. I think that in many ways he's a very good fellow. And I like Mrs. Bellamy as well. On occasions she can be charming. But since if I stay I shall inevitably be drawn into talking shop I shall instead go to my own home and read a little before dinner.'

'All right. Then we shall meet to-morrow at the Koski's.'

Da Costa nodded. He lit a cigarette and went away. Lushington examined the white waistcoat. It had several black marks across the front. He understood now why Pope had put out his dinner jacket to wear that night. It would now be necessary to find another waistcoat. He went into the bedroom and began to go through the drawers. There were no white waistcoats. Then he pulled a box from under the bed and began to throw its contents on the floor. He was lucky and in a few minutes found a garment that was not too crumpled to wear. While he was putting the buttons in the telephone bell rang.

'Hullo?'

It was Flosshilde from the desk in the hotel lounge. She said in her slow English:

'A gentleman to see you. And two ladies.'

'Ask them to come up.'

Lushington fumbled with the last button of the waistcoat. He wondered who the other lady was. He said:

'It is Mr. Bellamy, of course, of the British legation?'

'Please?'

'It is Mr. and Mrs. Bellamy? The English *chargé d'affaires*? The gentleman who often walks about without an overcoat?'

'The gentleman said that his name was Count Bobel. He did not tell me the names of the ladies.'

'Count Bobel! Tell them to wait for a moment. Tell them that I am engaged and can see no one for the time being.'

'For the time being? Please I do not understand.'

'Now! Now! Stop them!'

'They have started on their way up.'

'Prevent them quickly.'

'They have already ascended in the lift.'

The knock came at the sitting room door at the exact moment at which Lushington was turning the handle to get out into the passage and send down his visitors in the lift from which they had emerged. The door opened inwards and Count Bobel entered holding out his hand and beaming. He was followed by two women. Count Bobel said:

'Mr. Lushington, *mon cher*, how splendid to see you again.'

To gain time Lushington took the hand and shook it. Count Bobel said:

'Mr. Lushington, I was about to make a little trip into the country with these two ladies. There is a small hotel along the coast that we could reach in time for dinner. Outside I have a sleigh. It occurred to me that with a fourth there would be more pleasure for all concerned. Will you not therefore join us? In that way we shall be *une partie carrée*.'

Glancing at the girls Lushington saw that they were the ones who had sat near his table the night he had gone to Maxim's with Da Costa, Waldemar and Cortney. The one who had worn riding costume on that occasion was evidently dressed at this moment in something of the sort under her coat, because she wore top boots and a three cornered hat that spoke of stag hunts in Normandy and the meet on St. Hubert's

day. The other, the blonde, was so encased in furs that he could barely
see her face at all but the features that were visible showed that she
still looked cross. The faces of both ladies were made up for the savage
glare of night club illuminations. Lushington, remembering that he
was in his shirt sleeves, took up his tail coat and began to struggle into
it. Count Bobel was looking round the room with interest. He said:

'This lady speaks English.'

Outside, the clock above the National Theatre struck the half-
hour. Lushington remembered that Da Costa had once reported an
observation made by Bellamy to the effect that unpunctuality in a
diplomatist spelled ruin. The Bellamys would therefore arrive at the
hotel at any moment now. It would be necessary to take action. Count
Bobel said:

'I will introduce. This is the Marquise Clothilde de Madragore.
And this the Princess Varvara.'

Lushington shook hands. The Marquise said:

'Yes, please. Speak English, mister.'

Count Bobel who had sat down on the sofa and was lighting one
of his amber cigarettes said:

'You understand that it is not so much English that she speaks and
thus it will not matter if I mention in front of her a little matter which
I do not wish to forget. The young girl at the desk downstairs. She has
been here long?'

'I don't know at all.'

'You have noticed her?'

'I have seen her, of course. What do you mean? I do not understand you.'

'You would not mind if I were to ask her out?'

'Why in the world should I?'

'You have not approached her, no?'

'Only for my letters.'

Count Bobel threw up his hands. He said:

'Ah, your English stiffness! When shall I become accustomed to it?
But I must tell you how I met the young lady who is at the desk downstairs. It was at a little cabaret on the river bank. She was with an Englishman, a good fellow, a Mr. Pope who said he knew you. He is perhaps a secretary at your legation, yes?'

'No.'

'Never mind then. Later I won a little money from him doing

tricks with matches. The young lady was with him. I am not a vain man but I could not help seeing that she had taken a fancy to me.'

'Indeed?'

The smell from Count Bobel's cigarette was filling the room. Certainly the moment to act was approaching. The Princess Varvara had begun to repair her face and patchouli was added to the scent of amber. The Marquise produced a lipstick from her vanity bag. Lushington took Count Bobel by the lapel of his coat and led him into the corner of the room.

'Count Bobel I must speak to you plainly. It was a misunderstanding that they showed you up here. I am busy. I must inform you that the door opposite leads to my bedroom.'

'Ah-ha?'

'You are disturbing me. I cannot come on this trip. I am not alone. I am occupied. This is an important moment in my life.'

'You mean, Mr. Lushington——'

'Exactly.'

'*Une femme*——?'

'Must I put it more bluntly?'

'But——'

'Have I said enough?'

Count Bobel fell into an armchair and began to roar with falsetto laughter. He said:

'You English! You English! When shall I become accustomed to your way? But why did you not say so at once? And I myself was so slow that I thought you were putting your clothes on. Never for one moment did I guess that you were taking them off. You are cunning, *mon cher.*'

Still laughing he began to explain the situation to the ladies in a language that was unfamiliar to Lushington. They agreed with the Count that it was a good joke. Even the blonde relaxed a little. They were still enjoying it when the telephone bell rang. Lushington took up the receiver:

'Hullo?'

'Mr. and Mrs. Bellamy,' Flosshilde said.

'Will you ask them to wait for one moment?'

'They said that you expected them and that they would make their way up.'

Lushington snapped down the receiver. He took Count Bobel by the arm.

'And now, Count Bobel——'

The Count could hardly speak he was laughing so much but he managed to get up and to say:

'One moment, Mr. Lushington. I have here some postcards which I had intended to show you. I feel certain that they will amuse you. They are free but for that reason they are none the less funny. I brought them specially with me to-night that you might see them because I forgot to show them to you on the voyage. They are here. One moment——'

'Count Bobel, some other time. I must insist.'

'But look just at this one.'

'Not now!'

Lushington put him through the door and the Marquise and the Princess after him. As he shut the door behind him he heard the clang of the lift as it arrived at his landing. He had time hardly to stamp out the cigarette that Count Bobel in his amusement had left lying on the edge of the table and to throw the stub of it into the waste-paper basket when he found that the Bellamys had arrived.

Later in the evening Mrs. Bellamy said:

'Of course some people prefer the Bristol to this hotel. It may not be so comfortable but it is certainly quieter. You see some very impossible people in here at times.'

'I have noticed some odd people in the lounge on occasions.'

Mrs. Bellamy said: 'We passed three very extraordinary people in the corridor just outside this room when we arrived. A man and two women. Did you notice them, Trevor?'

'Well I hope they won't any of them decide to come in here,' Lushington said. 'As a matter of fact I had thought of moving to the Bristol. It would be, as you say, quieter. But then I shan't be staying here so very much longer.'

27

And then one day Count Scherbatcheff died. For a long time he had looked more and more ill and the troubles with his stomach had become increasingly serious. He could be seen in the streets, hunched up and wearing his astrakhan cap, as he hurried along, returning from a visit to some other member of the Russian colony. This was his occupation although he also sat sometimes in bars or sipped tea in the lounge of the hotel. He never appeared at diplomatic gatherings and all his friends were Russian. His grandmother sent Lushington an invitation to the funeral which took place in the orthodox cathedral. Ortrud sent a wreath but did not attend the ceremony because of what her husband felt about Russians. After the service they followed the coffin to a cemetery in a distant part of the town, further even than the Scherbatcheff flat, and they passed by the stacks of empty petrol tins and the big shells of uncompleted buildings with cranes on top of them. Da Costa and Cortney came too and wore top hats. Pope offered to lend Lushington a top hat for the funeral but, as the weather was cold, Lushington said that he would prefer to wear his own fur cap. He walked in the procession next to Count Scherbatcheff's uncle, the man with the shaved head who wore a grey military overcoat and the cross of St. George. On the way home Lushington saw him put his hand in the pocket of the overcoat and take out some cigarettes which he evidently carried loose there, instead of in a case. Count Scherbatcheff's grandmother walked in the procession too and wept into a small lace handkerchief.

Later that week there were political disturbances and someone hit someone else in the House of Deputies. There was also a riot at one of the timber yards up the river and the mounted gendarmes were called out. Some people said that there was going to be a revolution but this was considered to be unlikely because General Kuno was known to have such matters well in hand and more often the topic of conversation was the ball at the House of the Knights which was to take place soon and which it was intended to make more of a success than ever before, although Baroness Puckler had pointed out that whatever they did nothing could rival what these entertainments had been like when she was a girl. Sometimes it occurred to Lushington that soon he would be going back to England. He found that he talked less to Da Costa about Lucy. In fact on several occasions Da Costa himself had brought her into their conversations. He often saw Ortrud.

28

Coming down the stairs of the hotel into the lounge Lushington was surprised to see Professor Mavrin standing at the desk talking to Floss-hilde. Lushington touched him on the arm and said good morning. The Professor turned and said:

'Mr. Lushington, I am so delighted to find you at home. I am free this afternoon. I have no lectures. I hoped that perhaps you would accompany me on a walk.'

'I should like nothing better.'

Flosshilde said: 'Herr Lushington, here are three letters and a post-card for you. There is additional tax to pay on them. They have not enough stamps.'

Lushington glanced at the letters. All were from Lucy. He paid Flosshilde, put the letters in his pocket, and said to the Professor:

'That is the sort of thing that women never remember. To put enough stamps on a letter going abroad.'

The Professor laughed and stroked his tattered moustache which gave him something of the air of a sea-lion. He said:

'They are from your fiancée perhaps and therefore you do not mind?'

'Well, no. Not exactly. Just a friend, you know.'

They went out into the streets and walked down the steps that led to the river. It was a sunny afternoon with a sharp wind blowing inland from the islands. The Professor said:

'It is interesting to me what you said, that your letters came from a woman who was a friend. That is something that only England enjoys. The friendship between the sexes when the more deep relationship remains in the background. With all our advances in the sphere of modern thought we have not yet achieved such in this country. And you yourself, Mr. Lushington, do you never feel that a friendship of this sort may not become disturbing?'

'Of course one hears of instances where it may be said to have done so.'

'In this country it would seem impossible that such frankness can exist. The women themselves are not yet prepared for it. The men, too, hardly wish for it. And this brings me to a subject which I would discuss with you because I believe you to be a man of understanding. I wish to speak to you about my wife.'

Lushington assumed an expression of interest. He wondered whether the Professor was anything of a shot and if combatants were allowed to wear glasses in a duel. The snow in the early morning would be very dazzling to the eyes. Swords were clearly out of the question. The Professor continued:

'For some time I have noticed that she has not been herself. She is absent-minded. She weeps easily. Sometimes she is unnecessarily high-spirited. At other times she is sunk into deep despondency. Have you remarked these things? Indeed you cannot fail to have remarked them?'

'I thought that perhaps her temperament made her act as you describe. I have of course noticed that she has moods. But then I have known her for comparatively so short a time.'

'What do you think such behaviour signifies?'

'I cannot imagine.'

'But is it not only too clear?'

'Not to me, Professor.'

'Come, come, Mr. Lushington,' said the Professor, almost testily, 'you are a journalist. A man of the world. When do women behave in such a way? Is it not when they are in love?'

'Yes, I suppose it is now that I come to think of it.'

'Of course it is. And I will tell you. I think that such is the case with my wife.'

'But that is quite right surely? That she should be in love?'

'You misunderstand me. I cannot flatter myself that I am the cause of these manifestations. On the contrary.'

'No?'

'No,' said the Professor. 'And what is more than that, I believe that I know the man whom she loves.'

'Really?'

They were crossing the Nikolai Bridge now. An apprehension was raised in Lushington's mind that the Professor might have hired a gang to throw him into the river from this point. Singlehanded, he supposed, he could tackle the Professor himself, who could not be strong after the hardships he had undergone during the Revolution. When they were halfway across the Professor stopped, and for several minutes pointed out places of interest in the town which could be seen best from the bridge. Several suspicious-looking characters passed while he was doing this, but the further bank was reached without incident. The Professor said:

'But to return to the problem of domestic life, I will not ask you to guess who it is that I have in my mind, but I feel sure that you would guess correctly.'

'Oh, but on the contrary, I feel sure that I should not.'

'No, Mr. Lushington, you do not give your imagination due justice. But we leave that for the moment. For it is of the theory of the matter that I would speak to you and not of personalities. I wish to know from you how in England the situation would be considered?'

'Well, of course, situations of that kind have to a great degree to be judged on their own merits.'

'You think that?'

'Most certainly.'

'And such is the accepted English view?'

'It is and it isn't.'

'Exactly,' said the Professor. 'That is precisely what I myself feel. Sometimes I think this. Sometimes that. We must for example recognise that the economic position of women has altered in the last few years in a way which it is impossible to estimate. Woman has become her own master.'

'And very often someone else's mistress.'

'Very good!' said the Professor. 'Very good! Excellent! I must remember that and write it down. Will you repeat it once more? The modern woman is not only becoming her own master, she has already become another's mistress. I shall say that when I have to attend the dinner of the senior professors which takes place next week. It is a most true and profound saying. It will entertain them greatly and no doubt add in some measure to my popularity. But to return to a more serious view of the question, do you hold with me that women should be allowed considerable liberty?'

'Naturally I agree with you.'

'I am glad that you agree on that point. Yet this liberty must not be allowed to develop into licence. You agree there too. Not licence.'

'Oh most certainly not.'

'But who is to tell where liberty may end and licence begin?'

'That must surely remain a question for each individual to settle for him or for herself?'

'But is it not possible in the case of a husband and a wife that what may appear a necessary relaxation to the one, bears to the other all the marks of unjustifiable conduct?'

'Do you think so?'

'It would appear most apparent.'

'I had not thought of that. Perhaps you are right.'

'And yet I do not wish, Mr. Lushington, that for one moment you should think that I am out of touch with the ideas of the present day. On the contrary I have myself always been a steadfast upholder of advanced thought. But it is impossible to disregard the intricacies, the compromises, which must accompany any reconciliation of the teachings of the doctrinaire who may content himself with hypothetical cases of comparative simplicity, with the more complicated and personal problems of the individual world in which we live. You yourself will surely be with me in admitting the considerable range of obstacles which are on the road to a better understanding?'

'I quite agree with you there. I think that you are quite right.'

'Very well then. We may proceed. But first you will not mind my telling you why I choose you for these confidences. It is this. I have noticed that my wife speaks always of you and to you, Mr. Lushington, with considerable asperity. I feel sure that she likes you but I cannot blind myself to the fact that there is at the same time something about you that affects adversely her nerves. You do not, I hope, mind my telling you these things? You do not mind, Mr. Lushington?'

'Not in the least.'

'I am glad. It is for this reason that I said those words. You know my wife and yet because she is always so brusque with you she cannot fail to have caused you annoyance and therefore there is less breach of confidence on your part if you tell me what you think of her. You comprehend my meaning?'

'But——'

'One moment, please. I believe that the reason of her attitude towards you is this. You are a friend of Mr. Da Costa. It appears to me that she is *jealous* of your friendship with Mr. Da Costa. I do not think that she herself even is aware of this. It is all in the realm of the subconscious. I do not know indeed whether she is even aware of her own feelings for Mr. Da Costa, but I am confident that it is towards him that she feels a strong attachment.'

'Da Costa!'

'You are surprised. You cannot accustom yourself to the idea of a married woman feeling drawn towards a man who is not her husband. That is in many ways the right point of view for you to take. I admire it but I cannot say that I share it. My reading and my experience have taught me otherwise. But having told you so much you will not perhaps mind my asking you a question about your friend? Do you think, Mr. Lushington, that the feelings of which I speak are in any way reciprocated by him?'

'I feel sure that they are not. There is nothing of which I feel more certain. You can set your mind absolutely at rest on that point.'

'You can really assure me?'

'I am confident of it.'

The Professor said: 'In that case I feel greatly relieved. Because although I am a student of advanced thought I cannot conceal from myself that I still retain many unprogressive prejudices.'

'But even were anything so unlikely, so distasteful, the case as that my friend Da Costa and your wife possessed the feelings for each other that you suggest I cannot see why my friendship for him should make your wife jealous?'

'My dear Mr. Lushington, you do not understand. In the realm of the sub-conscious there are dark and secret places, strange emotions that do not distinguish, as does our waking consciousness, between such kindred feelings as love and friendship. These have power over the actions of the individual of which he himself or she herself is wholly unaware. I tell you this from the depths of my experience.'

'But, my dear Professor, I cannot allow the implications of what you have said to pass without protest. I feel justified in objecting most strongly to your suggestion that your wife is jealous of me on account of my friendship.'

'My dear Mr. Lushington, jealousy is far too definite a word. I used it only to indicate the general tendency of her attitude to give support to what I had already told you about her. Perhaps I expressed what I mean in a way that was not good. You must remember that I have but a limited knowledge of your language.'

'No, you are wrong. You speak English excellently. I am astonished at the degree of excellence with which everyone in this country speaks English.'

'You are too kind. But you understand that we must learn the language of the larger countries. It is necessary. As I was——'

'At the same time, Professor, I feel a little vexed that you should have made the remarks which you did. I think I am right.'

'My dear Mr. Lushington, I cannot imagine why you should think that. That indeed was the very last impression that I should like to give. Why, often people have asked me if I am not jealous of Baroness Puckler. In jest, naturally. And that was the spirit in which I took their remarks. Nevertheless, if you understand me——'

'Exactly, Professor. You have said enough. But do not let us discuss the matter further. I would rather not.'

'Perhaps you are right, Mr. Lushington. Perhaps I was going too far in what I said. Although I must assure you that I intended to convey nothing of what I fear may have been in your mind. I can only apologise——'

'No, no. Please do not apologise. We have said enough about the matter. Let us talk of something more pleasant. On such a lovely day as this, is it not a pity to discuss psychology? A little morbid, do not you think?'

'You are indeed right, Mr. Lushington, and again——'

'Please, my dear Professor, please say no more about it.'

They walked on for some time in silence. The wind was blowing the powdered snow off the parapets of the river's embankment. There was a fresh scent in the air of wood smoke. Lushington said:

'You have always promised to take me to the National Museum. Shall we go there now as we are about to pass it?'

'An excellent idea. Excellent. And besides the wind is becoming cold.'

29

They went up the steps of the museum and worked systematically through the halls of national costume, folk lore, pottery, agriculture, industries, and fossils. In this last room they found Da Costa. He was leaning heavily on one of the glass cases which creaked under his weight so that any moment it seemed possible that he might fall through it. He looked up when Lushington and the Professor entered and laughed so loudly that an attendant hurried in from the next room to see what had happened. Da Costa said:

'Fancy meeting here! How are you, Herr Professor? And how is Frau Mavrin? It is quite a long time since I have seen you both.'

Lushington said: 'Professor Mavrin and I have been for a walk and as he has always promised to show me round here I thought it would be a good opportunity as we were passing. But I didn't know you were in the habit of coming here.'

'I'm not,' Da Costa said. 'To tell the truth I have hardly ever been here before. But since Scherbatcheff's funeral I have become interested in death. I can't tell you why exactly, but there it is. It occurred to me that this would be a good place to consider it in.'

He laughed again and the whole of his face worked up and down. The Professor said:

'You are too young a man to think about death, Mr. Da Costa. You should think about life, love, your career. Death you should leave to old gentlemen like myself.'

Da Costa said: 'I think about those things too sometimes. But on the whole I find thinking about death a better mental exercise. For one thing one knows less about it than the other three.'

Lushington said: 'I was very sorry about Scherbatcheff myself. I don't think you knew him, did you, Professor? He was a Russian who travelled out here with me on the same boat.'

The Professor said: 'As a Russian I should not have known him. I know no Russians. But for your sake I am sorry that he is dead.'

Da Costa said: 'He was a nice man and whatever people may say about it one does not want to die. Anyway not just yet. At least that is the conclusion that I have just come to.'

The Professor said: 'You are right, Mr. Da Costa. The instinct of self-preservation remains with us in spite of all melancholies and discomforts. Only yesterday I was speaking to General Kuno, who as you must know has many times been threatened with death, about this very subject.'

Da Costa said: 'Well fortunately no one dislikes me enough yet actually to assassinate me although I must say I caught Bellamy looking at me in a very funny way the other day. Perhaps he will bribe Pope to poison me.'

Lushington said: 'I suppose they will get General Kuno in the end?'

Da Costa said: 'Nonsense. People like that bear charmed lives. Tons of dynamite get thrown at them every year and only the public standing round get damaged.'

The Professor said: 'I repeat, Mr. Da Costa, that you should not think of such things. You are too young. You have much time yet. Rather let us examine these fine specimens of the rare chromate of lead which come from Siberia and this meteorite which fell near this very town in the middle years of the last century. After that you will perhaps permit me to invite you to tea for I feel sure that my wife will be delighted to see both of you.'

Da Costa said: 'That is very kind of you, Professor. I have some things I particularly want to talk over with Frau Mavrin.'

30

The façade of the House of the Knights was ornamented with wooden carving and gargoyles. Inside it had not been redecorated for many years and it was a pleasing mixture of tastes. The ballroom was large and long, not unlike a drill-hall, and along two sides of it were alcoves in each of which a figure in armour had been placed. Most of the suits were Seventeenth Century in style. A few had casques with long tails and projecting visors and one or two, of Russian or Polish origin, curved up to points like Persian helmets. On the capitals of each of the pillars of the hall the arms of a noble family had been carved and painted and gilded. These also were late in date and some of the coats florid in design. At one end of the room the band from the Café Weber was playing Strauss and at the other the President sat, a small man wearing too short evening trousers. He had been given a high Spanish chair so that his feet were just off the ground but he sat there looking happy and interested in everything that was taking place. A group of cavalrymen stood behind him, leaning romantically on their sabres, mopping and mowing at their friends in other parts of the hall and assisting the room's chiaroscuro with a solid background of red breeches. Everyone of any importance seemed to be present although Ortrud had not yet arrived. Lushington was standing next to the British military attaché who had manœuvred himself behind a high backed chair under cover of which he was undoing the top button of his trousers which were, he explained, the ones he had bought at the time when he had first joined his regiment. Lushington who had been extending his sympathy, said:

'Is there anyone in the town who hasn't come to-night?'

'Only one that I know of,' said the military attaché absorbedly. Lushington heard the button unfasten with a click. The major gave a sigh of deep relief, straightened his tunic, and emerged from behind the chair. Lushington said:

'Who is that? Who hasn't come?'

'A fellow I got into conversation with in the lounge of your hotel. He seemed not to have had an invitation. In fact he asked me if he could come with me and get in on mine. He said he was a count. Bobel or some such name. Ever heard of him? He seemed a bit of an outsider.'

'I seem to have heard the name.'

'You have?'

'Somewhere or other. I don't know.'

'Well, I mean socially he may be an A.1 lad and all that, but you just can't go about doing that sort of thing. I mean it's all wrong. You'd think a fellow would see that.'

'Absolutely wrong. A fellow like that needs snubbing.'

'I snubbed him all right. Don't you worry. He got his snub.'

'I'm delighted to hear it.'

At that moment a diversion was caused by the belated entry of the French diplomatic representatives, a remarkable quartette consisting of the minister, a Charley Chaplin-like little man with the pointed beard of the stage Frenchman, round-shouldered with the weight of the *légion d'honneur* round his neck, and glancing nervously at his wife, whose immense proportions seemed as if they might at any moment evade the neo-classic creation she was wearing. Behind her came the secretary, the second-empire baron, who had recently had so narrow an escape at the hands of the Deputy-Chief of the Air Force, and beside him their military attaché in a uniform of remarkable shape and elastic-sided boots on to the heel of which spurs had been screwed. Ushers shepherded this cortège to the President's throne and when Lushington turned round again he found that the major was now talking to the American and Japanese ministers. The former of these plenipotentiaries was saying:

'No sir, I do not. The tongue of Shakespeare and *The Saturday Evening Post* is good enough for us and you can take it from me, Colonel—and you, Viscount, you bear this in mind too—if people are worth talking to they talk *English*.'

Lushington moved away through the crowd. He wondered why he had not yet seen Ortrud because it was late in the evening and he knew that she was coming to the ball. That night in his bath he had begun to realise that he was going away and would never see her again. The thought of this disturbed and frightened him. He was going away. He would not see her again. Passing the buffet he saw General Kuno, very spick and span, wearing the riband of a recently conferred order across his chest. He and Lushington bowed to each other and as conversation was impossible went through some amicable dumb-show beginning by Lushington offering the General a cigarette which was accepted and ending with the General offering Lushington a sandwich from the buffet which was refused. Waldemar was fussing about behind the General and, in his capacity of A.D.C., wore heavy gold aiguillettes which he continually trailed into the ices and drinks of those standing anywhere near him. He kept on adjusting his pince-nez and bowing to people who came up to speak to the General. Lushington said to him:

'How are you enjoying your new job?'

'I am worried. Worried. I will tell you a secret. It is a great shame. It is no joke. Almost I am ashamed to tell you.'

'I must know the worst.'

'The armour round the room. It comes from the National Theatre. It is not genuine armour.'

'Why not?'

'It is false. A mere trick. I would tell no other stranger but you. I am angry with my country. But the committee insisted that it should be so. They were very adamant.'

'But this is the invariable practice in all countries. The use of stage properties on such occasions as these.'

'You astonish me?'

'I assure you.'

'I am much relieved.'

'But don't tell Cortney. He had better not know.'

'You are right. Above all not Mr. Cortney. It must at all costs be kept from him.'

The waltz ended and Lushington saw Da Costa hand back Mrs. Bellamy, with whom he had been dancing, to her husband. There was some clapping but the band did not play an encore. Instead there was a pause and some picked dancers began to form up for the mazurka. Da Costa stood talking to the Bellamys for a few seconds and then made his way round the wall to the place where Lushington was. He looked hot.

'Very exhausting this sort of thing,' he said.

'How long will it go on?'

'Until about breakfast time to-morrow. It gets more amusing later in the evening when the diplomats from the larger countries have gone away. Last year the Bulgarian consul-general did some awfully clever conjuring tricks in the Hall of the Grand Masters. Unfortunately he broke one of the clocks on the mantlepiece and there was rather a row because it turned out to be valuable.'

'Was he the man who said, "May I join this little circle of rose-buds?" when he sat on the sofa between Mrs. Bellamy, Madame Theviot and Baroness Puckler the other night?'

'That's the one. He hasn't been asked this year. It's rather a shame really. But he has no sense of proportion.'

The band had begun to play again and the dancers moved towards each other in the opening movements of the mazurka. This dance was the highwater mark of the evening. As soon as it had taken place people would begin to slip away to bed, unless they had decided to make a night of it. General Kuno was watching the mazurka beside the President and Waldemar, left to himself for a few moments, came up to them, leading a girl by the arm. He said: 'Let me present my fiancée or as you say in English, my sweetheart. This English gentleman is Mr. Da Costa and this English gentleman is Mr. Lushington, Hedwig.'

Hedwig was a sensible-looking girl dressed in brown velvet and like Waldemar she wore pince-nez. Lushington shook hands and was about to ask her for the first dance after the mazurka was over when, seeing Ortrud across the room, he slipped away and left this duty to Da Costa. He moved with difficulty round the crowded floor, getting caught up in evening dresses and tripping over spurs. Once he nearly upset one of the suits of armour. As he made his way round he watched her, still thinking how he would soon see her for the last time. Ortrud was talking to two men, one of them a Swedish officer who held tucked under his arm a cocked hat with yellow plumes and the other the German first secretary, an ex-flying ace, whose evening clothes were plastered with crosses in black and white enamel. These men stood by her in the clockwork, angular attitudes required of Teutonic gallantry. Lushington watched her. She was dressed in black, too dramatically, but suiting her style and figure. Once again as on the boat when he had seen her first he thought of Lucy. But Ortrud was taller, thinner and her features were less subtle. Now as he looked at her she seemed like a sleek cat. He saw her straighten the gold lace that had become disarranged on the Swede's epaulette. As she did this her face did not alter but he felt angry that she should touch another man in this way. He pushed on through the crowd. She saw him and nodded, still talking to the Swede. Lushington waited by the wall, glancing at the mazurka which was becoming now more complicated and breathless as its leader shouted aloud the sequence of its movements. Then he felt her touch his arm. He turned—she was standing beside him. She was in black with a white flower fastened to her dress.

'My husband is not here to-night. He said that he had a *migraine* and would not come.'

'When will you dance with me? After this?'

'Two after this.'

'Two? Why not at once. After all this is almost the last time I shall see you.'

'I know but I have two duty dances. You understand?'

'No.'

'Is it to be one of the nights when we quarrel?'

'I hope not.'

She smiled at him, making him think that perhaps he would give up his job on the paper and try to find a post on the spot, a waiter's or something of the sort where it would not be necessary to learn much of the language. Anything so long as he could stay with her. They moved towards the doors of the ballroom. The mazurka clattered and stamped behind them. Its leader had allowed the dancers to get more than a little out of control and he himself began to shout more shrilly than ever. He was an old man with white dundreary whiskers and he was so thin and shrunken that if any of the dancers had collided with him he might have cracked in half.

Ortrud and Lushington went up the stairs. On one of the landings they turned into an alcove and sat down under the picture of a Swedish king, some benefactor of the knights, in a wig and with Roman armour fitting into the contours of his highly developed figure and wearing round his neck the Order of the Cherubim. They sat there and watched people passing up and down the stairs. Da Costa appeared, half-running, behind the daughters of the Dutch minister. He was taking these girls towards the buffet and all three of them were laughing a good deal. As he went by he shouted:

'Let me warn you that someone has poured vodka into one of the jugs of claret cup.'

He went off in pursuit of his two yellow-haired débutantes, shaking with laughter. Ortrud said:

'So you are going to leave me and go back to England?'

'We talked of that before. Don't let's talk about it again. What else can I do?'

'Will you be sorry that you are not going to see me any more?'

'Don't be silly.'

'You will go back to your English miss.'

'She is not a miss and hasn't been for some time.'

In the ballroom the mazurka came to an end and there was a great deal of clapping. They heard the Master of the Ceremonies making a short speech. People began to come through the doors in a stream. The American minister passed the alcove and pausing for a moment to point his finger in the shape of a revolver at Ortrud said 'Bang!' and walked with great deliberation down the stairs. Baroness Puckler went by with Countess Arnhfeldt and, smiling at them, went up towards the Hall of the Grand Masters. Ortrud said:

'Will you ever come back?'

'Of course I shall.'

'My lover, you are going away. You are going to leave me. What shall I do? I have only been happy with you. And now you are going away.'

'Why don't you come with me?'

'You know that I cannot. And you know that you do not want me to. It is you who are to blame for going away. You are treating me shamefully. I shall be annoying to-night. I shall annoy you. There will be time to make it up before you go. I shall come down then to the ship and wish you good-bye very nicely.'

'All right.'

'The girl you are going back to? Are you in love with her?'

'You will annoy me if you start all that again.'

'You are in love with her then?'

'Must we have all this over again?'

'You mean that it does not matter? Because you are going away from me in any case? Do you mean that?'

'If you like.'

'I shall take another lover.'

'Oh?'

'That nice young Spaniard.'

'Yes?'

'Spaniards are better lovers than Englishmen. Did you know that?'

'I feel sure they are.'

'Am I annoying you?'

'Yes.'

The American minister came up the stairs again, slowly, and with one hand on the banisters. He pointed his finger at Ortrud and saying 'Pop!' disappeared into the ballroom. Waldemar passed them with his fiancée on his arm. In the distance Lushington could hear Da Costa's neighing laugh. In the ballroom the band began to play *Weine nicht, mein liebe, weine nicht* in a sudden burst of sound, a musical caucus race, the result of refreshments in which each player began where he wished and went as far as he judged suitable. Ortrud rested her hand on his knee.

'What are you thinking?' she said.

'Let's go and try some of this famous claret cup?'

'No. I have to dance with General Kuno.'

'At once?'

'Yes.'

'Blast General Kuno to hell. I hope he is blown up by some of those old school chums of his who are always trying to get him. Why should he want to dance with you at this moment? Get rid of him as soon as you can.'

More and yet more curious sounds echoed through the building from the direction of the band. Lushington went down with her as far as the ballroom where they found General Kuno twisting his moustache and grinning fiercely like the villain in a melodrama. Lushington watched them dance away together into the middle of the crowd and then turned again towards the refreshment room. He found Cortney and Da Costa standing by the table smoking. Cortney held out his cigarette case:

'Have a *Lucky*?' he said. 'Isn't this party great? It takes you back somehow. The pictures, the armour, the old panelling. Even the dresses and the uniforms. Why we might be at the court of Catherine the Great or the *Roi Soleil*. Don't you get me, Lushington? See how I mean?'

'This sandwich takes me back even further than the armour.'

Da Costa said: 'You've done nothing but grumble ever since you came out here. Besides that joke is in very poor taste and not really at all funny. All the sandwiches I have eaten seemed to me very good, though I don't know why they had put caraway seeds in one of them. But with you nothing is ever right. Either Pope is annoying you or it is too hot indoors, or too cold out of doors, or your skis have come off, or the food has upset you. I should think you will be thankful to get back to England. As a matter of fact I shan't be sorry to get back there myself soon. I'm getting rather tired of this sort of thing. After all life must have something more to offer than a series of waltzes with Mrs. Bellamy, Frau Kuno and Waldemar's fiancée. I couldn't have been sent into the world for that.'

'Oh I don't know. I should think probably you were.'

Cortney said: 'Well I think you are a pair of grouchers and I'm off to find Frau Mavrin and take a dance with her.'

Lushington said: 'You won't manage it because she's booked up for the rest of the evening.'

But Cortney did not hear this and he went away from the refreshments. Lushington and Da Costa followed behind him to the ballroom. The floor was clearer now. Waldemar and his fiancée were among the couples dancing. They saw Waldemar's lips moving as he passed, counting to himself:

'*One*-two-three, *two*-two-three, *three*-two-three, *four*-two-three.'

Da Costa said: 'I am serious this time. I have done as much of this sort of thing as I can stand. I am going to resign and arrange to go out on an archæological expedition. Anyway it would be a change.'

'I should.'

'There's an oppressive feeling in the air to-night. I am tired of all these people. I shall be glad to get home to bed.'

'So shall I,' said Lushington. But he knew that he was not speaking the truth.

The dance seemed to go on for ever with endless encores and the one that followed it was equally drawn out, while Ortrud danced with the Chancellor of the University, a fat old man, who held her at arms length while he walked round the room. Lushington danced with Baroness Puckler who was enjoying herself a good deal and was full of stories of what the British ambassador had said in 1903 when he had met one of the secretaries walking down Unter den Linden in brown boots. She said:

'But it is so sad that you are leaving us. I do not know what Ortrud will do. It is very necessary for a young married woman to have someone to take her about. More especially when her husband is a clever man who has important national work to perform. It is very necessary for his sake that she should be kept contented. Cannot you stay for that reason?'

'I wish that I could.'

'You must stay. We all wish it. Cannot it be arranged?'

The band boomed on aimlessly and it was late before he managed to see Ortrud again. They danced once round the room and then went upstairs to the alcove where they had sat before. That night she was in one of her moods. They sat there in silence watching the people passing up and down the stairs. The air was heavy with the scent of women's make-up and the animal smell of the men, sweating into their thick uniforms. Soon the ball would be finished and they would be going back to their homes again and another of the times when he was with her would be over, the few times that still remained to him. People had been leaving steadily since the mazurka and now the House of the Knights was becoming quite deserted. All around him was the used-up atmosphere of the end of a party. Then the band began to pack up. Da Costa came up the stairs. He saw Lushington and Ortrud and said:

'I'm off now. Can I take you back?'

Ortrud said: 'Yes, it would be nice.'

'I'll get my coat then and find a drosky,' Da Costa said. He went away down the stairs.

Lushington said: 'Why am I not to take you back to-night?'

'No. Not to-night. I am in bad mood to-night. We will meet again before you go.'

'You certainly are in bad mood to-night.'

'You must not mind. I just do not want you to come back with me to-night. I would rather go with him. He will talk all the time and I shall not have to answer. I am tired and I want to get away from here soon.'

'All right.'

'Wait a moment,' she said. Very quickly she took the flower from where it was pinned to her dress and put it into his hand. He took it, not knowing at first what she had given him.

'For me?'

'Yes,' she said. 'For you.'

Da Costa reappeared. He said:

'I have got a cab. Can I take you too? Or do you want more gaiety?'

'No, I go in the opposite direction. Anyway I would like to walk some of the way, I think.'

Da Costa said: 'The cloak room here is a disgrace. I handed in my ticket and the attendant gave me a plumed helmet and a sky-blue cloak. I have got my own hat and coat at last but my goloshes seem gone for good, so we may be delayed a few minutes in getting away because goloshes are things that you cannot buy more than once in a lifetime.'

Lushington said: 'I shall go now then. Good-night. Good-night.'
'Good-night,' they said.

He went down the stairs. Putting his hand in his trouser pocket he felt the flower that she had given him.

31

The hard blue night, dissolving now patchily in the sky behind banks of cloud, was clear under the street lamps and Lushington went through the snow, piled up on either side of the steps and archways of the High Town. There had been a light fall less than an hour before so that some of the steps were slippery and the snow balled on the soles of his shoes. Two or three soldiers staggered past, drunk early or returning from drinking late, and one of them shouted after him and half-heartedly threw some snow. In the distance he heard the noise of firing, carried through the empty streets across the town from the barracks, or perhaps from among the islands along the shore where a gunboat might be scuffling with smugglers. But he did not trouble to make up his mind which of these it was most likely to be because he was thinking of Ortrud and how it would feel to see her no more when he was back in England and what he would say to her when he saw her soon again to say good-bye.

A few lorries had already begun to appear in the streets and one or two of the shops were beginning to take down their shutters but the town was still very silent. The lorries churned up the slush and made a noise with their gears as they came up the steep streets. Somewhere nearby men were shouting in a confused way as if they were calling papers. A few cars and droskies passed and the street lamps caught the decorations and polished buttons of guests returning from the ball. The walk back seemed interminable or rather it took place in the course of one of those passages of time that seem indefinitely extended and during which the destination approaches no nearer although more and more ground is covered. At last Lushington reached the hotel. With a great effort he pushed open the outside door.

In the lounge the servants had begun to appear and some of them with handkerchiefs tied over their heads were sweeping the floor with handleless brooms and talking to each other in shrill voices that jarred against the thin atmosphere of morning. Flosshilde had not yet arrived at her desk in the hall. Nor had the lift boy appeared, and for some reason the gates of the lift were locked, so Lushington walked up the stairs slowly and across the landings lit only by nightlights. He reached his room, took off his overcoat, and began to undress, throwing all his clothes on the floor. He was tired but with all the uneasy wakefulness of what he had come from, so that when he fell asleep, which was immediately, it was into a hagridden trance like sitting up at night in a railway carriage when burning pains run suddenly through the body and cold alternates with stifling heat. His clothes lay in a heap beside the bed.

He embarked at once on to a scene of nightmare, as if he had walked into a room not before entered that evening. It was a complicated, noisy affair, all bright colours and people moving quickly about and talking a great deal. Once he felt that he was falling through space. Through the conversations and strident musical instruments of his dream he could still hear the gurglings and detonations made by the room's radiators, hydraulic disturbances which always took place at this time in the morning.

32

It seemed almost at once that the telephone bell rang, at first in his nightmare, and then, becoming more conscious of the dryness in his throat and actuality, he got out of bed and went into the sitting-room, falling over the great coat lying on the floor and banging into chairs. He did not turn on the light but, groping, blundered about the room until he found the receiver.

'Hullo?'

'It's Pope, sir. Pope.'

'What do you want? When is it? Why haven't I been called?'

'There's been an accident, sir. Mr. Da Costa.'

'An accident?'

'Yes, sir. An accident. It is very serious. Can you come round at once?'

'Come round? Now? Where? What accident?'

'Mr. Da Costa's flat, sir. It is serious. If you could come round at once, sir?'

'But I am in bed. What is the time? When did this happen? Is it to-day or to-morrow?'

At the other end of the line Pope gobbled in a kind of ecstasy of fright and refinement, at intervals making a sort of clucking noise as he poured strings of unconnected, ingratiating words into the transmitter. Lushington could hear that Pope had his mouth pressed against the instrument as he gasped into it, hectic with melodrama:

'I take it I can count on you to come round, sir. The matter is most urgent.'

His voice faded away before Lushington could say any more.

Lushington stood in the middle of the room and wondered what had happened to Da Costa. He felt his way to the wall and round to the electric light switch. The glare dazed him and he sat down in an armchair and rubbed his eyes for a few seconds. The whole room seemed to be throbbing as if the band from the House of the Knights was playing in the bedroom but with muted instruments. Then he looked at his watch. He had been in bed less than an hour. Still feeling stupid with sleep he began to put on his clothes, aimlessly dressing once more in the stiff shirt and white tie which he found on the floor. He noticed that the white waistcoat had stains of claret cup on it. Only when he was fully dressed again it occurred to him that these were not the clothes in which to begin the day, but he was too heavy eyed to take them off and dress in something else. He picked up the overcoat from the floor and put it on as he went down the stairs.

When he arrived in the lounge the hotel had been given its usual appearance. The signs of early morning had been withdrawn. Flosshilde was now at her desk. She expressed surprise at seeing him so early and was about to begin a conversation as he passed but, smiling discouragingly, he moved on into the street and beckoned a drosky. He got into it and gave Da Costa's address. It was not yet light. There were more people in the streets now and twice a detachment of soldiers tramped past with fixed bayonets and wearing steel helmets. The drosky crossed the railway square and drove by the immoderate, Germanic nymphs, straining on their plinths under the station's architrave.

There were two gendarmes at the entrance to the block of flats. These, stage policemen out of a knock-about farce, stopped him shaking their heads. They stood in front of the door, grunting and intransigent, making signs that he could not go in, their expressions that of highland cattle. Lushington showed them his passport, but he had to add to it a press card and the membership voucher of a defunct London night club before they would let him pass. He went up in the lift, working it himself, and rang the bell of the flat. There was a long wait and then Pope opened the door.

'Well?' said Lushington, 'what is wrong?'

Pope could hardly speak. He was only half dressed, and Lushington noticed that he was wearing Da Costa's dressing gown over his shirt and trousers. He had no collar and his hair was not brushed. He fluttered with his hands.

'Mr. Da Costa, sir,' he said, 'Mr. Da Costa has been shot.'

And then Lushington saw that two more gendarmes were standing in the hall behind Pope fingering their belts and the holsters of their revolvers, dimly aware that they too were of dramatic importance in the setting of something that had taken place not long before. Lushington said:

'What do you mean?'

'Come here, sir. This way.'

They went into the sitting-room where a lot of people were standing about and almost all of whom were talking. Waldemar, very white in the face, was there and a police captain. There was a faint smell of antiseptic like a nursing home. When Lushington came in everyone stood up and clicked their heels. Waldemar came forward and taking Lushington by the arm, introduced him to several people, some of whom were doctors. Lushington shook hands all round. Pope stood behind, shuffling with his feet and swallowing. The blinds of the room were drawn and the electric light was on. The bedroom door was open. Pope shuffled. Waldemar made a movement with his hands. Lushington saw that they intended him to go into the bedroom. He went towards the doorway and looked through it. The people in the sitting-room went on talking but less loudly. The blinds were drawn in the bedroom as in the sitting-room and the lights were on. Lushington stood on the threshold of the bedroom and looked into the room. Then he said:

'Is he dead?'

'He's dead, sir. Dead.'

Pope swallowed.

'But what happened?'

'He was shot, sir. Shot.'

Pope clasped the dressing gown round him. He was very upset. Lushington stared into the room. Waldemar moved forward. He said:

'This is a grave and tragic episode. The men who have done this thing have committed an act of murder. Under the new code abolishing the death penalty they render themselves liable to a sentence of fifteen years forced labour. When they are apprehended the law will most surely exert its full rigour.'

Lushington stood and looked through the doorway of the bedroom. Here then was that rather astonishing mystery about which so much had been said that when the fact itself was there no further comment was possible. For the moment no near at hand formula seemed at all adequate. This was something well-defined and at the same time not easy to believe in. It seemed absurd, overdone. Lacking in proportion, like other people's love affairs. Here were all the signs of a loss of control. A breakdown of the essential machinery. The sort of thing no one could be expected to be on the lookout for. He rested one of his hands on the side of the door. He did not turn to hear what Waldemar was saying. The smell of disinfectant, he noticed, came from the bedroom.

In the room behind him the hum of enquiring talk continued. Pope said:

'That was the only covering I could find that was extensive enough in size.'

'I see.'

'I was about to search for something else when you rang the bell, sir.'

'How did this happen?'

It took some time to find out the answer to this question. Waldemar told most of the story with interruptions from Pope who had not been present and from one of the doctors who understood but did not speak English. The other people in the room talked to each other in their own language or made noisy telephone calls. The atmosphere, the fumes of sweat and disinfectant, was midway between an operating theatre and a corner of the monkey house. The mauve and Venetian red cushions were all crumpled up at one end of the sofa. One of the shelves of the bookcase had collapsed and some heavy books had slid on to the floor where they had remained in a heap. There was no blood.

The story came out by degrees. Da Costa, they said, had left the House of the Knights in a drosky. Crossing the square in front of the University a car driving away from the ball had drawn level. In this car were General Kuno, Waldemar, and two detectives. As the car was passing the drosky two men had run out from a side street and had begun to fire revolvers at General Kuno. General Kuno and his civilian bodyguard had replied with their automatics and Waldemar had drawn his sword. The gendarme on duty at the corner of the square blew his whistle and also opened fire. The two gendarmes who patrolled the street at right angles to the square were near the operative end of it and were soon able to join in with the others. The horses drawing the drosky had run away. That was how it had happened. When they stopped the drosky they had found Da Costa dead. Waldemar said:

'Also a drunk man was seen brandishing a revolver but after his arrest it was found to be but a cardboard pistol that they distribute at Maxim's on the nights of gala. Nevertheless he has been detained for further interrogation by the police. It is said that he is a count.'

Lushington thought about it all and while he thought about it he remembered something that up till then he had forgotten. He said:

'Was anyone else killed?'

Waldemar said: 'Alas, the lady——'

'The lady? What lady?'

'Frau Mavrin——'

'What happened to Frau Mavrin?'

Waldemar stammered. He said:

'She too is dead. She lived for a few minutes. But she died as they were taking her away.'

'Do you mean she was shot?'

'Yes, she was shot.'

'By these men?'

'Indeed.'

One of the fat men in black coats who crowded the room could not get the number he wanted on the telephone and he kept on tapping the instrument so that the bell gave out a number of little tinkling rings. Another of these men had taken down a book from the bookcase and was looking at the pictures in it. Lushington fingered his white tie wondering dimly why he had come in evening dress to what seemed to be an inquest. The police captain had sent for the two gendarmes and was giving them instructions which he made them repeat after him, like children learning a lesson. The faces of everyone in the room were shiny and looked like badly made models in wax.

Pope said: 'Two peasant women on their way to the fruit market were wounded by the shots of these men who are believed to have been communists. The porter from the flats opposite came out to watch and was grazed by a bullet. That was from the guns of the general's plain clothes men.'

Waldemar said: 'It is of great credit to the police that they were the cause of no grave casualties. None of their shots caused anyone a serious injury. They are in pursuit of the murderers and have high hopes of apprehending them.'

'Have they?'

'It is indeed certain.'

The heaviness of the room was almost insupportable. There seemed to be no air in it at all. Several of the men had not taken off their overcoats which were damp from the fall of snow. The fat man at last had been put through to the number he wanted on the telephone and he was now giving a complicated message, spelling out most of the words. When he had finished he gave the message again but in a different language. Waldemar was very upset. He took off his pince-nez and wiped them. He said:

'What must you think of my poor country, you with your English sense of constructive and far-sighted political philosophy. But here it is not understood to compromise. General Kuno had enemies. In England never have I heard that the chief of police is shot at. No matter how much the discontent with existing laws. But here of compromise little is known among the parties of the Left.'

Reviewing momentarily the situation Lushington found that he was not thinking of Ortrud as dead. He was surprised to find that at present he did not think of her as that. And in the same way it hardly seemed that Da Costa too, was dead in spite of what he had seen and what he could see at any moment again if he went back to the doorway of the bedroom. He himself felt a little dazed and rather sick and he could only think that he had missed an eye-witness account of the thing for the paper and that now he had been given orders to come back to England things were beginning to happen out here. Besides everyone was talking so much that it seemed useless to attempt to take in what they were saying. He tried to pull himself together and to decide upon something efficacious to say or to do. The first flush of excitement was dying down among the others and Waldemar was returning to his normal state of mild embarrassment. Lushington said to him:

'I am so sorry. I haven't congratulated you on your own escape yet.'

'Thank you, thank you.'

'And General Kuno.'

'I will bear your congratulations to him. It shall be done at once.'

'And the legation? Do they know there yet?'

Pope said: 'Mr. Bellamy is on his way here. I communicated with him by telephone.'

One of the men in the room, perhaps the fat one who had been doing so much telephoning, came across to Lushington and began to talk to him in a language that Lushington did not understand. He talked for a long time and Lushington nodded at appropriate intervals. When the man had finished and had gone away to talk to someone else Lushington said:

'Is it light outside yet?'

He seemed to have been in the room so long that he wondered if it was late afternoon. Pope heard him and walked quickly across the room holding the dressing gown round him like a mannequin displaying a dress. With one hand he held the dressing gown round him and with the other he pulled the curtains aside from the window, but the door bell rang before he had time to put out the lamps and he went to open the door while the sunlight came in through the double panes, into the room which was already filled with a yellow glow. Outside although the sun had scarcely risen some rays of its light caught the gilt domes of the Russian cathedral and with their coruscations accentuated the chill that was in the morning air. There were splashes of light now all over the harbour. A lot of people were moving about among the docks and several of the smaller boats were puffing up clouds of black smoke. In the streets officers carrying black portfolios under their arm were walking along to the Ministry of Defence, and boy and girl students in peaked caps were starting off for the University. Lushington thought that although he was tired it would be no good going to bed again that day. He would soon have to get some fresh air, he thought. He took a handkerchief from his pocket to blow his nose and some petals of a flower dropped on to the carpet. He sat down on a chair and began to pick them up one by one.

33

Lushington was doing his packing. The sitting-room was filled with his clothes and objects of little value acquired during his visit, none of which would fit into the available boxes. Cortney, who was helping with advice, pushed away the larger suitcase from the armchair and sat down. He fingered his moustache thoughtfully. The Baltic sunlight streamed in through the windows. Cortney said:

'Well, you'll be glad to get back. Away from all this trouble and turmoil. Back to quiet old England where the trees will soon be getting green again. I know how you'll be feeling about it.'

'Do you?'

'You bet I do. We've all of us had to face a deal of trouble out here and you most of all. There were two persons, young, promising, handsome, socially exclusive, aristocrats in the best sense. And now they are gone. Did you ever know either of them say an unkind word, do a dishonest action, or behave in any way meanly, pettily or so that you might be ashamed of them? I think, Lushington, that you did not. It's the passing of such as these that makes me think "see here, Cortney, what will you have to say for yourself the day you come to hand in your checks? How will it feel when the Recording Angel calls your bluff for the last time?" How many of us will make the grade? It's a question that I am not man enough to answer, and I think, Lushington, that you'll say with me that you are not man enough to face up to that question either.'

Lushington who had been straining to shut the fastenings of the bag he had been packing gave it up, took some of the things out and began to pack another one. Litter of all kinds covered the floor. There was just room for him to kneel down while he packed. He said:

'Do you mind getting up for a moment? I think you are sitting on my stiff shirts. Or rather what the laundry have left of them.'

'Scherbatcheff, he's gone too. The poor old count. He's gone to rest with his ancestors. Well, perhaps he's better where he is. He's gone where count and commoner are all the same.'

'I shall miss him on the voyage back.'

'What is it, Lushington, that makes you travel by sea when you

143

could do the journey in half the time and three times the comfort by land?'

'I thought the sea journey might make a story for my paper.'

'I daresay you're right. I love the sea myself. We Anglo-Saxon races have it just naturally in our blood. I often think I should like to be buried at sea when I have to make my reckoning with the Old Man with the Scythe. That strange old guy who gets us all in the end.'

Pope, who was in the deepest black, appeared silently in the room. He watched Lushington kneeling before the suitcase. He looked more wistful than ever. He said:

'If you wish, sir, I can complete your packing.'

'No thanks. I prefer to do it myself.'

'I think you would be wiser to allow me to complete it, sir. I have great experience of packing. My late master, sir, poor Mr. Da Costa often used to compliment me on my packing. He used to say that he knew no one like me. He didn't really. I hope that now that I am going to Mr. Cortney he will find me equally satisfactory.'

Cortney said: 'Pope, I am a reserved man. I come of a reserved family. We don't let our tongues run away with us. We leave most of the talking to our women folk. But at least I'll say this. If I can rely on you to serve me with the respect, the rectitude, the integrity, and the devotion that you were accustomed to accord to Mr. Da Costa I think that neither of us will have any cause for regrets.'

Cortney rose and taking his hat and stick from the bedroom, where they had been put in case Lushington should pack them, went towards the door. Pope inclined his head. Cortney said:

'So long, Lushington. I shall next see you on the quayside.'

'So long.'

Pope said: 'I was in the next room, sir, and I could not help overhearing that Mr. Cortney was speaking about death. When I was in the War, sir, of course one had to be prepared for it at any moment. My duty often took me within a few miles of the front line and a stray shell might easily have got me. But then we soldiers knew that such things were all in the day's work. We got used to it. We even used to joke about such things. I often look back on those days almost with regret. But then I was popular in the army. I don't know how it was. The men seemed to look up to me somehow. There are one or two experiences I should specially like to tell you, sir, as you'll be leaving this country soon and I may not have another opportunity.'

34

The boat sailed late, after dinner, and it was dark and cold down by the docks. Lushington leaned over the side and talked to Waldemar and Cortney who had come to see him off. Pope was there too, carrying a walking stick with a heavy, coloured-glass nob and he wore an unusually wide-brimmed black hat. He had been running about quickly, giving orders to porters, and for a few minutes he confused everybody so much that all Lushington's heavier luggage was taken on to a cargo boat bound for Stettin. However it was recovered without much difficulty. Now Pope stood in the background leaning on his stick. When Lushington tipped him he had said, 'A *bientôt*, sir,' which made Lushington wonder whether he had given him enough. The quayside was deserted except for a few loafers and some soldiers and gendarmes, watching to prevent anyone from committing a nuisance or blowing up the docks. A strong wind was blowing inland from the sea. They talked to each other awkwardly as they had been dining together and topics for conversation had run out earlier in the evening. At last a party of nondescript characters, supers from a tableau of haulers on the Volga, removed the gangway laboriously. The steam hooter sounded and a minor official in a peaked cap wound a hunting horn.

'Cheerioh, Mr. Lushington!' Waldemar shouted and saluted.

Cortney took off his hat and raised his arm in the fascist salute. In the background Pope brandished his stick.

The boat began to move away from the side, and down the watercourse. Lushington took off his hat and waved it. Waldemar and Cortney remained at their respective salutes. It was so dark that they and Pope were soon out of sight and the boat, zigzagging, passed on through the wharfs. There were cranes and low warehouses on either side and lighted flares at intervals which showed up the red and yellow wood of the buildings. On one of the quays three drunk nightwatchmen were dancing hand in hand round a fire. The boat went on past a fort and from here the harbour widened into open sea. This was the last outpost of the unreal city and, prodigally dramatic, a soldier was standing on one of the bastions of the central tower leaning on his rifle, humped out by his helmet and pack into a gargoyle against the snowy castellations and pale stars. It was the final and rather masterly shot of the reel.

The night air was very cold. This ship was smaller than the one on which Lushington had come out. It was little more than a cargo boat but there were half a dozen cabins that opened on to the dining saloon. Lushington decided to go below and have another look at the poky smoking room. He wondered if his brain would ever work again or if he would be obsessed for ever by the thoughts that he was thinking then.

In the smoking room a fat man was sitting with his back to the door, sorting packages which he had taken from a gladstone bag. When Lushington came in the man turned round. It was Count Bobel.

'Hullo,' Lushington said.

Count Bobel did not get up nor remove the cigarette from his mouth. He continued to arrange his samples. He said:

'Mr. Lushington, *mon cher*, I was delighted to see your name on the list of passengers and I have persuaded the Captain who is a self-willed and somewhat disagreeable man to allow you to share my cabin. He made difficulties but at last he consented and your effects have been removed there. In that way we can converse and thereby the voyage will have less *ennui*.'

'Are we the only passengers?'

'We are the only two. How fortunate that we should be already acquainted.'

Lushington stood and watched Count Bobel arranging his brown paper parcels. The smoke from the amber cigarette swept upwards and into his left eye. He said:

'Are you going to England this time?'

'Yes, yes. I begin with the towns of the North. Sheffield, Halifax, Bradford. Later you must give me all the *addresses* that you know in these towns. But there will be time for you to do that when we come nearer to England. My friend, what tragedies we have been through in the past weeks! What escapes! Do you know that for three hours or more I was in the hands of the police? They questioned me, *ces sales types là*, and all because I happened to be passing by when the tragedy took place. It is scarcely believable. And indeed you can well imagine how shaken were my nerves by the firing alone, without any of the police interrogation that followed. But these small nations are always *comme ça*. They find a man of the world like myself and immediately suppose that he is a revolutionary. *C'est rigolo*. And poor Madame

Mavrin! Do you remember how she was our companion on the out-wards voyage?'

'Yes.'

'You must know that I always thought that Madame Mavrin was attracted to you. A little *béguin*? No? Perhaps not then. But such is a thing that we men must always be on the look out for, because how much easier it is if a woman is already half won. You especially should be on the look out, Mr. Lushington. You have a way with women. The Princess Varvara often spoke of you after our visit to your hotel. Ah, what a humorous occasion that was. How much I have laughed over it since. You are a lucky man. I myself must not grumble. I had my share of romance. *Une jeune fille très comme il faut.* But I forget. You know her. The little reception clerk at your big hotel. And she was called Flosshilde, which is so pretty a name, more especially for me for whom Wagner will always be the supreme *maestro*. You remember her, yes? At the desk of your hotel?'

'Yes.'

'Alas,' said Count Bobel. 'Alas, the poor girl finds herself in a very difficult position. Very difficult. But she is a clever girl and no doubt she will find a way out. For my part I put such difficulties from my mind. A good friend of mine, a Brazilian, once told me that the rich men in his country, when they smoke a cigar, take only the first two or three puffs. Then they throw the cigar away. Those puffs are the best and when they want more they can buy another cigar. Sometimes I think that it is good to be with girls as my friend was with his cigars. It is the sentimental who do most harm in this world of ours. You are no doubt familiar with the works of Nietzsche? You are? I thought so. And besides I did not forget that this girl of whom I speak was fiancée to that charming compatriot of yours whose name I cannot recall.'

35

When they looked through the portholes the next morning snow was drifting down on to the sea. It was rough all the time on the voyage home. Lushington lay on his face in his bunk with one arm hanging down at the side and his hand touching the floor of the cabin. When he thought at all he thought about Ortrud who had been shot and Da Costa who had been shot and Lucy who had not been shot and whom, if he did not die of sea-sickness, he was soon to see again. Count Bobel, who was at that moment smoking one of his amber cigarettes, said:

'I should like some day to go to Corsica. I have seen some of the women of Corsica. They are splendid women. I should like to go to a public house in Corsica.'

'There are no public houses in Corsica. It is like France in that respect. No public houses and no Virginian cigarettes.'

'A public house. *Une maison close*. You understand me, yes? It is in the women of that island that I am interested.'

The boat heaved very slowly, climbing with great deliberation up one side of a wave. When it came to the top of the wave it paused and for a few seconds it seemed that it would remain suspended permanently on the crest of the swell. Then it came down again suddenly, moving more quickly as it began to rise once more and to approach another apex. The beams creaked. Count Bobel nearly lost his balance and, steadying himself by clutching Lushington's ankle, said:

'If one had enough money, that is to say if one was successful enough at one's business, which is really the same thing, it would be pleasant to make a trip with the object of ascertaining the relative beauty of the women of Europe. For my part I like young girls. *Les jeunes filles en fleur*. To me they seem more fresh. There are others who think differently. I know men who will speak only of the mature woman as a possible mate. They wish for experience, sophistication, in a word the *femme du monde*. But to me there is but slight beauty in such a one. Little romance.'

Lushington, musing on those fields of asphodel through which he felt that he might soon be wandering, turned over on his back and swallowed. Very slowly the waters beneath raised his bunk at an angle so that he could watch through the porthole the greenness of the sea and the creamy foam driving along the crest of the waves. Drops of water coursed interminably down the thick glass of the porthole. The boat's engines sounded only faintly like the distant buzzing of bees. Here too there was a smell of cocoanut oil. Count Bobel said:

'There is one method and one alone of avoiding the sea-sickness. Always I employ it. You wind this material round the waist. There is a great deal of this material and always you wind it round the waist. It has the effect of keeping the internal organs of the body in a position of constancy. The more tight you can bear it, the more effective is this remedy. Can I draw your attention to this method of avoiding sea-sickness, Mr. Lushington? I would be glad indeed to wind it round for you myself. Sea-sickness is a most distressing malady. Once I can remember many years ago it happened that I was *en touriste* at Nice and I had invited a young lady to accompany me on a trip in a motor boat. She had one of those very full figures that have in these days gone out of fashion to some extent. Her very fair hair went well with her style of dress. She was a remarkable girl in her way and very attached to me. I remember for example how much she was looking forward to the trip. Then as soon as she got out to sea she began to complain that she was feeling unwell. It was no use my telling her that the whole thing was her imagination. She insisted that she felt faint. I recall how sorry I was that I had not warned her beforehand that all would have been satisfactory if she had taken the very simple precaution of wrapping round her just a few yards of the material that I have here. In that way all would have been well. The delicate machinery of the body would have been kept in place. There would have been none of the unpleasantness that followed. I was sorry because the girl was genuinely attached to me. I tell you this story about myself only because it occurs to me that you might profit by this simple contrivance.'

Count Bobel dropped the stub of his amber cigarette on the floor and stamped on it with his foot. He wore shoes made of imitation snake skin and with patent-leather toecaps. The wind passed quickly along the sides of the ship and made a whistling noise through the cracks of the porthole. The beam in the cabin next door creaked continuously. Lushington sat up in the bunk, supporting himself by holding on to the curtain at the side. Count Bobel retreated slightly. He said:

'In Russia we have an expression—*nitchevo*. It is difficult to render into another language. It is in reality untranslatable. It means *nothing* or more freely *what does it matter?* It is a very popular expression, characteristic in a way of our people. I tell you this because I think this is a moment when such a philosophy of life might be of value to you. Say to yourself—*nitchevo*.'

It was rough all that day and all the next one too. Owing to bad weather they were almost twelve hours longer on the sea than the scheduled time.

36

Lushington went along the stone passages into which the sun never penetrated. They had told him downstairs that there was a new literary editor. He waited, talking to Miss Arnold in the outer office, while the new literary editor finished some stuff. Then he went in. The new literary editor, who looked if possible more shifty than the last one, said:

'Who did you say you were? Yes, I remember your name. Didn't you go off somewhere? I can believe you it was cold. Wasn't there a row? Someone got shot or something? Booth was talking about it. Were you in on that? No, you missed it. Well these things will happen, but all the same an eyewitness account is the only thing that cuts any ice when it's a small affair like that. It brings it home to the public, you know. People feel that they can get their teeth into it. Of course in the old days there'd have been a terrible to-do about that young chap. *Civis romanus sum* and so on. But all that's done with now and a good thing too, I expect. I suppose you knew him well being English and about the same age in a small place. They shot a lady at the same time, didn't they? They did? Yes, I thought so. I saw something about it. Was she a friend of his?'

'Yes.'

'I expect you knew her too. That's the thing about a small place. You know everybody. What was she like? A nice girl?'

'Yes, she was.'

'Sad,' the literary editor said, making some marks in blue pencil on a typescript. 'Hanging's too good for fellows like that who massacre women and children. And by the way, Miss Arnold, you will find that I shall be shooting you or something of the sort if I catch you muddling up those files again. It took me half an hour yesterday to collate the material for the historical competition. It just isn't good enough. You must get that into your head. It's all a question of having a system and sticking to it. After all it's not much to ask.'

Lushington said: 'The envelope in that pigeon hole? It looks like my writing. May I——?'

'Anything you like, old man. It was all there when I took over. Found a treasure trove?'

'No, no. Just some stories of mine. I don't know how they can have got there. I've mislaid them for some time. I'll look through them and then perhaps you might be able to use them. Anyway I'd like you to see them. They might do for the feature page.'

37

Going eastwards there was a place beyond the Tower where they could sit and overlook the river. It had been Lucy's idea that they should go there. Lushington had once proposed to her on that verandah and after she had met Da Costa the three of them had been there together on several occasions. Perhaps as a sort of mourning for Da Costa she was wearing country clothes, tweeds and low heels. The place was reached with some difficulty because she had made up her mind that the way there should be an expedition, a pilgrimage, and they arrived later than they had intended. They walked through the bar and beyond it on the wooden platform. It was too cold to sit out in the open but that was what Lucy had decided that she wanted to do. The evening was drawing in and lights were appearing along the river and on the few boats that passed by them. The water below the verandah had the slimy, viscous quality of the Thames and it seemed a denser liquid as it sucked and swelled beneath the boards. The rows of warehouses opposite, simplified by dusk, took on coherent, almost intellectual, forms. In each direction these shapes ended among the mists that were drifting up from the marshes. Sometimes fog signals sounded. A Scandinavian ship, done up in cream and green paint, had been moored to the right of them. The fog signals went off three at a time. Lushington said:

'It is much too cold to have come here.'

Downstream, on one of the larger buildings, there were cranes jutting out with a cloud behind them that caught and held for a moment the ochre-coloured light, across which dark flights of gulls sometimes passed. A ridiculous boat like a coracle with a triangular red sail passed them and floated on with the current. There was no sign of life on the big cream-and-green Scandinavian but three men in a dinghy with set expressions on their faces were rowing against the tide towards her. Lushington pointed to them and said:

'Look. Treasure Island.'

Lucy said: 'This woman who was killed at the same time. Was there anything between them?'

'No.'

'Are you absolutely sure?'

'Absolutely.'

'Did you know her well?'

'Quite well.'

'Was she attractive?'

'Yes.'

'You're sure he wasn't in love with her?'

'Yes.'

'What was she like?'

'Oh, I don't know. Rather sweet. She was the wife of a professor. They had only been married a few years.'

'How wretched.'

For some reason the situation seemed suddenly to have become easier. He did not know why he felt that. Before now he had not made up his mind about Ortrud. He had known what he had thought when he was on the sea, but there such feelings might have had their origin in being on the sea. But now it all seemed very clear. Lucy said:

'Now there are only us.'

And at once, not leaving any time for him to answer, she said:

'From what you say it must all have looked rather like this?'

'Do you remember when we saw the ships through the trees as if they were growing in the field?'

'Was it like that?'

'Only less real.'

'How do you mean real?'

'I don't know exactly.'

'The people or the places?'

'Both.'

The damp came up in a strong gust from the bed of the river. More gulls dipped across the cloud. The men in the dinghy had reached the ship and one of them was making passes at a rope ladder with his boat-hook. Lushington shivered. He said:

'Have another?'

'Yes.'

There were a few more people now in the saloon bar. Among them was the man who asked people their names when they came to the office and who controlled the house telephone without much success. This man saw Lushington at once and said:

'Back to the army again, sergeant?'

'That's it.'

'Seen you before down here.'

'Have you?'

'It's a nice little place. We get all sorts down here. You wouldn't believe. Artists. One of them got fifty pounds for a picture he did. I remember him well. He was down here at the time of the lightermen's strike. Used to sit out there all day. An artist, you know. Did some pictures. He got fifty pounds for one of them. That was time of the lightermen's strike. All sorts we get.'

'What will you have?'

The man stroked his face in meditation and said:

'Thanks, mine's a bitter with a drop of old in it.'

Lushington handed the man with the birthmark his drink and took his own and Lucy's. When he went outside again she was standing up and leaning her hand against one of the posts that supported the wooden roof of the verandah. She was looking across to the other side of the river where the warehouses were now almost hidden by the sallow mist. She said:

'I suppose I am more or less yours now.'

'Yes.'

'If you still want me.'

The mist was thickening and carried with it the acrid scent of fog and brought a smarting to the eyes. The cold had become intense. One of the men from the dinghy had at last succeeded in getting on board by way of the rope ladder. The other two remained in the boat, gloomily watching him. Lucy said:

'Who were you talking to in the bar?'

'The porter from my office.'

'The paper?'

'Yes.'

'Does he always come here?'

'I don't know. He said he had seen me here before.'

'I expect he thinks I'm a tart.'

'I was just wondering.'

Agents
&
Patients

For VIOLET GEORGIANA

'*So in every possible case; He that is not free is not an* Agent, *but a* Patient.'

WESLEY: Sermon lxvii.

1

Chipchase, judging it prudent from an increasingly set expression on Maltravers's face, to bring the story of his emotional life to an end, said:

'I don't pretend that my love affairs are not sordid. They are. They always have been. I like sordid love affairs. What I object to is the assumption that just because one's love affairs are sordid it doesn't matter whether or not they go wrong.'

Maltravers said: 'Naturally, naturally. It's far worse. People who have unsordid love affairs have extraneous things to fall back on. Sordid love affairs have to be their own reward.'

After he had said that Maltravers leant forward in the direction of his coffee, stiffly, because his movements were circumscribed by the heavy overcoat he had not removed in spite of the comparative heat of the room. He said:

'The handicaps that I myself have had to contend with in life have been enormous. Simply enormous. But I have come through. I am at one with myself. For example, I don't want money any longer.'

They sat in a high narrow room crowded with chairs and small tables where men and a few women came to drink coffee in sober surroundings. A pleated red curtain, set a foot or two back from the plate glass and rising to half the height of the window, gave the exterior of this coffee-room the appearance of a tailor's shop. The uncurtained window at the back of the room looked out on to a whitewashed wall, so close that even on fine days the place was in twilight. When there was fog about, the inside, only brightened by the reflections of the gas fire on the metal of the massive funereal urns in which the chicory stewed, was like a cave; and the linoleum floor a vein of grey-pink rock, some volcanic substratum. The time was nearly half past three in the afternoon and Maltravers and Chipchase had the room to themselves.

When Maltravers talked like this Chipchase knew that he was hard up. Chipchase had suspected this during lunch and now he felt sure of it. Both of them were post-war types, already perhaps a little dated. This was more immediately apparent in the case of Chipchase, whose emaciated physique and severe expression gave some indication

of his historical background. He was an art-critic by profession and an
amateur of psychoanalysis. Maltravers, who was tall and in a genial way
distinguished-looking, had connections with the film industry and might
easily have been a better-class gangster figure of any period. The black-
and-brown check pattern of his overcoat, the thick striped scarf wound
round his neck, and the cloth cap he wore, recalled indistinctly an
owner-driver of the early days of motoring. They gave no hint of intellectual aptitudes.

Chipchase said: 'When do you go to Berlin?'

'Not for some months. It may even fall through. Meanwhile my
Hollywood intrigues continue.'

'I may be crossing the Atlantic in the autumn myself.'

'A lecture tour?'

'On sub-normal psychology. But that may fall through too.'

'What I need,' Maltravers said, 'is new and vital experience. As
when I sold religious books from door to door to atone for having lost
all my savings gambling with stocks and shares.'

'Why not sell them again?'

'It would lose its virtue by repetition.'

'Pay me to put you right psychologically. I share none of your feelings about not wanting money, and you obviously need treatment.'

'Too late.'

Chipchase nodded several times to himself. Since Maltravers had
left the government office in which he had begun his career he had had
several professions. The most substantial of these had been his film
work. He wrote dialogue and adapted scenarios. Like Chipchase he too
had dabbled in journalism, which had left both of them with its
attendant paranoiac leanings. Chipchase had published a short book
on psychoanalysis in relation to automatic writing but its sales had not
been large and it looked as if his life work was to be writing weekly
articles on the galleries for a respectable provincial paper. This had
been a bad year. Both he and Maltravers were feeling the effects of the
trade depression which had set in.

Maltravers drank off his coffee at a gulp.

'When I find a rich man to put up the money for my film,' he said,
'I will employ you.'

'Thank you. As an actor?'

'In a sense. Since you say that you need money.'

'What I really want,' Chipchase said, 'is a suitable patient to experi-

ment on for a new system of psychological and psychoanalytical treatment that I am developing. Why not pay me to begin on you?'

'It is in your capacity as psychoanalyst that I should need you if
I wanted you at all. I want my film to be a document of behaviour
founded to a considerable extent on the findings of psychoanalysis. I
take a small group of people. I show certain salient features of themselves. Dreams. Desires. I illustrate their behaviour.'

Chipchase coughed.

'I see,' he said.

'Now you must have noticed,' Maltravers said, 'that a great many
of the best films are pictures in which professional actors play minor
rôles or no rôle at all. Russian peasants acting Russian peasants. Chinese looking oriental. Children being childish. It's by now a recognised
system. My extension of it is to collect a cast of, let us say, intellectuals
without previous training and watch them behave intellectually. All I
need is a little backing.'

'There must be a great many rich men who would be only too glad
to lose a few thousands in that way.'

'You like the idea?'

'Very much. It would fit in well with my own ambitions. If I could
find my patient and you your backer we should work excellently in unison. We might even make some money.'

'That,' said Maltravers, 'would be a purely secondary consideration. But think of what tremendous use to the human race a film of
such a kind would be.'

'What about Schlumbermayer?'

'Schlumbermayer would not do. Besides he is not really rich
enough.'

'Come, come,' Chipchase said.

They paid, left the coffee-room, and began to walk up the street.
Maltravers took long swinging strides as if he were trying to shake himself free from his overcoat. Chipchase, in a black hat and carrying a
rolled umbrella, hurried along beside him, blown about like an autumn
leaf. On the whole the fog had lifted in this part of London but it hung
about in wisps here and there like weeks-old poison gas. The bitter
wind scraped agonisingly against their faces. The street ended in an
open space and in the south-east corner people had collected to watch
certain mysteries which were being enacted there. Maltravers and Chipchase joined the crowd and saw that a man in chains was lying on the

ground. Nothing about the day could be said to recommend his dress and his position. He was almost blue-coloured from the cold. Above him stood another man holding a sword.

'What a grand couple,' said Maltravers.

Chipchase stood on tiptoe to see over the shoulder of an elderly negro in spats and a brown bowler hat who was obscuring his view of the performance.

'This is magnificent,' Maltravers said.

The rectangle in which they stood, enclosed on one side by the back of a theatre and on another by red-brick tenement buildings with asphalt courtyards between them, had small shops which sold sweets and groceries and newspapers on the remaining two sides, fronted with posters along their upper stories. Passages and narrow streets inter-sected these last blocks of houses. A number of dissociated objects col-lected together in the middle of the square supplied a surrealist back-ground to the various performers who paused in this place to do their stuff. These objects also added notably to the claustrophobia already induced by the disproportionate height of the surrounding buildings. In the centre of the open space a pile of stones lay beside a wigwam in which a man sat all day long, awaiting the completion of some un-achievable labours on the cobbles. Behind him was a small palisade by which a few cars had been parked unevenly and beyond these rested ornate pieces of scenery depicting the sea, delayed in their removal through the back entrance of the theatre. The rectangle was divided in such a way that its four corners were made individual entities in each of which widely opposed activities could be pursued without disturbing one another.

At the moment the man with the sword and his colleague, gagged and handcuffed on the ground, had attracted the bulk of the crowd. In the northwest corner the Hindu with the tripod, attempting to sell an ointment of his own invention for the cure of cutaneous diseases, had only two young men, his *claque*, listening to him. Even these seemed to have heard his speech so often on past occasions that the words held no longer any magic for them. They stood watching his agita-ted gestures without attention, sagging forward in their mauve over-coats.

'Rousseau was right,' Chipchase said, 'as regards chains.'

Maltravers said: 'It certainly looks as if nothing in life would sever the one that is round him now.'

Blore-Smith, on his way home from the City, where he had lunched with his solicitor, was already one of the audience. He stood on the other side of the ring of people, opposite Maltravers and Chipchase, whom he did not know, although he noticed and admired Maltravers's overcoat. He was a slightly Jewish looking young man with huge ears and an impediment in his speech, who had come down from Oxford at the end of the previous summer term and whose big brown eyes and shapeless face still suggested an undergraduate. At present he was reading for the Bar, but he was not much interested in law and did it to have something definite to tell people when they questioned him about himself. He had few friends in London and when he was not at his crammer's nor in the courts, listening to cases which he hoped would teach him about life, he wandered along the streets, sometimes going into art galleries or cinemas. Entertainments like the one he was witnessing at the moment were a great help in getting him through the day.

The man with the sword, an ape-like primeval character, stripped to the waist and tattooed intermittently, came deliberately towards the fair man lying on the ground and prodded him. The sword was an unimpressive weapon for use with court dress and the ape-man inserted it carefully between the coils of chain with which the fair man's body was gallooned. The chains had made dark marks on the fair man's arms and back, noticeable when he writhed and dragged up the vest he wore, showing the flesh beneath. The man with the sword was an athletic type with black hair growing low on his forehead and a sore on his face. He continued to prod, muttering all the time to himself. Then he turned unexpectedly, startling almost to flight Blore-Smith, who was standing nearest to him, and shouted as loudly as possible and as if overcome with disgust and loathing for the spectators:

'Can't you see what the poor chap's suffering? Aren't there any sportsmen here? What's the good of one-and-a-tanner?'

Response to this appeal was not immediate. Blore-Smith, although he had already contributed sixpence, would have given something more if he had not been so embarrassingly close. The ape-man, exasperated, threw the sword on the ground and, grinding his teeth, walked slowly to the other side of the open space, where a dilapidated small car stood by the tenements. Putting his hand under the number-plate, he lifted this from behind and shook it so that the car rattled and showed signs of dissolution.

Maltravers left Chipchase on the outskirts of the crowd behind the negro and pushed his way to the front row, where he stood among a group of small children, some of whom watched the show while others fought among themselves.

The ape-man returned from shaking the car. He picked up the sword from the ground and leant over the other man. While he did this he rolled his eyes in a paroxysm of fury. He said:

'You tied me up in Piccadilly and left me there for three hours, did you? Well, now you're going to see what it's like.'

Turning again to the crowd, he said:

'Come on, isn't there a gent among the lot of you to give a poor fellow more than one and eight-pence? Why, I've been doing this turn for fifteen years and if it wasn't a fine decent entertainment would I be doing it to this day, I ask you, ladies and gentlemen?'

He showed his teeth. There were flecks of grey foam round his mouth. A girl watching from the first floor window of one of the sweet shops threw a penny that rolled up to his feet.

'Thank you, missy, thank you.'

The ash-blonde who had thrown the coin smiled and swallowed shyly to herself. A car passed, slowing up to avoid running over the man in fetters. The man with the sword made towards it savagely as if he were going to seize it by the footboard and overturn it by force. Changing his mind, however, he allowed it to pass. The man in fetters struggled to his knees. For a time he rocked from side to side. A board with spikes in it was strapped firmly to his back.

Maltravers, watching with interest, began to unbutton his overcoat. Feeling in his trouser pocket, he found five coppers and threw them to the man with the sword. He threw them singly and slowly—one—two—three—four—five.

'Thank you, sir, thank you.'

The ape-man now passed the sword through the elbows of the other so that the flat of the blade pressed against his back. The fair man began to groan and to struggle violently as if he were on the point of having a fit. His position and gestures recalled some high-renaissance picture of Jacob wrestling with the Angel in which the Angel is not pictorially represented, being suggested only by the contortions of Jacob. After a time the fair man freed his arms from the chains and threw aside the spiked board. Then he loosened the gag and spat it out on to the cobbles. He stood squirming with the handcuffs. The ape-man said sternly:

'At the close of this remarkable exhibition my friend will oblige with a display of eating coal and candles.'

He put down the sword among a heap of assorted instruments of torture, which with his coat and hat lay on a piece of newspaper, and picking up a comb he began to tidy his hair. Chipchase, who had a bad circulation, was getting chilly, and he entered the crowd in search of Maltravers. Stepping over one of the smaller children who had fallen to the ground, he said:

'Shall we go? I don't think this is so good a show as the organ and the transvest male dancers.'

'It has its points.'

'Well, I'm off.'

'All right, I'll come too. Do you want a lift?'

'Which way are you going?'

'Home.'

'No,' said Chipchase. 'You're no good to me in that case. I've got to cover a show at the Frott Gallery. I missed the private view.'

They went off together towards the side street where Maltravers had parked his car, a torpedo-shaped gamboge machine bought second-hand from the editor of a motor paper. Tuned-up, she was rumoured to do eighty-seven. Maltravers climbed up and stepped in to avoid opening the door.

'Give Reggie my love,' he said.

'And mine to Sarah.'

Maltravers waved his hand and drove away. Chipchase turned up his coat-collar and slunk off, keeping close to the walls of the houses to avoid the wind.

Blore-Smith, having nothing better to do, stayed to watch the candle-eating. He was an unexceptional young man whose head was too large for his body. The lower grades of the civil service or an assistant mastership at a public school would have provided a suitable rôle for him. Both his parents, midland business people, had died when he was a child, and on coming of age he had inherited an income of several thousands a year so that he was faced with the task of finding an occupation more in keeping than these with his station in life. His guardian had insisted on a short allowance at the university during his minority, with the result that Blore-Smith had made fewer friends than might otherwise have been the case. His own temperament had caused him to choose these few friends from the dullest circles available during his residence. Life at Oxford had been lonely and obscure but his solitude and a lack of distinction did not become apparent to him until he had lived for some months in London. At the same time he preferred London. It was bigger and there were more cinemas. Sometimes he went to see his sister, older than himself and married to a nose specialist, or he attended dinner-parties given by people who had known his family. These made a change but they did not constitute much of a framework for the adult life which he had supposed that he would lead when finished with his education. The young men whom he met on these occasions led compact, hearty little lives of their own and the girls were bouncing or half-baked. Blore-Smith had even hoped on coming down from Oxford that he would have opportunities for friendship with the opposite sex. But although in London this was not openly put a stop to by the authorities it seemed no less difficult to achieve. He kept up with some of his Oxford friends. Secretly he had begun to look upon them as a grim crowd, now that they appeared in the chiaroscuro of London, unrelieved by a background of dreaming spires, and lately he had seen less and less of them. A great deal of his time was spent in his room reading, or looking at the illustrated papers at the Royal Automobile Club, for which his brother-in-law had put him up. His comparative affluence seemed no help. In the first place he disliked the idea of spending a lot of money all at once, and in the second he could think of nothing that he wanted to spend it on which would not complicate life in a way which alarmed him. He took rooms in Ebury Street because he had heard of it as a place where bachelors lived, and although he managed to pay about double their market value his income was still far in advance of what he needed. He was interested in a rather pedantic way in contemporary art and letters and he had sometimes considered making a collection of modern pictures or even, in his wilder moments, founding a magazine. He could never bring himself to lay the foundations of the former hobby and the latter he knew to be a purely romantic conception, because he had no idea what the magazine would be about nor who would write in it. A larger establishment would involve dealing with servants; he was unable to distinguish one make of car from another and he knew only too well that he would never be able to drive one; wearing new clothes made him feel embarrassed; expensive restaurants were not places to go to alone; he had once got drunk at a Bump Supper and had scarcely tasted alcohol since; he never lent money to his friends because he had once been told that to lend money to a friend was a sure way to lose him and although he now, in fact, wanted to lose his present friends, a system of multiple loans seemed the least advantageous method of setting about it. All the more obvious ways of getting rid of increment were therefore closed to him and his money remained on deposit account at the bank. Blore-Smith knew that there was a good deal to be said for this but at the same time he was dissatisfied. Life showed every sign of being a disappointment.

It was because of this consistent lack of incident in his day that Blore-Smith was so absorbed by the candle-eating. On the whole this was a success and it was followed by the swallowing of fire and lighted cigarettes. After a while, like all things good and bad, the display came to an end. The crowd dispersed. Blore-Smith walked away, ruminating on what he had seen. It had given him food for thought. He too felt himself chained. Chained by circumstance. Again he toyed in his mind with the idea of collecting hour-glasses or first editions or something of the sort. He knew that a little decision was all that was necessary. But steps of that kind needed a command of initiative. He decided that at least he would drop in to an art gallery before it was time to go home and have another go at Cheshire's *Modern Real Property*.

Maltravers drove north in the direction of his flat. He went through Bloomsbury and soon he had passed the gothic spires of some railway stations and was driving along grey steep roads that led uphill. While he jarred his wheels over the tram-lines he thought about the interlude that he and Chipchase had seen performed in the space beside the tenements. He wondered whether he could get from it any ideas that might prolong his connection with the film trade. From practical matters he moved on to the scene's symbolic aspects. Like Blore-Smith, he had been impressed by these. They were several in number and he gave careful consideration to all of them.

In this part of London the light was always of a thin quality and passing through its streets gave the illusion of cinema. The wind swept by him down the hill and blew noisily through the exhibits outside the shop where they sold tombstones. Maltravers glanced in the direction of the memorials in this yard, as he did whenever he went by it, to remind himself of man's impermanence. On the right was the green embankment of the reservoir and later the statue of Sir Hugh Myddelton. He turned off down a lane that led to a wide treeless square and stopping in front of one of the houses at the far end he opened the door and went up the stairs to the top floor. In the sitting-room Sarah stood by the window, eating a slice of bread spread with Gentleman's Relish and holding a cup in her hand.

There were two or three tables in the room, littered with sheets of foolscap, books and tea-things. On one of these were three typewriters and on another a gramophone. A number of newspapers lay about, some of which had been crumpled up and left on the floor. A wide sofa stood in front of the fire, also covered with typescript and books, while the two armchairs were piled high with gramophone records. The two remaining chairs were chromium-plated and had no back legs, the seats being supported by the front legs alone which curved back and united below them. Press-cuttings, invitations, and snapshots were stuck in the sides of the gilt empire mirror which hung over the mantelpiece.

Stepping over two cats and paying no attention to Sarah, Maltravers walked across the room. Without taking off his cap he went to one of the typewriters and sat down at it with his feet stretched out in front of him. Then he sighed and began to type. Sarah finished her bread and Gentleman's Relish. She put down her cup on the gramophone and said:

'Do you want some tea?'

'No.'

'What sort of a day have you had?'

Maltravers did not answer. He gritted his teeth and went on typing. Sarah poured out for herself another cup of tea. She said:

'Did you lunch with Oliver?'

'Yes,' said Maltravers, making no secret of the effort it was for him at that moment to answer questions.

'How was he?'

'I had to listen to a lot of stuff about his girl.'

'Poor dear.'

'Him or her or me?'

'All of you.'

Maltravers grunted. Then he sniffed several times and began to type away again. While he did this he listened to Sarah gulping her tea. Nearly a minute passed before she said:

'I'm going out to-night.'

Maltravers jumped up from the chromium-plated chair, tore the sheet of paper out of the typewriter, crushed it in his hand, and threw it into the waste-paper basket. He said:

'Why can't I ever have two minutes' peace? Must I be bothered every moment of the day and night by you and your incessant chattering?'

'I only said that I was going out.'

'Well, what of it? I don't care. What business is it of mine? I don't mind whom you go out with. You always talk as if you were going to run away with someone.'

'I probably am.'

'Well, what do you expect me to do about it?'

'I thought you might like to have some warning.'

Maltravers took off his cap and threw it on to the table. It fell with its peak in the butter. He said:

'This afternoon I watched a man with a sword who was prodding another man who was gagged and chained and lying on the ground. That's what I feel like in our married life. I lie on the ground gagged and chained and you prod me with a sword.'

'Where on earth did you see all these extraordinary things happening?'

'Who are you going out with to-night?'

'I don't expect it would interest you.'

'It doesn't interest me. I'm ordering you to tell me.'

'I don't see why I should.'

'I'm your husband.'

'You seldom treat me like a wife.'

'Who is it?'

'I shan't tell you.'

'Who is it? Come on now.'

'It's Nipper, if you really want to know.'

Maltravers sat down heavily on the chair, which vibrated beneath him.

'Heavens above,' he said. 'Heavens above.'

Sarah began to clear up the tea-things.

'Shall I leave the tea?' she said, 'or shall I put the kettle on and make you some more?'

Maltravers said: 'It's not that I mind. I don't care who you make friends with. Zulus, condemned criminals, Scotch nationalists, they'd all be the same to me. It's only that I can't conceal my surprise that you should be able, far less choose, to spend a single moment more than necessary with a creature like Nipper.'

He stared hard at Sarah, who stood beside the wireless set, holding a tea-pot and watching him, but showing no interest in what he was saying. She said:

'You've only met Nipper once and then he was in fancy dress, wearing a mask.'

'That was enough for me. God forbid that I should ever spend any time in his company when he's not wearing one.'

'Anyway it's me that's going out with him to-night, not you.'

'You can't go.'

'What do you mean?'

'I forbid you to go.'

'You—forbid—me—to—go?'

Sarah began to roar with laughter. She repeated the phrase several times. Maltravers turned away from her and occupied himself with his typewriter, inserting another sheet of foolscap. Sarah put down the kettle for a second and lit a cigarette with a spill. Then she went out of the sitting-room and the noises of washing-up came from the kitchen. Maltravers concentrated on the scenario he was mapping out. The two cats who until now had been asleep rose simultaneously and pompously made for the door. Maltravers let them out and sat for some time, brooding in front of the typewriter, sometimes tapping out a few sentences.

At last he shouted:

'Sarah.'

There was no answer. He shouted again. Nothing happened. He got up and went out into the passage. The noise of running water came from the bathroom. Maltravers went as far as the bathroom door and tried to get in. The door was locked and he hammered on it. From inside the bathroom Sarah said:

'Hullo? What do you want?'

'Is there anything to eat in the house?'

'I can't hear.'

'Is there anything to eat in the house?'

'What?'

'Turn the water off.'

'Now what is it?'

'Is there anything to eat in the house?'

'Yes, lots.'

'What time does Mrs. Doon come back in the evening?'

'You told her we shouldn't want her to-night.'

'Hell.'

'There's lots of cold food. You can easily manage by yourself.'

Maltravers did not answer at once. He was too angry. Sarah turned the water on again and began to sing and splash about. Maltravers, putting his mouth to the crack in the door, said:

'You're a magnificent wife for a man to have, I must say.'

'What?'

'Turn the water off.'

Sarah again stopped the tap running. Maltravers said:

'I only wanted to tell you that I think you are a magnificent wife for a man to have.'

'Well, you were out every day last week.'

'What if I was?'

'Well, it's my turn to go out to-night.'

'When I go out and leave you alone it's because I'm trying to persuade influential people to give me a job. It's not because I want to go to the cinema with a little rat of a man who wears his jumper tucked inside his trousers.'

'Why shouldn't he? It doesn't look half so funny as some of the clothes that you wear. Besides, you told me yourself that on Tuesday you gave that beastly Swedish girl dinner and on Wednesday you had dinner with Mendie. I don't suppose you expected to get a job from either of them.'

'Shut up.'

'Go away then and don't disturb me in my bath.'

'All right,' said Maltravers, 'I will go away. And it will be some time before you see me again.'

'I don't care.'

Maltravers went back to the sitting-room and put on his overcoat. While he was rubbing the butter off the peak of his cap he heard Sarah calling from the bathroom. He took no notice. After slamming the door

of the flat as loudly as possible he went downstairs again and got into
the car.

Chipchase continued to walk in the direction of Bond Street. He
stopped to look at many shopwindows as he passed, absorbed by
money-making phantasies. He varied these with thoughts of Caroline
with whom he had broken off relations finally the night before, tor-
menting himself with images of his potential successor. Caroline being
given a good time by stockbrokers or minor poets; by cads with high
powered motor-cars or rather tousled painters; sitting in the rooms of
undergraduates who did not really care for women at all; having dinner
with very very old clubmen with complicated desires, refined American
who played polo, or tanned and stuttering colonial officials home on
leave; with intelligent men, with appalling men, or with saintly men
who just went about doing good; guardees and naval officers and sec
retaries from the Latin-American legations; with Parsee students, White
Russians, Jewish actors or nestling in the arms of some strapping Sene
galese. Filled with gloom he reached the doors of the Frott Gallery.

Inside by the entrance was a notice *Catalogues* 1s. and a plate for
the money. Chipchase took a catalogue without paying for it and went
towards the inner room. Reggie Frott, the owner of the gallery, was
standing in the corner talking to a tall man with a curly moustache be
ginning to go grey, who wore a single eyeglass and leant against the wall
with one hand on his hip and the air of an Elder Statesman. Reggie
when he saw Chipchase, came closer to his client and, lowering his
head, grimaced diabolically through the space enclosed by the older
man's ribs and the flying buttress of his elbow. Chipchase raised his
eyebrows and smiled and then moved about the room looking at the
pictures, an *avant-garde* selection in which canvas and paint were helped
out by the adhesion of small pieces of looking-glass, sea-shells, match
boxes, and newspaper. Touching one of the seascapes with his hand
Chipchase loosened a bead but found himself able to stick it on again
without attracting Reggie's attention. He killed some minutes in this
way, making pencil notes in the margin of his catalogue, until the man
with the eyeglass had succeeded in edging his way to the door of the
gallery and subsequently out into the street without being persuaded
to buy the more-than-life-size statue of Pomona, executed in green ba
salt by a German sculptor, which Reggie was bent on selling him.

Chipchase sat down on the low sofa and waited. Reggie shut the

door and ambled across the room again. Reggie that afternoon was
looking more than ever himself, an intemperate little boy of twelve
years old or, alternatively, an octogenarian jockey left over from the
Phil May period, threatening reminiscences of Romano's and the old
Pink 'Un gang, ageless but at the same time heavily dated. For a time
he stood in front of Chipchase, rolling from side to side and belching.
At last he said:

'Well, you old swine, how are you?'

'Just ticking over.'

'Do you know what time I got to bed this morning?'

'When?'

'Eight o'clock. And it wasn't my own bed then.'

Reggie put his hands in his pockets, swivelled round on his heel,
and began to chant in a tuneless sing-song:

> 'Beds—beds—beds—beds—
> And it wasn't my own bed then.'

Then he took a small bottle from his pocket and smelt the grey
liquid inside.

'Time to take my medicine,' he said. 'Have some?'

'No.'

'Do. It's awfully good for you. Gets rid of all the poison inside.'

'I prefer to keep mine.'

'Just as you like, you old devil.'

Reggie opened a cupboard concealed in the wall and took a tumbler from the shelf inside, where it stood with several other glasses, an
empty gin bottle, some aspirin tablets, and a broken piece of negro
carving. Putting it on a flattish piece of sculpture resembling a miniature model of the Blarney Stone, he poured out some of the medicine.
He said:

'I had a damn good dinner on Schlumbermayer last night. And
the best three-shilling cigar in the whole of London.'

He drank off the medicine, gently belched again, and put the glass
back into the cupboard. He said:

'And we rounded it off with half a bottle of Napoleon brandy.'

'Did you manage to sell your host anything at the end of it?'

Reggie slipped his arm round the waist of the statue of Pomona.
He said:

'He's coming in to-morrow and should buy something really wortl while. And, by the way, why weren't you here to write up the privat view?'

'I've come to do that now. Is anything selling?'

'Not a thing. Mind you say something polite.'

'They won't print it if I'm too kind. I can't risk losing my jok Money's much too scarce. Who was that you were trying to land Pc mona on?'

'Why, Algy Teape, of course. You must know the gallant Colone Teape?'

'So that's Colonel Teape, is it?'

'One of the best-known faces along the old *Côte d'Azur*!'

'*Ah, oui, oui. Je comprends.*'

'That's just as well for you,' Reggie said. He put his other arm round Pomona's waist and, looking up into her face, said:

'She's an ugly old girl, isn't she?'

'Not my type.'

'The colonel didn't think she was his either.'

'He's a friend of Pauline de Borodino's, isn't he?'

'Yes. In fact he said that he thought Pomona was more in her lin than his.'

'Did he, did he?'

It was at this moment that Blore-Smith came into the gallery. A though he had stayed to watch the candle-eating he walked quicke than Chipchase and he had not delayed his progress by looking into s many shop-windows. He took a catalogue, put a shilling in the plat and began to inspect the show, beginning at the exhibit marked *No. 1* Reggie, not seeing him arrive, or seeing and not caring, moved his arm lower down the body of the statue, at the same time retreating his fee so that in a few seconds he had lowered himself to the level of the carpe where he lay with his head resting sideways on Pomona's pedestal. H groaned several times and said:

'What I need is a good lie down.'

'That's exactly what you seem to be having.'

Blore-Smith, out of the corner of his eye, watched the scene ner ously, and delayed for several minutes among the smaller pictures t allow Reggie to resume a more conventional posture.

While he was doing this Blore-Smith came to a great decision. H too would break away from the chains that bound him. On that afte noon he would lay the foundation-stone of a more serious life. He would begin to make a collection of modern pictures. Suddenly he saw quite plainly that what he wanted was a hobby. He watched Reggie rise from his knees and light a cigarette.

'What have you the impertinence to ask for this object?' Chipchase said, tapping Pomona on the behind.

Reggie reached for a book that lay on his desk and began to turn over the pages. He said:

'I have to be careful about answering that sort of question. I sometimes get our code muddled up and the other day I sold a picture for eighteen guineas that ought to have been a hundred and eighty. So you see I have to be absolutely sure even with an old friend like you.'

Blore-Smith had by now come up quite close and with his back to them stood listening to their conversation. Reggie ran his finger down the page. At last he said:

'To you—and to you only, mark you—we could do this for—let me see—shall we say three hundred guineas?'

'Yes,' said Chipchase, 'let's say that.'

'It's really awfully cheap,' Reggie said. 'It would fetch almost that in Paris.'

'Somebody may buy it.'

'You never can tell,' Reggie said. 'Why, I sold a thing nearly twice that size once for the same amount. It's in a museum now so thank goodness it won't pass through my hands again.'

In the background Blore-Smith was trying to collect all his courage. His mouth had gone dry. His legs shook under him. Clutching his umbrella, he stepped forward awkwardly in the direction of Reggie and said:

'How much is that picture? That one there.'

Reggie shut the price-book with a snap and eyed Blore-Smith disapprovingly. Then he looked him up and down slowly as if he were valuing an unsaleable piece of sculpture.

'What picture?' he said, after he had given Blore-Smith time to flush painfully.

'That one.'

Blore-Smith pointed with his umbrella and accidentally touched one of Pomona's arms.

'Mind,' said Reggie. 'Mind. Don't break the whole place up.'

He went over and had a look at the picture which Blore-Smith

had indicated and returned to his book, turning over the pages very deliberately. Blore-Smith leant with all his weight on his umbrella, trying
to give himself confidence. Reggie put his head on one side and stuck
out his lower lip, a favourite mannerism.

'That's two hundred guineas,' he said.

He shut the book noisily again and glared at Blore-Smith.

'I should like to buy it,' Blore-Smith said. The room went black
all round him.

For the moment Reggie was taken off his guard. For a brief second
the veil was torn aside and all his knowingness became wide-eyed uncertainty, like a frightened child's. Blore-Smith, now that he had said
the words, felt much better. They had acted as a spiritual purge. He
stood looking at Reggie quite sternly. Chipchase folded up the catalogue on which he had been making notes and put it into his pocket.
He wondered whether Blore-Smith was in full possession of his facul-
ties. It was almost inconceivable that a total stranger both to Reggie
and to himself should be prepared to pay two hundred guineas for a
picture of that sort. Almost at once Reggie recovered himself and said:

'The frame would of course be a little extra. It's a special one as
you see.'

'Naturally.'

'That would only be a matter of a pound or two.'

'Quite.'

'And now,' said Reggie, almost his old self, 'you must give me your
name and address, for although I know your face very well and I'm sure
we must have met, I can't remember any details. I expect I may have
been a bit boiled at the time. Have you got a cheque-book with you?
No? Then we have some blank forms here.'

Reggie pulled back the chair at the desk for Blore-Smith to sit on
and at the same time handed him a fountain-pen.

'Who shall I make it out to?'

'Well,' said Reggie, 'I should think you might make it payable to
R. Orlebar Frott, Esquire'; and turning to Chipchase he added:

'It won't do my private account any harm to have a little money
circulating through it again.'

'And how much is the sum exactly?'

'As we haven't had any previous dealings it's customary to pay a
third in advance, which would be—let me see——'

'Oh, I'd rather pay the whole lot now.'

Before replying Reggie turned in Chipchase's direction and puffed out his cheeks.

'In that case,' he said, 'that will be two hundred and seventeen pounds, thirteen shillings and ninepence. That will include carriage to within a mile from here.'

'And when shall I get it?'

'The show closes at the end of the month.'

'Will you send it to the Ebury Street address?'

'We'll send it right along.'

Later, Blore-Smith never knew how he got out of the gallery. He felt faint and his legs seemed about to give way. There was a loud humming in his ears. As he closed the door behind him he could hear Reggie giving peal after peal of laughter. He wondered what he had done that seemed so funny and tried to feel convinced that after all it could not be himself that Reggie was laughing at. He made an effort to pull himself together and concentrated on trying to remember which direction he should take in order to return to his rooms. He was dazed but at the same time rather happy.

'Who was it?' Chipchase said, when Reggie had stopped laughing.

Reggie looked at the address. He said:

'That was Mr. Blore-Smith, that was.'

'He seems anxious to get rid of his money as soon as possible.'

Reggie rubbed his hands together. He said:

'We've got to see if his money is any good first and when we've done that we'll sit back and show him some more pretty pictures.'

'I want to meet a man myself with some money he wants to get rid of.'

'I'll introduce you one of these days.'

'I wish you would.'

'What do you want to do with him, anyway?'

'A little scheme he might be interested in.'

'Something dirty?'

'No,' said Chipchase. 'Something eminently clean. As clean as driven snow. Cleaner if possible.'

Reggie, who had collapsed by now on the sofa, put his feet up and was about to go to sleep when again he was disturbed by the sound of someone coming into the gallery. This time it was a woman. She was tall and fair-haired and wore an overcoat of military cut. As she came in she unbuttoned this and put her hands on her hips, showing a tweed skirt and jumper under her coat. Stepping out like a man, she strode across the floor towards them. Her carriage suggested that she was unable to decide whether she wanted to be taken for a discontented tragedy queen on a holiday or a careless tomboy caught up through no fault of her own in serious bohemian life. Whichever it was she was unmistakably a beauty. Reggie jumped up from the sofa.

'Mrs. Mendoza!' he said. 'How are you?'

Chipchase stood up too and the woman laughed and kissed both of them. She took off her hat and threw it onto the desk, patting her hair.

'How's Mrs. M.?' Chipchase said.

'Pretty bad.'

'What is it this time?'

'Everything. Money chiefly.'

Reggie said: 'I've had a man in here who gave me a cheque for two hundred guineas for one of the worst pictures I have ever hung in my gallery—and between you and me that's saying a good deal. What do you think of that for a business coup, Mendie?'

'Obviously it will turn out to be a dud.'

'He wasn't the sort of young man who gives stumer cheques.'

'What sort a young man was he?' said Mrs. Mendoza, showing some interest for the first time since she had been in the gallery.

'Well,' said Reggie, turning to Chipchase, 'what sort of a young man was he?'

Chipchase said: 'He looked as if he would do for Mendie very well. He must be over fifteen and he's evidently got some money. He'd be all right if he had his hair cut and changed his tailor and was taught a little about art.'

'You always want everybody's individuality taken away from them,' Mrs. Mendoza said.

'Fortunately this young man hadn't got any.'

'I don't believe you.'

'I see you have fallen for him already.'

'I think he sounds sweet.'

'He is. You'll adore him. Reggie will have to arrange a meeting.'

'What have I got to do?' said Reggie, who was again attempting to go to sleep on the sofa. He groped about with one arm in the air in the direction of Mrs. Mendoza.

'Go to sleep, my pet, that's all you have to do,' she said, patting him on the head.

'How's the flower business, Mendie?' Chipchase said.

'So-so.'

'Don't talk so much,' Reggie said. 'I can't sleep with so much noise going on.'

Mrs. Mendoza pulled his hair. Reggie writhed.

'Don't be so ungrateful,' she said. 'I happened to be passing and out of sheer kindness I came in to relieve your boredom and all you do is to go to sleep.'

'It was very sweet of you, Mendie darling. Let's all have dinner together?'

'I can't,' said Chipchase. 'I've got a date.'

'Neither can I,' said Mrs. Mendoza. 'I'm dining with the Commodore.'

'Cut him.'

'He'd be furious.'

'He'd get over it.'

'No, he wouldn't.'

'Of course he would.'

'It would spoil his week.'

'He'd forget about it.'

Mrs. Mendoza said: 'An elephant *never* forgets.'

'I must go now,' Chipchase said. 'There are several things I want to do before dinner.'

He got up and walked once round the room to have a last look at the pictures. He was about to leave the gallery when Mrs. Mendoza said:

'Wait a moment. I'll walk with you some of the way.'

'Don't leave me all alone,' Reggie said. 'I can't bear it.'

'You've brought it on yourself,' Chipchase said.

They put an overcoat on top of Reggie and some rugs imported from Paris and left him lying on the sofa. By the time they had reached the door he had begun to snore. After the warmth of the gallery the street seemed cold and dispiriting.

'When is your date?' Mrs. Mendoza said. 'Why not come back to *la cattleya* for a bit?'

'All right.'

After some discussion as to whether they could between them afford a taxi, it was decided that they should walk, and they went along Piccadilly, striking south at Hyde Park Corner and passing through Belgrave Square.

Having no immediate objective ahead of him, Maltravers sat for several minutes in the car in front of his house, reviewing the drawbacks of married life. He had wanted to get some work done that afternoon but since Sarah had made work impossible there seemed nothing for it but to call on one or another of his friends. That was if he had any friends. He began to go through the list. There was Griffin Griffiths, but he did not feel altogether in the vein for Griffin Griffiths who, besides, lived a long way away. Gubbins, three-parts crazy, was always ready for a talk. When Maltravers had last dined with him Gubbins had spent the greater part of dinner trying to balance a loaf of bread on his head. That would be worse than Griffin Griffiths. Maltravers was in no mood for the repetition of such behaviour to-night. He dismissed all thought of Gubbins from his mind. Chipchase would be somewhere between his flat and the Frott Gallery or prosecuting some depressing love affair away in the suburbs. There was McConochie; Twysleton-Carbery; Schlumbermayer; or Ingrid? And then suddenly Maltravers had a good idea. He would go and see Mrs. Mendoza in her flower-shop. He started up the engine.

Mrs. Mendoza's flower-shop, *la cattleya*, as she had portentously named it, was in the neighbourhood of Sloane Square and about this time of day she was usually at home. Even if she should be out there would be someone left in charge to whom it would be possible to talk. Either Commander Venables, a retired naval admirer of hers, or Scrubb, the medical student who lived in a small flat at the top of the house and who, when he was behindhand with his rent, was made to sit for hours together in the shop surrounded by medical books, grudgingly selling flowers to customers who might drop in while Mrs. Mendoza was out with her friends.

Maltravers drove off. He wanted to talk to someone, anyone, as soon as possible. He drove the gamboge car in and out of the traffic, skidding along once more over the tram-lines on the way down the hill. The evening light made visibility bad.

It was later, when he had reached the S.W. district, that the accident occurred and then, as it happened, the light had almost nothing to do with it. The fault lay entirely with Blore-Smith, who had walked in a dazed condition all the way from the Frott Gallery, facing death more than once while he did so from lorries and errand-boys on bicycles. Maltravers's speed was excessive but he knew that his brakes were reliable, so that Blore-Smith's sudden decision to step off the pavement almost under the wheels of the gamboge car found him quite prepared, although Blore-Smith had been standing on the edge of the kerb for several seconds, watching the street and showing only very faint signs of wanting to cross to the far side.

The collision was sufficiently violent to knock Blore-Smith off his feet, but he fell very slowly, landing on his hands and knees, and although covered with mud he was able to get up by his own efforts. Maltravers got out of the car at once and ran round to the front.

'Really that was too bad. I am so very sorry. Let me brush some of that off. It was a most unfortunate thing to have happened.'

Inwardly Maltravers composed a line of attack in case Blore-Smith should turn nasty.

Blore-Smith, still winded, said something about it all being his own fault and not mattering in the least. He picked up his umbrella and tried to get away, but Maltravers, seeing the spirit in which Blore-Smith proposed to accept the accident, took him by the arm.

'You can't possibly go away like this,' he said. 'Why, I've hardly had time to apologise to you at all. You must come and have a drink with me so that I can make some amends for having done this. Are you in a hurry? Are you on your way to an important engagement?'

Blore-Smith was surprised by all this. He was still rather shaken by his picture-buying as well as his fall. He said:

'I was on my way home.'

'What were you going to do there?'

'What was I going to do?'

'Yes. Had you anything to look forward to?'

'I hardly know. I think I was going to read a little before dinner.'

Still holding his arm, Maltravers led Blore-Smith into the car.

'In that case,' he said, 'you must certainly come and have a drink. It will do your nerves good after the shock they have had. There is a place I know of just round the corner.'

Slipping into reverse, Maltravers shot back the car quickly, throwing Blore-Smith down into the seat, which was low and sloped at so sharp an angle that already he felt almost horizontal to the road. Then they drove rapidly up a side turning and stopped.

'Here we are,' Maltravers said.

It was the first time since he had been in London that Blore-Smith had entered a public house. He had always imagined that such places were filled with drunken navvies and old women wearing men's caps and smoking clay pipes. It was something of a surprise for him to find himself in a room that reminded him of a seaside teashop.

'What will you drink?' Maltravers said.

'Oh, anything.'

'But you must have some preference.'

'Oh, beer, I should think,' said Blore-Smith desperately.

He had begun to wonder whether he would ever escape from this man. He still felt a little stunned.

'A pint of bitter and a double White Horse,' Maltravers said. 'Let's sit down by the fire. It's more comfortable.'

Not many people had spoken kindly to Blore-Smith in the course of his life. Incompetence at games had soured his schooldays, causing him to be disliked equally by masters and boys at the small public school to which he had been sent. Although he had come into his money in time for his last term at Oxford and there were those who, if properly approached, might have been prepared at an earlier period to help him enjoy it, his personal appearance and his shyness caused both them and himself to feel that any such opportunity that there might have been had come too late. He had worked hard and had tried to please the dons but even his tutor could not conceal his conviction that he had a right to expect of his pupils a higher standard of looks than Blore-Smith could offer. In the circumstances Maltravers, who depended on shock-tactics as one of his chief means of earning a livelihood, made a distinctly favourable impression. Soon after the second round Blore-Smith had told him most of his life story, though natural caution made him minimise the extent of his income. Maltravers listened and nodded his head at intervals to show that he understood about all these things.

'What college were you at?' he said.

Blore-Smith told him.

'Yes,' Maltravers said. 'Yes. I knew someone who was there. You've had a hard time.'

'London is such a disappointment,' Blore-Smith said.

He felt that he had now gone so far that he had better tell Maltravers everything. He said:

'One doesn't seem to get any of the things one expected.'

'What sort of things?'

'Well, I mean life and so on.'

'But you seem to get plenty of excitement. For instance, I've just knocked you down in my car.'

'Oh, I don't mean things like that,' Blore-Smith said.

He hesitated.

'Women,' he said, and then felt that he had gone too far. In fact he saw by Maltravers's face that he had.

'Women?' Maltravers said. 'Women? Why, the whole place teems with them. They're impossible to get away from.'

'Oh, I don't mean tarts.'

'Neither do I. I think it rather insulting of you that you should suggest that I did.'

'I'm sorry,' Blore-Smith said, much embarrassed. 'I know I oughtn't to have said that. I suppose I really oughtn't to have mentioned the subject to an absolute stranger anyway. But you seemed the first person that I've ever met who understood what I meant when I talked about these things.'

His solicitor had given him a light stand-up lunch and the unaccustomed quart of beer he had just drunk made Blore-Smith feel full of self-pity.

'And besides,' he said, 'I didn't only mean women. I meant life and excitement. Meeting people who count and doing important business.'

'Like one of Balzac's heroes.'

'Yes, I suppose so,' said Blore-Smith, wondering whether he ought to admit that he had never read any Balzac.

Maltravers nodded his head slowly.

'Ah-ha,' he said. 'Ah-ha.'

'I'm sure you do all these things,' Blore-Smith said.

By now he was quite breathless.

'Yes,' said Maltravers. 'I do all these things.'

He sat, still wearing his cap and scarf and oppressively big overcoat, and looked hard at Blore-Smith. There was a pause in which Blore-Smith tried to regain some breath. Maltravers said:

'You are quite right. I *am* one of the people to whom things happen. Things happen to me all the time. This evening, for example, I left my wife.'

'You left her?'

Maltravers nodded. Blore-Smith did not know what to say. He could not make up his mind whether a serious matter was being treated by Maltravers with heroic restraint or, on the contrary, with almost inconceivable frivolity. Maltravers said:

'She is young and lovely and as good as she is beautiful. In fact she's better. But all the same I am going to leave her.'

'Why?'

'Because,' Maltravers said, 'it is right that I should.'

He leant forward suddenly with his elbows on his knees and his chin in his hands. After a time he sighed deeply. Blore-Smith wondered whether it was his duty to say something. Thinking it better to change the subject he said:

'Didn't I see you watching the men with chains this afternoon?'

'You may have done. How like all of us.'

'Did you think so too?'

'Psychologically speaking.'

Maltravers leant forward so that his face almost touched Blore-Smith's. He said with intensity:

'Do you think that what you really need is to be put right psychologically?'

'Psychoanalysed, do you mean?'

'Something of the sort.'

Blore-Smith faltered. He had read of such things. Somehow he had never associated himself with a need for them.

'I don't know,' he said. 'Perhaps.'

Suddenly Maltravers jumped up.

'But you want life, women, a good time,' he said. 'It's no use our staying here. This isn't the sort of place where one can find any of those. Come along with me and I'll introduce you to the most beautiful woman that you have ever seen.'

By this time Blore-Smith had made up his mind that there was no escape. He was not even sure that he wanted to escape. Perhaps this was indeed what he had been looking for. He was surprised to find that, now that adventure had come his way, he was not at all certain that he was going to enjoy it. He put down his glass. Maltravers hurried him into the car again and a few minutes later they stopped in front of a flower-shop.

A coloured sign hung outside inscribed *la cattleya* and underneath these words was a conventionally unconventional representation of the flower, executed by the same painter whose work Blore-Smith had seen at the Frott Gallery. Maltravers pushed at the door which rang a bell when opened and they went into the front of the shop. No one was there and Blore-Smith followed Maltravers towards a curtain which shut off the further end of the room. From the other side of the curtain came Mrs. Mendoza's voice. She was saying:

'After all, why shouldn't I live in Basra if he does get a job there? It probably won't be worse than anywhere else. I shouldn't have everybody nagging at me there, living on my vitality, telling me all about themselves and their beastly affairs, and bothering me, and never giving me a moment's peace. Nor should I have to look after this wretched shop. It might be rather nice. I should be able to ride.'

Maltravers and Blore-Smith went beyond the curtain. Mrs. Mendoza and Chipchase were sitting in front of a gas fire. Chipchase, who had talked about himself all the way from the Frott Gallery, was now listening gloomily to Mrs. Mendoza's troubles. He said:

'A camel? Or a dromedary?'

'Hullo, Mendie,' Maltravers said. 'I've brought someone to see you.'

Mrs. Mendoza turned round.

'Why, Peter,' she said, 'how are you, darling? I heard the bell and thought it must be a customer.'

She stared at Blore-Smith, who wondered if he had ever felt so embarrassed. Maltravers said:

'This is Mr. Blore-Smith. I've just run over him in my car. To make up for doing this I thought I would bring him along to see you, Mendie.'

'But how nice.'

Mendie took Blore-Smith's hand and gave it a good squeeze while she looked at him. Blore-Smith decided that Maltravers was right. She was certainly the most beautiful woman he had ever seen. He did not know at all what sort of a person she was. Her clothes were simple and she was hardly made-up and yet at the same time there was something about her that was very arrogant, an air that he imagined rich spoilt women would have. He noticed that she had taken off her stockings and sat with her feet in a man's pair of woolly bedroom slippers. He knew that he had gone red in the face. He said:

'I hope you don't mind my coming in like this?'

'This is Mr. Chipchase,' Mendie said. 'Have a cigarette?'

Chipchase offered a limp handshake. Blore-Smith said that he did not smoke. Mrs. Mendoza took a cigarette herself. Chipchase said:

'I've just been admiring your taste in pictures.'

'My taste in pictures?'

'I was in the Frott Gallery just now.'

'Oh, yes,' said Blore-Smith. 'I think I remember seeing you there. I'm so glad you like the picture.'

'It seemed to me just a little expensive. Just a little. Of course the Frott Gallery's prices are sometimes a trifle high, there's no doubt. But they always have the best stuff.'

'I thought it a bit expensive myself,' Blore-Smith said, 'but I didn't want to miss it altogether.'

He hoped that he was giving an impression that buying pictures meant nothing to him.

'Oh, you were quite right,' Chipchase said. 'Quite right.'

Maltravers dragged a small settee closer to the fire and they sat down.

'How is Sarah?' Mrs. Mendoza said.

'I've left her,' Maltravers said. 'My married life is over.'

'I on the other hand am contemplating matrimony.'

'The Commodore?'

Mrs. Mendoza nodded and laughed. No one had made any effort to light her cigarette and it had remained all this time in her mouth while she moved it up and down. Blore-Smith watched this for some minutes. At last he plucked up sufficient courage to rise and take the box of matches that lay on the table beside her elbow and strike one. Mrs. Mendoza smiled beautifully at him and he began to blush again. Maltravers said:

'It would make a change if you married, Mendie.'

'I can't see that it would at all,' Chipchase said.

'I think it would be a change for the better,' Maltravers said.

Mrs. Mendoza said: 'You're both of you in a ghastly mood to-night. What on earth is wrong?'

Turning to Blore-Smith she said:

'I think he must have run over you on purpose.'

'Oh, no, I'm sure he didn't,' Blore-Smith said, and hoping to turn the conversation to something less personal added: 'Is that a Picasso hanging up there?'

Chipchase laughed harshly.

'Shut up,' Mrs. Mendoza said to him, and to Blore-Smith: 'No. It was painted by a friend of mine. I think it's rather good, don't you? I know some people don't think so. But if you're interested in pictures you must come and see the ones upstairs. I haven't space to hang them all down here.'

'I should like to very much.'

'Come along then. Some of them are in Scrubb's room. He's my lodger. He may be working now and so will be rather bad-tempered when we disturb him but don't take any notice of what he says.'

'Oh, but if it isn't convenient——'

'This way,' Mrs. Mendoza said. 'Mind the step.'

Maltravers and Chipchase were left alone. When the others could be heard moving about upstairs, Chipchase said:

'What is this you've got hold of?'

'I've no idea. I thought I'd bring it along.'

'Do you know that it's boundlessly rich?'

'How did *you* discover that?'

'It came into the Frott Gallery and paid a couple of hundred for the least inspiring picture you ever saw in your life.'

'All I know about the young gentleman is that he's bored with life and wants amusement. Women and so on. That's why I brought him here.'

'To get off with Mendie?'

'Odder things have happened.'

'You're preposterous.'

'Also I thought you might take him in hand as your first patient.'

'That, on the other hand, is a brilliant suggestion.'

'Isn't it?'

'Why shouldn't he put up the money for your film too? He's probably rich enough for that.'

Maltravers, who had been lying, apparently in a state of nervous collapse, on the sofa, sat up all at once and reached out for the cigarettes.

'That's also a very good idea,' he said. 'A very good one. How altruistic one is.'

'Will you tackle him first?'

'It's worth trying. Meanwhile you must be less morose.'

'It's important that he should respect me to get the best results.'

The bell in the shop rang again and they heard someone come through the door. Maltravers, who always seized any opportunity of serving customers if Mrs. Mendoza was not there, got up to see who had come in. Before he had reached the shop a man put his head through the curtains and said:

'Evening, everybody.'

'Hullo,' said Maltravers and Chipchase together.

The man was about fifty. He was heavily built, with a purple weather-beaten face, and was dressed in a blue mackintosh and a bowler hat. He carried a thick malacca walking-stick.

'Mendie in?' he said.

'She's upstairs,' said Maltravers, 'showing someone the pictures. I expect she'll be down in a second.'

'Anyone I know?' said the big man, taking off his hat and mackintosh and propping up the stick against a small bookcase.

He sat down heavily and looked around the room with some suspicion. He did not seem to be altogether comfortable. Chipchase said:

'No. None of us knows him.'

'Is he a new friend of Mendie's?'

'I ran over him a short time ago,' Maltravers said. 'That is how we got to know him. I brought him along as a compensation.'

'Oh,' said the big man. 'Yes. I see.'

Cautiously he took out a pipe and began to fill it.

There was silence. Maltravers got up and, going to the foot of the staircase, shouted:

'Mendie!'

From upstairs Mrs. Mendoza yodelled.

'Someone to see you!' Maltravers shouted.

Again Mrs. Mendoza yodelled.

'Tell her not to hurry,' said the big man uneasily, and began to light his pipe.

Once more there was a long silence.

'What do you think about the slump?' said Maltravers.

The big man struck several matches and threw them away one after another, pulling away at his pipe all the time and shaking his head, by now enveloped in smoke. Before he had time to make a pronouncement Mrs. Mendoza came into the room again followed by Blore-Smith. She said:

'Hullo, Hugo.'

The big man stood up.

'How are you?' he said and held out a wide red hand. Mrs. Mendoza took it and at the same time gave him a small kiss low on his face.

'I'm grand,' she said. 'Do you know Mr. Blore-Smith, Hugo? This is Commander Venables.'

Commander Venables shook hands with Blore-Smith but before he sat down he went across the room to where he had hung his mackintosh on a peg and felt in one of the pockets. He found a small parcel and held it out to Mrs. Mendoza.

'This is for you,' he said.

'Hugo, the cigarette-case?'

'Yes.'

Mrs. Mendoza tore off the paper. She was excited. There was a chamois leather envelope inside. She opened it. Inside the envelope was a cigarette-case.

'Oh, Hugo, it's not the one!'

Commander Venables looked startled.

'Not the one?' he said.

'Of course it isn't!'

'But you said the modern-looking one?'

'Well, this doesn't look modern, does it?'

Commander Venables took the cigarette-case in his hand and examined it. He clearly found it altogether impossible to decide whether or not it looked modern.

'Oh, put it away,' Mrs. Mendoza said. 'It doesn't matter.'

'I can easily change it,' Commander Venables said.

'No. It doesn't matter in the slightest. This is a very nice one. It looks as if King Edward might have designed it for Queen Alexandra.'

'But I want you to have the one you like.'

'Don't let's say any more about it.'

'No, but look here, I say——'

'No more, Hugo, for goodness' sake.'

Mrs. Mendoza was displeased and the face of Commander Venables showed that he was only too well aware of the depths of stupidity and ignorance of which he had shown himself capable. Blore-Smith felt that as neither Maltravers nor Chipchase showed any signs of finding the situation at all awkward it was perhaps no business of his to try and ease the tension of which he himself was so conscious, but as no one spoke for some minutes he could not prevent himself from saying at last:

'I thought the pictures upstairs very interesting.'

'They are,' Maltravers said. 'I was looking at them the other day. I think they show a very strange side of Mendie's character. You know, Mendie, I think you ought to be psychoanalysed.'

'I agree with you,' Chipchase said. 'I was thinking the same myself only the other day.'

'I suppose you are going to suggest that you should do it?' Mrs. Mendoza said.

Chipchase said: 'Well, why not?'

'When I get psychoanalysed,' Mrs. Mendoza said, 'I shan't become a client of yours.'

'Very well. There is no need to be so bitter. I shall remain friends with you even if you do happen to prefer another practitioner.'

'Have you been psychoanalysed, Captain Venables?' Maltravers said.

Commander Venables showed genuine amusement for the first time since he had come into the room. He gave several deep muffled snorts. His body shook all over and his face contracted so that it looked like a huge shrivelled fruit. Mrs. Mendoza looked at him sternly. She said:

'If you are laughing at psychoanalysis it might be as well to find out about it first.'

'I wasn't laughing at it. I was laughing because he was asking me whether I had ever had it done to me.'

'It might do you a great deal of good,' Mrs. Mendoza said. 'In fact I believe it is just what you need.'

'I think it would do you good, too,' Maltravers said. 'That is, if you don't mind my saying so. It would make you enjoy life tremendously.'

'Don't talk nonsense,' said Mrs. Mendoza, speaking as in defence of her own property threatened with outside interference. 'If Hugo decides that he wants to be psychoanalysed he can talk it over with me. I know all about it. Far more than you.'

She was in a thoroughly bad temper by this time. Suddenly she turned on Blore-Smith and said:

'I'll tell you what psychoanalysis would do for you. It would cure your stutter.'

Blore-Smith wished that the ground beneath would open and swallow him up for ever. His stutter was a subject he was particularly sensitive about and although he could tell from Mrs. Mendoza's tone that she was only letting off steam he felt horribly uncomfortable. Before he could answer, Commander Venables, who was evidently anxious to change the subject, said:

'What I really came in about was to know what time you wanted to dine?'

'Come here at a quarter past eight,' Mrs. Mendoza said.

Commander Venables looked uncertain.

'Shall I be here at a quarter to?' he said. 'Then there would be a margin of time if you weren't ready.'

'Come at a quarter past eight. How many times do you want me to repeat it?'

Commander Venables inclined his head.

'Give me the cigarette-case,' he said, 'and I'll change it.'

'All right. If you insist.'

Commander Venables took his hat and mackintosh from the hook and his stick from the bookcase.

'Then I shall see you at eight-fifteen,' he said. 'Ready?'

'Oh, goodness me, yes,' said Mrs. Mendoza.

Commander Venables turned in the direction of Maltravers, Chipchase, and Blore-Smith. He made a movement as if to bow.

'Good hunting, gentlemen,' he said, raising his stick.

He turned about and passed through the curtain out of their sight. The bell rang once again as he opened the door of the shop. Mrs. Mendoza sat down on the sofa beside Maltravers and sighed, at the same time putting her arm around his shoulder. Chipchase said:

'I suppose I ought to be going too.'

'Why?'

'I've got to change. I'm going to the ballet.'

'Ring me up soon.'

Chipchase turned to Blore-Smith and held out his hand.

'Good-bye,' he said. 'I expect we shall see more of each other soon. I hope so anyway.'

Blore-Smith was surprised at these words because on the face of it nothing seemed to him more unlikely than that he should ever set eyes again on Chipchase. But in spite of feeling this he said as heartily as possible that he hoped it would not be long before their next meeting.

'Ring me up,' Chipchase said, giving his number. 'We'll have a meal together and talk about pictures or psychoanalysis or something of the sort.'

Chipchase then kissed Mrs. Mendoza and disappeared through the gap in the curtain. Maltravers looked at his watch. He said to Blore-Smith:

'Why not have dinner with me if you have nothing better to do? We might go to a movie afterwards if you liked?'

'But really it's awfully kind of you. Of course if you want me to I'd like to dine with you enormously.'

'That's what we'll do then,' said Maltravers. 'We'll leave when Mendie decides to go upstairs to dress.'

It was approaching nine o'clock when they reached Maltravers's club. The dining-room was empty except for waiters who stood about it in formal groups of two and three like pieces of debased classical statuary. Maltravers led the way to a table in the furthest corner of the room. From here the door they had come in by was almost out of sight. Blore-Smith knew that his cuffs were distinctly dirty and tried to forget this by staring up towards the white and gold ornamentation of the ceiling. He noticed that Maltravers's check suit seemed out of place in these surroundings but as Maltravers seemed unconscious of any incongruity he decided that it must be all right and that perhaps it would not matter after all about his cuffs.

'Who exactly is Mrs. Mendoza?' he said.

Maltravers thrust the toast across the table in his direction. He said:

'It's not very easy to define her in three words. You've seen her so you can judge for yourself. Nothing I could say would help very much, any more than I could describe what caviar tastes like.'

'But what does she do?'

'As you have seen, she runs a flower-shop. *la cattleya*. She has had lots of jobs and been married more than once.'

'She is certainly very beautiful,' Blore-Smith said, and although he feared that it might be indiscreet he could not prevent himself from adding:

'And who is Commander Venables?'

'He's at the back of the shop. He's in love with Mendie as you may have noticed. He was in the navy. Now he's got some job connected with civil aviation, I believe.'

'Oh, I see.'

'She may be going to marry him.'

'But he's years older than she is.'

'Yes,' said Maltravers, 'he is. It's all very unsatisfactory. Don't let's talk about it. We may depress ourselves. Tell me, what did you think of Chipchase, the drooping man who was sitting in the arm-chair?'

'He seemed very nice.'

Blore-Smith said this out of politeness because what slight impression he had carried away with him of Chipchase's personality had not been favourable. Supercilious was the adjective he had applied mentally to Chipchase's manner. Supercilious and bad-tempered.

'He's a clever fellow,' Maltravers said. 'You know, if you don't mind my saying so, there was something in what Mendie said about your consulting a psychologist. Do you remember that I had suggested it just before we arrived at the shop? You might do worse than get Chipchase to take you on. That is if he would.'

'But whatever would he do to me?'

'The mind, or rather the Ego,' said Maltravers, 'needs care as much as the body. You tell me that you are dissatisfied with life. How can you hope to enjoy life if your Ego is wrong? I ask you?'

'I suppose you can't,' Blore-Smith said, confused, 'but I still don't see what he could do.'

'If I could tell you that I should be doing it myself. But don't let what I've said worry you. It was only a suggestion of the most conversational kind.'

'But I should like you to tell me more.'

'No, no,' Maltravers said, 'I wasn't really very serious. But if the idea interests you, talk to Chipchase about it when next you see him. He will explain everything.'

'But does he charge to do this?'

'Naturally he doesn't practise out of sheer philanthropy. What a strange notion.'

'Has he many patients?'

'I believe that he could get as many as he wants and that so far he has refused to take anyone on owing to his extreme, and to my mind rather absurd, modesty,' Maltravers said. 'But I feel that I should not have introduced the subject. I see that it has disturbed you.'

'Not at all. I am most interested in it.'

'In that case you should talk to him. But now tell me about yourself. What are your chief amusements?'

'I hardly know. I read. I walk in the park. I go to the cinema.'

'You go to the cinema? Are you interested in films?'

'Certainly I am. Aren't you? I think it's'—Blore-Smith blushed as he said this—'the most living of the arts at present.'

'It's my job,' Maltravers said. 'I write scenarios and help direct them sometimes. But it's not so much as a money-making concern that I care about it. I just use that to keep me alive. The important thing, as you say, is the film as art.'

'Oh, yes,' said Blore-Smith.

This was safer ground than discussing Maltravers's friends with him.

'The difficulty is,' Maltravers said, 'to get together all the people who feel this about the cinema. To get them together and produce uncommercial films of real social, scientific, artistic, literary, dramatic, human, and philosophic interest. That is what I hope to do one of these days.'

'It has been done to some extent already, hasn't it?' said Blore-Smith, who had by this time no idea what Maltravers was talking about.

Maltravers said: 'What I intend to do has, so far as I know, never been done in a serious manner. My proposal is nothing short of this: that I should photograph people existing.'

'What?'

'I surprise you,' Maltravers said. 'I thought I should. It is a daring scheme. Only an extension, of course, of a system that has shown itself successful in innumerable other branches of human life. But it has had to wait for me to apply it.'

'Who will you apply it to?'

'I suggest beginning on a small party of intellectuals.'

'How would you approach them?'

'To some extent psychoanalytically.'

Blore-Smith started at the repetition of this word. Maltravers said:

'A small group of people. Simply watch them behave. But no, I must not allow you to think that I am being flippant. My scheme is to represent certain human relationships in slow motion, so to speak. The films would, at present at least, have no commercial value whatever. But they would be of immense use in spreading an understanding of psychology if privately shown.'

'When are you going to begin doing this?'

'I have already a great deal of material collected.'

'Soon then?'

'I must admit that considerations of a financial kind make themselves felt. I must find someone to produce, or to cause to be produced, enough money to cover the expenses that these experiments would involve.'

'Would that be a large sum?'

'Comparatively, no.'

'But you don't know exactly how much?'

Blore-Smith's voice shook a little.

'Naturally it would be hard to say accurately,' Maltravers said. 'Let me see——'

He took a small gold pencil from his pocket and began to do some calculations on the back of an envelope. After some minutes he passed the envelope over to Blore-Smith and said:

'It's nothing really. Unfortunately I have not got it to spare at the moment.'

'But surely such a brilliant idea stands a good chance of success? People who have got money will come forward when they hear about it?'

'Ah,' said Maltravers, 'there you are quite right. Lots of people would come forward. But they would be unsuitable people. At heart their real interest would be in making money. One would be back again in the old world of the commercial film. What I am in search of is sincerity.'

Maltravers sighed when he said this and allowed his head to fall into his hands. Blore-Smith watched this and was moved. He too sighed. He was, indeed, genuinely interested in the film as art. He said:

'But there must be someone interested in the cinema who is both rich and sincere?'

'Find him,' Maltravers said, with intensity but without raising his head. 'Find him and bring him to me.'

'Well, but that's absurd. I told you that I hardly knew anyone at all in London. Of course I don't know of someone like that when you yourself have not been able to find them.'

'I thought you might know of someone just down from Oxford. It would not matter what age he was. In fact it would be a good thing if he were young. We should have to keep in touch with the younger generation.'

Up to then Blore-Smith had estimated Maltravers's age at twenty-

eight but now he pushed it on to thirty or even more. He did not want
to be questioned too closely about Oxford for fear that the dullness of
his own life there might be revealed in full, so he said:

'I don't think there is anyone who has just come down who would
do for what you want. They weren't a very exciting crowd up with me.
But what a wonderful thing it would be to help direct something like
that.'

'It would have to be someone of intelligence and taste, who could
supply a lot of the ideas himself.'

'I'd give anything to be able to do that.'

'Ah,' said Maltravers, 'I expect so. And you would be a very suitable
person too. What a pity you have not got the money. How often one
feels that about oneself and one's friends.'

Maltravers emptied the decanter into Blore-Smith's glass.

'But—but——'

Blore-Smith knew that again he was getting red in the face. It had
been a day of strain and excitement of a kind to which he was quite un-
used. Habitually he found it difficult to make decisions about which
restaurant he would eat his lunch at or what book he wanted to take out
of the library. And yet the last few hours seemed to have been packed
with resolutions about life of the most weighty sort, all formed on the
spur of the moment. He said:

'If you meant it when you said that the venture would only cost
that amount, I think—I mean, I daresay—possibly, if there was no sort
of complication that turned up later—well I might be able to find the
money myself.'

'You could?'

'Of course I wouldn't have mentioned such a thing if you hadn't
said that you thought that I should be a suitable person.'

'I thought so as soon as I met you. But I hardly imagined that you
would be able to find the financial support.'

'Well,' said Blore-Smith, rather overcome and wondering whether
perhaps he had had too much to drink, 'in that case I should be prepared to say that I would certainly put up the money. Provided, that is,
that I had a certain amount of control over the concern.'

He felt it safer to add this last condition and to make his importance clear from the start. Maltravers tapped with a fork on the table.
He said:

'Wait a minute. We must not go too fast. Do you realise the

amount of trouble and hard work that this will let you in for? You are suggesting that you should take on what is almost a sacred trust. Are you sure that you will prove yourself worthy of it?"

'Of course I can only say that I will do my best. I'm awfully keen, if that——'

'Once decided you will not be able to turn back,' Maltravers said. 'Think it over. Do you want to spend your money in the cause of Beauty? Wouldn't you rather invest in something more gilt-edged?'

Blore-Smith made an effort to control himself. He muttered:

'Is there anything more gilt-edged?'

Maltravers banged on the table so that the group of waiters posed near him all jumped at the same time like a perfectly trained *corps de ballet*.

'Excellent,' Maltravers said. 'Excellent.'

Blore-Smith knew that for once he had said something worth saying. For perhaps the first time in his life he had come up to scratch.

'Will I do then?' he said.

'Yes,' said Maltravers, 'I think you will do.'

He sat in silence with his eyes staring at the table-cloth, turning his wineglass between his finger and thumb. Blore-Smith was silent too. He was thinking of Maltravers's words: 'Once decided, you will not be able to turn back.' He was finding it difficult at that moment to reason at all clearly. He made a mental reservation that he would certainly turn back if things showed signs of going in a way of which he disapproved. This had become a great adventure. Perhaps he had begun to live. He lost himself in wild speculations until at last he heard Maltravers say:

'We will go back to my flat now and I will show you some of the stuff. Then you can think about things all to-morrow and we can meet on the next day or later in the week and discuss the views that you yourself hold. What about that?'

'There is nothing I should like better.'

'Then we can really make a start. Waiter, the bill.'

'Sit down,' said Maltravers. 'Throw those papers on the floor if they are at all in your way. It's only the manuscript of a novel my wife is writing. If you will wait here for a second I will go and get the notes I have already collected and we can run through them together.'

He went out of the room and left Blore-Smith free to examine the photographs and invitations on the mantelpiece. Blore-Smith had never before seen a room at all like this one. It surprised and to some extent shocked him to find that anyone lived and worked among all these newspapers, typewriters, and gramophone records. At the same time it made him ashamed of his own sitting-room with chintz curtains and Medici prints on the walls. He knew that after seeing this place he would never again enjoy spending an evening there reading *Vision and Design*. He would be thinking all the time of this, the wider life. He decided that he would move Van Gogh's *Sunflower* into the bedroom as soon as he reached home again. He crossed to the window. The curtains remained undrawn and he looked out on to the dark square. While he watched, a long sports car drew up in front of the house and someone got out. Then the car left the square, fast and with deafening noise. A few minutes after, Blore-Smith heard the door behind him open. Expecting that it was Maltravers who had come back to the room he turned and found that a young woman in a blue leather overcoat was standing in the doorway.

'How-do-you-do?' she said.

Blore-Smith did not know what to answer. If Maltravers had not told him earlier in the evening that he had left his wife Blore-Smith would have assumed that this was Maltravers's wife, but in the circumstances no such assumption seemed possible. At the same time he felt that, should this indeed be Mrs. Maltravers, some explanation of his own presence in the room was called for, so he said:

'Mr. Maltravers will be back in a minute. He has gone to get some papers.'

'Oh, has he?' said the young woman. 'Do sit down. I hope that he hasn't forgotten that he has left you here and gone to sleep. He sometimes does that.'

Before Blore-Smith had time to consider this possibility Maltravers came into the room again.

'Hullo,' he said to the young woman. 'You're back early.'

'Yes.'

'This is Mr. Blore-Smith, Sarah,' Maltravers said. 'You haven't met my wife yet, have you?'

Although Blore-Smith had been much impressed by Mrs. Mendoza's beauty, which was far in advance of that of any woman to whom he had previously been introduced, Sarah's appearance had an almost stronger effect on him. She was small and had her hair cut short, and the collar of her coat was turned up. There was something about her that attracted him in a disturbing way. Later he decided that it was her manner that he found so irresistible. Maltravers said:

'And how was Nipper?' and turning to Blore-Smith added: 'My wife has been dining with a racing motorist. Isn't that romantic?'

'He had a slight headache,' Sarah said, 'so he went to bed early to-night. That's why I'm back now.'

Maltravers raised his eyebrows and pursed his lips together.

'Oh?' he said. 'Oh?'

'What have you been doing?' Sarah said. She offered her cigarette-case to Blore-Smith.

'Mr. Blore-Smith has come here to discuss some business matters,' Maltravers said politely. 'Is there anything you want?'

'No,' said Sarah, 'there isn't. Except this.'

She took up one of the typewriters and held it under her arm. Blore-Smith, thinking of the smile that Mrs. Mendoza had given him for a similar act, struck a match and lit her cigarette.

'Thanks,' said Sarah. 'Good night.'

She shut the door and a few minutes later they heard the tap-tap of typing coming from the next room.

'She's writing a novel,' Maltravers said. 'I'm the hero.'

Blore-Smith could think of no suitable reply to this piece of information so he said nothing. He had begun to feel exhausted. Maltravers's energy seemed to increase rather than to diminish as time went on, and clearing a space on one of the tables he set out some typewritten sheets of notes and began to explain them to Blore-Smith, who did his best to listen but without much success.

'Of course this is very provisional,' Maltravers said. 'It will all have to be done in much greater detail before anything like a start can be made. At the same time it gives some idea of the scheme.'

He handed the sheets of paper one after another to Blore-Smith, sometimes making pencil notes on them as he did so.

'The pattern scenario is temporarily called *Œdipus Rex*.'

'I see.'

'It merely describes, as you see, a situation that might be photo-graphed in certain stages of development.'

'But how would you get the people together?'

'My present scheme is that, once a good situation between a group of suitable people has been discovered, we collect them together in the same house and await developments, shooting when we think best. It's their actions that count. With the best will in the world one can't photograph a passive man subconsciously hating his father.'

'Shall we have to take a house specially for this?'

'I think that can be arranged satisfactorily. A friend of mine has a house that would be very suitable.'

'Has he agreed to lend it?'

'Not yet. But he will.'

It was after midnight by the time Maltravers had come to the end of all he had to explain. Blore-Smith was so sleepy that he wondered if he would ever have the strength to get home. The noise of Sarah's typing had stopped. Maltravers threw his pencil down on the table.

'There we are,' he said. 'That makes a beginning.'

He stood up and stretched his arms above his head.

'Are you hungry?' he said. 'I am. We'll get Sarah to cook some bacon and eggs.'

'Oh, but——'

'Sarah,' Maltravers shouted. 'Sarah!'

He went to the corner of the room and reached down behind some boxes, from the back of which he pulled out two bottles of beer. While he was opening these Sarah came into the room. She was wearing a Chinese dressing-gown over pink pyjamas.

'What do you want?' she said, rubbing her eyes. 'I was just going to sleep.'

'Will you cook us some bacon and eggs?'

'Now?'

'Of course.'

'All right. I might cook some for myself too.'

'Well, don't be long. We're famished.'

'What a life.'

'Please don't trouble as far as I'm concerned,' said Blore-Smith. 'I really don't think I want anything at all to eat. I ought to be going back, at once. Shall I be able to get a taxi outside?'

'You can't go yet,' Maltravers said. 'You must stay and have something. We can call you up a taxi at any time.'

'No, don't go,' Sarah said. 'The eggs will be ready in a second. I've begun to feel quite hungry myself.'

'Can't I help you?' said Blore-Smith, although he had only a vague idea of how to cook bacon and eggs.

'Oh, don't bother to be polite,' said Maltravers, who had gone back to the papers on the table, but he took no active steps to prevent Blore-Smith from following Sarah into the kitchen.

'Look,' she said. 'Do you mind giving these plates a bit of a polish up with this cloth?'

For some minutes he stood watching the eggs being cooked and handing her objects she asked for.

'There,' said Sarah, 'will you take yours? I'll bring these along on the tray.'

They returned to the sitting-room, where Sarah laid the table. Maltravers poured out some beer.

'How is your book getting on?' he said to Sarah.

'It's finished.'

'Why haven't you shown it to me?"

'I only finished it this morning.'

'Well? I've seen you since then, haven't I?'

'You didn't show much sign of wanting to hear about it when you came in this afternoon.'

'You never mentioned it.'

'I didn't think it would interest you.'

'I take a great interest in your work,' Maltravers said. 'More than you do in mine, I'm afraid.'

Blore-Smith noticed that Maltravers, perhaps experiencing a reaction from the energetic mood he had been in all the evening, now seemed to be working himself up into a rage. Feeling nervous as to the consequences of this, should it be the case, Blore-Smith said to Sarah:

'What sort of book are you writing?'

'A novel,' Maltravers said. 'I told you. I'm the hero.'

'You're not,' Sarah said. 'You're not in it now at all. I had to take you out. You were such a boring character.'

'What?'

'You are just mentioned right at the end as a half-mad tramp who comes into a public house and frightens some commercial travellers.'

'So that's what you think of me, is it?'

'That's all you are in the book.'

'Of course I've known for ages that that is how you regard me,' Maltravers said, putting a lot of pepper over his egg.

The three of them ate in silence for some minutes after he had said this. At last Blore-Smith, again speaking to Sarah, said:

'We've been talking about the film.'

'What film?' Sarah said.

'*Œdipus Rex.*'

'I haven't seen it. Where is it on?'

'The private uncommercial film your husband thinks of organising.'

Blore-Smith was surprised that he had to explain this. Maltravers said:

'You haven't heard about it yet. I shall tell you in due time.'

'Are you blossoming out into a film director?'

'Ask no questions. I shall inform you when I think fit.'

'How frightfully exciting.'

'Meanwhile you must try and learn to cook bacon better.'

'What is wrong with this?'

'It doesn't taste like bacon.'

Sarah turned to Blore-Smith.

'What do you think?' she said.

Blore-Smith stuttered:

'I? Well, it seems to me very good on the whole. Perhaps a little salt. Excellent really.'

After he had said this Blore-Smith looked with apprehension at Maltravers, who showed no mark of having heard what he had said. Sarah smiled at Blore-Smith, who at once felt glad that he had taken her side and even regretted that he had not said more in defence of her bacon. Maltravers put down his knife and fork.

'I'm going to bed now,' he said. 'I'm rather tired. I've had a busy day. Will you ring me up when you have thought all these things out?'

He held out a hand to Blore-Smith, who shook it and was too surprised and tired himself to say more than good night. Passing his hand across his forehead, Maltravers sighed and left the room. Sarah began to clear away the plates.

'Poor dear,' she said. 'He hasn't been very well lately.'

'Is he often like this?'

'Not well?'

'No—I mean—at least—yes. Is he often not well?'

'On and off.'

Sarah yawned.

'I really must be going now,' Blore-Smith said. 'I'm afraid I've been a great nuisance staying so long.'

'Nonsense. Do you want a taxi? There's the number.'

While he was waiting for the taxi to arrive Blore-Smith nerved himself to say:

'I do hope that we shall meet again.'

'Of course we shall. Especially if the film gets under way.'

'Yes,' said Blore-Smith, remembering the film. 'Of course.'

'You must ring me up and come to see me.'

'May I really do that?'

'Do you think you will be able to find something for me to do in the film? Writing dialogue or designing sets or something?'

'Oh, but I'm sure that your husband will arrange for that, won't he, if you'd like something like that?'

'I'm not so sure.'

'You see, it will all be more or less extempore, I suppose. No studio work. But do you do much work for films?'

'No. None really. I'm motoring correspondent for *Mode*. Did I tell you that? Are you interested in cars?'

'Well no, not much,' said Blore-Smith. 'But I suppose you are?'

'I go down on my knees to them.'

'To cars?'

'They're my religion.'

'Oh.'

'I'll take you out in my car some time,' Sarah said. 'Be sure and ring me up.'

Outside in the square the taxi hooted a few times. Blore-Smith said good night again and groped his way to the foot of the stairs. On the way home he went to sleep, and when they arrived at Ebury Street he was roused by the taximan shaking his arm.

The next morning Blore-Smith found that he had a slight headache. He lay in bed thinking about the previous day, trying to recall all that had taken place. After a time he contrived to sort out in his mind some of the things that had happened to him.

Pondering over them, he became convinced that he had behaved in a silly manner. He got out of bed. While he was shaving he decided that if Maltravers tried to get into touch with him he would excuse himself on the grounds that he had had too much to drink and in this way extricate himself from the entanglement.

He sat indoors all the morning and every time the telephone bell rang he prepared himself for making a speech to this effect. But all the telephone calls turned out to be wrong numbers, and by the end of the day Blore-Smith found himself in a highly nervous state. As usual he had dinner alone. Not in his rooms, to which he found that he had taken a sudden dislike, but at a small restaurant in the neighbourhood controlled by distressed gentlewomen. Contrary to his usual custom, he sent out for half a bottle of St. Emilion but this did not cheer him up so much as he had hoped. After dinner he went to a cinema but the film was so poor that he came out half-way through and walked about the streets for some time to avoid arriving home before it was time to go to bed.

The next day passed in much the same way. He heard nothing from Maltravers. By this time Blore-Smith had tried to reconsider the situation and had begun to think that perhaps his first conclusions about the scheme had been justifiable after all. Since meeting Maltravers time seemed to hang on his hands more heavily than ever before.

On the second evening he stayed in his room and read but he found that he was unable to concentrate on either law books or novels. That night he slept badly.

He woke up on the third day convinced that he was behaving like a fool. Maltravers had given him the chance of a lifetime and he had taken no steps to follow up a suggestion which he realised now had been presented to him in so unblatant a form that many of its best points had at first escaped him. He made up his mind that if he heard nothing of Maltravers during that day he would write to him in the evening and ask when it would be convenient for them to have another discussion about the matter in hand. He would have telephoned if he had not felt too embarrassed to use this form of communication. Again the day passed so slowly that he thought the evening would never come. Apart from anything else he wanted to see Sarah Maltravers again. After tea Blore-Smith sat down and began to compose a letter.

While he was doing this the telephone bell rang. Blore-Smith lifted the receiver. It was Chipchase, asking if he might pay a call.

Blore-Smith's first sensation on discovering the name of the speaker was a renewal of his earlier suspicions, but as Chipchase did not mention Maltravers and because Blore-Smith was only too anxious to have someone to talk to at any price he said:

'Yes, yes. Of course I remember meeting you. Do come round. I was meaning to ring you up but I mislaid your number.'

'All right,' Chipchase said, speaking very indistinctly. 'I'll be round quite soon.'

Blore-Smith sat down and tried to size up his hopes and fears. He wondered whether or not he should take Chipchase into his confidence. Chipchase was the only person he knew who could possibly tell him anything about Maltravers. At the same time Chipchase was Maltravers's friend and would therefore be biased in his favour. When the front-door bell rang Blore-Smith was still unable to make up his mind. He felt thoroughly uneasy. Chipchase's manner did not reassure him.

'Won't you put your hat and coat there?'

Chipchase did so and sat down in silence. Blore-Smith was uncomfortable. He had the impression that Chipchase's bearing was intended to convey in suitable terms the arrival of a gloomy genius in this humble place. He remembered suddenly that there was nothing to drink in the house. He said:

'I'm afraid I haven't got anything to offer you to drink. I'm so sorry.'

'I don't want a drink, thanks very much,' Chipchase said. 'I have indigestion as a matter of fact.'

'Oh? I'm so sorry.'

'It doesn't matter,' Chipchase said. 'I shall get over it. It's a form of compulsion-neurosis due, I think, to jealousy. I suppose the Frott Gallery haven't sent your picture along yet?'

'Oh, no. I can't expect it for a long time yet. The show has only just begun,' Blore-Smith said, wondering whether he should ask Chipchase straight away what he thought of Maltravers's proposal.

This problem was solved by Chipchase himself, who said:

'Did you have an amusing dinner the other night after you left Mendie's?'

'Very enjoyable. How nice Mr. Maltravers is. Afterwards I went back to his flat. In fact I had bacon and eggs there at the end of the evening.'

'Did you meet Sarah?'

'She cooked the eggs.'

'Didn't you like her?'

'She's charming,' Blore-Smith said. 'Awfully nice.'

'I think they are such a good couple,' Chipchase said. 'Made for each other.'

This view of the Maltravers household had not immediately recommended itself to Blore-Smith, who was so surprised at what Chip-chase had said that he looked closely at his face to see if he might perhaps be joking. As Chipchase's features had all the appearance of seriousness, Blore-Smith replied with some remark about Sarah's attractive way of dressing. Chipchase agreed.

'They are lucky to have found each other,' he said.

'Have they been married long?'

'About two years. There was a lot of opposition on the part of Sarah's family. Then her old father died suddenly. I think she must have poisoned him.'

'What?'

'Well, perhaps not. Anyway the old man must have had his suspicions because he left most of his money to found a home for fallen women or something of the sort. That was because he disapproved of Maltravers.'

'Why did he disapprove?'

'Well,' said Chipchase, 'you've seen him, haven't you?'

'Maltravers?'

'Yes.'

'But was it just his clothes?'

'That sort of thing and the way he talked and the things he did. Maltravers gave up the civil service and got a job in pictures, which Sarah's father considered to be falling as low as it is possible to fall.'

'Did he sell pictures or paint them?'

'Not that sort of picture. Films. He went into the movie business.'

'Oh, of course. I knew he was doing that.'

'His own family wanted him to become a colonial governor or a permanent under-secretary or something of the sort but I expect that in their hearts they realised that in the long run he would do much more harm to more people in a job like that than he would ever be able to do in the cinema trade.'

'But why should he do harm?'

'I don't mean harm in the bad sense, you know.'

Blore-Smith wondered what other harm there was but he did not like to ask repeatedly for explanations of everything that Chipchase said to him and so he did not reply. His interest in these facts about Maltravers's private life had made him forget about the projected scheme for uncommercial films. Chipchase continued to talk. He talked about Maltravers, about Sarah, about plays, about painting, about books, about food, and about women. Then he got up suddenly and said:

'It's been very nice meeting again. I must go now. Will you ring me up some time?'

He had taken up his hat and coat and nearly reached the door before Blore-Smith could collect himself sufficiently to mention the subject that was now uppermost in his mind.

'There was something that Maltravers said to me the other night ——' Blore-Smith began, and then he stopped, not knowing how best to word what he wanted to ask.

'Yes?'

'He said he wanted to make an uncommercial film. He said he wanted someone to put up some money——'

'Well?'

'He suggested that I should do this as I think I could probably raise the amount he mentioned.'

'I congratulate you,' Chipchase said. 'You must have made a very good impression on him. It sounds a magnificent idea.'

Blore-Smith was taken by surprise. He said:

'Yes. I think so.'

'I shall enormously look forward to seeing the film when it is shown,' Chipchase said.

Again he prepared to leave the room. Blore-Smith in some agitation said:

'I wanted to ask you—do you think—you see, I don't know Mr. Maltravers at all——'

'No, of course you don't. You only met him the other day when you came to Mendie's, didn't you?'

'Shall I do it?'

'But it's the chance of a lifetime.'

'You think so?'

'I'm sure of it.'

'I—I suddenly became suspicious.'

'Why?'

'I don't know. I sometimes get like that. I think I'm rather nervy.'

Chipchase began to take off his overcoat.

'Look here,' he said, 'I'll stay a bit longer. You tell me all about yourself.'

'How do you mean?'

'Your nerves.'

'What shall I tell you?'

'Everything.'

'Where shall I begin?'

'Describe your symptoms.'

'I can't make up my mind to do anything. I'm bored. I can't sleep. I'm frightened of people.'

'In fact you have a strong feeling of inferiority? Yes?'

'At times.'

'The uncertainty that you feel about Maltravers and this film is typical?'

'Absolutely.'

Blore-Smith did not think it necessary to add that such problems as these did not arise in his life every day.

'People seem to be persecuting you all the time?'

'Sometimes.'

'You give way to day-dreams?'

'At intervals.'

'How often?'

'I don't know. Once or twice a day perhaps. I don't remember exactly.'

'Do you mean that you don't want to remember?'

'Yes—I mean no.'

'You are ambitious?'

'No, not at all.'

'Of course you are!'

'I suppose in some ways.'

'Do you ever have delusions of grandeur?'

'No.'

Blore-Smith was emphatic this time.

'You are sure?'

'Quite sure.'

'Do you,' said Chipchase, coming closer, 'ever feel an overpowering impulse to cruelty?'

'Good heavens, no.'

'A slight one then?'

'No, I don't think so.'

'Come, come,' said Chipchase. 'Admit you feel a slight one.'

'Perhaps,' said Blore-Smith, wretchedly.

There was a pause. Chipchase put his hands in his pockets and walked towards the window. Without turning round he said:

'Have you ever thought of taking any sort of psychoanalytical or similar treatment?'

'Well, Maltravers suggested something of the sort—and—and Mrs. Mendoza,' said Blore-Smith, remembering the reference to his stutter.

'It would be worth considering.'

'You think so?'

'Especially if you are going to embark on the film directing business. You will need to have strong nerves to stand the strain of the people you will meet in the movie world. Make up your mind to that.'

'Are you—do you do it yourself?'

'Do what?'

'Give treatment?'

'That is how I propose to demonstrate some of my own developments of the science.'

'And do you think it would make me feel better?'

'Of course no definite promise can be made. There is every reason to suppose that, given time and application on your part, your own state might be improved.'

'Would you take me as a patient?'

'Why?' said Chipchase. 'This is very unexpected.'

'I should be so pleased if——'

'I should have to think about it. Are you sure that you really want me to?'

'I think it would be a great help to me if you would.'

'It would cost you a certain amount of money, you know.'

'Naturally. But are the fees high?'

Chipchase took a card from his pocket and held it towards Blore-Smith, who took it and read the figures written on it.

'I see,' he said, 'I see.'

He thought for a few moments, remembering that he had other commitments on his hands. There was a pause. Chipchase lit a cigarette. At last Blore-Smith said:

'I think I could manage that.'

'It is very important,' Chipchase said, 'that treatment should continue uninterrupted for a reasonably long time. It would not do, for example, if you suddenly went away for a month in the middle.'

'No, I see that. But what should I do if I had to? In connection with the film, for instance?'

'The only thing would be for the treatment to be continued wherever you went.'

'By some local practitioner?'

'No, no. It is vitally important that there should be no change of that kind.'

'Perhaps you would be able to accompany me?'

'That would be the only satisfactory way.'

'Would you be able to do this?'

'It might be arranged.'

'There is, of course, no prospect of my going away at present.'

'Excellent. But one never knows. When would you wish to start the treatment?'

'Would the next week or so be too soon?'

'I think I could manage that,' Chipchase said.

He wrote down his address on the back of his tariff card. 'Come here at eleven o'clock on Monday week,' he said, 'and we will have our first session. I shall look forward to seeing you.'

He took his hat and coat from the chair.

'Good-bye,' he said.

'Good-bye,' said Blore-Smith, opening the door.

When he heard the front door shut, Blore-Smith crossed to the window and, drawing the lace curtains aside, he watched Chipchase sidling up the street. Once more his head was in a whirl. He wondered what had come over him during the last few days. He sat down in the armchair and clasped together his hands.

It was some time before Maltravers and Chipchase had the opportunity to meet again and discuss matters. This was because Maltravers had been offered a temporary job at some film studios which, although inconsiderable financially, was important from the point of view of keeping in touch and occupied most of his day. Chipchase had been busy with odds and ends of journalism. Both of them kept up with Blore-Smith, Maltravers by telephone and Chipchase at his own flat, where he held one or two preliminary examinations of his new patient's conscious and subconscious mind. On the whole the necessary arrangements by which they were to take over the reorganisation of Blore-

Smith's life seemed to be going forward in a manner satisfactory to all parties concerned. A hint of spring was in the air now, so that when at last Maltravers and Chipchase contrived to meet it was decided that dinner at a roadhouse would supply a suitable environment for talking over ways and means.

As they drove down a by-pass road between bright-coloured filling-stations and neo-tudor cafés, Chipchase said:

'Well? What are we going to do with this male Madame Bovary now we have got him?'

In the distance before them, growing obscure in the light of evening, there were trees behind the brick and tin houses that lined the macadam. Maltravers accelerated, jumping the amber light of the traffic signals. He said:

'It is now arranged that I go to Berlin next month.'

'And I shall be left here holding the baby.'

'I can't risk throwing up the Berlin job. You will have to keep him in play till it's over. It will only last a month or two.'

'It had occurred to me that I might take him to Paris for a few weeks. Half the trouble is that he has never been anywhere. He could shake off a few inhibitions there and then we could join you in Berlin for a little research work in the art of the cinema.'

'What a very good idea. By the way, Caroline is in Paris now, isn't she?'

'Is she? Perhaps we shall meet. One will be very busy, of course.'

'How serious a case do you think he is?'

'I shall earn every penny of my emoluments. I can assure you of that. No human being ever needed treatment more.'

'It always makes life pleasanter,' Maltravers said, 'to feel that one is living honestly. It is just the same about his attitude to the cinema. I know that I am combining business with genuine philanthropy. So often one has to get money in such sordid ways.'

'True.'

'As a matter of fact,' Maltravers said, 'I always look upon myself as a gentleman, however badly I behave. I'm like those women who after having dozens of lovers still secretly regard themselves as pure. Everything is done with a sort of mental reservation like having one's fingers crossed.'

Chipchase said: 'I don't feel like that any longer. I've sunk. I can therefore take far more credit for the few gentlemanly actions I do than persons like yourself who ought really to be doing them all the time.'

'Perhaps that is a wiser attitude. I suppose you will come to Berlin too?'

'Naturally.'

'By the way, in the course of your preliminary talks with him has he said anything about Sarah?'

'There is a woman who sounds uncommonly like her who is evidently obsessing him.'

'It is undoubtedly Sarah. I had a strong suspicion that he was going to fall for her.'

'Is she furious?'

'I don't think she knows anything about it yet.'

'Would she be coming with you to Germany?'

'I don't know. She may have engagements in London.'

'Nipper?'

'I take it.'

The road bifurcated and they turned left and roared up a hill and out into the country. Soon they were passing between hedges and fields. Chipchase said:

'Then I will go ahead with arrangements for visiting Paris without further reference for the moment to your plans.'

'Act quite independently. Paris should be very enjoyable at this time of year. The trees will be coming out.'

'We will start at the beginning of next week. I will keep you informed as to developments.'

'I shall look forward to Berlin too. You know I haven't had a real holiday since I've been married.'

'No?'

'I may let myself go,' Maltravers said.

He parked the car at the end of a row of other cars and took a numbered ticket from the hand of an attendant dressed in a green leather jerkin, a hood, and buckled shoes. They went up the steps and under a portcullis. A girl in a steeple hat and wimple took their coats. Sounds of music were coming from the room inside.

2

Blore-Smith sat in his room, attending respectfully to Chipchase, who stood in front of the mantelpiece, outlining their plan of campaign. Van Gogh's *Sunflower* and the miniature reproduction of the Colleone statue had been taken away, and Blore-Smith had fixed his eyes on a spot beyond Chipchase's head where the picture from the Frott Gallery, unexpectedly prompt in arriving, now hung. Some bottles were ranged along the sideboard. Blore-Smith had just ended his account of the nightmare he had experienced on Tuesday and he lay back relaxed and exhausted on the sofa. Chipchase shut his notebook and put his fountain pen into his pocket. He said:

'And so I shall leave all the arrangements in connection with our visit to Paris in your hands. It will bring you into touch with life and will encourage you to leave behind the dream world in which you have become accustomed to live.'

Blore-Smith gave a start and blushed.

'What exactly shall I have to do?' he said.

'Tickets. Passports. Money changing. I will show you my passport, which will tell you where to apply.'

'How are we going?'

'I think it will be best to fly. It is quickest. And on the whole the most comfortable.'

'Will you look through the things after I have got them?'

'I will check everything.'

Some days later, after running through the stuff, Chipchase was glad to find that all the items were in order.

It was sunny weather when they arrived at Croydon. Blore-Smith stood and listened to the fretful noise of the machines as they left the green lawns of the airport. He watched them uneasily as they swept up and disappeared at last in clouds. He had never before been in an aeroplane.

'Come on,' said Chipchase. 'Up the steps.'

Blore-Smith obeyed. Soon he was watching England splayed out enigmatically below him. Chipchase, reading *The Occult Review*, which he had bought at the airport bookstall, sat moodily beside him. For some time neither of them spoke, and then Blore-Smith said:

'Look. The sea.'

'Yes.'

'What are those mauve patches on the water? Are they seaweed? Is it so clear that we can see the bottom?'

'Cloud-shadows.'

'Don't they look strange on the blue water?'

'Like bruises on a body.'

Blore-Smith did not answer. He continued to look through the glass at the waves, which became more grey as they flew on. Chipchase said:

'We're running into bad weather.'

The plane began to rock about, sinking violently into air-pockets that seemed bottomless, racing through banks of dark cloud. Blore-Smith found himself tiring of the vibration and for a time he clutched a paper bag, wondering whether he would be able to hold out until they reached their destination. Chipchase had folded up *The Occult Review* and sat staring in front of him. His face looked like grey marble. He, too, toyed with a bag for some minutes but after a time he folded it up and returned it to its pocket on the wall. Several other passengers were less fortunate. At last they arrived at Le Bourget.

'Whereabouts are we going to stay?' Blore-Smith said, as they climbed into the bus.

Chipchase said: 'On what George Augustus Sala refers to as the Surrey side of the Seine.'

It was a small hotel and the hall smelt of cinnamon. After the boxes had been taken up to their rooms Chipchase grunted loudly.

'And now,' he said, 'we'll have a *fine* to settle our stomachs after all we have been through.'

'Can we go to the Latin Quarter?' said Blore-Smith.

'Yes. We will. We'll go and have a *fine* in the Latin Quarter.'

Blore-Smith followed Chipchase down the stairs of the hotel and out into the street. This was the first time he had been out of England. He looked around him with surprise, trying to remember any French that he might have learnt at school. He had never before felt himself so entirely in the hands of his psychoanalyst. A sinking despair overcame him as they left the long narrow street along which they had been walking and began to cross the Luxembourg Gardens. Everyone they had come in contact with since crossing the Channel had seemed to be in a bad temper. Life in this city of new smells and unfamiliar light was evidently lived on a different plane from anything he had been used to. He tried to cheer himself up with the thought that he was about to see Montparnasse of which he had heard so much.

'Shall we go to an artists' café?' he said.

'Yes, we'll go to an artists' café,' said Chipchase, 'but try not to over excite yourself. You must learn to develop a more level view of life.'

'I can't help feeling excited.'

Sometimes Blore-Smith felt almost petulant at the way Chipchase treated him. He only bore it in silence because he realised that in the long run it was all for his own good. He said:

'I've always wanted to see Montparnasse.'

'Well here you are then.'

'This?'

'All of it.'

They had debouched into a broad boulevard which at first sight seemed to be fronted entirely with super-cafés. Chairs and tables stretched away into the distance as far as the eye could reach. At this time of day the *terrasses* were almost deserted except for waiters who stood, flicking napkins at insects, real or imaginary, and watching the passers-by with sallow disapproving faces.

'Which one shall we go to?' Chipchase said. 'There is very little to choose.'

'Could we go to the Dôme?'

'Very well. We will go to the Dôme.'

They sat down at a table and Chipchase ordered drinks. Blore-Smith looked round him. A curious sweetish smell that he found sickly and not altogether agreeable hung about the place. Three Americans sat at a neighbouring table, hunched up and swaying in their thick tubular clothes, while they argued with each other about a poker game of the previous night. While Blore-Smith watched them they were joined by a fourth American, who, on his arrival at the table, said to one of those already seated: 'And did you make her?' To which the other replied: 'And did I make her?' at the same time knocking over and on to the floor with his elbow a pile of saucers, some of which broke while others rolled away along the pavement.

'Who are those?' Blore-Smith said.

'Artists,' said Chipchase. 'And now I want to say a little more about how we are going to live. We shall be very quiet but at the same time have a look at everything. There are certain barriers that you have got to break down but there is no reason, in my opinion, why you should go at them too violently.'

'No, no.'

Blore-Smith felt relieved by these words. Chipchase said:

'That is why I thought it best that you should come abroad with me first. I like doing things quietly. If you begin to feel that life with me is too slow, remember that there will be plenty of opportunity for more excitement when we meet Maltravers in Berlin in a few weeks' time. He has a great deal of energy.'

'Oh, but I like being quiet——'

'Yes'—Chipchase paused in his conversation to watch a *midinette*, carrying a cardboard hat-box with a bright flowered design all over it, pass their table—'at present that is all right. But there is danger that you may allow this taste to grow into a resistance to life. You understand what I mean?'

'Yes, but——'

'Very well then. There is no need to discuss it any more now. I thought I would just mention it to you.'

Before Blore-Smith could answer Chipchase had begun to wave his hand to a man who was walking up the street, and at the same time to shout:

'Gaston! Gaston!'

The man, who was tall and slim and dressed in a light grey check suit, was of indeterminate nationality. He had a slight moustache and was clearly intended to look English, but there was something unconvincing about this highly perfected character-part so that in the end he might have been a member of any cosmopolitan society, Scandinavian, Austrian, Hungarian, or American. His face was a flat dead white in colour and very smooth. When he saw Chipchase he paused, threw up his hands, and then vaulted over a café table to reach the place where they were sitting.

'Ah, *mon vieux*,' he said. 'How's life?'

'Have a drink?'

'Did I ever refuse?'

'This is Mr. Blore-Smith,' Chipchase said. 'Monsieur de la Tour d'Espagne.'

'*Enchanté*,' said the Frenchman, nodding formally, but at the same time managing to convey that he omitted to shake hands because he understood that it was an un-English habit rather than because he wished to be stand-offish. 'Are you over for long?'

'A week or ten days,' Chipchase said. 'Mr. Blore-Smith is a client of mine. I thought that a little Paris air might do him good while we proceeded with the psychoanalytical treatment that he is undergoing at my hands.'

M. de la Tour d'Espagne looked surprised. He said:

'Ah, le psychanalyse?'

'That's it,' said Chipchase. 'And how are you, Gaston?'

'Top-hole, old man.'

He talked really excellent English, flavoured with an occasional touch of pre-war slang which lent an old-world charm to his conversation.

'You have seen Schlumbermayer?'

'No. Is he in Paris?' Chipchase said.

'But of course. He is over on business. Buying pictures and furniture.'

'How very extravagant.'

'And what pictures do you think he is buying?'

'Dirty pictures.'

'No. You are wrong. He is buying the famous La Tour d'Espagne collection.'

'No?'

'Well he is having a look at it and he will certainly buy something out of it.'

'But why are you selling?'

M. de la Tour d'Espagne raised his hands.

'Well, you see, times are pretty rotten,' he said. 'And then I don't go there often. I am trying to let the house to some South Americans. After all, one must live.'

'I suppose so.'

'Why not meet us all to-morrow night? Pauline is giving a party A la Vache enragée. She would love to see you, I know. Bring your friend along. Everybody will be there, including Schlumbermayer, as a matter of fact.'

'That sounds perfect,' Chipchase said; and, turning to Blore-Smith, added: 'Pauline is the Duchesse de Borodino. You must certainly meet her. She is one of the most delightful people in the whole of France.'

'I should like to very much,' said Blore-Smith sincerely.

'Come about eleven o'clock,' said M. de la Tour d'Espagne. 'And now I must be going.'

He got up from the table, shuddered violently, and grimaced.

'I must go at once now,' he said. His face twitched a little. 'Awfully glad to have seen you. A *demain*.'

He set off up the street at a great rate.

'Why did he go so suddenly?' Blore-Smith said.

Chipchase screwed up his eyes.

'Goodness knows,' he said. 'I expect he had a date.'

'Who is he?'

'He's called the Marquis de la Tour d'Espagne. An anglicised Frenchman,' Chipchase said. 'Never an entirely satisfactory product for some reason.'

'Why not?'

'It's a synthesis that doesn't seem to work. I don't know why. But with all his failings Gaston can be very charming.'

'Why is he so white?'

'He smokes too much,' Chipchase said, and laughed.

They spent the morning strolling the rue de Seine, looking at the picture galleries. Blore-Smith found that after a night's rest he was on the whole feeling better, although the change of air had affected his inside and the alien surroundings still caused him some misgivings. He found that he had to keep his wits about him in case he might be called upon to speak French. Chipchase could on occasions produce some unexpected regional colloquialism, but apart from this his knowledge of the language was severely limited and he insisted on Blore-Smith doing all the talking on the grounds that it was psychologically good for him to make contacts with foreigners in this way.

'The first thing you must do,' Chipchase said, as they walked in the direction of the river, 'is to develop a healthier attitude towards women. Be firm with them. They won't bite you. Not immediately, anyway.'

'Will there be a lot of women to-night?'

'What do you mean?'

'At the Duchesse's party?'

'There will be some certainly. And there will be a lot in the places where we shall go.'

'Oh.'

'Littered about.'

'Professional?' said Blore-Smith with an effort.

'Of course.'

Chipchase did not pursue this subject. Instead he said:

'We will have a nice little lunch now and after that we will go to the cinema. Then we can return to the hotel and I will take some notes on your state. After that we will find somewhere pleasant for a drink and dine well and late so that we can go straight on from dinner and join the others. What do you think of that?'

'All right.'

'Here's a taxi.'

Chipchase told the man an address and got in after Blore-Smith, who sat in the corner and began to think about Sarah Maltravers. He found that lately his mind had dwelt more and more on this subject. He wondered what this could mean, and supposed that it had something to do with the changes that were undoubtedly taking place in his attitude towards life. He could not help wishing that his visit to Paris was over and that he was back in England again. He was roused from these musings by Chipchase's voice saying:

'Will you pay this fellow off, while I go and find a table?'

Blore-Smith did his best with the taxi-man. Then he went into the restaurant, where he found Chipchase, who had already begun to order lunch.

'Sit down,' said Chipchase, 'and I will tell you about some of the people we are going to meet to-night. What do you want to drink?'

'Vichy,' said Blore-Smith. 'Go on.'

'I think I might have half a bottle of something white. Well, first of all there is Pauline de Borodino. You remember Napoleon made them kings of Cyprus or some such place. She knows everyone in Europe of the slightest interest.'

'Does she talk English?'

'Better than Gaston. Now Gaston is rather another matter. He is not Napoleonic. He is mediæval in the worst sense, and when he has had a few drinks he sometimes behaves like a minor character in Proust who has got out of hand. When he begins to speak of the blood of Bayard flowing in his veins, don't argue with him.'

'I shouldn't dream of arguing——'

'Very well. But remember: the blood of Bayard is a danger-signal.'

'And who is Schlumbermayer?'

'Schlumbermayer,' Chipchase said, 'I shall not attempt to describe. It will be sufficient for you to know that he is a collector, has a large and hideous house near London, and is somewhere between the ages of forty and fifty. His character repays study, so, if you get an opportunity to-night, talk to him.'

'What does he collect?'

'Everything. Pictures, furniture, carpets, pots and pans, rare editions, armour, stamps, matchboxes, tram-tickets—everything.'

'What does he do with it all?'

'He sells a certain amount and keeps the rest in cellars.'

'Who else?'

'There will probably be some Americans with foreign titles. You must not be surprised at anything this crowd say or do.'

'I'll try not to be.'

'Some of them are distinctly eccentric. And, I warn you, French fairies are the last straw.'

The afternoon passed quickly and pleasantly. By dinner-time Blore-Smith had thrown off his depression and was feeling very happy. He continually reminded Chipchase of his gratitude at having been brought to Paris.

They dined, as Chipchase had suggested, well. The panelled room was dimly lighted, and sitting back in his chair, drinking coffee, Blore-Smith felt full of suppressed excitement at the thought of the evening before him.

'What shall we have now?' Chipchase said. 'Brandy? Armagnac?'

'I should like to try something I have not tasted before.'

'Very good. Excellent. That is just how you should be feeling. How about some calvados?'

'Yes.'

Blore-Smith was feeling better than he had felt for ages. Perhaps better than he had ever felt in his life before. He turned the liqueur glass between his finger and thumb and assumed as well as he was able the sluggish prudential expression of a connoisseur.

'How do you like it?'

'Excellent.'

'Another one?'

'Yes.'

'It will be time to start soon. You'd better begin asking for the bill. I'll be back in a second.'

Blore-Smith, out of sheer lightness of heart, ordered another calvados for himself while Chipchase was out of the room and drank it quickly before he reappeared.

'Did I leave enough?' he said later when they were in the taxi.

'Quite enough,' Chipchase said. 'Far too much in fact. Still it doesn't matter. One's only young once.'

Blore-Smith noticed that Chipchase as well as himself seemed to be in much better form than was usual. It was also clear from his manner that it was the calvados that had made him unbend. He had become rather flushed in the cheeks. Soon they arrived at the entrance of what was evidently a night-club of the most discreet kind. A small sign stuck out from above the door on which were the words, 'A la Vache enragée.'

The place surprised, and to some extent disappointed, Blore-Smith by the quietness of its black-and-gold decorations. A Cuban band, in coloured shirts and cummerbunds, was playing in muted pessimistic tones in one corner. The clients sitting at the tables round the room or up at the bar seemed on the whole equally subdued, but a certain amount of noise and laughter came from the corner of the room opposite the band where the Marquis de la Tour d'Espagne sat with a number of other men and women. When he saw Chipchase and Blore-Smith, the Marquis jumped up and said:

'Splendid of you to come.'

After the introductions, which left him hopelessly confused, Blore-Smith found himself separated from Chipchase and sitting between the Duchesse de Borodino herself and a young negro wearing a dinner-jacket. The rest of the party, only some of whom were in evening dress, included two middle-aged American women in expensive clothes, introduced as Princess Marquetto and Mrs. Rausch, a mousy little French-woman dressed in black who never spoke, a bald American man, possibly Mrs. Rausch's husband, the Colonel Teape who had been in the Frott Gallery just before Blore-Smith's arrival there, Schlumbermayer, whom Blore-Smith recognised at once; and two or three others, at the far end of the table, amorphous entities whom Blore-Smith was unable to distinguish one from another. Chipchase took his place among these last.

Pauline de Borodino sat at the head of the table, a tremendous

Rowlandsonesque Catherine the Great or Maria Theresa. She had a bottle of champagne in each hand and was filling all the glasses within her orbit. Whilst she did this she talked to Blore-Smith, who was thinking that never before in all his life had he seen anything like her.

'How long are you over here? It's so awfully nice of you to come to-night. I expect you know Paris well. I wonder why we have never met before. Do try some of this champagne. It's a special brand that I make them keep here for me. Have you known Oliver Chipchase long? Do you want a stick to take the fizz out? What do you think of it? It's dry isn't it, in the English way? He is a very old friend of mine. Do you know Peter Maltravers too?'

'Yes, I do. He and I are going to produce an uncommercial film together.'

Blore-Smith suddenly felt that he wanted to tell her all about his life.

'A film? You are going to produce a film with Peter? But how exciting.'

'I think it's going to be called *Œdipus Rex.*'

'Divine.'

The Duchesse talked such fluent English that it was almost impossible for Blore-Smith to remember that she was a foreigner.

'And Oliver is taking part in the film too?' she said.

'Well he may be,' Blore-Smith said. 'He's my psychoanalyst now, you see.'

'Ah?'

'He's an awfully good psychoanalyst.'

Blore-Smith had begun to feel strangely sentimental about Chipchase, and indeed about all the other people at the table or even in the room.

'Awfully good,' he repeated, sipping his champagne.

Glancing round he thought he had never seen so many pretty women collected together in so small a space. He was drinking in this uncommon vision when he became aware that Colonel Teape was staring hard at him. Blore-Smith gulped some more champagne to steady himself, because in spite of his high spirits Colonel Teape's eye had made him falter.

'Over for long?' Colonel Teape said, moving aside some bottles to get a better view.

'Just a short time.'

'Business?'

'Well—yes—at least I don't know whether you would call it business. I'm really over here to—to break some of my barriers down, if you know what I mean.'

Colonel Teape took a single eye-glass from his pocket and began to polish it with his silk handkerchief as if he wanted to make a more expert assessment of Blore-Smith's appearance than was possible after even prolonged staring with the naked eye.

'H'm,' he said. 'You're going to break down some barriers, are you? And where do you propose to do that?'

'I don't know. You see I am in the hands of my psychoanalyst.'

'And who may he be?'

With his eyes Blore-Smith indicated Chipchase, who was at the far end of the table, talking to a dark girl to whom Blore-Smith had not yet been introduced. Colonel Teape turned his eye-glass in Chipchase's direction. He watched him for some seconds and said:

'Your psychoanalyst seems to be breaking down a few barriers for himself at the moment, doesn't he?'

Blore-Smith did not wish to commit himself so he only smiled. Colonel Teape smiled too. Indulgently, Blore-Smith thought.

'You must come out with me one night,' Colonel Teape said, 'on a barrier-breaking expedition.'

'I should like to very much. It is very kind of you to suggest it.'

'Give me your address before we part to-night.'

'Certainly.'

A cabaret turn had now begun. A young oriental in mauve spangled tights was swinging about on a sort of trapeze that had been lowered from the ceiling.

'He's a splendid little fellow, isn't he?' said Colonel Teape.

Blore-Smith agreed that he was.

'He's called Aziz,' Colonel Teape said. 'We might go round and see him later.'

'Is he always here?'

'Yes. One finds beauty in strange places.'

'I suppose one does.'

The turn came to an end and Aziz withdrew after much applause. The Marquis de la Tour d'Espagne suddenly began to blow on a tin trumpet which he had produced unexpectedly from his pocket. Having drawn the necessary attention to himself in this way, he said:

'And now we will all go *Chez Zouzou. Allons.* Do you like that, Pauline?'

'*Il reste encore une bouteille, Gaston.*'

When they had finished it everyone made a move from the table and down the stairs.

The second taxi, which contained the negro, Mrs. Rausch, Colonel Teape, and the Duchesse, was the one into which Blore-Smith was hustled. As they drove along he felt someone pressing with great weight on his left foot just where he had a small corn. It was either Mrs. Rausch or the colonel. Which, he could not tell. At moments the pain was intense. Blore-Smith bore it in silence because he thought that the journey would not be a long one. He was mistaken in this, and it seemed an interminable age before the taxi stopped in front of a house near what Blore-Smith supposed to be the other end of Paris. Above the door was an electric sign, appearing and disappearing, on which were the words, '*Chez Zouzou.*' Along the street were other and similar signs. An old woman sat on a chair outside the entrance and mumbled some greeting to them.

'I'm getting sober, aren't you?' Mrs. Rausch said to Blore-Smith as they went in.

In this new wonderland red plush and gold provided the ascendant note in the general scheme of *décor*. A later hand had added some frescoes on the panels of the walls and door, more than life-size, executed in a light stipple of pastel shades, and conceived in a spirit of complete moral detachment. These frescoes so startled Blore-Smith that at first he was unable to prevent himself from staring at them, but as none of the rest of the party seemed to consider them in any way unusual as mural decoration he did not mention his surprise. This, indeed, was to some extent vitiated a short time later by his realisation of the appearance of the ladies present, of whom there were a great number. A few of these were in evening dress, but many seemed equipped for sun-bathing by the informality of what they wore. They sat about in groups of two and three, and some of them, because the room was certainly overheated, had lifted up their frocks well above their knees. At present there was no sign of Chipchase and the rest of the supper-party. The Duchesse led the way to a table and in a few minutes she was surrounded by buckets containing champagne, without which her background seemed incomplete. Blore-Smith was by this time experiencing the curious sensation of being dissociated almost physically from the life around him. It was as if he were sitting with his chair a yard or more off the floor. This sensation was increased perceptibly by the sounds that all at once burst out from a mechanical piano, which began to play *Valentine*.

'Here,' said the Duchesse. 'Have some wine, *mon cher*.'

'Why look,' said Mrs. Rausch. 'If that isn't Yvonne and Lulu.'

She pointed towards two girls who were waving from the other side of the room.

'So it is.'

Mrs. Rausch and the Duchesse jumped up and made their way across the room. Colonel Teape said:

'You know, between you and me, I don't care very much for this sort of place. It's Pauline who has these full-blooded tastes. I don't know why we couldn't have stayed at the old *Vache*.'

'Where are the others?'

'They will be along in a minute. I hope they bring Aziz with them. I told Gaston to ask him to join the party when his turn was over.'

'Who are the ladies the Duchesse is talking to?'

'Two American lizzies.'

'Oh.'

'Look here,' said Colonel Teape. 'I think I'll just take a turn up the street to have a word with Charley at the *Bar des Matelots*. If Aziz should turn up, tell him I'll be back in a minute.'

'All right.'

Colonel Teape picked his way through the room and Blore-Smith was left alone at the table with the negro, who grinned at him and showed his teeth in an alarming manner.

'May I pass you the wine?' said Blore-Smith, who felt full of friendly feeling to everyone, no matter what their pigmentation.

The negro said: 'Sure, you may pass me the wine, suh.'

Blore-Smith watched the negro drink a glass or two more of champagne, give a series of contortions with his hips and shoulders as if he were about to have a fit, and then jump up from his chair. For a moment the negro looked wildly round him and then, jerking his elbows and knees violently this way and that, he crossed the floor and was soon dancing with a tiny Jewish blonde. Blore-Smith was left alone at the table. The Duchesse and Mrs. Rausch had settled down, as if for ever, with Yvonne and Lulu. There was no sign of Chipchase.

Blore-Smith had never felt so benevolent. The room's bright colours seemed a trifle blurred to his eye and at times he found it difficult to focus on certain objects that attracted his attention; but all the same he had the sensation of being at peace with himself and with everyone else all round him. He became lost in reverie so thoroughly that it was several minutes before he noticed that someone else had come to sit at his table.

'*Eh bien, mon petit, tu penses* . . . ?'

She was a plump little creature with an Eton crop, who reminded him slightly of Sarah Maltravers. She took one of the bottles of champagne out of its bucket and began to wipe it with the napkin. Blore-Smith tried to collect his thoughts.

'*Tu permis?*'

'Why, yes. *Oui, oui.* At least, it really isn't mine. *Ce n'est pas à moi, vous savez,* but do have some all the same.'

The girl laughed and poured out a glass for herself and another for him.

'*Une cigarette?*'

Blore-Smith fumbled for his case, trying to remember whether or not this lady had been in the Duchesse's party.

'*On m'appelle* Yoyo,' she said.

'Oh, yes, I see. *Je comprends.*'

She took the box of matches from him after he had lighted her cigarette and wrote YOYO with matches on the table in front of him.

'*Charmante,*' Blore-Smith managed to say.

He realised now that she had not been one of the supper-party and he began to feel some embarrassment at the thought of Colonel Teape, due back any moment from his visit to the *Bar des Matelots*, finding him sitting with an unknown woman. He felt that Colonel Teape would be displeased by such a thing. He looked such a gentleman of the old school, and he had already expressed disapproval of the environment *Chez Zouzou*. It was for this reason that when Yoyo suggested, or seemed to suggest, that they should leave the table and explore the other rooms in the house he agreed to do so. He only intended to stay away from the mechanical piano for a few minutes because it was inclined to make his head throb more than was pleasant. He never intended to avoid deliberately the company of the Duchesse, Chipchase, and the rest of them. It never crossed his mind that he could do such a thing even if he had wanted to. Perhaps Yoyo worked the whole thing, even to helping him up the stairs. Afterwards he was never able to remember.

On the stairs he felt very happy. Yoyo was the nicest girl he had ever met and in many ways astonishingly like Sarah Maltravers.

They went up several flights of stairs and Blore-Smith found that the upper stories of this house resembled in some respects an hotel. An hotel, in fact, without anything to recommend it. The room they were shown into by a maid with only one eye was small and worse than stuffy. It contained a red divan, a screen, and some domestic fittings. At any other time Blore-Smith, shy as he was, would have made a fuss. Even now he felt that this accommodation was vaguely distasteful but he did not want to hurt Yoyo's feelings. Besides this the usual processes of time seemed suspended. They had spent an untold age getting here but now they had arrived matters became astonishingly speeded up.

Yoyo told him about her brother-in-law. Her brother-in-law wrote novels. The novels were in the style of Pierre Loti. He found it difficult, for some reason, to place them with a publisher. It seemed that he had written three novels in this style and none of them had been placed. Yet her brother-in-law was not discouraged. He believed in himself. Blore-Smith said that that was what mattered: to believe in one's self. Yoyo was the nicest girl he had ever met.

Later, months later, when he could look back in cold blood on the episode, Blore-Smith felt that the real mistake had been his falling asleep. But somehow an unspeakable drowsiness had overcome him, even though he could see that Yoyo was putting on her shoes. An intolerable heaviness against which it seemed idle to contend. He lay back and lost consciousness, with his head hanging over the edge of the red divan.

When Blore-Smith woke he was extremely cold. He rolled over on to the floor and, getting up, found his way to the window. Through the glass he saw rows and rows of grey houses with shuttered windows. The sun was rising behind these roofs which sloped away steeply below him. For a time he contemplated this district which he believed to be Montmartre. Then he turned back towards the room. Yoyo had gone. Through the wall on one side he heard snoring and on the other a whispered conversation. Blore-Smith dressed and went down the stairs. As he passed the lower landing he saw the one-eyed maid watching him through a *guichet*. He went quickly on down the stairs and found a small side door opening on to the street. Outside the air was full of a strange musty fragrance that he had never smelt before in any other town. He hurried through several narrow streets and came to a wide boulevard with tram-lines. A taxi cruised past. Blore-Smith shouted, 'Taxi! Taxi!'

When he got back to the little hotel on the Left Bank he found that his notecase was missing. There was enough small change in his trouser pocket to cover the fare and he felt too far gone to mind much about the loss. He stumbled up to his room and fell on to the bed.

The sounds which had been penetrating his consciousness for some minutes were clearer now and resolved themselves from a merely random acoustic nuisance to the active torment of words and music.

> *Elle avait un tout petit menton,*
> *Valentine, Valentine . . .*
> *Elle avait de tout petits tétons*
> *Que je tâtais à tâtons . . .*

At first, when he turned over, Blore-Smith thought that he was going to die. The agony of movement, the strange dryness in his throat, and the fact that he was still wearing his underclothes all pointed to some sudden and fatal seizure. The blinds of the bedroom were not drawn and the sunlight was playing on his face. The room looked out on to a well and it was from the well's depths that the boots or some other employee of the hotel was, like the statue of Memnon, greeting the dawn with a song. Blore-Smith shut his eyes and felt the bed slowly revolving on its own axis beneath him; from left to right; and then up and down.

'*Que je tâtais à tâtons . . . Valentine,*' fairly yelled the boots.

Blore-Smith tried to remember why the song was so familiar. For some time he lay like this, hoping that the end would come quickly. Never in his life before had he felt in such a state. His parched throat drove him at last out of bed. He almost fell to the ground. He managed to reach the washstand, where a bottle of Vichy stood, already opened, but still containing a little water. He drank this and broke out into a cold sweat. He sponged his face and lay down again on the bed. Later, looking at his watch, he saw that it was nearly lunch-time.

Slowly he put on his dressing-gown and made his way along the passages to Chipchase's room, which was on the floor above his own. He wondered with horror what he would do if Chipchase should turn out not to be there. He reached the door and knocked.

'*Entrez.*'

Blore-Smith heard Chipchase's voice with enormous relief. He stood for a moment on the threshold, trying to pull himself together. Then he opened the door and went in.

He stopped, petrified, staring at the bed. It seemed that in the night Chipchase had been turned by some fearful thaumaturgy into a woman.

A closer examination of the circumstances revealed that Chipchase was standing by the looking-glass, holding a tumbler in his hand, while the person in bed was a dark-haired girl who was drinking a cup of coffee. Chipchase turned towards the door.

'Come in,' he said. 'How are you feeling?'

Blore-Smith was unable to do more than stand and stare at the bed.

'This is Caroline,' Chipchase said.

Blore-Smith tried to speak but found himself unable to do so. Instead he sat down heavily on a chair.

'You don't look well,' Chipchase said. 'Will you have some Eno's?'

'Yes.'

Chipchase poured out the white powder into the palm of his hand and from there into a tooth-glass. He held this towards Blore-Smith.

'What happened to you last night?' he said.

'I can't tell you. I want to go back to England.'

'Where?'

'To England. To England!'

'At once?'

'Yes. As soon as possible.'

'But why? There are lots more things you ought to do here in the way of widening your outlook. The Louvre. Versailles. The Musée Carnavalet.'

'No there aren't. I want to get away at once.'

Chipchase took the tumbler from Blore-Smith's hands, rinsed it out, and began to fill it with mouthwash.

'But this is absurd,' he said.

'I can't stand it. I can't stand it, really. Come back to my room and I'll tell you about it.'

'Well, all right, if you wish,' Chipchase said. 'Are you ready to make a move to England, Caroline?'

'I suppose so, if that's where everyone wants to go,' said the girl, who all this time had been drinking her coffee and eating a brioche. She brushed her hair away from her face and smiled happily at Blore-Smith.

'I'm frightfully ill,' Blore-Smith said.

'So am I,' said Chipchase. 'Frightfully ill. I haven't often felt worse.'

He threw back his head and began to gargle.

'But I mean really ill.'

'So do I. What did you think I meant? A little food will put us right.'

'I can't possibly touch food.'

'You'd better try a little. Something really tempting. I know a place where the *pâté maison* is excellent.'

'Do come to my room,' Blore-Smith said. 'I can't tell you everything here.'

He felt near to tears.

'All right. I'll be along in a minute.'

Blore-Smith returned along the passage and lay once more on the bed. This was the last straw. He lay on his face, trying to make his mind a blank. He was still in this position when Chipchase came in. Blore-Smith did not look up. He heard Chipchase walk across the room to the window, open it, and take several deep breaths.

'Have you ever noticed,' Chipchase said, 'that after a thick evening it is always very difficult to shave properly? The hairs seem to recede under one's razor.'

Blore-Smith made an effort and sat upright on the bed. He was feeling very near the end now.

'Listen,' he said. 'This is what happened to me.'

He told Chipchase about *Chez Zouzou*. Chipchase sat on the edge of the bidet, nodding his head at appropriate moments.

'And now,' said Blore-Smith, bringing the general trend of the narrative to a close, 'I can't find my pocket-book. Somebody must have stolen it.'

'How much was there in there?'

'About a thousand francs.'

'Well, well,' said Chipchase. 'Well, well.'

'Do you think that it was stolen?'

'Of course. Unless in a moment of generosity you presented her with it.'

'I'—for a moment confused memories of a prodigal impulse clouded Blore-Smith's mind—'I can't have done.'

'Well there it is.'

'But it's dreadful.'

'Do you know what it's called?' said Chipchase. 'It's known in certain circles as *buying experience*. Now you see how sensible it was of me to insist on taking charge of the letter of credit you brought with you. But don't you worry any more. Accept my heartiest congratulations.'

'Whatever for?'

'Don't you feel much better?'

'I never felt so awful in my life.'

'Never mind what you feel like now. You've your life before you. As I said before, I'm feeling far from well myself. You can't expect to feel well after drinking even a small quantity of the filthy champagne they supply at those places.'

A wave of illness, a sensation of burning in his cheeks and of nausea welling up from within him, passed over Blore-Smith, spurring him to profound irritation.

'And who is this woman?' he said.

'Which woman?'

'The one in your room.'

'I've told you. She's called Caroline. A very old friend of mine. Incidentally I met her coming into the *Vache enragée* just as we were going out. That was why I didn't show up at *Chez Zouzou*. We spent the evening together. She's been here for a week or two on a job. She's a trained student of psychoanalysis and she can do typing and shorthand too. She will be invaluable in my treatment of you in committing to paper reports on your state and so on. The additional expense will be very slight.'

'But do you expect me to pay for her?'

'Well you can't expect me, out of my meagre income, to pay for your own mental and subconscious treatment, can you?' Chipchase said, rather testily.

Blore-Smith rose up suddenly from the bed, moving in the direction of the basin. Chipchase stepped aside and turned again to the open window, through which he leant and inspected the street below. Some minutes later he withdrew his head and said:

'I expect you are feeling easier now.'

'I must insist on going back to England as soon as possible,' Blore-Smith managed to say.

'All right. If you really want to. Mind you, I concur only because I am so delighted to see you take a firm line about matters.'

'When can we go?'

Chipchase looked at his watch.

'We should just be able to catch the afternoon plane,' he said.

'Oh, no, I can't do that!'

'But you said as soon as possible.'

'I'm sorry. Can't we start to-morrow?'

'That would certainly be more convenient. Caroline will want to collect her things from her flat.'

'What? Is she coming too?'

'I've already told you that she is engaged as my secretary to help me in my treatment of your highly complicated state. You must try not to give way to these resistance compulsions. Of course it shows that the treatment is taking effect, and, so long as you realise that, it is all right. It is, however, important that you should convince yourself of the na-ture of the difficulties you seem so anxious to put in my way.'

'Then we go to-morrow?'

'If you really wish it. We ought to pay a call on Pauline de Boro-dino and thank her for her delightful party.'

'Must I come too?'

'Perhaps I might do that in the morning and we could fly back in the afternoon.'

'I can't go in an aeroplane so soon again.'

'Really,' said Chipchase, 'you are making things very difficult. In that case we will travel by one of the later boats. Will that suit you?'

'I suppose so.'

'And now you must dress and come out. We are having lunch with Schlumbermayer. Food will do you a lot of good. Remember that I have your interests at heart. Pull yourself together and come to the *Deux Magots*. You remember the café? I showed you where it was yesterday. Caroline and I will be sitting there.'

Chipchase half-lifted Blore-Smith from the bed and began to remove his dressing-gown. Blore-Smith struggled feebly, muttering that he would be along at the café as soon as possible.

'Very well,' said Chipchase. 'I will go and drive that slut out of bed.'

He left the room, slamming the door.

After the soup Blore-Smith refused to eat any more. The others did not press him and he sat back, watching the rest of the luncheon-party as through a mist, sometimes catching snatches of their conversation, but more often hearing the words as if they were part of the irregular buzzing of insects in a garden, the heat of the restaurant providing an additional illusion of high summer. Schlumbermayer sat immediately in front of him, and, although his outline was from time to time obscured by clumps of black spots that would appear suddenly to block Blore-Smith's line of vision, his general aspect and personality conveyed themselves with some force across the table. He was about forty-five, tall and getting fat, with greyish hair and a short black moustache. He wore a black suit, no hat, and carried a stick. He spoke seldom, leaving most of the conversation to Chipchase; but he continually eyed Caroline through thick spectacles with steel rims. Blore-Smith thought that he had the largest nose he had ever seen.

'And so Gaston is coming over to stay at Broadacres some time this summer?' Chipchase said.

Schlumbermayer started slightly and said:

'Just for a short time he may be.'

'I don't expect it will be for a short time when he gets there.'

Schlumbermayer laughed uneasily and began moving about the knives and forks. He had a fleshy face that arranged itself in folds and was the colour of an old document. Upsetting the French mustard-pot, he said:

'Why not come down for a few days at the same time? You and Gaston always seem to get on pretty well together, and I want him to enjoy himself.'

'We should like to enormously,' Chipchase said. 'Shouldn't we, Caroline? But there is this point. Would you mind extending the invitation to Mr. Blore-Smith here? You see he really needs my treatment all the time.'

Schlumbermayer turned his glasses on to Blore-Smith and looked him over suspiciously.

'It's very quiet down at Broadacres,' he said slowly. 'There is nothing much to do there.'

'Oh, he doesn't expect a party like the one we had last night all the time,' Chipchase said. 'You like being quiet sometimes, don't you?'

Blore-Smith found that he was just able to nod his head without prejudicing his physical state.

'Of course he does,' said Chipchase. 'None of us want to be racketing round all the time. It's very kind of you to ask us. I'm sure it will be very enjoyable.'

'As I say,' said Schlumbermayer, addressing himself to Blore-Smith. 'As I say, there is nothing to do there and so I don't know how you will amuse yourself.'

He contrived to look so menacing when he said this that Blore-Smith was startled into saying:

'I should like very much to stay, but I'm afraid that we shall be in the middle of taking our film.'

'I was coming to that,' Chipchase said sharply. 'Don't be in so much of a hurry.'

Blore-Smith lay back in his chair and Schlumbermayer, still morose, said:

'What film is this?'

'A psychoanalytical film,' Chipchase said. 'Nothing less.'

'What is that?'

'You will see when it is produced.'

'Who is doing it?'

Chipchase nodded his head in the direction of Blore-Smith.

'In connection with Maltravers,' he said.

'Peter Maltravers?'

'Who else?'

Schlumbermayer pressed his lips together and raised his eyebrows. Then he moved his head from side to side with slow regularity as if he were a human metronome. He said:

'Where is it going to be taken?'

'That depends.'

'What on?'

'Several things. It must be, for example, a place where the psychological state of my friend here will be in suitable surroundings. We've got to find the right house. If we are coming to stay with you in the summer, we might look about in your own neighbourhood.'

'Will you rent the house?'

'Goodness, no. That won't be necessary. You see, the film will get so much publicity that many people will be only too glad to have the advertisement of making their house into a film studio.'

'Do you think so?'

'I know it.'

There was a long pause. Then Schlumbermayer, after spitting from his mouth a number of grape-skins, said:

'Look here, I'm going to give you a surprise. I'm going to suggest that you all come down and take the film at Broadacres.'

He pushed back his chair and, putting both his fists on the table, beamed at Chipchase.

'It's awfully kind of you, but I'm not at all sure that a previous offer will not have to be considered first,' Chipchase said.

Schlumbermayer's face fell.

'Oh, come on. After all, we've known each other for a long time. Why not come to Broadacres? I'm asking you as a favour.'

'I'm not sure that it's quite the house.'

Schlumbermayer leant forward wheedlingly across the table. He said:

'But you couldn't have more room. It's an absolute barrack. And there's plenty of space in the grounds. Do come.'

'Of course if you ever wanted to sell the place it would be famous all over England after the film was released.'

'It's not that.'

'Why should it be such a good turn then?'

'I want Gaston to stay there until all our negotiations go through. They may take some time. Something like that going on might keep Gaston quiet while we transact business.'

'While you buy his pictures and furniture?'

'Exactly.'

'I see what you mean,' Chipchase said. He stroked his chin. 'Then I may take it as fixed that I can discuss the matter further with Mr. Blore-Smith when his health is better, and with Maltravers—with the object in view of making Broadacres our headquarters?'

'Yes.'

The rest of lunch passed without incident. Afterwards Chipchase and Caroline set out in the direction of the bus which would take them to the Bois. Blore-Smith, on his way back to the hotel, where he proposed to lie down, walked beside Schlumbermayer. At the end of the street Schlumbermayer waved his stick to a taxi.

'I have to see relations in Passy,' he said. 'You had better have my card in case you want to get in touch with me about the film.'

He handed a card to Blore-Smith and got into the taxi. As the taxi began to move, Blore-Smith ran forward and said:

'But this card says *Mr. Joseph Simpson*, and there's no address.'

The taxi stopped. Schlumbermayer leant out.

'Oh, does it?' he said. 'I must have given you the wrong one.' He fumbled in his notecase and handed out another card, which was inscribed *Mr. E. E. Schlumbermayer. The Bibelot Club. S.W.*

'The others sometimes come in useful,' he said, and laughed angrily. Then he banged on the glass to make the taxi move forward again. Blore-Smith put the new card in his pocket and found his way to the hotel.

3

Maltravers opened the front door, and, after stepping out into the square and looking up and down it, followed Chipchase up the stairs and into the sitting-room.

'I passed three people with goitre this morning,' Maltravers said. 'I thought I'd just glance round the neighbourhood to see if there were any more about.'

Chipchase examined the invitations in the looking-glass. He said: 'Why am I asked to none of these? And who is this?'

'I don't expect you know her,' said Maltravers, taking the snapshot from him and putting it in his pocket. 'On second thoughts I think it may be better undisplayed. But now tell me all about Paris. Why have you returned immediately? I leave for Berlin at the end of next week. No hitch of any kind, I hope?'

'On the contrary.'

Maltravers listened, filling his pipe, while Chipchase described the Paris trip.

'Where is he now?' he said, at the end of Chipchase's narrative.

'He's retired to bed, and says he isn't going to get up for two or three days.'

'Any specific malady?'

'No. A sort of general protest against what he has undergone.'

'The best place for him,' said Maltravers. 'He'll get up feeling a new man.'

'That was what I told him. The other important thing is that Gaston de la Tour d'Espagne is coming over to stay with Schlumbermayer, who wants to buy most of his pictures and furniture as Gaston is broke and is selling up. Schlumbermayer has invited you to make your film at Broadacres.'

'What in heaven's name has induced him to do that?'

'He thinks that a film studio on the premises will keep Gaston quiet. It's good that, isn't it?'

'Good? It's absolutely superb. Quite apart from anything else, we ought to be able to get some revealing psychological shots of Schlumbermayer and Gaston bargaining together.'

'That hadn't occurred to me, as it happens, but it has immense possibilities, I can see at once.'

'I shall go to Berlin feeling much easier now that is fixed,' Maltravers said. 'I don't think there is any hurry for you and him to come out there. Give him a long rest. You can have a look round the place and then come back to England and we can take the film with summer well begun.'

'And then I've brought a secretary back from Paris.'

'Indeed?'

'She's called Caroline.'

'Not——?'

'Yes.'

'Tell me how it happened.'

'Well,' said Chipchase, 'if you don't mind a rather long story, it was after we all left the *Vache enragée* . . .'

Although the sulkiness which he had felt during the Channel crossing lasted until the day after his arrival in London, where he went straight to bed, Blore-Smith found that he was soon able to face the world again and that Chipchase had been right in his prediction. He surprised himself by his own awareness that he was in the best of form. Paris in retrospect had become not so much a bad dream as the memory of a refining experience. An ordeal by torture which he had survived. He could see some of its episodes as having even a funny side. He rang up Chipchase, intending to ask him round. The voice that answered the telephone he recognised as Caroline's, and for a moment he experienced a recrudescence of his former horror. Pulling himself together he asked if Chipchase was in, and was told that he was already on his way to Ebury Street.

'How are you liking your work?' Blore-Smith said.

'I've been spending the morning typing out the notes on some of your dreams in Oliver's case-book.'

'What do you think of the reports?'

He could not hear whether Caroline said, 'Very full,' or, 'Very foul,' and, not liking to ask her to repeat herself, he said good-bye and rang off.

While he waited for Chipchase to arrive he found that his talk with Caroline had made him think again of Sarah Maltravers. Dimly at the back of his mind he had the impression that all this thinking about her was going to result in his developing a definite attitude to some problem that had been troubling him for a long time. He was still trying to collate his mental images when Chipchase arrived. Blore-Smith jumped up to meet him.

'You were quite right,' he said. 'I feel ever so much better now.'

'I said you would.'

'I'm awfully glad we went to Paris. Really I am.'

'Now look here,' said Chipchase, reaching across for the cigarette box. 'I'm very pleased to hear this, but you mustn't think that because you feel like a million dollars now, life is nothing more than staying up late and gadding about to night-clubs and giving treats to gay women. It's nothing of the sort, I can assure you. You must buckle down to something serious now that you are back in London, otherwise you will soon find yourself getting depressed again.'

'Oh, I never thought——'

'Maltravers starts for Berlin at the end of next week. When the film is launched it will provide just the right sort of mental occupation at your present stage of development.'

'I'm looking forward to it very much.'

'In the meantime we will continue treatment along the prescribed lines, and I should recommend some quiet intellectual occupation for your mind.'

'Shall I go on collecting pictures?'

Chipchase covered his eyes in thought for a few moments.

'I think, if I were you, I would avoid the dealers,' he said. 'Go to the public galleries and take some notes.'

'Why not small shows?'

'You never know who you may meet at places like the Frott.'

'There was something else'—Blore-Smith hesitated—'I wanted to ask you——'

'Go on.'

'There's a woman——'

'Yes?'

'A married woman I know——'

'Well?'

'Her husband doesn't spend much of his time with her——'

'Some husbands don't.'

'I rather like her——'

'Why not?'

'She's often alone——'

'Too bad. She ought to make some nice friends.'

'Yes, that's what I mean. Well I wondered——'

'Now look here,' said Chipchase. 'I'm not altogether following all this. There is a married woman, whom you know and like, whose husband doesn't spend much time with her so that she is sometimes lonely. What else?'

'Do you think I might—well—become friends with her myself?'

'Ah,' said Chipchase. 'I see.'

He shook his head and stroked his chin. He was looking in better health after the Paris trip, but was still pale.

'You really feel like that about it, do you?' he said.

'I think so.'

'Are you sure?'

'Practically.'

'Well my advice is, be careful. Very careful.'

'But you think I might—well—try? You see I seem to feel somehow different after—after Paris.'

'So I gather.'

'So what do you think?'

'Does she live with her husband?'

'He sometimes goes abroad.'

'For long?'

'I don't know exactly.'

'The important thing in matters of this kind,' said Chipchase, 'is to think it out for yourself. Nothing would be more absurd than for you to importune a married woman simply because I advised it. If you want the best results you must decide for yourself.'

'I suppose I ought to have thought of that first?'

'No, no. It does no harm to tell me these things. In fact it is all for the best that you should. The important point is that the ultimate decision should rest with you. After all, matters were left entirely in your own hands in Paris, and look what a success you made of them.'

'Yes,' said Blore-Smith, and he could not help a note of pride creeping into his voice. 'Yes.'

'I must take down a short account of this conversation,' Chipchase said, opening his notebook, 'because it may have direct bearing on other aspects of your case. When I have done that we will continue the treatment along the usual line. Have you had any more dreams about the Prime Minister of the kind you had the week before last?'

Later on in the afternoon Chipchase pushed open the door of *la cattleya*. Scrubb was sitting behind the counter with a pile of books in front of him. He was a high-shouldered sour-faced young man whose skin went red in patches whenever anyone spoke to him. He peered at Chipchase from behind a pot of yellow tulips that stood beside him.

'Mendie is out, I suppose?' Chipchase said.

Scrubb put down Eden and Holland's *Manual of Midwifery* and took off his pince-nez.

'She will be back soon,' he said. 'If she isn't the shop will be left without anyone to look after it, unless you care to take the job on, because I've got a date with a jane at five o'clock.'

'I wouldn't have thought it of you,' Chipchase said, 'but I don't mind taking charge for a bit if you tell me what everything costs.'

'There's a list of prices she wrote out for me in the drawer. You're just back from Paris, aren't you?'

'In a manner of speaking.'

'Do any good?'

'I always do good.'

'You know what I mean.'

'On the contrary.'

'Yes you do.'

Scrubb came from behind the counter.

'Any nice little bits of skirt?' he said, at close range.

Chipchase shuddered, and said:

'You'd be surprised.'

As if to loosen it, Scrubb pulled at his already unduly grubby collar.

'If I had the money to go to Paris,' he said.

Chipchase walked across the shop away from Scrubb to a vase of madonna lilies, and, thrusting his face forward, inhaled deeply. He said, after some minutes:

'I hope, for your sake, you never will.'

Scrubb, who had by now returned to his seat, put his feet up on the counter. He tipped recklessly backwards.

'Not that I have to go as far as Paris,' he said.

'No?'

'They're after me all the time.'

'The police?'

'The hotsies.'

'Are they, are they?'

'I should rather say so.'

'Accept my congratulations.'

'I remember the first time,' Scrubb said reflectively. 'Everyone else always tells me they were petrified. Do you know I didn't give that?'

He snapped his fingers.

'You showed great fortitude.'

'It was just like the first operation I was on,' Scrubb said. 'Two of the younger students fainted. Another was sick out of the window. Do you know what I thought?'

'You've got me guessing.'

'Meat.'

'Was that so?'

'That was all it was to me.'

'Ah?'

'Take gallstones, for instance——'

'No, please not.'

There was a pause. Chipchase picked up Ross's *Post-Mortem Appearances*, and glanced through it quickly to see if there were any pictures. He said:

'It's getting on for five o'clock. I mustn't make you late.'

'Here's Mendie, anyway.'

Mrs. Mendoza, holding several parcels, came into the shop hurriedly. Scrubb began to gather up his books. He said:

'I'm off now. Here's the list of people who telephoned, Mendie. They all said that you had specially told them that you would be at home if they called you up this afternoon.'

Mrs. Mendoza snatched the list from him and said: 'Hell.' Scrubb took *Post-Mortem Appearances* away from Chipchase and shambled off and up the stairs towards his room. Chipchase said:

'When are you going to give that deplorable young man notice?'

Mrs. Mendoza looked up.

'Oh, hullo,' she said. 'Do you mean Scrubby-wub? He is a bit awful, isn't he? Still he's rather sweet sometimes.'

'No he isn't. He's horrible. You must get rid of him. Why not poison him? With a scented flower.'

'All right, darling, I will. Just to please you. And how was the *ville lumière*?'

'Not bad.'

'How are you and Peter getting on with your new boy friend?'

'Admirably.'

'You're both so secretive about him. He's becoming one of London's mysteries. No one ever talks of anyone else.'

'Why all this interest?'

'You both seem so determined to keep him for yourselves.'

'Oh, nonsense. He's very neurotic. You shall see him when his condition has improved a bit. But what intrigues you so? Isn't the Commodore pulling his weight? No Nelson touch?'

'We may be going to Paris for a week or so soon.'

'Come to Berlin. It's far gayer in these days. We are all going there.'

'Who does that include?'

'Peter, myself, and our—what shall I call him?—our patient.'

'What about your new secretary?'

'Ah-ha? So you know about her too. You are well-informed. Well, since you ask, Caroline is not coming with us.'

'Nor Sarah?'

'Nor Sarah.'

'I might consider a change of plans. Paris with Hugo would be deadly, I'm sure.'

'Bring him to Berlin. It would broaden him.'

Mrs. Mendoza sighed.

'Don't let's go on standing here, anyway,' she said, and Chipchase followed her through the curtain to the back of the shop.

Sarah Maltravers stood on the pavement for a few seconds, watching Nipper's Bentley, borrowed from a friend of his in the motor business, disappear round the corner. Nipper turned and waved to her just before he went out of sight, and she blew a kiss after him. Then she got into her own car, which was parked a short way from the entrance to the track, and drove in the direction of her home. Her driving style was modelled on that of her husband, but she had added certain mannerisms of her own to this notably uncommonplace handling and she shot quickly in and out of the traffic, barking out little crepitations of censure when pedestrians or tradesmen's vans did not get quickly enough out of her way. When she reached the garage she spent some time conferring with the garage-hands. After they had sufficiently discussed her own car, and also the new Chrysler that had been brought in for repairs that afternoon, she walked across the square to the flat, planning out the article on continental car models which she was going to write that evening. In the flat she took off her airman's helmet, her goggles, her gauntlets, her leather overcoat, and her leather jumper, without which essential minimum she never attempted to drive a car. After giving the cats some milk, she settled down at one of the type-writers.

It was about half an hour later that the telephone bell rang. Sarah took up the receiver.

'Hullo?' she said.

Her voice sounded enchanting to Blore-Smith, who was at the other end of the line. He felt all at once so nervous that he wished he had never initiated the call. He would have rung off immediately if he had had the presence of mind to do so, but instead he introduced himself, muttering that he supposed that Sarah did not remember who he was.

'But of course I do,' said Sarah. 'How absurd of you to say that. Why haven't you come to see me?'

This question left Blore-Smith at a loss for a reply, because he could think of no good reason why he had abstained from visiting someone to whom he had taken so great a fancy, except that he had felt too nervous to take the initiative. He did not like to admit this to Sarah herself, so after a second's thought, intending to suggest that he should come and see her then and there, he said:

'What are you doing now?'

'I'm writing an article on French bodies,' Sarah said.

'French what?'

Blore-Smith could hardly believe his ears. Had Chipchase been spreading scandals behind his back, and were Sarah's words intended to convey an oblique reproach to him for his way of life? It was only too possible. He began to tremble all over.

'Bodies,' Sarah shouted down the line. 'Bodies. What did you think I said? Car bodies. Don't you know that I am motoring correspondent for *Mode*?'

'Yes, yes. Of course, you told me.'

'Of course I did. It's the thing in my life I'm most proud of.'

'It's—it's a great achievement,' said Blore-Smith. He had made a fool of himself again.

'Why don't you come in and have a drink this evening? It's rather a long way for you, that's the only thing.'

Blore-Smith pulled himself together with an effort. He said:

'I really rang up to know if you would dine with me to-night?'

'I'd like to very much.'

'Will you really?'

'What time? Can you come and pick me up here? Don't come before seven and then I can get this thing finished.'

'Your bodies?' said Blore-Smith, who had begun to feel quite jocular now that matters seemed to be going so easily.

'Yes,' said Sarah. 'My bodies. Good-bye, my dear. I'll see you later.'

Blore-Smith pushed the telephone away from him, and, jumping up, began to pace the room. Now that the step was taken there were a thousand things in connection with offering hospitality to a woman of Sarah's sort, if indeed there were others like her, about which he knew himself to be entirely ignorant. Many of these uncertainties could have been settled by a few discreet enquiries before embarking on such a venture. He made up his mind that this was the last time that he would take such a plunge without previously thinking out every detail of procedure. After much reflection he decided that he would not wear evening clothes. He hoped that Sarah herself could be persuaded to suggest the name of a restaurant that she liked. Wild visions of hitherto undreamt of successes suddenly beset him and he poured out a glass of beer to steady himself.

Dinner seemed an easier matter than Blore-Smith had imagined it could turn out to be. Sarah took him to Soho and did most of the talking herself. He enquired after Maltravers's health, and was told by her that her husband was away for the week-end and that she would not see him until Monday, when both of them were having lunch with Chipchase.

'Why not come too?' Sarah said. 'I'm sure Oliver would be only too pleased.'

'Oh, no,' Blore-Smith said. 'I couldn't possibly. He hasn't asked me, and I'm sure he would be very angry if I did that.'

'How is your psychoanalytical treatment going?'

'He says he's very pleased with me.'

After dinner they went to a cinema. During the news reel, at a moment when a racing car had failed to take a corner and turned over and over in a black woolly cloud of fumes, Sarah took his arm. She was excited. Blore-Smith felt excited too, because all at once his feelings for Sarah became plain to him. It was a revelation. Something transcendental. Later, when they came out of the place into the street, he said:

'Will you come back and have a drink at Ebury Street? I'd like you to see my rooms.'

'All right,' Sarah said. 'But I shan't stay long, because I don't want to be late to-night. I want to get up early to-morrow and watch some tests.'

Blore-Smith was too overwrought by his own thoughts to ask her who was going to test what, but he muttered that he did not want to stay up late himself. They got into Sarah's car and drove towards Ebury Street.

'The nights are getting warmer now,' he said, and Sarah agreed that they were.

In the sitting-room he held up a quart beer-bottle to the light and shook it to see if any liquid remained inside and not daring to look round said:

'What would you like?'

'Water,' Sarah said. 'A large glass of water.'

She took off several leather coats and began to comb her hair. Blore-Smith went to the kitchen and filled a jug. Then, to nerve himself, he finished off the beer, finding that it was very flat. Now he was not sure where to begin.

'Isn't life awful?' Sarah said, sitting down in the armchair and reaching out for *Si le grain ne meurt*, which Chipchase had left at his last visit.

'Why, yes,' Blore-Smith said. 'I suppose it is.'

'It's about time something nice happened.'

Blore-Smith decided that this must be his cue. He walked firmly across the room to where Sarah was sitting sipping her glass of water, and placing himself beside her he put his arm round her shoulder.

'Will you——?' he began, and then he could think of no way of ending the sentence. Sarah in her surprise allowed a large amount of water to be spilt on the carpet.

'Will I what?' she said.

'Will you become my mistress?' Blore-Smith said, very loud and close to Sarah's face. He remained for some seconds looking at her fixedly and holding on to her shoulder.

"Will *I*?' Sarah said.

She seemed entirely unable to conceal even a small part of her stupefaction.

'Yes, you. Will you?'

For a moment Blore-Smith had thought of trying to get out of it and to pretend that he had not meant this at all. It might be possible to explain that it was only advice he was seeking with regard to someone else. After all, Sarah's sophistication would make such an enquiry permissible. The expression on her face had made him consider for a second this way of retreat but he dismissed the idea at once. He must stick by what he had said.

'Will you?' he said. 'Will you?'

'No,' Sarah said. 'Most certainly I won't. But thank you very much for asking me all the same.'

Blore-Smith allowed his arm to drop. He lay back on the sofa, white in the face.

'No,' he said, at last, 'I thought you wouldn't.'

'You just thought it worth making sure about?' Sarah said.

'No,' said Blore-Smith. 'No, no. You mustn't think that of me.'

'Why not?'

'Because it isn't true. I think I'm in love with you.'

'This is all very embarrassing of you,' Sarah said. 'You really shouldn't go on like this. There are lots of nice girls you could find without making this sort of scene. Besides I must be going home now anyway. Promise me that you won't be so silly when we next meet.'

'But——'

'I'm sure I can trust you not to be so silly.'

'I——'

Sarah began to put on her leather coats again. Before Blore-Smith could reach the door she had opened it and shouted:

'Good night! Good night!'

He heard the sound of her car going away up the street.

Maltravers leaned out of the window of Chipchase's flat and looked down.

'Any sign of her?' Chipchase said.

'Have you ever known her to be less than twenty minutes late?' Maltravers said. 'It was madness to arrange to meet here and not at a restaurant where we could have begun our meal. As it is, I daren't leave a message and go on, in case she misunderstands it. She's got all my tickets and money for Germany.'

'I saw Mendie the other day,' Chipchase said. 'She seems to be getting rather tired of the Commodore. I suggested that she should come to Berlin too.'

'What, and start life anew there as a man?'

'That's not a bad idea.'

Maltravers withdrew his head and Chipchase poured some more sherry into his glass, saying:

'Livery stuff this.'

He finished the dregs of the decanter. Maltravers returned to the window. He said:

'Here she comes.'

Sarah arrived in the room hurriedly. She was flushed and evidently bursting with gossip.

'You've arrived just in time,' Maltravers said. 'We've been drawing lots to decide which of us should kill and eat the other.'

'I've got something funny to tell you,' Sarah said.

Maltravers said: 'I'm in no mood for laughter. It's bread I want. Not circuses.'

'Do you know what that wretched little Blore-Smith friend of yours has done?'

'Good Lord, what?' said Maltravers. 'You haven't made him do something silly, have you?'

'I haven't. He did it on his own.'

'Well what is it?' said Chipchase. 'Don't keep us in suspense.'

'What do you think?'

'Oh, spill it,' said Maltravers, getting up from his chair. 'What are you being so arch about?'

'He's just tried to seduce me.'

Maltravers sat down again so violently that the sofa springs gave a rending sound. He said:

'Goodness, what a shock you gave me.'

'But, I say,' said Chipchase. 'What frightful cheek! Did he really now?'

'I believe you put him up to it,' Sarah said.

'My dear, don't be so absurd. You know perfectly well I shouldn't dream of doing anything like that. What a little ass he is. Really I'm most awfully sorry. I confess I feel indirectly to blame as I'm supposed to superintend his emotional life. But I had no idea that he would go and do a thing like that. He must have gone off his head.'

'What do you mean?' said Maltravers. 'I hope you aren't trying to suggest that Sarah isn't attractive.'

'This isn't a moment for your habitual bad taste,' Chipchase said. 'It's a preposterous thing to have happened.'

'But I like my wife to have successes. It gives me confidence in myself.'

'Is that really all you have to say?' Sarah said.

'What else do you expect me to say, darling? What did you do, anyway?'

'I didn't do anything. I was laughing too much.'

'There you are. You treat the thing as a joke yourself and then expect me to be furious.'

'But I'm your wife.'

'Of course you are. Could I ever forget it?'

'You seem to sometimes.'

'I must really speak to him seriously,' Chipchase said. 'He'll be trying to get off with Caroline next.'

'No, you'd better not say anything, really,' Sarah said. 'Poor little creature. I only told you because I thought it would make you laugh.'

'But I certainly shall speak to him about it.'

'What do you want us to do?' Maltravers said. 'First of all you treat it as the most awful experience you were ever subjected to, and now when Oliver wants to make a fuss you tell him not to.'

'Oliver won't make the right sort of fuss.'

'How do you know?'

'I will really,' Chipchase said. 'I'll make a frightful fuss.'

'But I don't want a frightful fuss made,' Sarah said. 'All I want is that he shouldn't go on bothering me.'

'Of course you're delighted really,' Maltravers said. 'I expect you ed him all the way up the garden.'

'Yes, I did, as a matter of fact. To annoy you.'

'But I've told you, it doesn't annoy me in the least. It shows me what an irresistible and at the same time reliable woman I have married.'

'Well I think you're the limit.'

'Shall I horsewhip him? He's probably much stronger than I am. Those little fellows are very wiry. Besides he's going to be our main ource of income for the next month or two.'

'And so I suppose you propose to sacrifice me to him?'

'That will not be necessary, as has already been shown. Or have you offended him so mortally that he will never see any of us again? There will be trouble if I find that you have done that.'

'I haven't offended him. He offended me.'

'Look here, Sarah, I hope you did not do anything silly.'

'My darling, don't be absurd. Think what he looks like.'

'Good heavens, you don't suppose I mean that! I mean were you so insulting that he will be frightened away for good? You're sure you didn't?'

'I only laughed at him.'

Maltravers again jumped to his feet.

'You only laughed at him! You stand there discussing a man who is admittedly such a mass of nerves that he has to get Oliver here to put him right psychologically and myself to find him a job, and you say that you only laughed at him, at what was probably one of the turning-points of his life. You've probably done irreparable damage. What happened? Did he foam at the mouth or shake all over or go into a trance?'

'He looked a bit green.'

'Poor devil.'

'What did you expect me to do? Go off for a week-end with him?'

'There you go, twisting everything I say as usual. You know as well as I do that I'm only too anxious for you to lead a life that won't bring my name into disrepute. It's an old name and until my marriage was a good one.'

'It's not your fault if it's remained good.'

'Couldn't you have shown a little tact?'

'That's just what I did do.'

'Well, why didn't you say so at first?'

'You didn't give me an opportunity.'

'Now look here,' said Maltravers. 'I've a jolly good mind to tell the whole story to Nipper.'

Sarah was getting angry now.

'What the hell's it got to do with Nipper?' she said.

'It would show him what sort of a girl you really are.'

'He knows already. Better than you do, I shouldn't wonder.'

'For goodness' sake don't let's begin discussing Nipper now,' Chip chase said. 'Even I know most of the arguments for and against him by this time. Both of you must know them absolutely by heart. The question is, how do we now stand as regards Blore-Smith?'

'Exactly as you stood before, however that was,' Sarah said. 'All that's happened is that he made a certain suggestion to me, was turned down, and we remain friends. Neither of you two brutes are involved in any way.'

'I'm involved,' Maltravers said. 'You're my wife.'

'Oh, shut up.'

'I think I'd better get in touch with him,' said Chipchase. 'Otherwise he will be getting into some other sort of mischief. What a life!'

Blore-Smith now was merely dejected. He had felt so embarrassed when first Chipchase mentioned the Sarah episode that he could only edge to the corner of the room with his back to the light. The embarrassment had passed now, leaving in its place an unbearable depression.

'I won't say any more about the matter now,' Chipchase said, 'but you can take it from me that you acted in a very silly way. A way that might have had grave consequences.'

Chipchase paused for breath.

'Judgment,' he said. 'That is the quality you must develop.'

'But you said it never did any harm to try.'

'Relatively. Of course I meant relatively. It may do a great deal of harm. Incalculable harm.'

'How could I know?' Blore-Smith said miserably.

'Anybody. Anybody but Sarah.'

'But if it had been someone else you would have made just as much fuss.'

'Certainly I should not.'

'Who wouldn't have mattered then?'

'Well that's descending from the general to the particular, and to give a purely negative example of this kind is always difficult. But Mendie, for example——'

'It would have been just the same.'

'On the contrary.'

'Of course it would.'

'Please don't contradict me,' Chipchase said. 'It would have been a matter between you and the Commodore. No one else.'

'So you say.'

'And I need hardly add that what I say I mean.'

'You didn't about all this.'

'Please do not try and shift the blame. And, above all, don't mis-
interpret me now and make a sudden assault on Mendie's virtue when
she is trying to sell some tuberoses to a customer.'

'Of course I shouldn't.'

'Good. I'm glad to hear it. But don't take all this too much to heart.
The Duke of Wellington said that a man who never made a mistake
never made anybody.'

'Does Maltravers know?'

'Of course he does.'

Blore-Smith groaned aloud.

'Don't worry about him,' Chipchase said. 'He'll get over it. It's you
I worry about. You sometimes seem almost unwilling to learn.'

Maltravers left for Germany and nothing more was heard of him
for some weeks. Then Chipchase received a letter from him, suggesting
that, now that he was satisfactorily settled in, Chipchase and Blore-
Smith should come out there. Maltravers's job was to continue for another month at least. He seemed very pleased with the way things were
going and implied that it would not be long now before he was at the
head of his profession. Chipchase read excerpts from the letter to Blore-
Smith when he next visited him.

'I expect you will like Berlin,' Chipchase said.

He folded up the letter and put it back in his pocket. For some minutes he stroked his long pallid face.

'It's not at all like Paris, is it?' Blore-Smith said.

'Not at all. But in spite of that you must keep your wits about you
all the same.'

'Oh, I will.'

'And now,' said Chipchase, 'I want some more details about what
you used to see from your night-nursery when your guardian had the
house next door to the seminary.'

Chipchase opened his notebook and took up his fountain-pen.
Blore-Smith said:

'There was one thing I wanted to ask before we begin. Do you—
is there any chance of there being any—any awkwardness about——'

'No, no,' Chipchase said. 'All that's quite forgotten now.'

'And Mrs. Maltravers?'

'Goodness, yes. I expect that sort of thing's happening to her all the time.'

Blore-Smith sighed with relief. He lay back on the sofa and began to piece together the high-spots of his childhood.

4

Although the journey to Berlin had been uneventful, Blore-Smith felt tired when he and Chipchase arrived at the Zoo Station. As they passed through the barrier a German girl, wearing a *béret* and a black oilskin coat, touched Chipchase's arm. She showed him an envelope she carried addressed to himself. Chipchase tore it open, and after reading the letter inside he shook hands with the girl and said to Blore-Smith:

'We're going straight down to the film studios at Niebelheim. This is Fräulein Grundt, who will take us there.'

Blore-Smith shook hands with Fräulein Grundt, who had light blue eyes and straw-coloured hair. Only her thinness prevented her from having the appearance of a typical German girl in a French comic paper. A Rhine maiden in a mackintosh. She said in slow and very accurate English that a motor was waiting outside. They followed her in silence and climbed into the back of Maltravers's gamboge car. There they sat without speaking while she drove along the wide streets between the red and yellow flat-blocks of Berlin Westen. Soon they left the town and began to pass through fir forests on either side of the straight white road. At one point Blore-Smith noticed stretches of water between the trunks of the trees and the coloured sails of little boats. Fräulein Grundt drove fast, much in the manner of Maltravers himself, scarcely slowing up at all as they went by occasional clumps of dark red-brick villas. At last she turned off into a narrow road and entered a lane that crossed it at right angles. At the end of this lane gates like those of a level-crossing blocked the way. On either side of the gates were lodges, and beyond them, at some distance off, stood a number of low square structures like aeroplane hangars. Rising out of the centre of these was a larger and more pretentious building, a sort of town hall, and beyond this again, on the horizon, the outline of Greek or Roman ruins stood out against the flat blue-grey sky. A triumphal arch stretched above the gates on which was written, in gothic characters, *Niebelheimnazionalkunstfilmgesellschaft*.

On recognising the car a porter came forward to open the gates and Fräulein Grundt drove through, gathering speed to about fifty-five along the asphalt way and passing on the left a group of tables and chairs like those of a café, where Blore-Smith noticed a few of Napoleon's grenadiers eating and drinking. The car drew up in front of the edifice that dominated like a citadel the rest of this film-town. Fräulein Grundt jumped out and opened the door for Chipchase and Blore-Smith to descend.

'Kommen Sie mit,' she said.

They followed her into a hall lined with fire-buckets and green doors. Going through one of the doors they entered a pitchy dark passage and, opening another door at the end, came out into a white-panelled room, full of Louis-Seize furniture and lined with eighteenth-century portraits. A curtain was drawn across the further side. The room had no immediate roof and looking up Blore-Smith allowed his eye to travel far away into a sombre vortex of beams and rafters, which sprouted up towards a roof, apparently vaulted like that of a cathedral. Chipchase and Fräulein Grundt disappeared beyond the curtain. Blore-Smith hurried on in case he should be abandoned by them and lost for ever. He pushed aside the heavy plush folds and went forward.

Beyond the curtain Blore-Smith found himself in the depths of the jungle. Tropical foliage hung down from above him so that he had to pick his way carefully along the narrow path between giant cactuses and spiky clusters of equatorial blossom. Once he caught his foot in the wire supports of a rope of orchids and fell headlong, causing the surrounding undergrowth to shake violently. This attracted the attention of Fräulein Grundt, who turned and put her finger to her lips to enjoin silence. They left this primeval forest by way of a sliding door in a hollow tree and in the distance, as he stooped to avoid a python that hung, swaying, from one of its lower branches, Blore-Smith heard the voice of Maltravers. It was raised in anger, and said:

'Very well. If you think that your way is right, do it your way. It doesn't matter to me whether the *Niebelheimnazionalkunstfilmgesellschaft* is a laughing-stock all over the English-speaking world. It is a subject to which I feel wholly indifferent.'

A muffled voice replied to this but not loud enough for the sense of the words to be plain. By this time Blore-Smith had caught up with Chipchase and Fräulein Grundt. All three of them at the same instant came out from behind a wing of scenery and into the blaze of light that shone from several powerful arc-lamps that were trained like searchlights on to a group of people wearing solar topis and carrying

rifles. There were also some negroes, shining and almost naked. Maltravers, with his hands in his pockets, stood in front of these, facing
an elderly man about four feet high who wore dark glasses and whose
right arm ended in a hook. At that moment, that is to say, the period
of time coinciding with Blore-Smith's grasp of the identity of the scene's
protagonists, the elderly man seemed to be in the act of threatening
Maltravers with his hook. Immediately after this realisation Blore-Smith
once more fell heavily to the ground, this time on account of a piece
of camera apparatus that trailed in his path when he pressed forward
to get a better view of the theatre of war. The noise that accompanied
this second collapse drew to him the attention of everyone present.

'Ah, here you are at last,' said Maltravers, turning from his dwarf
adversary. 'What sort of a journey did you have?'

'Lousy,' said Chipchase.

'I thought you would,' Maltravers said. 'But let me introduce you
to the Herr-Direktor. The greatest film-producer in Germany. Herr
Roth—Herren Chipchase and Blore-Smith.'

They shook hands with the dwarf who, although clearly in a fury,
clicked his heels together and offered his unhooked arm, and yelled
shrilly:

'Roth!'

'At the moment,' Maltravers said, 'Herr Roth and I have a small
disagreement about a point. Perhaps you might help with an outside
opinion.'

'We should be delighted,' Chipchase said.

Maltravers said: 'The scene is central Africa. The hero is, in the
German version, a Korps student who wants to be a soldier; in the
French version a soldier who wants to be a poet; and in the English
version an English gentleman who wants to be an English gentleman.
All are thwarted in their desires and adjourn to the great open (or,
to be more accurate, the great enclosed) spaces where they each meet
another Korps student, soldier-poet, an English gentleman respec-
tively, who is living with a native girl. They quarrel over this woman
and one of them is killed. As he lies dying while the surrounding tribes
of cannibals advance towards the hut, the German says: "*Muth verloren,
alles verloren, Da wär es besser, nicht geboren.*" The Frenchman says:
"*J'irai loin—bien loin, comme un bohémien, par la Nature, heureux
comme avec une femme.*" The Englishman says: "*Play up and play the
game.*"'

'There's something you can't improve on.'

'While the oncoming cannibals croon the refrain of the "Boating Song," from the jungle over which night is falling.'

'All of it?'

'Only the first two and the last verses.'

'Quite perfect.'

'They say it will take too long, because they will have to get the music from England.'

'Absurd.'

Maltravers turned in the direction of Herr Roth. He said:

'You see, this Englishman is in complete agreement with me, Herr-Direktor.'

Herr Roth had evidently had enough of Maltravers for the time being. He threw the script he was carrying on to the ground and shouted:

'Gross Gott!'

Then he spat on the floor and hurried off the set, making his way between two banana trees. He disappeared behind a native kraal. A buzz of conversation broke out among the people standing round the arc-lamps. Maltravers sighed.

'It's always the same,' he said in a lower voice to Chipchase. 'He simply can't keep his temper.'

'Foreigners don't seem able to, somehow.'

'I found everything in a terrible mess when I arrived here. At first no one would do what I told them.'

'There still seems some opposition.'

'There certainly is. Shall I show you round?'

'Look here,' said Chipchase, 'we've had a tiring journey. How about doing that some other time?'

'We'll go straight across to the hotel,' Maltravers said. 'Wait a moment, I'll introduce you to a few people. Herr Schrott, Herr Kuhn, Herr Rubenstein, Herr Israels, Herr Bondy, Herr Andersen, Herr von Neustadt, Mademoiselle Dupont, Madame Obolenska, Fräulein von Bernhardi . . .'

Chipchase and Blore-Smith shook hands all round, including the scene-shifters. It took a long time, and at the end of it Maltravers said:

'Come along. We will go back to the hotel for lunch. The food at the canteen is uneatable.'

'Where are we staying?' Blore-Smith said.

'At the Sans Souci Palast. It's a little hotel in the woods not far from here. Very convenient for the studios.'

'Aren't we going to stay in Berlin itself?'

'We'll move up there later. At present it is better to be near the scene of action.'

Blore-Smith was disappointed to hear that they were not going to stay in the heart of the capital, but he said nothing. He had learnt that it was better to be quiet when he was with Maltravers and Chipchase. He would have their eventual move as something to look forward to. They followed Maltravers by another route to the car.

'What has happened to Miss Grundt?' Chipchase said.

'Oh, Hedwig. She's got to see one of the actresses about something,' Maltravers said. 'She will find her own way to the hotel.'

'Will she indeed? Tell us about her.'

'She's got a walk-on part in the Napoleon film. But she's much too good for that. She has the makings of a great actress in her. If she was in my hands a bit longer she could do something big.'

'I have no idea what you mean,' Chipchase said, 'but are we to understand that the lady is under your protection at the moment?'

'I feel a little responsible for her.'

'Ah.'

They got into the car and drove once more through the gates and across the main road into some woods.

'Hedwig might come in useful when we begin to shoot Œdipus Rex,' Maltravers said, as they slowed up. 'There's the hotel. Just ahead of us.'

The Sans Souci Palast was on a corner where four roads met. It stood back, half hidden by fir-trees, a white building designed on modern principles with a wide enclosed verandah in front of it, the top of which made a balcony for the rooms on the first floor. On the gravel space in front of the entrance were some green tables and chairs, rusty and piled one on another. There was no sign of life, and at first sight the place seemed to be an isolation hospital or a hydro, rather than a hotel.

'Wait a moment,' said Maltravers. 'I'll get Adolf.'

He got out of the car and returned a few minutes later, bringing with him a tall waiter with a drooping moustache and a dark carmine-coloured nose. This waiter, who wore a short white coat, gave Chipchase a military salute, winked at Blore-Smith, and took charge of the luggage. Chipchase and Blore-Smith followed Maltravers up the steps which led to the verandah. Inside, seated at one of the tables, a very smartly dressed man was drinking benedictine. He bowed curtly to them as they passed.

'Who is that?' Chipchase said.

Maltravers said: 'That is Rowland Inglethorne.'

'The actor?'

'He is second lead in the main picture they are producing here now—the Napoleon film, not the tropical one—but he had a quarrel with the producer this morning and he is going back to England this evening.'

'But what will they do?' Blore-Smith said.

'They will have to wait until he comes back,' Maltravers said.

'But perhaps he won't come back.'

'Don't you worry,' Maltravers said. 'He'll come back all right. These are your rooms. What do you want for lunch? I'll go down and order it.'

'What is there?' Chipchase said.

'*Wiener schnitzel.*'

'What else?'

'Eggs.'

'Is that all?'

'Yes.'

'Eggs then,' said Chipchase. 'Is this the invariable menu?'

'And you?'

'What was the other?' Blore-Smith said.

'*Wiener schnitzel,*' Chipchase said. 'You had better have that to familiarise yourself with an important Teutonic contribution to the art of the cuisine. And, by the way, I observe that the running water in this hotel does not run.'

When he came downstairs Blore-Smith found Maltravers and Chipchase sitting at a table on the verandah. Inglethorne had joined them and was telling Chipchase exactly what had happened to make him decide to go back so suddenly to England. Chipchase was agreeing that the producer's conduct was simply a case of bad manners. Maltravers was reading the *Völkischer Beobachter*. He looked brown and in excellent health and Blore-Smith now found time to notice his clothes, on which the *Niebelheimnazionalkunstfilmgesellschaft* had already had a marked effect. He was dressed in a shirt and trousers of different, and equally loud, check pattern, both garments giving the impression that zip-fasteners wherever possible had been used in place of buttons. He wore no coat. Chipchase said:

'What are we waiting for?'

Maltravers said: 'Hedwig hasn't come yet, but I told them to bring food as soon as possible. She's hopelessly unpunctual that girl. I've often spoken to her about it but it does no good. I'll give her hell when she does arrive.'

Inglethorne had another benedictine and went upstairs to pack.

'He won't get further than Hamburg,' Maltravers said. 'They can't do without him.'

While he was speaking Fräulein Grundt came running up the steps. Maltravers said:

'Why are you late again?'

'I could not get away.'

She talked slowly and smiled as she spoke, moving aside to allow the red-nosed waiter to put food on the table.

'I had to speak to Fräulein Levinska. The Herr-Direktor was angry. He caused her to be delayed.'

'The Herr-Direktor was certainly in a bad temper this morning,' Maltravers said. 'I'll grant you that.'

'Do you often have rows with him?' Chipchase said, beckoning to the waiter.

Maltravers said: 'As a matter of fact I do. He finds the greatest difficulty in controlling himself. He tore away all the seat of a camera-man's trousers with his hook the other day.'

'Why did he do that?'

'Wanted to draw attention to his own importance. The man is a megalomaniac. Still we are great friends really.'

Chipchase had by now secured the attention of the waiter and was trying to explain that he wanted some salt. He was met with a flood of German. Maltravers said:

'Adolf is saying that he has been to England and understands English. That isn't, strictly speaking, true. If you will tell me what you want, I will do my best to explain.'

'Salt.'

'Ah, yes. There is always some difficulty about salt.'

Maltravers and the waiter conferred for some minutes. Maltravers said:

'Adolf also wants me to say that if you smoke Kurfürst cigarettes will you give him the coupons, because he is collecting them. When he has fifteen thousand he can apply for a free trip in an aeroplane to Munich.'

'And back?'

'He said nothing about the return journey.'

'Tell him I'll do it if he gets me the salt.'

During the next few days the weather became hotter. Maltravers spent most of his time at the N.N., as the film company was commonly called. His job there was to last a few weeks more. The final date was still uncertain. Chipchase and Blore-Smith walked in the woods, bathed, spent mornings in Berlin, or loitered about the film studios. Fräulein Grundt was usually there to conduct them round or sit in the open-air canteen drinking beer and explaining why none of the better-known stars were taking part in N.N. productions at the moment. She herself would ask such questions as: 'Please to tell me how in London the serious problem of traffic mobility is ordered?' or, 'Does the Youth-Movement still advance itself well in England?' or, 'How good is the chance that the surtax duty on optical glass shall be lowered?' These questions could not always be answered on the spot. At Chipchase's suggestion, Blore-Smith was accustomed to undertake the task of expounding matters to her as clearly as he was able. Meanwhile Maltravers argued with Herr-Direktor Roth, gossiped with the actors, or joined the others in the canteen.

Inglethorne, as predicted, had returned from Hamburg and was now back in his former part. He had received an apology from Herr Roth and he looked in better health after a day or two away from his work. He was a thin man, with hair going grey, who at one time or another had played with efficiency every dramatic part from Hamlet to the Widow Twankey. In this way he found himself in early middle-age provided with a pattern of behaviour for any eventualities that life might provide. Although most of his time was spent in a *terrain vague* between these and other strongly contrasted rôles, he was prepared for farce or tragedy at a moment's notice. Lines from Congreve, Ibsen, Edgar Wallace, Pirandello were always ready. Inglethorne was a man absolved forever from being himself. He had become very friendly with Maltravers, although they often quarrelled, and used to discuss with him and the others the filming of *Œdipus Rex*. It was even suggested that if he had time Inglethorne should help in its production.

Blore-Smith found that he was enjoying himself. Sometimes he thought with shame and regret of Sarah Maltravers, but he made a great effort to keep her from his mind. To some extent he was successful.

It was at the beginning of the following week that Maltravers came back from the studios early and suggested that they should dine that night in Berlin. When approached Inglethorne agreed to come with them. After Inglethorne had changed his clothes twice and Fräulein Grundt had decided whether or not she should wear a hat, the party started off along the Avus in the gamboge car.

Blore-Smith registered in his mind the fact that the first place they went to was called the Eden Bar. After that they seemed to visit at least once most of the establishments in the Kurfürstendamm. When they had dinner he was vaguely aware of the atmosphere of an aquarium. Or at least the immediate proximity of goldfish housed on a larger scale than he had ever before seen in a restaurant. After dinner Maltravers had a quarrel with Inglethorne because Inglethorne tried to pay the bill and Maltravers said that Inglethorne was his guest. In order that honour should be satisfied they went on to several more places at Inglethorne's expense. It was about three night-clubs further on that Fräulein Grundt began to cry because she said that Maltravers was taking no notice of her. Maltravers had just ordered her to find her own way home when everyone's attention was distracted by the arrival of Herr-Direktor Roth with an immensely beautiful girl rather more than six-foot high. They began to dance as soon as they came into the room. Chipchase said:

'How does he get them? The hook?'

'It's mostly bluff,' Maltravers said.

When Herr Roth saw them he stopped dancing and asked if they would join him at his table. He seemed to have forgotten any differences he might have had with Maltravers and pinched his ear as if he had been Napoleon with one of his grenadiers. In the excitement at having the Herr-Direktor at the same table Fräulein Grundt forgot her troubles. Herr Roth noticed her and asked Maltravers who she was. He seemed glad to hear that she was employed at the N.N. Soon after this Herr Roth's partner said that she was tired of this place and, as Inglethorne still bore a grudge against Herr Roth in connection with his recent rustication to Hamburg and had assumed the face he made when about to pick a quarrel, it was generally agreed that another move might be a good thing. Blore-Smith had some coffee to steady his nerves. One or two other people joined the party and the name of their next port of call was passed round. As they left, the band played *Rule, Britannia*, softly.

'Don't get lost this time,' Chipchase said in Blore-Smith's ear, giving what Blore-Smith thought a rather nasty laugh.

'We can walk,' Maltravers said. 'It's just round the corner.'

Two brownshirts were selling papers in the street when they went outside. Maltravers said:

'Heil Hitler.'

'Heil Hitler,' said the brownshirts.

'They'll be coming into power soon,' Maltravers said. 'Just as well to be the right side of them.'

Maltravers led the way through side streets until they came to a doorway by which stood a notice saying that this was the Real Berlin. The notice said this in several languages, and some highly coloured effigies in cardboard, larger than life and only a little less natural, stood on the threshold, presaging what might be found within. Maltravers, Chipchase, Blore-Smith, Inglethorne, Fräulein Grundt, Herr Roth, Herr Roth's girl, and several anonymous supers went along a passage and into a small ante-room with a bar. Beyond this was another room, very wide and high, containing tables and a band. As he was following the others into the big room, Maltravers took Blore-Smith by the arm. He said:

'I want to introduce you to Herman. We can join them later.'

He led Blore-Smith across to the bar, which was presided over by a supercilious young man in a mauve-silk Russian shirt. Maltravers said:

'Good evening, Herman. How are you this evening?'

Herman's face brightened up when he was spoken to. He had sad pencilled eyebrows and flashing teeth. He shook hands with Maltravers and then with Blore-Smith.

'So,' he said, 'you have now a new friend? That is nice. One sees that it is nice. I knew that you would not always bring girls to see me. Did not I tell you?'

Herman looked closely at Blore-Smith. He said:

'So nice a boy. You will bring him to see me often, yes? You would like that?'

He addressed his last sentence to Blore-Smith, who mumbled that he would be very pleased to come again if he could. Herman leant over the bar and took the sleeve of his coat. He felt the material between his finger and thumb. Then he shook his head.

'The cloth is not so good,' he said to Maltravers. 'It is fair but not so good as yours. I will tell you. There is a shop not far from here where I find the cloth so good as English cloth. Indeed excellent suits. You must take your friend there. In Berlin, you see, it is easy if you know the good places to get good English suits. Not perhaps so good as yours but than this far better. And ties'—Herman let go of Blore-Smith's arm and turned his attention to his tie—'for two marks fifty you can have ties that are so much better, yes, so *much* better than this one——'

'I'll take him there to-morrow,' said Maltravers. 'And now we must hurry on and join our friends.'

'And his shoes. Let me see, please——'

'Another time, Herman,' Maltravers said.

'But, yes,' Blore-Smith heard Herman say as they left him, 'it is so cheap and your friend will be so nicely dressed——'

'Herman is charming, isn't he?' said Maltravers, as they entered the big room.

At first sight this seemed to Blore-Smith much the same as the night-club they had just left except that it was on a larger scale. It was indeed larger than any of the places they had visited that evening. The band was playing a tango and several couples were dancing. Blore-Smith was surprised to notice in the middle of the floor two business men in black-striped suits, one of whom wore pince-nez, while the other's head was closely shaved and shiny. The effect was so unfamiliar that he was tempted to ask Maltravers about them, but he decided that he would wait until something else attracted his attention so that he could put all his questions at once. However he could not prevent himself from stopping and watching, and in this way he blocked the route to the table where the rest of the party were sitting.

'Come on,' said Maltravers. 'What has happened? Have you seen a ghost?'

Blore-Smith moved on and they sat down. The party had thinned out and only Inglethorne, Herr Roth's girl friend, and an anonymous extra remained with Chipchase. Herr Roth's girl friend seemed to be getting on very well with the extra, a sallow young man, thought to be a Russian.

'Where is the Herr-Direktor?' Maltravers said.

Inglethorne said: 'The Herr-Direktor has seen fit to go behind the scenes with Miss Grundt. Not before I had mentioned to him a few points with regard to what are considered good manners in England.'

'He seems to have taken a fancy to Hedwig,' Maltravers said. 'I suppose you lost both of us our jobs by what you said to him.'

Inglethorne jumped up from his chair.

'Are you aware,' he said, 'that you are the rudest man I have ever met?'

Before Maltravers had time to answer, Chipchase said:

'Why, look, there's Mendie.'

Maltravers turned in the direction in which Chipchase pointed. He said:

'And the Commodore. What a small world it is, to be sure.'

'What, do you know that vision?' said Inglethorne, sitting down again.

Mrs. Mendoza had seen them simultaneously, and already she was hurrying down the room leaving Commander Venables alone at the table.

'How are you, my dears,' she said.

She took, in spite of their protests, a spare chair from a table where five little young men were sitting and drew it up between Maltravers and Chipchase. She said:

'How wonderful to see you all here. Of course this is the only quiet place in the whole town. We are staying at the most awful hotel. Too uncomfortable for words. I can't think why Hugo stands it. No one else would for five minutes.'

She sighed. Maltravers pushed his drink across to her.

'Have that,' he said. 'I'll order another one. What on earth are you doing here anyway?'

'Well, Hugo suggested Paris and I told him no one ever went to Paris now anyhow, and that Berlin was the only place with any gaiety left, and so we came here.'

'And now you don't like it?'

'Herman in this place is rather sweet. I just like coming here and talking to him a bit in the evening. What do you do?'

'We don't have much time for frivolities of this sort,' Maltravers said. 'We're here on business. I spend my days telling the directors of the *Niebelheimnazionalkunstfilmgesellschaft* where they get off.'

'That must be lovely for them,' Mrs. Mendoza said. 'And what are you doing here, Oliver, may one ask?'

'One may,' Chipchase said. 'Although you seem to forget that it was myself who advised you to come here in the first place. I am making observations for my new book on psychology. For example, if you will look round for a moment, I will ask you to note the effect of Berlin on the Commodore.'

Commander Venables was indeed no longer alone. He had been joined on one side by a tall blonde in evening dress, carrying an ostrich-feather fan, and on the other by a young person in a dinner jacket with wavy dark curls and a precise little mouth. Maltravers said:

'Why, if he hasn't collected Willi and Fritzi. He's making a big evening of it.'

'Really,' said Mrs. Mendoza. 'Isn't Hugo the limit? I don't mind the girl so much, because they seem impossible to get rid of in this town. You literally have to hit them before they will leave you in peace. But at least he might tell that little wretch in a badly cut tuxedo to sit a little further away.'

'My dear Mendie,' Maltravers said. 'I think you have fallen into the common error of thinking that Fritzi is the boy and Willi the girl. You should have learnt by this time that it is the other way about. The Commodore seems to share your misapprehension.'

It was only too clear that Maltravers was right. While Commander Venables was having a brisk and apparently amicable conversation with the blonde, under cover of the ostrich-feather fan, he had turned away with a look of aversion from Fritzi, who had to content herself with stroking his shoulder. Mrs. Mendoza said:

'I can't have Hugo going on like this the instant my back is turned.'

She beckoned violently in Commander Venables's direction. It was some minutes before he caught her eye. When he saw that she intended him to leave the table and come down the room to where she was sitting, Commander Venables got up at once obediently. But Fritzi and Willi were not to be shaken off so easily. Each linked an arm in his and all three arrived at Mrs. Mendoza's side in this formation.

'Won't you and your friends join us?' said Maltravers. 'How are you, Willi? And you, Fritzi?'

'*Guten Abend*, Herr Maltravers,' Willi and Fritzi said.

They unlocked themselves from Commander Venables and found places round the table. Commander Venables did the same but he looked cowed and sat as far as possible from Mrs. Mendoza, though he gave an occasional apprehensive glance in her direction. Mrs. Mendoza's attention had been captured by Inglethorne, who was leaning across the table and telling her that he had always admired her from a distance but that he had never dared hope that his luck would bring him to the same table as such beauty. For the moment this served to cover Commander Venables's tracks. Inglethorne made his statement to Mrs. Mendoza several times, very slowly and distinctly. His repetition made it clear that professional worries and the lack of air in the room had begun to tell on him. Blore-Smith, himself rather dazed, listened to Mrs. Mendoza, who was telling Inglethorne he had always been her favourite actor. All at once he felt someone touch him on the head. He turned and found a tall man with a single eye-glass standing behind him. For a moment he could not place this figure, although he was conscious of a sense of uneasiness.

'Teape,' said the tall man. 'Teape. You're not going to say that you've forgotten me?'

'Oh, of course not.'

The memories that Colonel Teape called up made Blore-Smith break out in a cold sweat. Colonel Teape said:

'What a gay life you lead. Are you never out of a night-club? And how are your barriers? Most of them pretty well rased to the ground by this time I shouldn't wonder?'

Blore-Smith laughed uncomfortably. Colonel Teape's eye strayed past Blore-Smith to Willi, and then to Fritzi. His brow puckered. He passed on to an examination of Inglethorne. While he was doing this Inglethorne looked up from his conversation with Mrs. Mendoza and caught sight of the Colonel's eye-glass trained on him. For some seconds they watched each other, and then Inglethorne began to make faces. He raised his eyebrows, screwed up his nose, and forced out his lower lip with his tongue. Colonel Teape also raised his eyebrows and glanced away shyly like a frightened doe.

'Why does he look at me like that?' Inglethorne said. 'I don't like it.'

When Inglethorne said this he addressed himself to Commander Venables, who had sat down next to him. Commander Venables laughed nervously. Inglethorne said:

'You know when a man looks at me in a way I don't like I have something to say to him.'

He got up slowly and walked round the table to Colonel Teape. Maltravers followed him, saying:

'Don't be so unreasonable, Inglethorne. You're behaving like a drunken governess.'

Inglethorne swung round on Maltravers. Chipchase at once got up from the table, and, taking Fritzi by the arm, began to dance. Willi, not to be outdone, by sheer force of character and in the face of Mrs. Mendoza's exasperated gasp of 'Hugo!' seized Commander Venables and made him do the same. Blore-Smith, thinking it advisable to follow Chipchase's example, and get away from the table, turned to look for Herr Roth's girl friend. He found that she and the Russian super had disappeared.

'Look here,' said Inglethorne to Maltravers. 'I've already told you you're the rudest man I've ever met.'

Colonel Teape now bustled forward and said:

'Surely it's Peter Maltravers, isn't it? Didn't we meet a long time ago with Pauline Borodino?'

'Of course we did,' said Maltravers. 'This friend of mine is a little over excited.'

'You call me over excited!' Inglethorne said. 'My dear sir, are you aware you are addressing Maltravers, the well known public nuisance? You must be confusing him with someone else of the same name or you would never claim his acquaintance.'

It was immediately after this that Blore-Smith heard Mrs. Mendoza saying to him:

'Come and dance with me. I can't stand this any longer.'

Before he fully realised what he was doing Blore-Smith found himself in the centre of the room clasping Mrs. Mendoza in his arms. He was so overwrought that he could scarcely move one foot in front of the other, but she steered him firmly until they had reached the other end of the room.

'You must take me away from here,' she said. 'Will you do that for me? I'm sure you will. My nerves just won't stand it. Please do this for me.'

Blore-Smith was so astonished by this request, and by the tone of voice in which she spoke it, that he could only say:

'Of course, of course.'

'We'll sit outside somewhere for a bit,' Mrs. Mendoza said. 'The Romanisches Café isn't far from here. We'll sit there until we feel better.'

'Are we going to leave all—all——'

'All these beastly people? Do you want to stay with them? I shall go in any case.'

'No,' said Blore-Smith. 'Of course I shall come with you. Perhaps we might pick them up later. It's still quite early.'

'Come on then,' said Mrs. Mendoza.

Sitting in the Romanisches Café they looked out, as from the bastion of a neo-gothic fort, at the crowd. A steady stream of dolled-up girls—Dietrich, Garbo and Harvey the prevalent styles—passed underneath the café's parapet and crossed towards the spiky grey church or to the other corner where a stunted Nazi with galloping consumption was selling newspapers. It was a warm night. Because the café was raised above the level of the street it was out of reach of the beggars who were unable here, as at other cafés and restaurants, to approach and stand close up to the tables with bowed heads. This architectural exemption was advantageous. Berlin beggars, neatly dressed for the most part in gloves and plus-fours, would remain immote for lengthy periods, distressing but somehow repellent from the limitations and Germanness of their methods. Like all their countrymen they were hopelessly technique-bound.

'Do you know,' said Mrs. Mendoza, who had sat for some time in silence watching a child prostitute, with a face like a white mask, passing and repassing along the pavement below them. 'Do you know why I should most like to have been born a man?'

Blore-Smith blushed, a habit he still found it impossible to throw off entirely, and said that he had no idea. He was more than a little frightened at finding himself alone with someone as dazzling as Mrs. Mendoza, and the course of action he had followed in leaving the night-club reminded him of his behaviour when he had gone to Paris.

'I could have learnt Greek,' Mrs. Mendoza said.

Blore-Smith caught his breath with surprise, and tried to cast back his mind so that he could remember the advantages that had accrued to him from his smattering of classical scholarship.

'Is it too late to take lessons?' he said.

'Don't be absurd,' Mrs. Mendoza said, so crossly that in order to cover his mistake as quickly as possible Blore-Smith added:

'Some of Herodotus was very amusing, I remember.'

But Mrs. Mendoza was not listening.

'The Greeks knew how to live,' she said. 'If they heard music they danced; if they saw a stretch of golden sand they raced along it; if they came to blue sea they swam in it. They were natural, beautiful, free. They didn't live horrible constricted fussy little lives like us.'

Mrs. Mendoza clenched together her hands and held out her arms stiffly on either side of her, looking, Blore-Smith thought, with Greece in the fore-front of his imagination, like Artemis carved on the prow of a ship.

'Don't you like Berlin then?' he said.

'Like it? I hate it. Every minute I stay here is sheer hell.'

'But why not go back then?'

Mrs. Mendoza put down her drink so sharply on the table that she chipped off a small piece from the glass's base.

'My good man,' she said, 'how do you suppose I can do that? Do you think I should be here at all if I were my own mistress? Try not to be quite so dense.'

'I'm sorry, but——'

Suddenly, to Blore-Smith's great surprise, she stretched out her hand and took his.

'I know,' she said. 'Don't mind what I say. Why should you bother about why I am here? It's very sweet of you not to have gone raking about for gossip. You see I really have to do more or less what Hugo wants because—well I'm rather in money difficulties at the moment.'

'But surely if you want to go back to England he will take you back, won't he?'

'You've no idea how selfish men are.'

'But I mean if he——'

'Anyway I'm not sure that I want to go back to England—with Hugo.'

'Do you'—Blore-Smith prepared himself for another snub—'want to get away from him?'

Mrs. Mendoza shut her eyes and shook her head from side to side.

'Sometimes——' she said. 'I don't know.'

There was a pause. Mrs. Mendoza played with the stem of her glass.

'And what about you?' she said. 'Do you like Berlin?'

'Oh, yes, at least what I've seen of it,' Blore-Smith said. 'And of course I more or less have to be here too. But we shall be going back soon to make the film.'

'Tell me about the film.'

'Well, you see, it's to illustrate the workings of psychoanalysis. Photographs of types and states of mind. I expect some of them will be of me. I'm—I'm rather a neurotic subject.'

'You can't tell me anything about neurasthenia,' Mrs. Mendoza said. 'But how are you going to do all this?'

'Well, I don't exactly know just yet, but the plans are all prepared, and of course a certain amount of the work will have to be rather opportunist.'

'Is that what Peter and Oliver tell you?'

'Yes. They said that,' Blore-Smith said. And he added: 'Naturally it would be bound to be like that.'

'Where are you going to do all this?'

'A Mr. Schlumbermayer has asked us to use his house. Very kindly.'

'Gracious!'

'Do you know him?'

'Of course I know him. But whatever made him agree to this?'

'I don't know exactly. The others arranged it.'

Mrs. Mendoza sat for some time apparently thinking. Then she said:

'I suppose you must rather want to get back to London and your girl? Or do you really rather enjoy being on the loose for a bit?'

Blore-Smith winced.

'My—how do you mean?'

'Well I suppose you've got some sort of steady company?'

'Hardly any—that is—not really. No.'

'Don't you like women then?'

'Oh yes. I think so.'

Mrs. Mendoza raised her eyebrows.

'You are a funny boy,' she said. 'Are you just too lazy?'

Blore-Smith fidgeted.

'They don't seem to like me,' he said.

'Nonsense.'

'They don't.'

'But I like you.'

To Blore-Smith's great surprise Mrs. Mendoza suddenly kissed him in the middle of the Romanisches Café. For a moment he was stunned. He knew of no words for such a situation.

'Don't you like me a little?' she said.

The people passing in front of the café seemed to move quicker and quicker like a merry-go-round. The gothic spires of the church swayed forward and then violently from side to side. Blore-Smith felt that his head would burst.

'But why should you?' Mrs. Mendoza said. 'You must think me the most awful woman in the world from what you have seen of me.'

'No, no,' said Blore-Smith, 'I don't.'

He took her hand. An intolerable agitation was taking place inside him.

'You see there is no one I can turn to for help,' Mrs. Mendoza said.

She removed her hand for a second, and then replaced it with a rolled-up handkerchief in the palm.

'Look here,' said Blore-Smith, through his teeth. 'Why not come back to England with me?'

'What?'

Mrs. Mendoza was so stupefied by this suggestion that Blore-Smith was confused and said no more.

'But do you really mean that?' Mrs. Mendoza said. 'Will you take me back? You'll have to look after me when I'm there, you know. I can't go back to *la cattleya* at present because the bailiffs are in.'

'Then will you come?'

Mrs. Mendoza laughed.

'I haven't said so,' she said. 'But why shouldn't I? It might work. Do you really want me to?'

'But I shouldn't have asked you if I didn't.'

'But what about the film you are going to make?'

'That can be arranged later.'

'What will Peter and Oliver say?'

'I don't care.'

'They will blame me, of course.'

'Do you mind?'

'Well, they're both rather sweet, you know.'

Mrs. Mendoza paused for a moment as if she were estimating in her mind the value of concord with Maltravers and Chipchase. Then she laughed again, more quietly, and said:

'All right then. I will come with you. When shall we go? As soon as possible? We can't manage to-night, can we? I suppose it's too late.'

'To-morrow then?'

'All right we'll go to-morrow. How will you get away from Niebelheim?'

For a minute this problem presented itself to Blore-Smith as insoluble. It came as the icy dip after a Turkish bath. Then he remembered something that Maltravers had said earlier in the day.

'I can take the train before they get up to-morrow,' he said. 'It was agreed that we should all stay in bed late after to-night's party. But what about you?'

'Take your things to the station and put them in the cloak-room. Then come round to the hotel and ask for me, and we will take the night train.'

'And hide in Berlin during the day?'

'We'll keep out of the way, up the Unter den Linden end of the town.'

They sat there in silence, still holding hands. Two groups of Nazis, walking in Indian file and coming from opposite directions, passed each other and saluted, as if about to initiate a game of oranges and lemons. At last Mrs. Mendoza said:

'You must take me back to the hotel now, sweetie, otherwise you will miss the last train back.'

She held his arm while they walked away from the café. After he had said good night to her at the entrance to the hotel Blore-Smith wandered for a time through the streets. The crowds, who in this town seemed never to retire to rest, jostled by him. At last, after being accosted twice by a tall woman who wore pince-nez and shiny vermilion-coloured riding-boots, he made an effort to collect his senses and managed to find his way to the station where the trains left for Niebelheim.

As he came down the dark avenue of fir-trees that led to the Sans Souci Palast Blore-Smith saw that the windows of the bar were still lit up. There was also a distinct sound of singing echoing from the same room. It appeared that in spite of the lateness of the hour the rest of the party had not yet gone to bed. He wondered if he would be able to get up to his bedroom without being seen, and he went very quietly up the steps and through the door. In the hall, where the light was not turned on, he collided violently with someone coming in the opposite direction. This person, whom he was at first unable to identify, took him by the arm and, talking all the time rapidly in German, led him to the bar, before he could make an excuse to escape. As they came through the door together he saw Chipchase, who said:

'Why, hullo? Whatever happened to you? Have you been following up your Paris experiments?'

Chipchase took Blore-Smith's other arm, partly to steady himself, but did not seem interested in obtaining an answer to his questions. Blore-Smith was now able to recognise the figure who stood on his other side. It was Adolf, the red-nosed waiter, who was dressed in a black suit with an artificial flower in his buttonhole. He carried a bamboo walking-stick and a soft grey hat. Like Chipchase, Adolf was swaying slightly. On the other side of the room, where seats ran along the walls, sat a large group that included Maltravers, Inglethorne, and several actors, actresses, camera-men and dressers from the N.N. From this group the sounds of singing recurred intermittently. Maltravers, whose face was brick-red, waved affectionately to Blore-Smith and asked for no further explanation beyond saying: 'Where did you get to?' The room was hot and Inglethorne was giving an imitation. Blore-Smith sat down, determined to get away as soon as possible.

Adolf followed and sat down on the chair beside him. Blore-Smith moved his own chair to make more room. Adolf leant forward across the table to where Maltravers sat, and, cupping his hands to his mouth, shouted:

'Not a waiter to-night!'

'What?'

'Not a waiter,' Adolf said. 'Night out.'

'Have a drink?'

Adolf nodded. He turned to Blore-Smith.

'Not a waiter, Herr Blore-Smith,' he said. '*Verstehen Sie?* Night off.'

'Yes, I see.'

Adolf turned to where the other waiter, a stunted character with an obstinate red neck, was drawing the beer. He shouted to him in German to hurry, and banged on the table with his walking-stick.

'Lazy man,' he said. 'Idle. Bad service here.'

The other waiter brought the tankards along while Adolf threatened him with the sack.

'Where did you get to?' Chipchase said, burying his nose in his beer.

Blore-Smith said: 'Oh, Mrs. Mendoza said she was feeling so hot in that night-club that she wanted some fresh air, and then of course I couldn't get away for some time as she wanted to sit for hours in a café.'

He surprised himself by the fluency with which he was able to say this.

'I wonder she didn't keep you up all night,' Chipchase said, snapping down the tankard lid.

Adolf leant across the table again.

'You are a fine character, Herr Maltravers,' he said. 'A fine character. An English gentleman. I'm not a waiter to-night. I am a gentleman.'

'Naturally, naturally,' Maltravers said. 'Have another.'

'On me this time,' Adolf said. 'We are all gentlemen. Herr Chipchase, he is a fine character. He is an English gentleman.'

'Of course he is.'

'Herr Blore-Smith is a fine character. He is an English gentleman.'

Maltravers inclined his head.

'I am no waiter,' Adolf said. He banged on the table with his stick.

The other waiter brought the beer, and as he was walking away Adolf caught his ankle with the crook of his walking-stick and caused him to fall down.

'He is a lazy fellow,' Adolf said.

Inglethorne, who had finished his imitation, said:

'Look here, Maltravers, don't you know it's damned rude to talk while someone's doing something he's been specially asked to do for the amusement of the assembled company?'

'I didn't like what you were doing. It was bad theatre.'

'Look here——'

'Mr. Inglethorne is a fine character,' Adolf said.

'No, he isn't,' said Maltravers. 'He's a good actor but a bad man. I know some stories about Mr. Inglethorne I couldn't repeat. And anyway what he's just been doing was bad theatre.'

'Now look here, Maltravers——'

'Do you have some Kurfürst cigarettes?' Adolf said.

Blore-Smith said that he did not. He watched Adolf get up and go round the table, asking everyone in turn whether or not he or she smoked Kurfürst cigarettes. Maltravers said:

'I really can't make up my mind whether I'm pleased or furious about Hedwig and the Herr-Direktor. I suppose it will solve a lot of problems.'

Chipchase said: 'He'll probably turn her into the new German film star and then she will be bribed to go to Hollywood and we will all go over there and stay with her.'

The room was getting hotter. A camera-man began to sing, *Wien, Wien, nur Du allein*. One of the dressers, an elderly Balt, began to cry. Adolf had gone down on his knees under the table and was searching for Kurfürst cigarette coupons to further his aerial trip to Munich.

It was clear that no one, except perhaps Adolf, would rise early on the following morning. Soon Blore-Smith found an opportunity to slip upstairs and do his packing.

The Berlin zoo seemed as crowded as the Berlin streets. The weather was still intensely hot. Chipchase took off his hat and held his hand for some seconds to his forehead. Maltravers said:

'And now we will go and take a look at the gorillas.'

'Wait a bit,' Chipchase said. 'Vertigo has intervened.'

'Walking will do you good. Besides they are lovely creatures.'

Chipchase said: 'I cannot make up my mind as to which of us was wrong. I admit I was a bit severe with him in the beginning. That seemed to work very well. Then he came under your more lenient methods. That seemed to work very well too. What on earth can have made him go like this without a word?'

'Don't worry. Come and see the gorillas.'

'I can't understand it. Does gratitude mean nothing to his generation?'

'I expect he's gone straight back to his flat. He'll soon get sick of sitting alone there.'

'But should one go back at once and patch things up?'

'Well I can't for a week or two until this job's finished.'

'But should I?'

'We must think things over.'

'I can't afford to go on staying out here indefinitely at my own expense.'

'It's all very annoying.'

'Wait a moment. I must sit down again. I'm losing ground.'

They found some chairs under a tree within sight of the gorillas' cage, in front of which there was as usual a large crowd. The male gorilla was swinging on his trapeze, very slowly backwards and forwards, facing the people with an expression heavy with hatred and contempt. He had caught something of the national character of the race he found himself among, and his demeanour suggested a Prussian captain of industry at his morning exercises. Maltravers stretched himself back in his chair.

'I'm not feeling too well myself,' he said. 'But isn't that a familiar face? Near the gorillas?'

He pointed to where a figure stood apart from the rest of the crowd facing the cages. The outline was that of a tall man, with drooping shoulders, who wore a bowler. His pose recalled a minor work of Rodin. The stoop suggested in a too obvious way that he was playing a rôle in tragedy. Chipchase, who had taken off his hat again, shaded his eyes.

'Is it the Commodore?' he said.

'Who else?'

'Sent to the zoo while Mendie lives in guilty splendour.'

'It looks like it.'

While they watched him Commander Venables turned away from the gorillas. For a time he stood still, looking in front of him at a blank wall. Then he began to trudge in the direction of the chairs on which Maltravers and Chipchase sat.

'I'm not sure that I'm up to conversation,' Chipchase said. 'Shall we climb a tree and pretend we're animals?'

'Let's talk to the old boy and hear about all Mendie's evil doings.'

Commander Venables advanced, staring in front of him glassily like a sleepwalker. He had almost passed the chairs when Maltravers said:

'Ahoy, there.'

Commander Venables drew up slowly and did not at once look round. When he turned towards them it was with the fixed unbelieving expression of a sceptic at a séance, convinced that trickery is at the bottom of the manifestation.

"Isn't it a lovely afternoon,' Maltravers said. 'Do come and sit with us for a bit. It's much too hot to walk all the time.'

Commander Venables moved grudgingly forward towards the chair that Maltravers offered him. He said:

'This is a funny place to meet.'

'Not at all,' said Maltravers. 'Have you been watching the gorillas? We often come here and do that. I think animals have such a lot to teach one.'

Commander Venables grunted. He began to feel for his pipe.

'It's good to meet you,' he said. 'I thought I was the only person who talked English in the whole of Berlin, except the barman at my pub.'

'How's Mendie?' Chipchase said.

Commander Venables struck a match. He said:

'So far as I know she's very well.'

'Hasn't she got up yet? Really, at five o'clock in the afternoon! You oughtn't to allow her to indulge herself in that way!'

'She's gone back to England,' Commander Venables said.

He drew at his pipe.

'She's left me,' he said.

Maltravers sat up in his chair. He said:

'This was rather unexpected, wasn't it?'

Commander Venables said: 'Look here, you two, you both know Mendie pretty well. I wouldn't go off the deep end to any stray blighters I might happen to meet, but you both know her pretty well. What do you think of it? She leaves a chit in my room saying that she doesn't want to be disturbed till lunch-time, and when I go in there at one-thirty I find another chit to say that she can't stand things any longer and has gone back to England.'

He pushed back his chair, grinding its back legs deep into the gravel.

'Gone back to England,' he said. 'What do you think of that?'

'I think it's hard,' Maltravers said. 'Decidedly hard.'

'I wouldn't sound off like this just to anyone,' Commander Venables said. 'But, after all, you know the girl. I don't expect her to be a blooming plaster saint or whatever you call it. I'm not that myself. Besides I know I'm no oil-painting. I suppose I'm not particularly clever either. I've spent most of my spare time chasing a ball——'

The thought of his own honest simplicity so affected Commander Venables that for a few seconds words were inadequate to express his feelings. He could only stare in front of him with steel-blue eyes that seemed to have sunk far back into his head from the strain of scanning immeasurable tracts of sky and sea and which refused to focus on the caged beasts by which he found himself encompassed. At last he said quite low:

'I thought she was my girl.'

'Didn't she give you any sort of warning? No danger signals?'

'Only that she went home by herself last night. But she's done that before now.'

'No other men?'

'No—unless that fellow Herman at the bar last night—she's always talked a lot about him—if it's him——'

Commander Venables went a deeper crimson in the face and clenched his fist dramatically. Maltravers said:

'No. It wouldn't be Herman. I can guarantee that.'

'There's been no one else. She went back to the hotel with that little chap who runs round with you, whatever his name is. No. It isn't another man here. It may be someone in England.'

Chipchase fanned himself with his hat. Maltravers leant forward with his elbow on his knees. He said:

'Look here, you are going to dine with us to-night. You want companionship. It wouldn't do for you to be wandering about Berlin after dark in the state of mind you're in now. You look as if you want some sleep too. Why not go back to your hotel and have a snooze, and we will pick you up about eight o'clock and gnaw some food?'

Commander Venables blew out his cheeks and frowned terribly. He said:

'You know, you two are being damned good to me.'

'That's a date then?'

'I don't know why you want to bother about me.'

'You make tracks for your hotel, and we'll have a binge later.'

Commander Venables stood up. He said:

'I believe you're right.'

He was looking better already.

'In the bar,' he said.

'Right.'

Commander Venables waved good-bye and retreated at a fair pace considering the heat.

Maltravers and Chipchase watched him disappear among the crowd. Then they sat down again. Maltravers said:

'I need not explain to you what has happened?'

'You certainly need not,' Chipchase said.

'Of all the pieces of infernal interference!'

'It's in her nature. She just can't help it.'

'If I ever had anything to do with her again,' Maltravers said, 'I'd do something to her that would mark her for life.'

'I would at the same time point out that you originally produced him for Mendie's benefit.'

'True, true. However we now know where he's got to, and we can make plans accordingly.'

'Where does the Commodore come in?'

'I had to pack him off in a hurry to make sure that he would not remember that Mendie will probably be leaving on the night train and can therefore still be intercepted.'

'You mean that our game is to allow them a few weeks of each other's company before we weigh in again?'

'Exactly.'

'Excellent,' said Chipchase. 'Excellent.'

'After living with Mendie for a week he will be more in need of treatment than ever. After a fortnight we shall be able to dictate unconditional terms.'

'And so in the long run everything may turn out for the best.'

'Quite likely.'

Chipchase held his forehead again for several seconds.

'And have we really got to entertain the Commodore to-night?' he said. 'I was hoping for an early evening.'

'I know of a place in the country where one can dine outside, overlooking a lake.'

'That should do us all good.'

'And now,' said Maltravers, 'let's go and look at the snakes. They may remind me of Hedwig and the Herr-Direktor.'

5

Sarah Maltravers, coming rather suddenly out of the entrance to *Mode's* offices, where she had been to deliver personally an article on car mascots, saw Schlumbermayer immediately in front of her. He was standing half-way up the steps that led to the doorway, inspecting a photographer's show-case full of sepia prints of the year's débutantes. He was leaning forward on his stick, peering with anxiety at one of these. There was not room to pass unnoticed and it was too late to retreat up the stairs again so Sarah lunged at him with her umbrella and said:

'Seen something nice?'

Schlumbermayer shrank away from the umbrella's touch and ever so slightly slanted his face to the right so that he could see out of the corner of his eye who had accosted him.

'I thought you were a beggar,' he said, turning when he recognised her.

'I am.'

Schlumbermayer laughed and looked at his watch.

'What about some lunch?' he said. 'Since you're so indigent.'

'That would be very nice.'

'Where shall we go? The Ritz? Savoy?'

'What about the Ritz? It's close.'

'As a matter of fact,' Schlumbermayer said, speaking slowly, 'I have a certain reason for not wanting to go to the Ritz to-day. I think there may be someone there I'm trying to avoid.'

'The Savoy then?'

Schlumbermayer ran his finger round the inside of his collar. He craned his neck forward. He said:

'It's rather far away. I want my lunch at once. I'm hungry, aren't you? I'll tell you what, shall I take you to Bazzi's?'

'All right.'

'Do you know it?'

'I've had lunch there twice this week.'

'You like it then? We'll go there.'

Later, over some *ravioli*, Schlumbermayer said:

'Your husband comes back next week, doesn't he?'

'He told me to expect him soon on his last postcard.'

'Only about this film,' Schlumbermayer said with some caution. 'He wrote to me with various details——'

'Yes?'

'Well, you know about this Blore-Smith being at the back of it?'

'I'm vague about anything except the general idea.'

'Blore-Smith is in Berlin with them now, isn't he?'

'So far as I know.'

'You're sure of that?'

'Oliver Chipchase is still treating him, isn't he?'

'In Berlin?'

'Yes.'

Schlumbermayer's face, as usual the tint of a page from Domesday Book, became in his excitement a thing almost of flesh and blood. He said:

'He isn't in Berlin any longer. He's in London. And who do you think he's living with?'

'How on earth should I know?'

'With Mrs. Mendoza.'

'Mendie?'

Sarah was thoroughly surprised.

'Yes,' said Schlumbermayer. 'What do you think of that? I've seen them together myself.'

His news had made him triumphant.

'Have a *zabaglione*?' he said. 'They are expensive here but very good.'

'No. Coffee.'

'And yet,' Schlumbermayer said, 'Peter writes as if Blore-Smith were still in Berlin. At least he implies that arrangements are to go ahead without alteration.'

'If Peter says so he means it.'

Schlumbermayer looked uncertain.

'I don't want to get involved in a lot of unnecessary expense,' he said. 'I've had a very unprofitable year. One's always paying out. Charities and so on. Constant demands on one.'

'But what difference does this make? His living with Mendie?'

Schlumbermayer pursed his lips together and shook his head slowly from side to side, raising at the same time his eyebrows.

'Perhaps he won't feel the same about the film. He may want to spend all his money on Mrs. Mendoza.'

'You are very anxious to have it taken at your house then?'

Schlumbermayer shrugged his shoulders. He said:

'You know I'm having business negotiations with Gaston de la Tour d'Espagne?'

'So I hear.'

'Something of the sort might occupy his mercurial temperament in a way that I could scarcely hope to do if I was alone in the house with him.'

'Have you laid in a stock of poppy and mandragora and all the drowsy syrups of the world?'

Schlumbermayer laughed so much that he spilt his coffee all down the front of his coat. Then he stopped laughing and looked disturbed. He said:

'Surely he'll bring his own supplies, won't he? He can't expect hospitality to extend as far as that.'

'It would be very awkward if he was stranded without any. People can be very tiresome when that happens.'

Schlumbermayer thoughtfully rubbed with a torn pocket handkerchief at the coffee-stains on his clothes. He said:

'I'll have to risk it.'

'How was Blore-Smith looking when you saw him?'

'Ill.'

'Poor little brute.'

'Then you think everything will go forward as arranged?'

'I'm sure it will. When is Gaston arriving?'

'He hasn't let me know yet.'

Schlumbermayer brought to an end his efforts at dry cleaning and sank back in his chair. He was evidently thinking of the Marquis de la Tour d'Espagne's probable idiosyncrasies as a guest. Sarah began to collect her hat, bag, and other belongings. She said:

'I shall have to be getting along.'

'Come to a movie?'

'No, thanks. And thank you for lunch.'

'I hope you will come down to Broadacres when the film gets going.'

'I shall look forward to it.'

Sarah left the restaurant and, after he had found a mistake in the bill, Schlumbermayer took a taxi to Somerset House to look up the personnel constituting the directing board of some companies he was interested in.

'But I thought you told me that you couldn't live here a moment longer and that the only thing to do was to give notice at once,' Blore-Smith said. 'You did say that, I know. You said if you found that I hadn't given notice when you came back you would jump into the river.'

Mrs. Mendoza clenched her hands. She said:

'Whatever does it matter what I said? Where are we going to live if we leave here before finding somewhere else to go? You must tell Mrs. Pinkus that you've changed your mind and that you want to stay at least a month longer.'

'But I pay by the week.'

'That doesn't matter. She will be only too glad to have you for a bit longer.'

'I don't think she will.'

'Why not?'

'When I gave notice Mrs. Pinkus said that she was just coming up that very evening to say that she would be needing these rooms for another tenant. She said she'd spoken to you about it.'

'I told her the place was kept in a disgraceful state. She was very impertinent.'

'You never mentioned this.'

'You don't suppose I tell you every time I have to put someone like that in their place, do you? As a matter of fact we should have had to go in any case. I couldn't stay in the house of a woman who had been as rude to me as that.'

'What did she say?'

'What do you think she said? What do people usually say when they are angry and know you aren't married to the man you're living with?'

'Oh, I didn't know——'

'Well, you know now,' said Mrs. Mendoza. 'You see how I'm treated. Perhaps it may make you a little more considerate in future. What are we doing to-night?'

'Nothing that I know of.'

'But haven't you made any plans? It never seems to occur to you that a woman wants some amusement.'

'What about a cinema?'

'A cinema? Didn't we go to a cinema last night and the night before? What else is there that one could possibly see? And then we've got to make some plans about where we're going to live. Why not take a cottage somewhere for a bit?'

'In the country?'

'That's where cottages usually are, isn't it?'

'But do you want to live in the country?'

'Do I want to live in the country? Do you know that the only place I have ever been happy in for more than five minutes has always been the country? Can't you see that I like the country? Do I look the type who likes living in towns?'

'But you always seem to have lived in towns——'

'Don't be absurd. I've lived in towns because I've had to. Not because I liked it. You arrange to have your odds and ends stored somewhere and we will find a furnished cottage.'

'But I don't like the country.'

'You don't like the country? You must be mad. You've probably never lived in the country. You feel quite different when you live there. We'll keep a horse and lots of dogs. It will be lovely.'

Mrs. Mendoza put her arm round his shoulders and looked at him in a way that made him ashamed of the objection he had raised to leaving London.

'You'll be much happier there,' she said. 'Don't you want to be happy?'

The moderation of her request in asking for a cottage instead of a palladian house or a ruined castle impressed Blore-Smith. It was this streak of simplicity in her which he found so hard to resist. He remembered that for some time now he had been tiring of these rooms in Ebury Street. If he went to the country he would be less likely to encounter Maltravers and Chipchase. Perhaps if he stayed there long enough they would forget about him and find some other means of earning a livelihood. He said:

'All right. But where shall we be able to find a cottage?'

'I'll take the car and have a look round to-morrow.'

At the mention of the car Blore-Smith winced. It had been Mrs. Mendoza's first and, at present, most expensive necessity which he had had to supply.

'Shall I come too?'

Mrs. Mendoza pulled the hair at the nape of his neck.

'You can come and see when I have found something nice,' she said. 'Not before.'

Blore-Smith hesitated.

'You won't go too far,' he said—'I mean in making arrangements about taking it—before I've seen it?'

'Do you mean you don't trust me?'

'No, of course not. I mean—well——'

Mrs. Mendoza stamped on the floor.

'Why did you ever take me away from Hugo?' she said. 'Why did you bring me all the way from Berlin, where at least there was Herman, to come back to London, where it has rained every day for a week and I have to live in this most dreary of all streets in the world? What have you done to make my life possible to endure, as some return for my having come to live with you? After all I don't ask much from you. I haven't ordered a mass of clothes or asked for a lot of jewellery. Not that I expect I should get it if I did, as I never see so much as a bunch of daffodils or a bottle of scent out of the penny-in-the-slot machine. Do you suppose I haven't given up something by doing this? And not so little either. What about my friends? Am I never going to see Peter and Oliver again? Why I used to get more amusement out of five minutes with them than you've managed to supply in three weeks. And then just because I ask if we can live in the country and offer to try and find somewhere to do it you become beastly to me at once. Why men have gone down on their knees to me—literally their knees—and asked me to live with them in the country. Sometimes I wonder if you aren't just raving mad. In fact that's the only explanation.'

Mrs. Mendoza jerked back her head and gave several rather wild fits of laughter.

'Just mad,' she repeated.

She stood posed with her legs apart, staring at Blore-Smith, who was trembling violently.

'My friends, my real friends,' Mrs. Mendoza said, 'must be laughing. How they must be laughing! How Peter and Oliver must be laughing! And when I think of what I've done it makes me laugh too. I take you away from them and leave poor dear lumbering old Hugo, who would have carried me home to England on his back if I had asked him to, just in order to live in some poky little rooms surrounded by law books and Medici prints. Well, nobody can say that I can't see a joke, can they? And I don't mind telling you that this is just about the best joke I have ever had an opportunity of seeing.'

Mrs. Mendoza sat down on the rug in front of the fender and laughed and laughed. She laughed until the tears began to pour down her cheeks. Blore-Smith could only say:

'I'm sorry. Really, I'm so sorry.'

Then he knelt down on the floor beside her and took her hand. She allowed him to hold it, but for a time she continued to laugh. He tried to tell her that he was really only too ready to live in the country. He tried to explain, in the manner of Chipchase, that his first apparent unwillingness had been caused by deep-seated inhibition emanating from the subconscious.

Schlumbermayer's home, Broadacres, was about thirty miles from London in a residential neighbourhood that appealed to stockbrokers. It was a large red affair, build about 1900, and surrounded by closely cut grass, circular flower-beds, and high banks along which ran clipped yew hedges. There was a lawn in front of the house and on the further side of the drive a wide stretch of meadow where the previous owner had played polo. Neighbouring estates were hidden by a high wall that surrounded the grounds. The big bare rooms were furnished for the most part with stuff that Schlumbermayer had picked up cheap from a country club that had gone bankrupt. There were no pictures to speak of. Sometimes when Schlumbermayer bought something that was an unmanageable size it would stand about or hang on the wall for a month or two, but for the most part he kept his collection in the cellars. Upstairs in his own sitting-room, which was always locked, there were ikons in glass cases let into the walls and some favourite pieces that Schlumbermayer could not bring himself to sell. There was also a life-size portrait of himself, so incompetently executed that its painter was generally supposed to have been some art student with whom Schlumbermayer had once been in love.

It was a warm evening. Maltravers, Chipchase, and Schlumbermayer himself were strolling up and down the lawn after dinner. The air was still and the whine of traffic on the arterial road that passed about a quarter of a mile from the house rose and fell in the distance. Maltravers said:

'So that is all fixed then. We all come down here on Friday and on Monday we set to work.'

Schlumbermayer took a cigar-case from his pocket. He said:

'I still don't see how you are going to get him down here. After all you've been in London some days now and you haven't even tried to see him.'

'Do you think we don't know his measure?' Maltravers said, putting out his hand for a cigar.

'It's not him so much as Mrs. Mendoza.'

'Do you know her?'

'Not well. But I know about her. I used to know Mendoza a bit. We once put through a bit of business together.'

'And your experience teaches you that she may be difficult?'

'She may not want to let him go.'

'You would, I presume, have no objection to her coming along too, if necessary?'

Schlumbermayer moistened his lips and readjusted his spectacles.

'I daresay we could find room for her,' he said. 'She's certainly a good-looker.'

'In that case,' Maltravers said, 'you may rest assured that everything will start on Monday as arranged. I have already given orders for the necessary gear to be sent down by car. It may not even be essential to ask Mrs. Mendoza. On the other hand your permission to do so will make negotiations easier.'

'Yes, do ask her,' Schlumbermayer said. 'I should certainly like her to come now that I've thought it over. Be sure to ask her. I should like to ask her one or two questions about Mendoza.'

'I expect she will enjoy answering them very much, if she comes,' Maltravers said. 'But I can't make any promises either way at present. She may come and she mayn't.'

Chipchase, who had stopped walking and was now leaning against an urn that stood at one of the corners of a small lily-pond, said:

'He has probably done himself incalculable harm psychologically by stopping treatment in this way. Heaven knows what he will be like when I start again.'

'All the better from your point of view,' Maltravers said. 'I should increase your fees for the additional trouble involved.'

Schlumbermayer said: 'You both seem to do pretty well out of him. Do you think he would be interested in my collection?'

'I'm sure he would.'

'To purchase, I mean.'

'Ah, that's another matter. One can't say. He's not as rich as all that, you know.'

Schlumbermayer sighed.

'I suppose not,' he said. 'Still he might like to see some of the things.'

Maltravers said: 'If Gaston is coming over on Wednesday let's all meet and have dinner together on Thursday.'

'That would be all right. Gaston and I are dining at the Ning-Po that night. You can join us there,' Schlumbermayer said.

'Why the Ning-Po?'

Schlumbermayer fidgeted from one foot to the other.

'Well,' he said, 'supplies seem to be rather low and Gaston thought he might meet a man there who would put him in touch——'

'Ah, I see. But I thought he had knocked off the stuff lately. He seemed quite *désintoxiqué* when we met him in Paris.'

Schlumbermayer said: 'I hope so. I don't want a lot of nonsense of that sort down here.'

'Naturally.'

'Still we must go to the Ning-Po if he wants to.'

'All right,' said Maltravers. 'We'll be there.'

They walked towards the former polo ground.

'Listen,' Chipchase said. 'The nightingale.'

The removal-van had arrived two hours later than the time appointed, but Blore-Smith had only a small amount of furniture so that his belongings were soon stowed away inside it. He stood on the doorstep, watching the remaining odds and ends which lay round about him on the pavement being secreted into empty spaces. Van Gogh's *Sunflower* was propped against the railings and Blore-Smith went down the steps towards it, thinking that he would put it in himself to make sure that the glass was not broken. As he stooped to pick it up he heard a voice behind him say:

'Why, you seem to be moving house?'

Turning, he saw Chipchase, who with Maltravers stood watching him. It was Chipchase who had spoken. He was leaning against the pillar-box. Blore-Smith could think of no reply. Chipchase took a small notebook from his pocket and wrote something in it with a stump of pencil. Maltravers said:

'If only we had known earlier that you were making a move we could have come along and lent a hand. Where are you making for? Or is that inquisitive?'

'Well, we've taken a cottage——'

'We?'

'Mendie and I.'

'Really? But how very nice. You will be able to go over there for week-ends. It's not far from London, I suppose. Kent? Sussex? Not, I hope, Essex?'

'Sussex. But——'

'The film starts at Schlumbermayer's house on Monday. We thought it might be better to go down a day or two before. To-morrow, to be precise. Will that suit you all right?'

'But Mendie——'

'She is invited too. Will she come, do you think? By this time, though, you will have realised that when dealing with Mendie one can't really tell until the last moment.'

'No, she——'

'Where is she now?'

'Down at the cottage. It's a furnished one. These things are going to be stored.'

'You have your personal belongings still here? Your clothes and so on?'

'Yes.'

'Then how would it be to send Mendie a wire? You can spend the night in my flat on the sofa and we will go down to Schlumbermayer's to-morrow. I will run over to the cottage in my car and explain to her why you were unable to turn up. I expect that she didn't realise that we should be ready to begin making the film so soon. Time means nothing to her. You didn't really realise that yourself, did you?'

'No, I didn't,' was all Blore-Smith found himself able to say.

'Or perhaps you would prefer that Mendie should not be invited?' Maltravers said.

'Well——'

'Anyway,' said Chipchase, putting away his notebook, 'that can be decided later. What I want to know is, how have you been? Your nerves? Have you been sleeping all right for example?'

'Not altogether. I——'

'I feared that would happen,' Chipchase said. 'You know it was a very natural reaction of yours to leave Berlin like that. In some ways one

couldn't have had a better sign that you were beginning to assert yourself. But it was a risky thing to do. I don't want to indulge in recrimina-
tions but it was very risky.'

'I've felt the bad effects of it,' Blore-Smith said.

He could not prevent himself from saying this. He had not meant
to speak of himself at all to Chipchase but he felt suddenly that renewed
treatment might after all be a good thing.

Chipchase said: 'I can't say I'm surprised. But we must have a long
talk about all that some time later. I see the van is now ready to start.
Get your luggage and we will put it in the car and run it up to the flat,
sending a wire to Mendie on the way.'

'But——'

'Have you a better suggestion?'

'All right.'

'You are dining with us to-night,' Maltravers said. 'On us, in fact,
to celebrate our reunion. Gaston de la Tour d'Espagne will be there and
also Schlumbermayer, so that any little things you want to hear about
can be explained at dinner. We're dining at the Ning-Po. Do you know
it?'

'No.'

'Personally I wish we had made it somewhere else,' Chipchase said.
'I like the Ning-Po and when one goes to restaurants with Gaston it
often has to be one's last visit.'

'Oh, Gaston will be all right,' Maltravers said. 'He's as mild as a
lamb these days.'

'Is it Chinese food?' Blore-Smith said.

'Of course,' Maltravers said. 'You'll like it immensely.'

The Ning-Po Restaurant was a dark L-shaped room, full of Asiatic
students sitting two or three together, talking and arguing. Two negroes
were at a table in the corner with a pair of very blonde girls in front
of them. Maltravers, Chipchase, and Blore-Smith were in the other
corner, examining the menu and waiting for drinks to arrive from the
public house on the corner. They had been there about five minutes
when Schlumbermayer appeared at the door and came slowly up the
room. He stood uncertainly by the table as if he could not make up
his mind whether or not he would sit down at it.

'Well?' said Maltravers. 'A drink?'

Schlumbermayer shook his head sourly. He said:

'I'm on a diet.'

'Nonsense,' said Maltravers. 'A little drink will do you good. Anyway hang your hat up and come and sit down in peace where you can consider the question.'

Schlumbermayer hung up his hat and overcoat and sat down. He said:

'The worst has happened. Gaston has run out of supplies and he was in an awful state when I last saw him. I don't know how I'm going to get him down to the country or deal with him when I've got him there. He's worse than he was five years ago. I thought he had turned over a new leaf.'

'Don't worry,' said Maltravers. 'We'll handle him all right.'

'I'm not so sure,' Schlumbermayer said, blowing his nose noisily.

The Marquis de la Tour d'Espagne was late. It was nine o'clock when he made his arrival known by poking his head round the door and giving a piercing whistle. His bowler hat was tipped over his eyes in the manner of a masher or johnny of some generations earlier and he wore a check suit and carried a rolled umbrella.

'Ah,' said Maltravers, 'I suppose one ought to have known that he would arrive in this state.'

The Marquis walked unhurriedly across the restaurant, winking at one of the waitresses as he passed the service lift. When he reached the table he stopped suddenly and, assuming a melodramatic attitude, he raised his umbrella above his head and began to intone in a low rich voice:

> *'Je suis le ténébreux, le veuf, l'inconsolé,*
> *Le Prince d'Aquitaine à la tour abolie . . .'*

'You're very late, Gaston,' Maltravers said. 'Where have you been drinking?'

'Drinking?' said the Marquis, drawing off his saffron-coloured gloves. 'Drinking? What can have put such an idea into your head?'

He removed his bowler and, placing it on the end of his umbrella, rested the whole on his forehead, balancing the two objects in this position for nearly half a minute, at the end of which time the hat fell off and into a dish of pork pellets with sour-sweet sauce that an elderly Chinese at the next table had just begun to eat.

'Gaston!' Maltravers and Chipchase spoke at once.

The Marquis snatched the hat from the sour-sweet sauce. Almost no damage had been done. He said:

'Sir! How can I sufficiently apologise? It is the first time in all my life that I have done such a thing. It is middle age that approaches. We lose our former dexterity. Ten thousand regrets.'

The Chinaman smiled and bowed. He understood, he said. Everything was O.K., he said. But the Marquis was not satisfied. The Chinese gentleman must drink a cocktail with him. Or if not that anything that might take his fancy.

'For heaven's sake come and sit down, Gaston, and don't be a nuisance.'

It took some time but the Marquis was at last induced to join the others at their table and, after trying to kiss Schlumbermayer, he settled down fairly happily to humming aloud to himself the English version of the menu. Blore-Smith was too embarrassed to look more than once or twice in his direction. The others seemed to find nothing specially out of the way in this behaviour. Under Chipchase's direction food was ordered. Maltravers said:

'Now before we go any further I think I had better outline once more the general design of the scheme that we propose to follow in making the first of our documentary films. When I say that the relative importance of cutting will be even greater than when an ordinary commercial film is being made, you will have some idea of the weight that I attach to this side of our work. The juxtaposition of sharp contrasts will be all important.'

Turning to Blore-Smith, Maltravers said: 'You will, in a sense, be the hero.'

Blore-Smith nodded and bowed his head towards the plate of food that had been put in front of him by the waitress, not herself Chinese, who wore an unusually short skirt and had long heavily mascaraed eyelashes. The Marquis suddenly began to make a noise that made the rest of them turn their attention to him.

'Chopsticks,' he was saying. 'I must have chopsticks.'

'Bring some chopsticks,' said Maltravers. 'Now first of all we shall have to take suitable pictures of the setting. Broadacres must be shown from all its angles.'

'I hope you won't try and show it in anything but a favourable light,' Schlumbermayer said. 'After all you yourself suggested that if I ever wanted to sell the place——'

'It will be shown from all its angles,' Maltravers said. 'In the same way all the principal actors, notably ourselves, will be taken separately in characteristic pursuits. They will then be shown in relation to each other. We propose from time to time to import certain persons specially chosen for their significance to throw into high relief the behaviour of the protagonists.'

'Look here,' said Schlumbermayer, 'you never said anything about these additional people.'

Maltravers raised slightly his hand.

'On the contrary,' he said, 'if you think back you will find that I most certainly did and in one case at least you were very much in favour of her coming over.'

'I don't seem to remember it,' Schlumbermayer said, but he showed no signs of active opposition.

Maltravers said: 'Perhaps the most important feature of the whole experiment—for we must confess it is at present only an experiment—will be the shooting of situations that arise quite fortuitously. Naturally these may occur during the preliminary studies of each character and everything will be subordinated to taking as many of these as possible. *Montage* will do the rest.'

'I will now,' said Chipchase, 'say a few words about the side of the production which will be under my own management. That is to say the psychoanalytical——'

He was interrupted by a shout from the Marquis de la Tour d'Espagne:

'Why do you look at me?'

It was a yell, a sound like a clap of thunder. The Marquis, who until a few moments before had been crooning happily, had half risen and seized the edge of the table with both hands, dragging the cloth towards him, so that Schlumbermayer's food was jerked violently from him at the very moment when he was making an effort to transport some of it to his mouth. The attention of everyone was in this way directed to the table where the negroes and their girls sat, because it was on them that the Marquis's now bulging eyes were fixed.

'What are you looking at?' he repeated, almost as loudly as before. 'Why the hell have you the impertinence to stare so at me?'

The nearer negro began to roll his eyes horribly. He shouted back: 'What do you say to me?'

The Marquis let go of the table-cloth, knocking two glasses to the floor, and getting up began to push back his chair.

'What do I say?' he said. 'I say that the blood of Bayard flows in my veins and I am telling you that I won't be looked at like that by a black man. A black man! A black man!'

The further negro now jumped up too. In a very refined voice he chattered:

'What you mean, black man? Don't you think I'm as good as you, you poor thing, you——'

'Oh stow it, Oscar,' said one of the blonde girls. 'Don't take any notice of his common talk.'

The Marquis had by this time reached the table where the negroes sat.

'Listen,' he said. 'I will pay you a compliment that will surprise you. My second will call on you to-morrow when you tell me your address. Think how fine a death it will be for you, a black man, to be shot by one——' He broke off and turned to the Chinese in whose sour-meat sauce he had dropped his hat. 'Sir, will you do me an honour? Will you be my second? It is in the interests of the civilised races of the world——'

By this time Maltravers and Chipchase had risen also and both laid hands on the Marquis. Maltravers said:

'Gaston, for goodness' sake——'

The Marquis shook them off. His face was as white as chalk.

'Lâche!' he yelled. 'You coward black man! Booby!'

Schlumbermayer sat very still with a faint acid smile on his face. He watched the scene but all the time he messed about with his fork the food on the plate before him. Blore-Smith did not know what to do. For the first time in his experience Maltravers and Chipchase, like Frankenstein, seemed unable to control this creature of their own contriving. Both negroes now stood shoulder-to-shoulder and jabbered in unison. The other blonde began to powder her nose. The owner of the restaurant, a small Chinese, almost a dwarf, had now joined the combatants. The Marquis stretched out his hand towards the hook on which his umbrella hung. At this moment the situation was taken in hand with extreme violence by the waitress with the long eyelashes. She took the Marquis de la Tour d'Espagne by the arm and said:

'Out! Go on, out you get!'

The Marquis turned and, seeing her, was so taken aback that at first she was able to drag him halfway down the room towards the door.

'Out you get, you!' she said.

The Marquis suddenly jerked himself away from her. He snatched his bowler and umbrella from the wall, leant forward and gave her a smacking kiss, ran towards the door, where he paused for a moment and shouted: 'Merde!' Then he bowed and disappeared into the street. All this happened so quickly that at first Blore-Smith could scarcely collate in his mind the sequence of events. When his brain cleared a little he saw that Chipchase was offering his cigarette-case to the negroes, while Maltravers was quieting down the owner of the restaurant. After a while they came back to the table. Schlumbermayer said:

'Shall we ever see him again?'

Maltravers said: 'I wonder whether we ought to go out and have a look for him. I don't expect he's gone far.'

'Let's see what we can do,' Chipchase said. 'Personally I don't want a Chinese meal much after all this.'

'Do you want me to come too?' Schlumbermayer said.

Maltravers said: 'Not unless you want to specially. Why don't both of you finish your dinners and then come up to my flat? Sarah will be there even if we haven't arrived yet. We'll have a look for Gaston and bring him along. Of course he may have gone for good, in which case we'll have to discuss ways and means without him.'

Blore-Smith, not liking the idea of having to force his way in on Sarah in the company of Schlumbermayer and thinking of the explanations he would have to give, tried to protest, but before he was able to take any practical steps to avoid this Maltravers and Chipchase had left the room and he was alone with Schlumbermayer. He noticed that the negroes and blonde girls had settled down to quarrelling among themselves. Schlumbermayer, who had for some time now turned his attention to his food, looked up.

'Silly, isn't it?' he said at last, fixing Blore-Smith through the thick lenses of his spectacles.

'Yes, isn't it?' Blore-Smith said.

They went to the Maltravers flat by bus, each paying his own fare. Blore-Smith did not speak much because he felt shaken after the scene in the Ning-Po and Schlumbermayer as usual had little to offer in the way of conversation. Sarah herself opened the door on their arrival. She was clearly surprised to see them together. To Blore-Smith's relief Schlumbermayer gave some explanation of what had happened.

'Come in anyway,' Sarah said, after she had heard something of the story of the Marquis de la Tour d'Espagne's behaviour, 'and tell me the rest upstairs.'

Outside in the street Blore-Smith had forgotten his earlier fears of embarrassment at meeting Sarah again. On the threshold of the flat these returned in an aggravated form. He sat down on one of the steel chairs, wondering what to say. Schlumbermayer made his way round the flat, examining everything, sometimes unhooking a picture from the wall and looking at its back, and turning up pieces of china or silver to inspect the mark on each. Sarah sat down beside Blore-Smith.

'What sort of a time did you have in Germany?' she said. 'Did you meet any nice girls?'

'Well there was a Miss Grundt——' Blore-Smith began, and then broke off, remembering that he could not very well tell Sarah of Fräulein Grundt without supplying at the same time a certain amount of compromising information about Maltravers.

'Oh yes,' Sarah said, 'but she was Peter's girl surely? Not yours? He wrote me all about her.'

'Well, I suppose she was in a way. But I mean I used to see a good deal of her too—not in the same way of course—that is, I mean, we all went about a lot together all the time.'

'I don't want to hear about her. The brute!'

'No, of course not, naturally, at least——'

Schlumbermayer came heavily across the room holding a mug in his hand.

'This seems quite good pewter,' he said. 'Where did you get it?'

While Sarah was explaining the mug's history the door opened and Maltravers came in, followed by Chipchase and the Marquis de la Tour d'Espagne.

'Why, Gaston,' Sarah said. 'What ages since we've met.'

The Marquis kissed her hand. He seemed considerably cowed. After he had said a few words to Sarah, almost in an undertone, he turned to Blore-Smith and Schlumbermayer and said:

'Before I do anything I must apologise to you for what happened at the restaurant Ning-Po. I get very excited sometimes. I am afraid that this happened to-night. You must accept my apologies and regrets. Will you?'

Blore-Smith and Schlumbermayer said that they would. The Marquis sat down at Sarah's invitation. He seemed, Blore-Smith was glad to notice, thoroughly exhausted. Chipchase said:

'I will now tell you something about the psychoanalytical side of the film. As I was about to when interrupted.'

He looked meaningly at the Marquis, who turned his eyes away. Maltravers said:

'Have we got any biscuits or anything of the sort in the house? We were forced to make rather a scrappy dinner.'

Chipchase said: 'The film is to be called *Œdipus Rex* for the obvious reason that a great deal of it will illustrate the practical workings of the œdipus-complex.'

He glanced at Blore-Smith, whose attention was at that moment distracted by the telephone bell. Maltravers took up the receiver.

'Hullo?' he said.

Chipchase stopped talking and watched the telephone grudgingly.

'Who is that speaking?' Maltravers said; and then, handing the receiver to Sarah, said:

'It's Nipper.'

'Nonsense,' Sarah said. 'It can't be.'

'I tell you it is.'

She took the receiver from him and said:

'Hullo?'

Someone at the other end of the line talked for some minutes while Sarah answered 'Yes' or 'No.' The others listened in silence. At last Sarah said:

'I must say good-bye now. See you on Wednesday.'

She hung up the receiver.

'So it was Nipper?' Maltravers said.

'No, of course it wasn't.'

'But I recognised his voice.'

'It's quite different.'

'Who was that then?'

'He's called Chummy.'

'Is he, indeed?'

'You've met him.'

'I thought the name seemed familiar,' Maltravers said.

However in spite of the name's familiarity Maltravers did not seem entirely pleased and he sighed deeply. Beyond this he made no comment. Chipchase said:

'Shall I go on?'

'Yes,' said Maltravers. 'But what about those biscuits, Sarah? Surely we've got something to eat in the house?'

'I'll try and find something,' Sarah said.

She went out of the room. Chipchase said:

'As to the psychoanalytical side——'

The Marquis de la Tour d'Espagne, who had up to now been listening quietly enough, at last began to show signs of agitation. Chipchase broke off in the middle of his sentence.

'What is it, Gaston?' he said.

The Marquis said: 'What is all this you are talking about? I don't understand. What is happening?'

'The film.'

'But I don't understand.'

The Marquis began to whimper. Chipchase said:

'It's the film, Gaston. The film we told you about. It will amuse you. It's all about psychoanalysis.'

'*Le psychanalyse?*'

'*Oui.*'

'But I don't understand,' the Marquis said in a broken voice. 'What have I got to do? What is it all about? Why have you brought me here?'

He began to cry gently in a small silk pocket handkerchief. Maltravers said:

'Cheer up, Gaston. What's the matter? You won't have to do anything. All you need do is to watch us make the film while you stay comfortably at Broadacres.'

The Marquis's sobs became louder and louder. His body shook all over. He was now definitely howling.

'I don't understand. I can't understand all about the film. What am I meant to do?'

Chipchase said: 'Look, Gaston. Here's Sarah with some chocolate biscuits. Have a biscuit. You'll feel much better.'

'What's happened?' Sarah said.

Maltravers said: 'Gaston's feeling a bit off colour. I think he'd really better go back to bed.'

'I'll see him home,' Schlumbermayer said, and added to Chipchase:

'You go my way, don't you? Perhaps you could come with us and lend a hand?'

'All right,' Chipchase said. 'Where's he staying? With you? Are you going back to Broadacres to-night?'

'At the moment he's in a furnished flat in the Jermyn Street part of the world.'

'What an extraordinary thing to do,' Sarah said. 'But how like Gaston.'

'I'm at my club. I'm not going back to the country until to-morrow so I can't do anything about him,' Schlumbermayer said.

'Well we'll see him home,' Chipchase said, 'and try and fix him up for the night.'

Schlumbermayer added in a lower voice, as if someone might be listening at the door: 'I believe there's someone in a neighbouring flat who might be able to assist as regards——'

'We'll find out about that when we get there,' Chipchase said. 'Now come along, Gaston. Bedtime.'

The Marquis was by now lying on his face on the sofa, heaving spasmodically. He was crying loudly and aimlessly like a child who has forgotten the original cause of its grief. He gulped noisily when Chipchase spoke to him.

'Cheer up, Gaston,' Maltravers said, and, taking out his handkerchief, wiped away some of the Marquis's tears.

They took him by the arm and he made no objection to being led out of the room after he had once more kissed Sarah's hand. Schlumbermayer said:

'Wait a moment, let me see if I've got enough money for the taxi.'

Maltravers took Schlumbermayer gently by the shoulder and pushed him from the room, saying as he did so:

'You'll find you've got enough. Take my word for it.'

'Well, good night all,' said Chipchase, 'and you will pick me up to-morrow and we'll all go down to Broadacres together.'

He followed them out of the room. Maltravers heaved a sigh and sat down on the sofa. Sarah said to Blore-Smith: 'If you are staying here to-night we must begin trying to fix you up with a bed. We might start by moving some of the typewriters.'

After passing an only moderately comfortable night on the sofa Blore-Smith had breakfast with Maltravers alone, as they were making an early start and Sarah had decided to stay in bed until later in the day.

During this meal Maltravers spoke on the subject of the Marquis de la Tour d'Espagne.

'Gaston has far too much energy,' he said. 'Nothing short of world upheaval provides sufficient occupation for him. During the war, for example, he did well. In fact I attribute much of his subsequent behaviour to the fact that his war record was so good. I suppose he feels subconsciously that if he kicks up enough fuss war will break out again as a result.'

'But he was quite all right when I first met him,' Blore-Smith said.

Maltravers said: 'He has his quiet periods. And of course opium is a great preservative. When it's scarce he raises hell. But come along now. We must start.'

They drove in the yellow car towards Bloomsbury, where they were picking up Chipchase. He was looking out of his window when they arrived and soon joined them with his suitcase. Maltravers said:

'Did you get Gaston back all right last night?'

'He seemed fairly happy by the time we left him,' Chipchase said. 'And Schlumbermayer rang me up this morning to say that he's arranged to have a twist of Gaston's favourite baccy at Broadacres when he arrives, so that should be an additional inducement to get him there.'

'That's very handsome of him.'

'He says that Gaston has got to make his own arrangements in future but he understands that it wasn't altogether Gaston's fault that he was left short this time.'

Maltravers said: 'You know this deal Schlumbermayer hopes to put through must be pretty important for him to take all this trouble.'

Chipchase said: 'I always knew Gaston had inherited some very nice things.'

The car drew up in front of the entrance to a small block of flats. Chipchase said:

'I think I'll wait down here. I had enough of Gaston last night to satisfy me for some time.'

'Shall I wait too?' Blore-Smith said.

'You go up,' Chipchase said. 'It may prove very instructive.'

Blore-Smith followed Maltravers into the lift and they went up several floors. Maltravers said:

'What a place to live.'

He rang the bell of a door with frosted glass panels at the end of a small passage. The door was opened by a charwoman, a depressed character, so over-equipped with the traditional badges of her profession that she had the air of an amateur stage-impersonator. Maltravers said:

'Is the Marquess in?'

The old woman did not speak but she pointed to the door on the left and nodded her head. As she did this several screeching sounds came from the further side. Isolated, creaking notes, as from some creature in pain. Blore-Smith felt his heart jump. Maltravers raised his eyebrows and tapped on the door. There was no answer beyond a weaker repetition of the same noises. Maltravers tapped again. There was silence for a moment.

'Who is that?' a voice said.

'It's the younger generation,' Maltravers said, 'knocking on the door.'

Another confused burst of sound came from the next room. Maltravers turned the handle of the door and Blore-Smith followed him across the threshold.

'My dear Gaston,' Blore-Smith heard Maltravers say.

The Marquis was sitting on the window-seat with a coaching-horn in his hand. He continued to make unsuccessful efforts to blow this and merely waved to them with his left hand as an acknowledgment of their arrival. There was a bottle of yellow chartreuse on the table beside him. The air was charged with a musty sweetish smell. Maltravers said:

'Is this your latest hobby?'

Blore-Smith looked round the room. It was furnished with heavy leather armchairs and had a brown and gold embossed wallpaper. Lace curtains kept out some of the sun but a few shafts of lights fell on a buhl cabinet on which stood an eastern maiden done in bronze, holding a lamp. Maltravers said:

'Let's hear the Last Post.'

Suddenly the Marquis jumped up from where he was sitting. He threw the coaching-horn to the floor. Grasping Blore-Smith by the hands he began to dance round the room with him. Blore-Smith was unprepared for anything of this sort and found himself dragged round and round and round in a dizzy whirl, while the Marquis began to sing:

> 'We are two funny men,
> The funniest ever seen,
> And one is Mr. Gallagher,
> And one is Mr. Sheen . . .'

After a few moments Blore-Smith lost his balance and fell heavily to the floor. The Marquis, breathless, returned to his place in the window-seat. Maltravers said:

'I suppose you haven't packed, Gaston? You know we are off to Schlumbermayer's this morning.'

The Marquis, who had begun to study with great concentration a newspaper that lay beside him, looked up. He pushed the paper across the table in the direction of Maltravers and pointed to a square at the bottom of the page which was divided up into eight compartments each of which contained a small picture depicting two or more objects.

'They are railway stations,' the Marquis said. 'I've got most of them. All the easy ones in fact. Basingstoke. Horsham. Leeds. Aberdeen. But this lion and the church. It seems impossible. Is there a town Lion-church? You see it is vitally important that I win this. Let me read out some of the prizes to you. The first prize: a two-seater car. Second prize: a radiogramophone. Third prize: a tandem bicycle. Now what I want is the *third prize*. Do you think, Peter, that if I win the first prize they will allow me to choose the third prize? You see if I can only get this picture of the lion and the church I am certain to win it. What do you think?'

Maltravers said: 'Gaston. If I tell you what that picture is will you promise to pack your things and come quietly to Schlumbermayer's?'

The Marquis looked uncertain.

'What do you think?' he said. 'If I win it will they let me have the third prize?'

'Of course they will.'

'What is it then?'

'Do you promise to come?'

'Eh bien?'

'Leominster.'

'What?'

'Leo means lion: minster, a cathedral.'

Maltravers spelt it. The Marquis wrote the name down laboriously.

'Now it's a certainty,' he said. 'Provided they see reason about the third prize.'

'And now you must go and pack.'

'But——'

'Gaston!'

'*Je vous demande un peu*——'

'Please, Gaston. You have given your word.'

The Marquis laughed and went to the door. They heard him giving orders to the old woman to pack a suitcase. When he came back to the room Maltravers said:

'Why do you want a bicycle-made-for-two?'

'That's my secret,' the Marquis said.

He went across to the radio which stood in the corner of the room and began to fiddle about with the controls. A voice began to speak:

'. . . Then wrote Rehum the chancellor, and Shimshai the scribe, and the rest of their companions, the Dinaites, the Apharsathchites, the Tarpelites, the Apharsites, the Archevites, the Babylonians, the Susanchites, the Dehavites, and the Elamites . . .'

The voice broke off sharply.

'Sunday morning,' the Marquis said, and switched over the wireless to a man reading out numbers in an unknown language.

'It's hopeless,' he said. 'Never anything one wants to hear on the damned thing.'

He sat down again, his face working.

'And then my pipe has disappeared too,' he said. 'I suppose someone has stolen it. No doubt some low baron is smoking it this very moment.'

'Never mind,' Maltravers said. 'Everything will be all right when we get to Broadacres.'

He went close to where the Marquis was sitting and said something that Blore-Smith could not hear. His words seemed to have a good effect on the Marquis de la Tour d'Espagne, who brightened up and even went so far as to supervise the latter part of his packing. When he had left the room Maltravers said:

'He'll be all right when he gets to the country. I'm afraid he's in a rather difficult mood now.'

'Yes.'

'I'm rather interested to see Mendie's reactions to him.'

'When will she see him?'

'I thought we might look in on her on the way down,' Maltravers said. 'We owe her an explanation you know. Yourself, especially.'

'But——'

Blore-Smith found difficulty in expressing how little this idea appealed to him. Maltravers said:

'Oh, don't be afraid that there will be any sort of awkwardness. Mendie is much too sensible for that. Anyway Gaston will make a very good foil to distract her attention from ourselves.'

A short time later Blore-Smith found himself sitting beside Chipchase at the back of the car while they drove through south London. The Marquis sat beside Maltravers, and Blore-Smith could hear him explaining the plans he had for the time when he owned his tandem bicycle.

'Is this the place?' Maltravers said.

The car was drawn up in front of a gate. Beyond stood a black and white cottage with a thatched roof. The cottage was set back at some distance from the road and it leaned picturesquely sideways.

'This is it,' Blore-Smith said.

Maltravers, Chipchase, and the Marquis de la Tour d'Espagne set off up the crazy pavement. Blore-Smith lagged behind a little, as he was not anxious to face Mrs. Mendoza. Maltravers opened the front door and they went in. There was no sign of life.

'Mendie!' Maltravers shouted.

From upstairs a man's voice said: 'Who's that?'

Maltravers did not answer. He sat down in one of the chairs and began to glance through some snapshots that were lying on the table. A few moments later someone came heavily down the stairs. Maltravers looked up.

'Hullo?' he said.

It was Scrubb, the medical student. He was in his shirt-sleeves and covered in sweat and dirt.

'Oh, it's you all, is it?' Scrubb said.

'Yes,' said Maltravers. 'It's us. Where is Mendie?'

Scrubb said: 'She's in the garden. I'm helping her to get moved in. It's a bit of a business. There's a bricked-up fireplace upstairs. I'm opening it up.'

'In that case,' Maltravers said, 'we mustn't disturb you. We will go out in the garden and look for her. Come along.'

The others followed him out of the door and round to the back of the cottage. At the far end of the garden Blore-Smith saw Mrs. Mendoza. Wearing a bathing dress, she was lying on a rug reading a book. When she saw them she shouted with surprise and came to meet them.

'This is a shock,' she said.

She kissed Maltravers and Chipchase. To Blore-Smith's relief she kissed him too, quite automatically, but without any sign of resentment. Maltravers said:

'This is Monsieur de la Tour d'Espagne. I expect you've both heard a lot about one another even if you haven't met before.'

'Why, of course we have,' Mrs. Mendoza said as she took the Marquis by the hand.

'We are on our way to Schlumbermayer's,' Maltravers said, 'to begin on the film right away. We were hoping we might be lucky enough to get your co-operation.'

'But, my dear, you know I'd simply adore to take part in a film.'

'I too hope for a small part,' said the Marquis, who seemed to have momentarily conquered his obsessions.

He put his head a little on one side and surveyed Mrs. Mendoza. Mrs. Mendoza smiled prettily.

'I shall be noises off,' she said.

The Marquis said: 'I could do that work too.'

'We'll do noises off together then,' said Mrs. Mendoza.

It was clear that the Marquis de la Tour d'Espagne had made a good impression on her.

Chipchase said: 'What is—I believe his name is *Scrubb*—doing here? I ought to warn you that when we arrived he appeared to be pulling the cottage down brick by brick. Is it your wish that he should do that?'

Mrs. Mendoza laughed and said:

'That's O.K. He will come in very useful looking after this place when I am over at Broadacres.'

'Yes. He can do that. But I should lock everything up if I were you.'

'Don't be horrible. Scrubby has been very kind.'

Mrs. Mendoza turned to Blore-Smith.

'I sent Scrubb a wire after I heard from you,' she said in a tone that gave warning that things were blowing up for a row. 'You didn't suppose I could move in here without any help, did you? You haven't told me anything about that yet.'

Maltravers took her by the arm.

'My dear Mendie,' he said, 'all that was entirely our fault. Entirely. We take all blame. We practically kidnapped him.'

Mrs. Mendoza laughed again. She was in a good mood that afternoon.

'I suppose I mustn't grumble then,' she said.

Blore-Smith was much relieved when she said this. He knew that the subject of his telegram was bound to be raised sooner or later. He had in fact felt very guilty about the whole matter. Now everything seemed to have passed off all right. Mrs. Mendoza turned to the Marquis. She pointed to Maltravers and Chipchase.

'Aren't these two awful?' she said.

The Marquis made a sweeping movement with his hands.

'Incorrigible,' he said, rolling the r's somewhat deliberately.

'And now what about some tea,' Mrs. Mendoza said. 'I'll tell Scrubb to make some.'

'I'll come with you,' Chipchase said, 'to see that he does what he's told.'

As they walked across the lawn Mrs. Mendoza said:

'Who is the Frenchman?'

'Gaston de la Tour d'Espagne. You must have heard of him. He's a friend of Pauline Borodino's. Schlumbermayer wants to buy the contents of his château. That's why he's over here now.'

'Is he married?'

'He's had at least three wives in his time. Whether or not he has one at the moment I can't say.'

'I'm mad about him.'

'I'm not surprised.'

'I suppose he has every vice?'

'Naturally.'

'How very attractive of him.'

Mrs. Mendoza sighed and they entered the cottage. Scrubb could be heard floundering about in the room above them. Mrs. Mendoza shouted:

'Scrubb, darling, come down and put the kettle on, will you? And get some cups and saucers out of the pantry. We'll have tea in the garden.'

Some muffled reply came from above and Mrs. Mendoza said:

'Well, be quick. We're all thirsty.'

She sat down.

'When do you want me to come over to Broadacres?' she said. 'To-night with all of you?'

'We hoped you might be able to manage that.'

'And Scrubby can look after this place for a bit.'

'How long have you taken it for?'

'Only three months.'

Chipchase said: 'I don't want to lecture you, but it must be understood that if you come to Broadacres you are not to take our hero away again.'

Mrs. Mendoza said: 'I know, I know. I was very silly. But it brought its own punishment, as you must see for yourself by now. It won't occur again. I can promise you that.'

'In that case it looks as if we should all have a very pleasant and interesting time.'

'Does Schlumbermayer know that I am coming?'

'He seemed most anxious that you should be taking a part in the proceedings.'

'Is Sarah there?'

'She may be arriving later.'

Scrubb came down the stairs and into the room.

'What was that you shouted?' he said.

'I asked you to get the tea,' Mrs. Mendoza said. 'Don't be all night. And I shall be leaving here this evening for a day or two. Will you hold the fort?'

'But look here, I say——'

Mrs. Mendoza said: 'Now don't make a lot of silly fuss. You told me yourself you wanted a week or two in the country where you could read your medical books without being disturbed. Now I'm going to give you an opportunity to get some real work done.'

'I don't want to be left here alone.'

'We'll come over and see you. Don't worry. It will only be for a day or two.'

Scrubb disappeared into the kitchen, grumbling to himself. Mrs. Mendoza said:

'Aren't men extraordinary?'

'They are very odd,' said Chipchase.

6

When Commander Venables came into the Long Bar he had had a depressing morning trying to clear up the mess at *la cattleya*. The flower-shop was in the hands of the bailiffs and the charwoman said that when last seen Mrs. Mendoza was driving away in a car with Mr. Scrubb, who had taken a suitcase with him. She gave Commander Venables the address that Scrubb had left for the forwarding of letters, but she was unable to tell him whether or not Mrs. Mendoza was staying in the same place. From something that Scrubb had said this seemed probable. Commander Venables thanked her and went away. He was in need of refreshment.

Inglethorne was already in the Long Bar when Commander Venables arrived. Unlike Commander Venables, Inglethorne was in the best of tempers. He had just signed a satisfactory contract and he had already had one or two on the strength of it. He gripped Commander Venables by the hand and, although he was a much smaller man, threw an arm round his shoulder and led him to the bar. Commander Venables put up no opposition. He needed sympathy. Inglethorne said:

'And how's the little lady we met with you in Berlin? Mrs. Mendoza. You don't meet girls like that growing on every rose-bush.'

Commander Venables put his drink back and ordered the same again. Then he took a deep breath.

'Well . . .' he said.

Inglethorne, suddenly switching over to a different sort of acting said hoarsely:

'Tell me, man. Don't keep me in suspense.'

Commander Venables was taken by surprise. He was not used to actors. He felt Inglethorne's fingers digging into his arm.

'It's like this,' he said.

Inglethorne was a good listener. He was accustomed to practise facial expressions when other people were talking, and in his disquiet at the series of studies in physiognomy that Inglethorne called up, ranging from nauseated ennui to uncontrollable passion, Commander Venables said more than he intended. He told the whole story, or as much as he knew of it. It took some time.

'And now she seems to be living in the country with a medical student.'

'Do you know him?' Inglethorne said.

'He's been her lodger for ages.'

'But, my dear old boy,' said Inglethorne. 'My dear old boy! There's probably nothing in it at all. Positively nothing. After all, why should she have waited until now? Take my advice and go down and see her as soon as possible.'

The possibility of a platonic relationship between Mrs. Mendoza and Scrubb seemed to have escaped Commander Venables's consideration.

'But she surely wouldn't do that,' he said.

'Why not?'

'Well what does she want to take him for then?'

'To help her get moved in perhaps.'

Commander Venables looked uncertain. Inglethorne took two steps back and looked down into his open palm with the gesture of one who has just received a tip and verifies the amount. He said:

'O, *beware, my lord, of jealousy;*
It is the green-eyed monster, which doth mock
The meat it feeds on: that cuckold lives in bliss
Who, certain of his fate loves not his wronger;
But, O, what damned minutes tells he o'er
Who dotes, yet doubts, suspects, yet strongly loves!'

'So you think——'

'*Poor and content is rich,*' said Inglethorne, '*and rich enough;*
But riches fineless is as poor as winter
To him that ever fears he shall be poor:
Good heaven, the souls of all my tribe defend from jealousy!'

Having said this, Inglethorne pulled his hat further down over his eyes, put his hands in his pockets and hunched his shoulders. It was a sign that he had moved on from his Shakespearian rôle.

'But what is the best way to tackle the situation?'

'Have you got a car?' Inglethorne said.

Commander Venables nodded. Inglethorne said:

'Buzz down to see her with a little present to-morrow. Something unexpected. Caviar and some fizz. Offer her that. She won't refuse.'

Commander Venables was not a demonstrative man but he could not prevent himself from banging with his fist on the bar so that he nearly upset a bottle of tonic water belonging to the young motor salesman next to him.

'I believe you're right, Inglethorne,' he said.

'Of course I am, old boy,' said Inglethorne. 'I should start at once. Have another before you go.'

It was still early afternoon when Commander Venables, driving a battered two-seater from which the hood had been removed some years before, approached the white cottage. On the seat beside him was a basket containing two magnums of champagne, a pot of caviar, some *foie gras*, and a tin of biscuits. Some enquiry was necessary before he found his way, and after being several times misdirected a woman pointed to where it could be seen through the trees.

'Young fellow lives there by himself,' she said.

Commander Venables grunted and drove on. When he reached the gate he stopped the car and looked about for a few minutes to see if there was any sign of Mrs. Mendoza in the front garden. No one seemed to be about so he took his basket and went up the crazy pavement. The front door was ajar. Commander Venables knocked sharply. He heard someone inside walking across the stone floor. The door was pulled open.

At first, because he had several days' growth of beard, Commander Venables did not recognize Scrubb. He thought it was the boy who cleaned the boots or looked after the garden.

'Is Mrs. Mendoza in?' he said.

After he had said this he saw that it was Scrubb, and added:

'Where's Mendie? Didn't recognise you for the moment. I brought her down a little present.'

Scrubb took the basket. He said:

'Is this food?'

'Just a few odds and ends.'

Without asking Commander Venables's permission Scrubb took a knife and began to prise open the biscuit-tin. He said:

'The last I saw of Mendie was a week ago. She went off to do this film. I've been here with no food except what I could get on tick, which wasn't much, no money, and no way of getting away. What do you think of that?'

Commander Venables did not answer. He watched Scrubb take a handful of biscuits and put them in his mouth. Scrubb said:

'She asks me to come down here for a couple of days to help her move in and says that she'll motor me back to London, and then what happens? She just goes off to let me starve to death.'

'But didn't she say when she was coming back?'

'Of course she said she was coming back the next day. A fat lot of good it does her saying that. Besides she's gone off with Maltravers and Chipchase and that crowd, so there's precious little likelihood that any of us will see her for some time.'

'But where's she gone to?'

'To Schlumbermayer's.'

'Who is Schlumbermayer?'

Scrubb had his mouth full and he made a disagreeable sound to indicate his contempt for Commander Venables's ignorance. Commander Venables said:

'But did she come down here to live by herself?'

'Live by herself? She came down here to live with Blore-Smith.'

'Blore-Smith?'

'The little chap she came back from Germany with.'

Although Scrubb was interested primarily in his own troubles, something about Commander Venables's face made him say:

'Why, didn't you know?'

'That—little——'

Commander Venables made no attempt to express in words the mental agitation that assailed him. He went to the basket and, taking out one of the magnums of champagne, said:

'Have you got a glass?'

'What's that? Bubbly?' Scrubb said. 'There are only tumblers but they will do.'

He hurried to the kitchen and came back with the glasses just as Commander Venables drew the cork. Commander Venables poured out two full tumblers and sat down.

'Where does this blighter live?' he said. 'Where Mendie's gone?'

'About thirty miles from here.'

'Are they all there?'

'All who?'

'Maltravers and Chipchase and Blore-Smith. All that gang?'

'Of course they are. They're doing this film, I tell you.'

'I don't give a damn whether they're doing a film or not,' Commander Venables said. 'I propose to go over there.'

'But look here,' said Scrubb. 'You can't leave me here. Now you've arrived you must take me back.'

'You can come with me if you like.'

'I certainly do like. I don't want to stay here any longer with the baker threatening non-delivery every day and no prospect of ever seeing Mendie again.'

Commander Venables poured himself out another glass of champagne and Scrubb held out his own tumbler. He was already flushed from the effect of the wine. He said:

'Wait half a minute and I'll put my pyjamas and tooth-brush into a suitcase and then we'll go anywhere you like so long as we get away from here.'

'Right.'

When Scrubb came downstairs again he found that Commander Venables had opened the second magnum.

'What about having some caviar with it?' Scrubb said.

'Any damn thing you like.'

By the time they set out for Schlumbermayer's there was little left of the original contents of the basket that had been intended as a present for Mrs. Mendoza.

The company at Broadacres were sitting and lying in various positions on the lawn in front of the house. They consisted of Blore-Smith, Maltravers, Chipchase, Schlumbermayer, Mrs. Mendoza, the Marquis de la Tour d'Espagne, and Sarah. Blore-Smith sat a little apart from the rest, watching Mrs. Mendoza and the Marquis, who lay on the same rug, holding hands. A camera, resting on a tripod, stood at some distance from the group. Maltravers, who was sitting in a deck-chair, held a sheaf of papers in his hand. On these he was making notes with a blue pencil. Without looking up, he said:

'As regards the individual studies we now seem to have a fairly comprehensive series of shots, taken both when the subject was unaware that he or she was being photographed and also when aware that this was happening.'

Turning to Schlumbermayer, he said:

'There are some specially good ones of you.'

Schlumbermayer rubbed his nose. He said:

'And so what?'

Maltravers put down the papers on the grass beside him.

'We must now wait for things to happen,' he said. 'My experience tells me that usually one does not have to wait long.'

He lit a cigarette and lay back in his chair. Sarah said:

'Here's someone coming to pay a call.'

She pointed to a small dreadnought-grey car which had appeared from among the trees at the beginning of the drive and was now skirting the wide stretch of grass that lay fenced off on the further side of the gravel. As it came nearer it was noticeable that the car had no hood and that both of the men who sat inside it were red in the face. Chipchase said:

'Do you know, for a moment I thought one of them was the Commodore.'

Maltravers shaded his eyes.

'You were right,' he said. 'It is the Commodore.'

'And the other is Scrubb,' said Sarah.

Chipchase said: 'Scrubb? What have we done to deserve him? Anyway, what does either of them want here?'

'Heaven knows,' Maltravers said. 'However, they will make a very suitable addition to our little group of behaviour-actors. Keep your eye on the camera for any developments.'

'Mendie,' Chipchase said. 'Two friends of yours are arriving by car. If the engine holds out they will be here quite soon.'

Mrs. Mendoza rolled over on the rug without loosening her grasp of the Marquis's hand. She said:

'What's all that?'

'The Commodore and Scrubb are chugging up the drive.'

'Nonsense!'

Mrs. Mendoza sat upright. Commander Venables and Scrubb moved painfully forward. At last there was a sound of squeaking brakes and the small car stopped. Without bothering to open the door Commander Venables threw his leg over the side of the car and climbed out. He came slowly towards them across the grass. Scrubb followed him. Both of them had a high colour. Maltravers nudged Chipchase and jerked his head in the direction of the camera. Then he jumped up and said:

'Hullo, Captain Venables. Why haven't you come to see us before?'
Chipchase crawled hurriedly in the direction of the camera.

Commander Venables took no notice of Maltravers. He went
straight to Mrs. Mendoza. Turning away from the group Maltravers said:

'Have you got your distance?'

'Half a minute,' said Chipchase. 'Now I have.'

Mrs. Mendoza said: 'My dear Hugo, this is a great surprise. You
aren't wearing very country clothes, though, are you?'

'Never mind about my clothes,' Commander Venables said. 'Come
here.'

He took her by the wrist and pulled her up from the ground. Mrs.
Mendoza cried out at the violence with which he did this.

'Shoot!' said Maltravers.

'O.K.,' said Chipchase.

The noise of the camera was lost in Mrs. Mendoza's flow of protest.
Additionally so on account of the vibrations from an aeroplane that was
passing in the sky above them. Mrs. Mendoza said:

'Are you drunk, Hugo?'

'No, I'm not drunk,' Commander Venables said, still holding her
tightly by the wrist. 'I've just come down to say a few words about the
way you've behaved to me, and not to me only. What about that
damned flower-shop of yours with the brokers in? What about the way
you treated me in Berlin? What about that filthy little brute Herman
and all the little brutes before him, and after him too? What about this
chap you left to starve to death at your cottage? What about all your
friends? All these? They are your friends, aren't they?'

By this time Commander Venables's voice was like a fog-horn. The
extreme passion of his rage was infectious and Blore-Smith felt himself
trembling all over while small electric shocks ran up and down his arms.
Scrubb, paralysed by what he saw taking place, stood with his hands in
his pockets and his mouth open. Mrs. Mendoza snatched her hand away.
She said:

'Are you mad?'

At this point Blore-Smith felt his arm seized so tightly that he
could not help gasping with pain. It was the Marquis de la Tour d'Espagne who held him. The Marquis had risen to his hands and knees,
and said in a hoarse voice, close to Blore-Smith's ear:

'Introduce me!'

'Who to?'

'To this man!'

'To Commander Venables?'

'Yes, yes. Quickly!'

'But——'

The pain caused by the Marquis's fingers in the fleshy part of his arm was so intense that in order to do anything to allay it Blore-Smith scrambled to his feet. The Marquis followed him quickly. Sweating with fear, Blore-Smith said:

'Oh, Commander Venables, this is the Marquis de la Tour d'Espagne.'

Commander Venables swivelled round and looked at the Marquis, who was standing stiffly to attention. From him Commander Venables turned his eyes again to Blore-Smith. As he did this the Marquis bowed smartly and took two little steps forward which brought him so close to Commander Venables that their noses almost touched.

'Sir,' he said.

Commander Venables shied away his face, like an angry horse. He said:

'And what can I do for you?'

'You must behave more politely,' the Marquis said, in a very quiet voice.

There was a stillness as before an earthquake, broken only by the ticking of the camera and the more insistent buzzings of the aeroplane that was now circling above the house. Mrs. Mendoza said:

'Don't take any notice of him, Gaston. He must have been drinking. It's not altogether his fault, because he has a very weak head.'

Commander Venables looked at the Marquis de la Tour d'Espagne for some seconds.

'Go to hell,' he said, also very quietly.

The Marquis de la Tour d'Espagne smiled. He began to fumble in his breast pocket. From here he took a notecase and, after a short search, he found a visiting-card. He handed this to Commander Venables.

'If you will give me your address,' he said, 'I will instruct my seconds to call on you. Choice of weapons will of course be with you.'

Commander Venables put his hands in his pockets and stared into the Marquis de la Tour d'Espagne's face. He pursed his lips. It seemed that he found this particular situation unexpected. He had taken the card in his hand and now he examined it without enthusiasm. The Marquis looked round at the others. Blore-Smith avoided his eye in case the Marquis should fix on him as a desirable second. Commander Venables breathed heavily. At last he said:

'You had better get out. We don't fight duels in England.'

He tore the card into four pieces and dropped them on the grass. The Marquis de la Tour d'Espagne's face began to twitch in a way that Blore-Smith could now recognise as a warning of trouble in the offing. He began to clasp and unclasp his hands in front of him. His cheeks became a shade less grey than was usual with him. He said:

'The blood——'

He was interrupted by Sarah.

'Look!' she said. 'Why, an aeroplane is coming down in the big field!'

Schlumbermayer now got up from the pile of cushions from which he had been watching matters. He took out his spectacles and put them on. He said:

'What do they mean by coming down here? It's private property.'

Maltravers turned again to Chipchase. He said:

'Hold hard. New material.'

'Just a moment,' Chipchase said.

He shifted round the camera. The aeroplane bumped along the length of the field, turned, and came to a standstill. For a time nothing happened and then a short figure climbed out. It was a man, and he turned and helped another passenger to the ground. The second arrival was swathed in coats and scarves. Some of these were removed and a woman was revealed. She took the man's arm and both began to walk away from the aeroplane in the direction of the house. Schlumbermayer said:

'Who do you suppose these are?'

He advanced a few steps to meet them. Maltravers said:

'One of them is remarkably like Reggie Frott.'

'And if I'm not mistaken,' said Schlumbermayer, 'the other is the Duchesse de Borodino.'

'What? Pauline?'

In the excitement the Marquis de la Tour d'Espagne seemed to have forgotten about the duel. Commander Venables, too, seemed cowed and half ashamed of his earlier fury. Maltravers said:

'Don't miss them as they climb over the railings, Oliver.'

Reggie Frott and the Duchesse de Borodino approached. Schlumbermayer, by way of greeting, made some uneasy passes with his hands in their direction. Reggie Frott waved him aside.

'It's Gaston we've come to see,' he said. 'I'll talk to you later, old boy. Business first.'

Blore-Smith found himself shaking hands with the Duchesse de Borodino. As usual she was beaming and telling everybody what an amusing time they had had.

'It's an air-taxi,' she said. 'We thought it was going to come down in the middle of the Channel.'

Reggie Frott took the Marquis de la Tour d'Espagne by the arm.

'Gaston, *mon vieux*,' he said, 'I'm acting as an agent for Lazarus Kolf. He wants to buy all your junk. Everything. The whole doings, lock, stock, and barrel. It's the best offer you're ever likely to get. House, pictures, tapestry, furniture, *droit de seigneur*. The whole bag of tricks.'

Reggie took a sheet of paper from his pocket and began to unscrew the top of his fountain-pen.

'Why not sign the preliminary thing at once?' he said. 'It's not binding in any way except that it gives Kolf a fortnight's option. Why, we've been hunting all over Europe for you.'

Schlumbermayer came hurrying forward.

'What's all this, Frott,' he said. 'You haven't come here to try to——'

'Just the odd spot of business,' Reggie Frott said. 'Nothing to get excited about.'

The Marquis said: 'Is it ready money?'

'If you come back to Paris you can walk straight into Kolf's office and get the cheque to-night. He's always there until past nine o'clock at night.'

'Look here,' said Schlumbermayer. 'What do you want butting in like this? Gaston and I are fixing up a deal——'

'Why not go back in our air-taxi, Gaston?' Reggie Frott said. 'Pauline and I are on our way to London. I thought that if I found you here I could fix things up satisfactorily, and we have ordered a car to come down from London and pick us up here. It should arrive at any minute now. In fact I expect it is already out at the back, waiting.'

The Marquis de la Tour d'Espagne put his hand to his forehead. He seemed to be making a colossal effort to come to a decision. Then he said:

'I go back at once in your plane.'

He turned to Mrs. Mendoza.

'*Tu viens, chérie?*' he said.

Mrs. Mendoza prided herself on her French.

'*Tout de suite?*' she said.

'*Pourquoi pas?*' said the Marquis.

He took her by the hand and they began to run towards the big field. At first Commander Venables, himself no French scholar, did not realise what was on foot. Even so he was the first of the others to take action. He began to run after them. His speed was remarkable for a man of his age and build. By the time the Marquis de la Tour d'Espagne and Mrs. Mendoza had reached the railings he was close behind them. Mrs. Mendoza climbed over. The Marquis turned and, lowering his head, caught Commander Venables in the wind, just as he arrived. The impact was considerable owing to the exertion of Commander Venables himself. Commander Venables went down. The Marquis vaulted the rail and caught up Mrs. Mendoza. Both of them hurried on towards the aeroplane. Commander Venables lay on the grass. Maltravers said:

'That's an apache trick.'

All this happened so quickly that Blore-Smith was aware of little more than a feeling of terror and nausea that had now become unbearable. All he could remember were Reggie Frott's words about a car waiting at the back of the house. He began to edge away in the direction of the front door. His things would not take long to throw into a bag. As he went he heard Schlumbermayer, shaking with rage, say: 'You'll be sorry for this, Frott'; and Maltravers shouting, 'Come on, don't miss anything'; while Chipchase again replied, 'O.K.'

Carrying his suitcase, Blore-Smith stumbled down the back stairs and went along the passage and out into the stable-yard. A large saloon car, with a uniformed chauffeur, was waiting there. The chauffeur touched his cap and took the suitcase from Blore-Smith. He said:

'And the lady, sir?'

'She won't be coming,' Blore-Smith said. 'I'm a bit late myself, so drive to London as soon as possible.'

'Very good, sir.'

'And leave here by the back way.'

'Yes, sir.'

As they went out of the gate Blore-Smith, looking through the window, saw an aeroplane mounting towards the clouds. He lay back in the seat. The car drove on, gathering speed. It was not long before they entered the outskirts of London.

'What address, sir?' said the chauffeur.

'Ebury Street.'

It was the only home he knew, and he had decided to throw himself on Mrs. Pinkus's mercy. Later, when they had reached their destination, the chauffeur said:

'It's down to the Duchess's account, isn't it, sir?'

'Yes,' said Blore-Smith.

He fumbled in his pocket, thinking that he ought to give the man a tip, but as he seemed to have only a few coppers there he just said, 'Good afternoon,' and, picking up his suitcase, walked towards the house.

Mrs. Pinkus herself opened the door. She heard all that Blore-Smith had to say. Then she waited for a time, feeling abstractedly her back-hair. She said:

'You'll be quite alone this time?'

'Quite alone,' Blore-Smith said.

'Because——'

'Yes, yes,' said Blore-Smith. 'I know. I shall be quite alone this time and I shall remain quite alone.'

'Well,' Mrs. Pinkus said, 'the old accommodation is free. But I've had to raise my terms. They would be five shillings a week more than you were paying before.'

'All right. I'll take them on again.'

'In that case,' Mrs. Pinkus said, 'you'll find everything much as before. You know when you went away so sudden you never told the telephone you were leaving nor the gas neither.'

When Blore-Smith left her in the hall, she was still feeling her heavily embankmented hair as if she feared that the whole affair might come away from its moorings.

Blore-Smith spent the next few days trying to make plans for going abroad. That seemed the best thing to do. He went to several travel agencies but he experienced his former inability to take action, now that the excitement of escaping from Broadacres was past. And then one evening after tea there was a knock on his door.

'Come in,' said Blore-Smith.

It was Maltravers and Chipchase. Blore-Smith got up quickly from his chair.

'What do you want?' he said.

'We came round to see you,' Maltravers said.

'Well, I don't want to see either of you.'

'That is very unfriendly of you. Besides you owe some sort of an explanation with regard to the virtual theft of a car.'

'I took it to get away from you.'

'You caused a lot of inconvenience.'

'I don't care.'

'That is a matter of taste. Meanwhile someone else has had to pay for your journey. In short there is an account to settle.'

'It's been the same all the way along,' Blore-Smith said. 'You've just been trying to get money out of me.'

'But good heavens,' Maltravers said, 'whoever suggested that we were doing anything else? We've got to live. Do you expect two ambitious men to devote their whole time to looking after you just for your *beaux yeux*? You seem to have exchanged your inferiority complex for paranoia.'

'The whole of this talk about psychology is a ramp. You've just used it as a way to swindle me.'

'It seems nevertheless to have had a very formative effect on your character. You don't suggest, do you, that you would have had the courage to talk to me like this when we first met?'

'You hadn't tried your tricks on me then.'

'And very apparent it was. Why you couldn't say boo to a goose when I first saw you.'

'Anyway,' said Blore-Smith, who had begun to shake violently, 'I'm through with you now—and you.'

Maltravers slowly bowed but said nothing. Chipchase walked across to the sideboard and began to mix himself a drink.

'Ever since I met you,' Blore-Smith said, 'my life has been nothing but worry and strain. I haven't known what peace of mind means.'

'Whose fault is that?' Maltravers said, putting his hat on and sitting on the edge of the table.

'It's your fault. Both your faults. That's what I am complaining about.'

Maltravers said:

'I could tell you weren't pleased about something. But surely the fact that you worry too much is largely your own fault. Or I prefer to say that it is something that time and a good deal of application may cure. I cannot see that either of us is to be blamed for that.'

'It is you who brought me into touch with all the people who cause me to worry. All the beastly people in this film, for instance.'

'I thought you wanted to meet a few people? You complained that your acquaintance was so limited when first we met and discussed such matters.'

'I didn't know the dregs I know now.'

'You showed every sign of wanting to.'

'I didn't want to be dragged down as you've dragged me down.'

'It would have been hard work dragging you lower than the niche you were occupying when we found you,' Chipchase said, finishing his drink and replacing the glass on the sideboard. 'You must admit that. In fact the obscurity would soon have become so inspissated that you would almost certainly have become completely lost sight of.'

'At least I wasn't paying away all my income to you and your sharks.'

'Come, come,' said Chipchase. 'Please remember that there is such a thing as slander and that the law in this country is for rich and poor alike. Beware the fury of a patient man.'

Blore-Smith's teeth began to chatter. He had lost all control of himself and could no longer speak.

'Mind you,' said Chipchase, 'it would be with real reluctance that I should put matters in the hands of my solicitor.'

Maltravers swung his legs up on to the table and turned round, and over, so that he lay along it, supporting his chin on his hands.

'But what is really the matter?' he said. 'When we met you your life was of a dullness so intolerable that you thought of suicide. You told me so. I repeat your very words. We take you in hand and in the space of a few months you are in the thick of everything. Love affairs. Business dealings of the most varied kind. Travel. Strange company. Adventure. What else do you want? What else do you imagine life has to offer? I admit that it has cost you some money, but, after all, the money is no good unless you use it for something. In your case you didn't even keep it in gold on the premises and count it every night. Even that would have been more fun than you got out of it by your own efforts.'

'Well, I want to be left alone now.'

'Alone,' said Maltravers, 'is precisely the state in which you are going to be left. It was to tell you this that we came round to-night.'

'Have you found some other fool to make money out of?'

'You have the coarsest way of putting things,' Maltravers said, 'but, in a sense, yes. I have. We both have, in fact. We are crossing the Atlantic at the end of next week.'

'Who are you going to sponge on there?'

'On Hollywood, it may interest you to hear.'

'Both of you?'

'No,' said Chipchase. 'I am giving a course of lectures on sub-normal psychology. I shall find some of my notes on your own behaviour of great use for purposes of illustration.'

'Then I am really going to see the last of you?'

In spite of himself Blore-Smith allowed his voice to sound apprehensive. He had been prepared for a row but hardly for something so final as this.

'And what are your plans, may one enquire?' said Maltravers.

'I shall lead my own life again.'

'I see.'

'Not the life foisted on me by you two. Something very different.'

'I can imagine that.'

'The real thing,' said Blore-Smith, rather desperately.

'If,' said Chipchase, 'you imagine that the Real Thing is ever going to be widely different from what you have already experienced, I fear that you may be disappointed. However——'

'I'll risk that,' Blore-Smith said.

'In that case,' Maltravers said, 'we will take up no more of your valuable time. There are, however, a few items here.'

He handed Blore-Smith a sheaf of bills. Chipchase said:

'And the tail-end of my own account.'

Blore-Smith took the pieces of paper hurriedly. For a moment it looked as if he were going to tear them up. Then he turned to his desk and, still standing, he wrote out a cheque and handed it over.

'Thank you,' said Chipchase, 'and good-bye.'

'Before we part, a small token of our regard,' Maltravers said. He handed Blore-Smith an envelope. 'Should you want us we shall be at Broadacres for the next few days. Poor Schlumbermayer needs companionship. He has had a shock.'

They went through the door, leaving Blore-Smith standing in the middle of the room holding the envelope in his hand. Blore-Smith heard the front door slam. He tore open the envelope. Inside was a snapshot of Maltravers and Chipchase sitting on either side of one of the urns in the garden at Broadacres. Blore-Smith looked at it for a long time. Then he threw it in the waste-paper basket.

Later, he picked it out of the waste-paper basket and propped it up on the mantelpiece. After that he sat down on the hard chair and looked out of the window. It had begun to rain and small drops of water were running down the glass.

When the telephone bell rang nearly an hour later he was still sitting there, in the same position. He took up the receiver.

'Hullo?'

'Is Mr. Blore-Smith there?'

The voice seemed familiar. It recalled faintly some out-of-the-way experience.

'Who is that speaking?'

'This is Colonel Teape.'

'Oh—I see—yes. This is me speaking.'

'What a piece of luck finding you,' Colonel Teape said. 'You remember me? I so hope you do.'

'Why yes—of course.'

'How frightfully clever of you.'

'We have met—several times.'

'Yes,' said Colonel Teape. 'We have.'

In the distance he laughed a little.

'How's life been treating you?' he said.

'Oh, I don't know. Nothing very exciting really.'

'A bit bored?'

'Oh well, I don't know——'

'Oh yes, you are. I can tell at once. Now will you do something for me? Something that will please me a lot?'

Blore-Smith was aware of a sinking feeling inside him.

'What?' he said, trying to prevent his voice from trembling.

'I've taken a little house in the south of France—not far from St. Tropez, as a matter of fact. Just for the summer. I want you to come and stay with me there.'

'Why——?'

'Will you come? It would be so delightful.'

'St. Tropez?' said Blore-Smith. 'I—— Look here, do you mind if I write to you about it. I think——'

'I don't mind if you write and tell me that you can come,' Colonel Teape said. 'But if you were naughty enough to tell me that you couldn't, I should be very cross indeed.'

'I must say,' said Chipchase, cutting the cards to Sarah Maltravers, 'I think it was very kind of Pauline and Reggie Frott to take Scrubb back with them to London. I feel a great sense of relief now that he has gone.'

Sarah began to deal. She said:

'Anybody else but Pauline would have made a fuss about the car being taken like that. Still I suppose she can perfectly well afford to ring up and order another one when that sort of thing happens.'

'It's a jackpot,' Schlumbermayer said.

Commander Venables, who was looking all the better for his stay in the country, said:

'I think our host ought to be congratulated too. On his good nature in letting me stay here.'

'Oh, he's the best natured man in the world,' Chipchase said, 'even though he hasn't ante-ed yet. Personally I can't open.'

Schlumbermayer pushed two chips forward. He said:

'Nor can I.'

'Peter?' Sarah said.

Maltravers sat without speaking, brooding over his cards. He said:

'You know I've been thinking about Blore-Smith. What is he going to make of his life?'

'Can you open?'

'Yes. I'll open for two,' Maltravers said. 'And please don't be so aggressive when you speak to me. As I have said before, I think that young man made a grave mistake.'

'I'll come in,' said Commander Venables.

'So will I,' Sarah and Chipchase said at the same moment.

Schlumbermayer took some minutes to decide. At last, unwillingly, he thrust two more chips forward. Sarah dealt out the cards. Schlumbermayer said:

'I don't see how I can expect to win. Luck goes in waves and I haven't had any now for two years.'

'You'd better come out to America with us,' Maltravers said, 'and try your hand there.'

He opened the betting with two. Commander Venables said:

'I'll see that. I wish it was America I was going to and not Basra.'

Sarah said: 'I'll raise you one.'

'I'll see you,' Chipchase said.

Schlumbermayer frowned horribly and fiddled with his spectacles.

Chipchase said: 'I'm not sure that I really want to go to America now that it is all fixed. I'm trying to arrange for Caroline to come as my secretary with all expenses paid but there seems to be some hitch. People seem to take a malicious pleasure in putting difficulties in one's way.'

With an effort, Schlumbermayer said: 'I'll raise that two.'

Maltravers began to count the chips on the table. He pushed two piles of his own counters forward.

'Raise you the pool,' he said.

Commander Venables put down his cards heavily and gave a deep sigh.

'I'm away,' Sarah said.

'So am I,' said Chipchase.

Again Schlumbermayer sat wrapped in thought. Commander Venables said:

'You know, there I shall be with a few other white men, all talking of tiffin and *chota-hazri* and sighing for Piccadilly, and do you know I shan't have a word to say to them? It will be awful to feel different. After all, one's the same breed. But somehow when you've been through a good deal and you find yourself a few thousand miles from civilisation, whether it's on land or on sea, and you've had dinner—it will be at half past six in those parts—and you're sitting there in your evening clothes—or rather your pyjamas, which is what you change into in the tropics—you look up at those stars and you can't help developing a sort of philosophy of life.'

Schlumbermayer threw in his hand. Maltravers began to rake the kitty towards him. Schlumbermayer said:

'Let's see your openers.'

Maltravers picked up his cards and, extracting two knaves, flicked them across the table.

E DU